THE MEMORY PAINTER

HARPERCOLLINS
PUBLISHERSLTD

The

MEMORY PAINTER

GWENDOLYN WOMACK

HarperCollins books may be purchased for educational, business,
or sales promotional use through our Special Markets Department.

HarperCollins Publishers Ltd
2 Bloor Street East, 20th Floor
Toronto, Ontario, Canada
M4W 1A8

www.harpercollins.ca

Designed by Jonathan Bennett

Library and Archives Canada Cataloguing in Publication
information is available upon request

ISBN 978-1-44343-389-1

Printed and bound in the United States of America
RRD 9 8 7 6 5 4 3 2 1

In memory of
Fukumi Mitsutake

I stand before the masters who know the histories of the dead, who decide which tales to hear again, who judge the book of lives as either full or empty, who are themselves authors of truth. . . . When the story is written and the end is good and the soul of a man is perfected, with a shout they lift him into heaven.

—*Egyptian Book of the Dead*

THE MEMORY PAINTER

ONE

The paintings hung in the dark like ghosts. Too many to count—not an inch of wall space remained. The canvas eyes looked alive in the darkness, staring at their surroundings as if wondering what alchemy had transported them to this place.

The artist's loft had an industrial air with its Lego-like windows, concrete walls, and cement floor. A dozen bolts of Belgian linen leaned in a corner next to a pile of wood waiting to be built into frames. Four easels formed a circle in the center of the studio, a prepared canvas resting on each. Their surfaces gleamed with white gesso that had been layered and polished to an enamel-like perfection, a technique used in the Renaissance to obtain a nearly photographic realism. This artist knew it well.

The paintings themselves were an eclectic ensemble. Each image captured a different time in history, a different place in the world. Yet the paintings had one thing in common: all depicted the most intimate moments of someone's life or death.

In one painting, a samurai knelt on his tatami, performing seppuku. He was dressed in ceremonial white, blood pooling at his middle. The ritual suicide had been portrayed in excruciating detail, the agony on the samurai's face tangible as he plunged the blade into his stomach. Behind him, his "Second" stood ready, his *wakizashi* sword poised to sever the samurai's head. In the next painting, an imperial guard on horseback dragged a prisoner across a field in ancient Persia. And further along the wall, an old man wearing a turban stared into the distance, as if challenging the artist to capture his spirit on the last day of his life.

The studio had three walls, and the entire space was closed off by an enormous partition of Japanese silk screens. On the other side was a spartan living area with a kitchen hidden behind a sidewall. Down the hall, there was a smaller room unfurnished except for a mattress on the floor. The artist lay sprawled across it on his stomach, shirtless and in deep sleep.

Without warning, he sat up and gasped for air, struggling out of the grasp of a powerful dream.

"I am here now. I'm here now. I'm here now. I'm here now." He chanted the words over and over with desperate intensity as he rocked back and forth in a soothing motion. But then, just as suddenly, his body went slack and his eyes grew distant as a strange calm descended over him. He got out of bed.

Entering his studio like a sleepwalker, he selected several brushes and began mixing paint on a well-used wooden palette, whispering words in ancient Greek that had not been heard for centuries.

His hands moved with a strange certainty in the dark. Time passed without his awareness. He painted until the hours towered above him, pressing down upon his body and begging him to stop. His feet grew numb, his shoulders stiff with pain. When the sun's glaring noon light reached his window, a piercing pain lanced through his head, jarring him out of oblivion like an alarm clock.

I am Bryan Pierce. I am standing in my studio. I am here now. I am Bryan Pierce. I am standing in my studio. I am here now. I am Bryan Pierce. He forced the words into his consciousness, grabbing onto their simple truth like a child reaching for the string of a kite. The words were the only thing that kept him from flying away.

Bryan's legs buckled and he sank to the floor, leaning against the wall for support. Hands dangling over drawn-up knees, his arms were streaked with every pigment on the studio shelf. His bare chest displayed similar stains.

He forced himself to study his most recent work, knowing that this was the quickest way to assimilate the dream. Only when he felt able to stand did he get up and walk over to the video recorder in his studio. It was the highest-end digital camera that money could buy and came equipped with an infrared setting to catch nighttime activity. He always kept it on. Bryan didn't need to review the footage to know he had been speaking Greek all night again. But the recording proved that it had happened.

Most mornings, observing himself on camera gave him some sense of peace. But today he didn't feel like watching it—his vision was still too present, like a messenger in the room. Somehow, this dream held answers. But to what?

Origenes Adamantius, a priest from ancient Rome, had invaded his consciousness a week ago, and every night since he had been painting memories from the man's life. He had delivered the first canvas to the gallery before it had even dried. He knew it had to hang in his next show, but he had no idea why.

The opening was tonight. It would be his first show in Boston since he had moved from New York, and all week he had been toying with the idea of going. But then he would dismiss it just as quickly. He could not justify the risk. Being surrounded by so many people, having to stare into their eyes as he shook their hands—his paintings a screaming backdrop—would most likely trigger an episode. And how could he explain that?

When he hadn't appeared at any of his openings in New York last year, the press had pounced, portraying him as some kind of arrogant recluse who spurned the public, when nothing could be further from the truth. He put his work out there with the hope that someone, someday, would recognize his paintings for what they were, that someone else in the world suffered from the same curse. But maybe that hope was delusional. He had been searching for years and was beginning to feel it was a lost cause. Hundreds of paintings and not one answer.

Bryan rubbed his eyes. He could feel a headache setting in—the need to shut off his thoughts had become too great. Maybe he should take the day off, go outside for a long walk.

But first he wanted to go to the exhibit at the Museum of Fine Arts. All week, colorful banners had been waving in the wind next to the streetlights downtown, announcing its arrival: "Mysteries of Egypt and The Great Pyramid." Every time he saw them, it felt as if the last remaining Seventh Wonder of the World had come to Boston just for him. He'd been planning to attend, and today would be the perfect day to go.

He grabbed his keys and left, passing one of his neighbors in the hallway—a young woman he had seen only once or twice before. She lived at the opposite end of the hall with her husband, and she was looking at him with a mixture of embarrassment and allure.

With a faint smile, he murmured a quick "Hello" and turned around to go back inside. He had forgotten to put on a shirt.

TWO

"The amount of stone in the Great Pyramid could build thirty Empire State Buildings, or a three-foot-high wall across the entire country and back."

Linz gazed up at the projections, wearing her headset, astounded by the facts the prerecorded guide was ticking off.

"The stones were cut with a tolerance matched only by our best opticians today. Every stone is the same. Expert stonemasons think ancient Egyptians must have used tools with a precision five hundred times greater than a modern drill. The exactitude they achieved is astonishing."

But how is that possible? Linz asked herself, growing more perplexed by the minute. The self-guided tour seemed to pose more questions than answers.

"Ancient Egyptians were purportedly unaware of the Earth's shape or size, and yet the Great Pyramid stands exactly one-third of the way between the equator and the North Pole. Its height and perimeter are in perfect ratio to the circumference of the Earth and radius of the poles. Its axis aligns to true North–South—even more accurate than the Greenwich Observatory in London. It is the largest and most precise structure ever built in the entire history of our civilization, and even today we cannot re-create it."

Growing restless, Linz took off her headset, abandoning the tour. The truth was she hadn't come to the museum to see this exhibit, but for a far more personal reason. Linz had only been a baby when her mother had passed away, and almost thirty years later she still felt drawn to this place that her mother had loved so much.

Linz had spent the last two hours roaming every gallery, but by the end of the morning she still felt melancholy. *Maybe I'll go play chess at the park*, she thought. It had been several months since she had moved back to Boston and she had not yet made the time to return to her old haunt at Harvard Square.

Heading toward the exhibit entrance to return her headset, she stopped to look at an exquisite Egyptian armband, meant not for a woman but for a warrior. A little smile flickered across her face. It looked just like the tattoo hidden under her sweater.

Just then another person touring the space came to stand beside her—not too close, but close enough to make her look up. He was the most arresting man she had ever seen with eyes an electrifying blue. They both stared at each other for a suspended moment. Then he walked on.

Linz stood rooted to the ground, watching him leave. She wanted to pull him back and replay the moment all over again.

As if he could read her thoughts, the man turned and stared at her once more before disappearing into the next room. Linz hovered, unsure of what to do. She felt a strange compulsion to follow him, to reenter the galleries and pretend that she had not just wandered through the whole thing. But it wasn't like she could just strike up a conversation about Nefertiti and ask for his number. She had never hit on anyone in her life, and she wasn't about to start at the MFA. With a sense of reluctance, she dropped off the headset.

When she exited the museum, the world outside felt different somehow. Playing chess at the Square didn't seem as appealing as it had five minutes ago, but she figured she would go anyway. Maybe focusing on a game would help still the strange flutter of her heart.

As she left, she couldn't quite brush off the brief encounter with the man inside or the odd feeling that she was making a mistake by walking away.

Harvard Square was a postcard come to life, where people from all over the city gathered to play chess. Her opponent, an old man wearing a golfer's hat, made his first move. Linz countered within seconds, listening to the quiet play from the other tables, and her pent-up tension gradually released. Within ten moves, she had won.

The old man grumbled and set up the board for another round. Linz won the next game too and he gave her a sharp look, obviously reassessing his assumption that the pretty girl would be any easy win.

What her opponent didn't know was that she had been Junior Grandmaster at age fifteen, the most prestigious title awarded young players. As a child, she had pursued chess with an all-consuming passion and had only relaxed her obsession when she entered high school, where she took care to downplay her various talents in order to fit in. Most teenagers didn't appreciate a know-it-all chess champion with a scholar's mind beyond her years. It was only in college that she embraced her eccentricities and found the confidence to allow herself to openly excel. And when she began a fast track to earning her PhD in neurogenetics, she was no longer self-conscious that she was the smartest girl in the room because everyone was brilliant.

The old man moved on to another table with a disgruntled look.

"This table open?" someone asked.

Linz looked up and froze. It was the man from the museum— her man, the one she had almost followed.

Her mind racing, she computed the likelihood of this outcome given the variables. Impossible. In a city the size of Boston, the chances of their meeting at the museum and then running into each other at another random location was one in a billion, if not more. For the first time in her life, she had no idea what to say.

"You're quite good," he said, sitting opposite her.

In disbelief, she watched him reset the pieces. They were going to play chess. She and Mystery Man were going to play chess.

He must have followed her here. But within seconds she torpedoed that idea. She would have noticed him trailing her, plus he had been deep inside the museum when she had left.

"The old man you just beat usually likes to boast that he's a top-ranked player in the Chess Federation," he told her with a quizzical smile.

"You've played him before?" she asked with surprise, wishing he would look up and meet her eyes, but he kept them fixed on the board.

"I've been coming here every week for the last couple of months."

The news came as a disappointment instead of a relief—he hadn't followed her. This was bizarre chance, nothing more.

Linz decided she would postpone winning to extend their time together. However, within the first three moves, two things became apparent: he was an expert at chess, and her strategy to prolong the game wasn't going to work.

They had completely different styles. He was lightning fast with his choices, mercurial even, while she was meditative. He won after six moves. Like her previous opponent had done with her, she had underestimated him.

Her ego thoroughly trampled, she vowed to annihilate him in the next round. "Again?" she asked sweetly.

He chuckled and nodded, studying her hands. His refusal to look at her was beginning to drive her crazy.

But then his eyes met hers. "Why were you at the exhibit?"

She stared back at him, her mouth suddenly dry. "My mother used to work there," she blurted.

He waited, as if knowing there was more to the story. Somehow, his unwavering gaze pulled the truth from her.

"She died when I was only six months old. Sometimes I like to imagine she's still alive and that we've lived a life together . . ." Linz trailed off. Although it had been muted by time, the ache of her mother's loss had always remained, and she never spoke to anyone about those feelings. Today seemed to be the exception.

"What was her name?" he asked gently.

"Grace." Linz could feel the lump rising in her throat and swallowed. "She was from England . . . she came here to help curate the Egyptian Art collection."

Dr. George Reisner had led the longest-running and most successful excavation in Egypt from 1905 to 1942, a joint effort by the MFA and Harvard. It had resulted in Boston becoming home to one of the largest collections of Egyptian artifacts in the world. Linz had thought it quite fitting that the visiting exhibit centered around Egypt too.

"When I was growing up, I would sometimes go there alone and pretend she was still here . . . that I would round a corner and bump into her," Linz confessed, astounded she was sharing something so intimate with a stranger.

But he only nodded and said nothing. There were no knee-jerk condolences or sympathetic remarks. He simply accepted and understood.

"Ready?" he asked softly.

Linz felt like he was talking about more than the game.

"Your move," he said.

She blushed and looked at the board, trying to recapture her determination to win. But as the game progressed, she began to realize it was pointless. He was unlike any player she had ever encountered. Most people mastered chess by remembering thousands of essential patterns and potential plays, but he played with no pattern, creating new ideas as he went. It was impossible for her to get ahead of him. Still, she retaliated with every tactical position and forced move in her arsenal. She caught him smiling on several occasions after one of her plays.

This went on forever. Neither said a word, until finally he spoke, "It's going to be a draw."

Linz checked the board, unwilling to admit defeat. A draw was not a win. But after a moment, she saw he was right. It irritated her that he had seen it first.

"I'm here every Friday if you want a rematch."

She glanced up at him, trying to see what he meant by that. Was he signaling that he wanted to see her again? Because she wasn't quite sure what to make of this whole encounter. But he was staring at the board again. Maybe the attraction she was feeling was all in her head.

Linz checked her watch and was startled to see that two hours had flown by. She had plans tonight and she needed to head home and change. She gathered her purse and stood.

"Thanks for the game," she said and held out her hand in goodbye, unable to explain her disappointment. Their strange meeting was about to end.

He stood too. Bowing his head, he took her hand and raised it to his lips. The slightest feather of his breath touched the skin at her wrist, and then her arm was once again dangling by her side.

"Until Friday, I hope," he murmured.

She felt her heart flutter inexplicably again. "Until Friday," she found herself saying.

As she walked away, she could feel his eyes on her the entire time, and it took all her willpower not to turn around and go back to ask him the one question she had meant to ask a hundred times during their game: she had never found out his name.

THREE

The reversal of our patients' symptoms has been staggering. I do not want to present our findings until we have drawn absolutely conclusive results, but we are on the precipice of obtaining a cure for Alzheimer's. Each patient shows a complete reversal of plaque formation as well as synaptic regeneration at levels far beyond our projections. However, it is the synaptic and glial cell activity that has been the most surprising.

One of the strangest side effects is that patients are recalling memories from early childhood and infancy. These are memories they had no recollection of, even prior to their illness. Are these memories real, and if so, why couldn't they be accessed until now?

We find ourselves in uncharted territory and I cannot help but ask the question: if the drug is this effective on a damaged mind, what would be its effect on a healthy one?

This question consumes me and my impulse to try the drug has become too great. I have become my own case study and have taken several doses, reassuring myself that I am not the first scientist in history willing to use his body in an experiment.

I have not discussed what I have done with the team yet, let alone Diana. I am worried they will think I've lost my mind. I plan to tell them tomorrow and perform a series of sleep studies on myself.

I've decided to keep a journal of results with as much transparency as possible, to leave a trail behind so I can remember where I started and why I began. What's happening to me now presents a truly unforeseen and confounding variable. My experiences are taking me beyond the scope of my imagination. I do not have answers. I am not even sure what the questions are.

MB

FOUR

Bryan stared at the chessboard and laughed. He had just met the most amazing woman—a woman who had gone to war with him for two hours and almost won—and he hadn't even asked her name. Somehow it hadn't felt necessary.

Her weakness, he could tell, was that she calculated to extremes instead of trusting her intuition. It didn't matter if she could see twenty moves ahead if she couldn't follow the thread in the game. Maybe one day he would talk her into playing blindfolded. Then she might be able to beat him.

He realized he was already assuming a future where they would meet again—because they would. He was sure of it.

Bryan had only been at the museum for a few minutes when he saw her. When he did, it was as if his world had stopped and then started again. He had taken those steps toward her involuntarily, needing to dissolve the space between them.

He had stood beside her, feigning interest in whatever she was looking at, waiting for her to notice him while his artist's eye memorized every detail about her. She was tall, her body frail and delicate like a dancer, the blond flyaway curls on her head careless and fresh. On some level he felt as if he already knew her, and yet he didn't know what to say. She was too lovely.

When she had looked at him, he had stared into her eyes, unable to look away as he recognized lifetimes hidden within them. And meeting her now, he knew without a doubt that the visions he had suffered since childhood were in fact memories. It was something he had tried to convince himself of all his life: that somehow his dreams were pieces of a past that belonged to his soul. Clinging to that belief had somehow helped him feel less insane. The people in his visions had actually lived, and he had found their lives chartered in history, but still he had always wondered if he was deluding himself—until now, because he couldn't shake his sense of certainty that she had shared those lives with him.

Bryan had been too stunned to speak to her, so he'd left, or pretended to.

His only course had been to follow her, although he had felt like a fool, lurking thirty feet behind. What would he say if she turned around and noticed him? How could he explain his actions?

He had almost lost her on the T, but had relaxed after he realized her destination was Harvard Square. Now he had an excuse to be there.

Ever since he had returned to Boston three months ago, he found himself at Harvard Square playing chess at least once a week. His love for the game had come after he had remembered the life of Pedro Damiano, a Portuguese chess master who lived in the fifteen hundreds. Pedro had written the first manual on chess strategy to be embraced by the Western world, and after Bryan had remembered Damiano's life, he had also inherited the man's expertise for the game—including his joy for playing blindfolded.

Those memories had come five years ago; and wherever Bryan had lived since, he had always sought out a park where players congregated to play. Within a month of moving back to Boston, he knew all the regulars at Harvard Square. Only two were good enough for him to bother playing, although they could never beat him. They were both men, and the man she had played today was one of them. Bryan had observed the pair from afar and whistled softly to himself when she had won.

Now as he watched her head back to the T, he stood up, feeling rejuvenated. His decision to move back to his hometown was taking on a whole new dimension, and for the first time in ages he couldn't wait for tomorrow.

Whistling a silly tune, he strolled for hours with no destination in mind, the cool breeze of Boston's autumn enjoyment in itself. The wind danced and caught him, making him walk farther than he had planned, until he found himself standing across the street from the gallery that was hosting his show. He waited for the crosswalk to turn green. *I'll go to the opening this evening,* he thought, *just for a few minutes. It'll be fine.*

He glanced at his watch and grimaced. The show was still a few hours away. Maybe he would grab a coffee and go browse the bookstore down the street. Then he could head to the gallery just as the doors were opening at five-thirty. He would pay the owners dutiful compliments about how wonderful the showroom looked, say hello to whoever happened to stop by early, and then be on his way. He assured himself the plan was sound. He could handle conversing with a handful of art lovers. People usually didn't start turning up at these things until eight or nine.

As he prepared to step into the street, he felt a searing pain behind his temple.

He hissed in shock and gripped his forehead. The woman waiting to cross next to him asked if he was all right.

Bryan closed his eyes, fighting the onset of a vision. Usually they came while he slept and days apart from one another, so to have two within twenty-four hours—and with no trigger in sight—stunned him. He needed to get home before he lost consciousness.

Muttering, "just a headache," he raced off, knowing he only had minutes before his mind took him somewhere else.

FIVE

Alexander stared out the carriage window and thought that if his life were a book and God had a pen, then George d'Anthès had been written to play the antagonist. Or perhaps the devil held the pen, for there was no doubt an evil heart hid behind the Frenchman's handsome looks and charming manner. Why else would Alexander find himself in a carriage at dawn on his way to duel with the man?

He only wished that he had the power to write today's outcome. It had been years since he had challenged anyone, let alone wielded a pistol. At thirty-seven, Alexander's world revolved around his wife, their four children, his writing, and whatever money could be earned by it. Yet he longed for the simple solace of his study to write his Peter the Great novel . . . perhaps his best work yet, if he could ever finish the damned thing.

With a heavy sigh, Alexander reached out to feel the pistol box. Perhaps it was folly to duel, but he refused to live out his days with the knowledge that he had done nothing to defend his wife's honor and his manhood. Ever since George d'Anthès had arrived in the city, he had robbed them of both. D'Anthès' ceaseless and open pursuit of Natalia could not be borne.

Hailed the beauty of Russia, Natalia outshone every woman at court. Such exquisiteness came with a price and he had been paying it for years, both mentally and financially. His wife was the belle of every party, and every party required a lovely gown and jewels. They had been living beyond their means and Alexander could not write fast enough to pay his debtors.

But money was the least of his worries at the moment; he hoped he would not shoot himself or create some other embarrassment, for he knew this contest would be talked about. He was not an egotistical man, but he acknowledged himself as a public figure. His writing had resounded with his countrymen—at least what had not been censored or denied publication.

The truth was, he wrote as he breathed and could not have stopped the words if he had wanted to. Even now he felt the beginning of a poem swirling among his dark thoughts.

He had forgotten his talisman today while getting dressed, a turquoise ring given to him by his good friend Nashchokin to protect him against harm. And he had to return to the house to get his coat. Even though he knew it would be terrible luck to retrace his steps, his feet had moved on their own accord.

These bad omens had started him thinking about the mechanics of destiny, and like an expert engineer, he had taken that notion and begun to craft a poem. If he had not been running late, he would have ordered the driver to pull over then and there so his pen could have free rein. He felt the words forming and only hoped to remember them later.

The carriage came to a stop and Alexander looked up with surprise. Here so soon—the time had vanished. He had hoped d'Anthès would be late so that he could have more time to gather his thoughts. But upon seeing his rival, the words dancing in his mind faded at once.

D'Anthès eyed him with a derisive sneer and bowed his head. "I thought you weren't coming. Old men don't do well in the morning."

Ignoring him, Alexander got out of the carriage and prepared his weapon. He breathed in the cold, marveling at how the snow-covered countryside resembled the one he had imagined for Onegin and Lensky when he had written their duel. Would he die just as his fictional poet Lensky had?

"Ten paces," he heard himself insist.

D'Anthès frowned. "But that's point-blank range."

Alexander nodded and stared at his challenger's face. Something in d'Anthès' eyes pulled at him, making him feel that they had played this part before—known hatred for one another before. Had their novel already been written? He felt the lines were there, destined to be enacted. And now here they both were. The ten paces felt like an eternity.

Turning to face the man who would kill him, Alexander knew his fate. It was as if he had left his lucky turquoise ring behind deliberately—as if somehow he had known in his heart's darkest chasm that nothing could protect him on this day.

D'Anthès' gun fired. Alexander felt the bullet flame in his stomach and dropped to his knees. As pain fogged his mind, he stared at the blood blooming in the snow and thought: *I am a winter rose.*

He saw that the bullet had hit exactly where Natalia had forgotten to sew a button back onto his coat and the realization brought his mind back to his duty. "My shot," he insisted, though his voice sounded faint.

D'Anthès stood still, but with a slight tremor. Though mortally wounded, Alexander still had the right to shoot. He aimed as straight as his shaking limbs would allow and fired. He saw d'Anthès drop to the ground.

Alexander fell back. The deed was done. He stared at the sky above him and waited for elation to take hold, but felt only emptiness. "Strange," he murmured to the clouds, "I thought I would be pleased."

Alexander floated in and out of consciousness until Natalia's screams roused him, and he knew he was back home.

He opened his eyes to find her crying on his chest, and tried to offer her comfort through his pain. "Do not shed tears, my love. It is over."

He stroked her hair, feeling her sobs against his body. The public—or the mob, as he liked to call them—had called her cold and selfish and questioned her devotion to him time and time again. But he did not have to explain their love; it filled his heart.

During the days that followed, he stayed lucid, but only for pockets of time, as eight doctors—including the Tsar's personal physician—visited his bedside in an attempt to save him. They all knew he was dying. His spirit lingered only because of Alexander's determination to leave this life without debt so his family would be free.

In the moments when he was awake, he dictated a list detailing his liabilities, along with a letter to the Tsar asking to be absolved of his obligations. The reply came within a day. Alexander smiled when he read it. The Tsar, who had clipped his wings and prevented him from going abroad, prevented his work from being published—prevented so many things—had freed him in the end.

He laid his head back on his pillow and stared at his library, where the books he had written sat next to others like old friends. He would miss this life, but he felt happy to leave behind his writing. They were the pages that contained his heart.

He heard Natalia enter the room. "We don't have cloudberries," she said, "but we have cloudberry jam."

Alexander held out his hand. "Feed it to me?" She sat beside him. He opened his mouth, feeling the spoon slip inside. The jam tasted like ambrosia. He swallowed it and said, "I want you to remarry." Natalia held the next spoonful midair, her lip quivering. Though Alexander did not want to continue, he did. "Mourn me and then let my memory go. Find a good man, someone who will provide for you better than I have."

Natalia broke down. "A good man? You are the only good man." She clenched her hand into a fist. "I wish I had been born a man. As God is my witness, if I were a man I would hunt down d'Anthès and kill him."

Alexander tried to calm her, but she continued to work herself into a state. "I should have been a man, then I could make him pay for what he's done!"

Alexander closed his eyes, unable to stop a smile, imagining his Natalia out for vengeance. How he would miss her. He had known innumerable women in his life, but he had wanted none of them for his own until Natalia. He loved her beauty, her charm, and her girlishness—how polar opposite they were, but how well they understood each other. No one could drive him madder or soothe his spirit more.

He hoped the world would be kind to her. She was not to blame for this fiasco. His friends had told him d'Anthès still lived, having only suffered a wounded arm. Just as well, he thought. He did not want to have the man's death on his conscience. Perhaps he was the lucky one. D'Anthès would have his death marked on his soul, a blemish surely impossible to erase.

Alexander's mind took him back to his poem. Two days had passed since the duel and he had not yet written it. Perhaps he should ask Natalia for his pen.

He tried to form the words on his lips, but became distracted as a light drew near, growing brighter with its warmth. The figure of a woman stood shining within it, holding out her hand for him.

Alexander gazed at her in wonder, knowing he must be dreaming. Lada herself, the ancient goddess of beauty and love, had sprung from a favorite folktale and come for him.

But her hair was black as night, her eyes a wondrous indigo. Jeweled bands spiraled up her arms and around her neck, and a golden headdress graced the crown of her head like an Egyptian queen. She spoke to him with her eyes, and somehow Alexander heard the words, *All that you are will be remembered.*

His entire being filled with peace as his spirit reached out to take her hand. With a last fleeting thought about the poem, he assured himself, *I will write it when I wake.*

Bryan opened his eyes and saw the painting of Natalia before him. She was lovely even in her grief, clutching her husband's hand as he took his final breath: He had just painted the moment of Alexander Pushkin's death.

Unable to fight the tide of memories, Bryan heard the Russian words pour from him as he cried for Natalia, for their children, for a life now irrevocably gone.

His rational mind tried to gain control. He forced his breathing to slow and whispered his mantra. "I am here now, I'm here now, I'm here now, I'm here now . . ."

But the words weren't working. Overcome by the urge to write, he found a pen and scribbled line after line. After ten minutes he stared at the paper—the writing was in Russian. And Pushkin's last poem, the one the world never saw, now rested in his hands.

Bryan ripped the paper to shreds. He didn't want Alexander Pushkin's memories. He had not yet recovered from remembering the lifetime of the priest in ancient Rome. Now he had the life of Russia's greatest, most prolific poet in his head too, all within the span of a few days. He felt besieged.

Unable to stop himself, he grabbed the nearest paint tubes and started to defile the painting, yelling obscenities in Russian. He didn't want to see Natalia, to love her, to feel her loss.

Repeated knocking at the door jarred Bryan from his rampage and saved him from destroying more paintings in the studio. He threw down the paint tubes, stormed over to the door, and whipped it open—screaming in Russian at the poor man standing there.

The pizza delivery guy took a step back. "Dude. Sorry, you order a pizza?"

Bryan stood there frozen, his mind blank.

The pizza guy tried again. "You order pizza? Speak-a-English? This number 401?"

Bryan shook his head in a daze. "Next door," he whispered and closed the door.

He walked back into his studio, becoming aware of his surroundings. The shredded poem littered the floor. His hands and clothes were streaked with paint.

He picked up the scraps of paper, grabbed the painting and his keys. He needed to get out.

Outside his building, he passed by the dumpster, threw the painting and the poem into it, and kept going. God, he needed some normality. The past week had been intense. Sometimes the visions came in fragments, like reliving chapters from an autobiography, and other times a life came all at once like a tidal wave. Alexander Pushkin and Origenes Adamantius had both been tidal waves. It felt like drowning.

For the first time, real fear hit him. He didn't know how much longer he could keep having these attacks and still function. What if he had one in public, what if he had one with *Her.*

There would be no way to explain it, and at some point he knew he wouldn't be able to hide them anymore. The episodes were growing stronger and becoming more frequent.

Consumed by these thoughts, he was unsure of how long he had been walking until he found himself heading to the wharf. He passed by street vendors selling their wares to tourists, and a Haitian woman behind a makeshift table displaying silver rings called out to him.

"Hey, I have ring for you."

Bryan turned and saw her holding it out to him.

"This one suit you," she said, her smile a riddle, and put the ring in his hand. "It protect you from bad spirits."

Bryan stared dumbfounded at the turquoise ring. It was almost identical to Pushkin's talisman. The only difference was in the marbling of the stone.

"How much?" he asked, reaching for his wallet.

She wanted twenty. Bryan gave her the bill and slipped the ring on his finger. It felt as if it were made for him. *Was it a sign?* If so, he couldn't imagine what the message might be.

As he walked on, he thought about the ethereal woman Alexander had seen moments before his death. This was not the first time she had materialized in the dreams of the people whose lifetimes Bryan had remembered. He wondered who she was and why she kept appearing. She looked like a picture he had once seen of the Egyptian goddess Isis, and this had been the real reason behind his visit to the Great Pyramid exhibit. He kept hoping to discover who she was.

Maybe he would try to paint her again. He had only attempted it once, years ago. With a sigh, he put his hands in his pockets—hands that should not belong to an artist but did—and for the thousandth time, he prayed for understanding.

SIX

Linz didn't usually attend art openings. A hermit by nature, she preferred curling up with a good book or working on a new puzzle whenever she gave herself downtime from work. And she did attend the symphony. It was her one foray into the arts.

She enjoyed going regularly, at least monthly, and had been doing it for years. In college, she had been teased by acquaintances for blasting Beethoven instead of the Black Eyed Peas. It was just one more thing that made her feel out of step with her generation and added to her shyness. So attending a cocktail party to discuss the latest in art was definitely out of her comfort zone. But Derek and Penelope were her oldest and closest friends, and she had promised to come see their new gallery as soon as she got back to town. That had been three months ago. So she had feigned enthusiasm when she received an invitation to tonight's event.

The Keller Sloane Gallery was high-end but modest and nestled on Newbury Street in one of Boston's most famous districts. After four blocks of inching forward in traffic, Linz finally spotted the marquee and pulled her car up to the valet sign. Handing her keys over to the young attendant, she maneuvered through a crowd in cocktail attire outside the gallery with wine and cigarettes in hand. She felt out of place already.

As Linz approached the entrance, the art critic for the *Boston Globe* held the door open, his eyes lingering on her as she passed. Linz didn't notice her effect as she walked in, but her arrival brought a breath of fresh air to the room.

She spotted Derek and Penelope sipping champagne in the corner. The gallery owners were quite the odd couple: Derek Sloane, flamboyantly gay and ramrod thin, loved to talk art and fashion at all times and could charm a rock; Penelope Keller was the business mind behind the dynamic duo and a quiet introvert with an obvious weight problem.

Derek swapped Penelope's full glass for his empty one and took a generous swig. "The reporter just left. I need a Valium." He turned to greet someone.

Penelope saw Linz right away and made a beeline to her. "Finally!" She hugged her. "You made it!"

Linz returned the embrace with a tight squeeze. It was good to see her again. Tears welled in her eyes, and she had to fight them back. What was wrong with her today? Ever since she had gone to the exhibit she had become hypersensitive. She saw Penelope give her a searching look and she tried to play off her strange behavior. "Sorry, I'm just happy to see you. I've been so busy trying to get everything up and running at the lab."

Even as she said it, Linz went back to thinking about today. After chess, she had gone to the office and cleared her calendar for Friday. No easy feat, there had been two important meetings that day—one with a colleague from Copenhagen who was flying in to review her study on a specific plasticity gene. That meeting technically couldn't be pushed back, but she had done it anyway. All for a stranger who she couldn't stop thinking about.

"Is that our mad scientist?" Derek joined them and kissed both of her cheeks. "About time we had our reunion."

"I'm sorry it's taken me forever to get over here. But this"— Linz motioned to the space—"is beautiful. When did all this come about?"

Penelope grabbed two more champagnes from a passing waiter and handed her one. "We were both in New York for the holidays last year and hatched the idea for the gallery over drinks."

"And voilà," Derek snapped his fingers. "Keller Sloane Gallery was born." His eyes scanned the room, looking at potential buyers. "Lord knows I needed to spend my money on something besides clothes."

Linz shook her head at his attempt at modesty. Derek had a graduate degree in art history from the Sorbonne and not only had an encyclopedic knowledge of the subject but was brilliant at spotting talent. Penelope was just as accomplished. She had an MBA from Dartmouth and had been looking for a challenge outside her family's successful real estate firm. Their partnership made perfect sense to Linz. But then she also knew them well. They had been inseparable in high school, sharing a special bond that came from four years of being labeled the fat girl, the gay guy, and the geek. Although the trio had gone their separate ways for college, they had managed to stay connected over the years. Now here they all were back in Boston.

Linz looked around the room. "This is quite a turnout." In fact, she could feel the buzz in the air—this was an event. For the first time, she became curious. "Who's the artist?"

The crowd had started to swell, and the noise level in the room had amplified. Derek had to lean in and raise his voice. "Bryan Pierce, came out of nowhere and made a huge splash in New York."

"Huge splash," Penelope agreed, eyeing an older gentleman in the corner making pencil notes on his card. "Buyers are even in from Europe and we have the exclusive."

Linz glimpsed a dramatic painting of a Japanese woman in an elaborate kimono. Her black hair fell like a silk curtain and trailed to the ground as she knelt at a koi pond, a lotus flower dangling from her hand. A reflection shimmered in the water as a man stood watching her from the bridge above.

The artist had signed his name in Japanese. Linz nodded to the painting. "He's Japanese?"

Penelope shook her head. "He signs each work with a different name. He won't explain why. We're guessing it's whoever's point of view the painting is from."

"Pretty wacky but original," Derek chimed in. "Part of his mystique."

Linz glanced around at all the men. "Which one is he?"

"Our man of the hour isn't here," Derek said, signaling a circling caterer to go refill his tray.

When a group of people moved aside, it offered Linz a glimpse of another painting nearby: the Palace of Versailles under construction. The detail in the sprawling image captured the transformation of King Louis XIII's hunting lodge to Louis XIV's opulent palace to perfection. Hundreds of workers had been painted in miniature, draining swamps, clearing trees, and expanding the building's core. On the periphery, the geometric expanse of the gardens was beginning to take shape, with the king himself overseeing its design.

Overcome by the urge to see everything, Linz abandoned her friends. "I'm going to take a look around," she murmured and wandered toward the first wall.

She lingered at the Versailles painting. The longer she stared at it, the more she was filled with a strange desire to be in seventeenth-century France. The painting was signed Louis Le Vau, and she wondered if he existed. She'd have to look him up when she got home.

Next, she moved to a rendering of Machu Picchu, the Lost City of the Incas, as it would have appeared in the fourteen hundreds. The artist had conjured a breathtaking vista thick with people in motion, in the midst of some kind of religious ceremony. Again, it was as if time had opened a portal so she could peer into the past. She bent down to study the signature. Instead of a name, it was a symbol of an eagle with a tiny feather in its claw.

The next canvas told another story, of a bedouin family on their way to lay offerings at the Treasury in Petra. The dawn light cast golden embers over the city, which was carved within a mountain. A young man stood high on a cliff, playing a wooden pan flute to the girl down below as she walked with her parents and her brothers. The girl was looking back at him, her head tilted upward with a smile. The moment had been captured so vividly; the song the boy played resonated in the paint.

Every painting was a masterpiece—even Linz could tell that. She assumed the artist must have traveled to each location in order to paint with such authenticity. But it wasn't just their beauty—something about the images pulled at her, making her want to be alone with them in the room.

She turned the corner, where a freestanding wall had been erected to hold a single painting, the largest and most dramatic piece in the gallery. The moment she saw it, her thoughts vanished and she was suddenly standing on a mental precipice that was threatening to give way.

Minutes stretched to their breaking point. Every brushstroke screamed back at her. Somehow this artist had reached into her mind and captured something known only to her.

"So what do you think?" Penelope had joined her.

Linz had trouble speaking as she tried to grasp what she was seeing. The horrific image looked as real as any photograph. It was a painting of a woman tied to a stake while a sea of prisoners and Roman soldiers watched her burn.

"He brought this one in two days ago," Penelope said. "It's magnificent."

Linz was still struggling to find her voice. "P, I know this sounds weird, but did you tell this guy about my dream?"

Penelope frowned. "What dream?"

"The dream. The one I always had. Remember, I was going to that therapist?"

"You mean in high school? That dream?"

Linz turned to her, trying hard not to sound as hysterical as she felt. "It's the same as this painting. Exactly the same."

"Why would I tell someone about a recurring dream you had in high school? That's crazy."

The dream had haunted her not just in high school but her whole life. More like a nightmare, it had started when she was five and plagued her for years—always the same vision of being burned alive. It was so real that she would wake up screaming.

Her father had taken her to therapist after therapist. They had tried hypnosis, sleep studies, medication, but nothing had helped. Then one day, it just stopped, right around the time she had left home and gone to college. Over time, she had filed it away as a strange childhood phobia and tried to forget it.

But now the nightmare had manifested itself in unbelievable detail on a canvas at her best friends' art gallery. Her gaze darted over the painting again. She could already count twelve details that no one but her could know. One—the black crow that had come to land on the wood at the woman's feet, wings spread as if to shield her from the flames. Two—a child and a young woman watching from the tower; they had shared a cell with the woman at the stake and were to die the next day. Three—the priest reaching out to stop the flames as guards held him back, swords at his neck. He had been the woman's friend and teacher. Linz even remembered his name. Her eyes went to the signature on the canvas and she gasped. *Origenes Adamantius*—the Roman priest's name. There was no way he could know it.

Unable to comprehend the coincidences in play, she stepped back from the painting. "I need to talk to this artist."

SEVEN

Fingering the new turquoise ring on his hand, Bryan walked on automatic pilot as his mind tried to force his new memories to settle. When he finally did look up, he saw he had headed down Atlantic to a restaurant near the wharf, Doc's Waterfront Bar & Grill.

Bryan hesitated at the door, wondering if he felt up to seeing anyone tonight. Just as he was about to turn around and go home, the door opened for him.

"Well look who Picasso dragged in." Lou Lou, the house manager, winked. "Your dad's in the back counting lobster."

"I'll wait at the bar." Bryan went and sat at the far end, away from the tourists enjoying cocktails. He glanced at his watch, surprised by the time. His stomach grumbled.

Patty, his father's longtime bartender, came over. "Hey Bry, your dad said you were back in town. What'll it be?"

Bryan grimaced. Most of the employees at his father's restaurant had worked there for years and known him when he was growing up. His father, Doc, inspired people to stick around. Doc was a big bear of a man with the kindest heart and was always the first to be anyone's friend. He was also a wonderful father, but Bryan could count on one hand the number of times he had seen him since coming back, even though he knew how much weight his father had placed on his homecoming.

It wasn't that Bryan didn't want to see his dad. The problem was that when he stared into someone's eyes for too long, he could recognize them as other people from his dreams. Needless to say, this complicated matters when he was around those closest to him. He'd always known he couldn't talk about such things or someone would lock him up for sure. Or maybe he did need help, he wondered for the thousandth time. He was no longer sure if he could keep struggling alone.

"Bry? You okay?" Patty was still waiting for an answer.

"Sorry. Stoli, straight up." It seemed only fitting after today.

Patty poured him a shot and left the bottle on the bar with a wink.

Bryan took the shot and poured another, already regretting his decision to come here. Then he saw his father walk toward him, beaming.

Doc enveloped him in a hug. Bryan closed his eyes and squeezed back.

His dad pulled away and slapped him on the shoulder. "Covered in paint, surprise, surprise. I knew you were working. Told your mom that's why you missed tonight. When we left, there was quite a crowd coming in."

Bryan shrugged, unable to explain the real reason he hadn't showed—that he was too busy reliving Alexander Pushkin's life. He grimaced and poured another shot. "Want to hang out and drink with your son?"

"Twist my arm," Doc said, but then tried to sound serious. "Just call your mother tomorrow. She was disappointed we missed celebrating your birthday last week . . . she even came to the gallery with a cake in the car."

Bryan gave a pained sigh. He was in for it. "I've had a lot on my mind," he said, knowing he sounded defensive.

"Hey now, don't shoot the messenger." Doc brought over a basket of peanuts. Bryan loved the fact that his father knew him well enough not to ask what had been on his mind. "Be right back," Doc said. "Let's round you up some real food." And he was off to the kitchen before Bryan could protest.

Bryan downed another shot, welcoming the burn of the vodka. His cell phone vibrated and he looked at the number. Apparently the same person had called earlier—twice. He also had a voice mail. On a whim, he picked up. "Hello?"

"Hello? I'm trying to reach Bryan Pierce."

Bryan stilled at the sound of the woman's voice, felt it reaching for him through the line.

"My name is Linz. I'm a friend of Penelope and Derek's, from the gallery. I made it to your show tonight."

He knew this voice. It was the woman from the park. Bryan grabbed on to the counter, unable to believe this was happening.

"Hello? Are you there?" she asked.

"Yes. Go on," he whispered.

"There's a painting I'd like to ask you about. Maybe we could meet?"

"Yes." He wanted her to never stop talking.

"You signed a painting Origenes Adamantius. Isn't that the priest who watched the woman burn?"

Tension began to coil in his body. "You know that?"

She didn't say anything.

"How do you know that was his name?" Bryan waited, holding his breath.

"I was going to ask you the same thing. Like I said, we need to meet."

"When?" He was ready to hang up and go now. Instead, she suggested her place in the morning. He agreed and wrote down the address, his hand shaking. This was why the painting had to be at the opening—he had brought it to the gallery for her.

He hung up and stared at the phone in disbelief. He now had her name, address, and phone number, and he was going to meet her tomorrow. He wouldn't have to wait until next Friday for their paths to cross again. They were already entwined.

He looked at his turquoise ring and, on impulse, kissed it for luck.

EIGHT

Bach's Air on the G String blared from the speakers. Linz sat at her dining room table, nursing a third cup of coffee and placing puzzle pieces together. Last night had been her worst sleep in ages. From the moment she had recognized the painting, she had been wired. Then an even stronger anxiety had gripped her after she had spoken with the artist. What had compelled her to suggest her place? A coffeehouse would have been better.

Already nervous, she looked around her immaculate living room but could find nothing to clean. She forced her attention back to the five-thousand-piece puzzle she had begun earlier this morning, now already half-finished, and tried to calm her nerves. The whole thing was probably just a strange coincidence, and no doubt this meeting today was entirely unnecessary. Maybe she should cancel.

She picked up her phone to call him but then hesitated. The clock already read ten minutes past ten. Most likely he wasn't even coming. It was probably for the best.

Unknown to Linz, Bryan had been standing outside her door for the last ten minutes, unable to ring the bell.

Just ring it, you idiot. He forced himself to do it.

Seconds later, Linz opened the door. Her "hello" died on her lips when she saw him standing there.

"You!" she exclaimed.

He saw the disbelief on her face, the accusation.

"You're the artist? Penelope and Derek's artist?" she demanded, incredulous, her mouth opening and closing like a fish.

"Yes. Bryan Pierce." He felt a twinge of guilt. At least he'd had some time to get over the shock after recognizing her voice on the phone.

"This is not possible," she said, her voice rising.

"I'm afraid it is." He tried to be gentle.

"We randomly meet three times?"

"We only met randomly once," he said, confessing, "I followed you to the Square."

"You followed me?" She crossed her arms defensively, blocking the door.

Inwardly, Bryan groaned. Now she thought he was dangerous. "I was intrigued," he said, settling on a miniature version of the truth. "The third time was your doing," he reminded her. "You called me about my painting."

"But that's still random. I didn't know who you were," she argued, not sounding mollified at all.

"Well, I didn't know who you were either," he said. "We're two strangers who happened to play chess together at the park and then you saw my exhibit . . . a little serendipity at hand, that's all." *Like hell*, he thought to himself, but he had to do something to put her at ease. She looked ready to scream and bolt the door. For good measure he added, "I'm perfectly harmless. I promise. You can call Derek and Penelope."

Hearing those two names seemed to have the desired effect. After a moment she visibly relaxed, most likely convincing herself this wasn't as improbable as it seemed.

"Serendipity." She stepped back with a wry smile, offering him entry. "Okay, then. We'll call it that. Thank you for seeing me."

Bryan came in and Linz shut the door, standing there for an awkward moment, as if hesitant to join him. Bryan wandered around, pretending to admire the view. Her place was a low-rise on Back Bay with a scenic view of Charles River. With its Zen-like atmosphere, walnut wood floors, skylights, and vaulted ceilings, the space felt serene yet luxurious at the same time.

Near the windows stood the most enormous, serious-looking home telescope he had ever seen. The metal plate said it was an observatory-class Celestron Pro, and it had probably cost a fortune.

"You're a serious stargazer," he guessed.

"I studied a little astronomy in college," she said. "Do you know anything about astronomy?"

The hint of a smile played on Bryan's face. "A little." He left it at that.

Linz eased away from the door. "Coffee?"

"Yes, please. Black," he said, watching her head into the kitchen. His body sagged with relief as she left the room, and he collapsed onto the couch. Closing his eyes, he put his head in hands and reminded himself: *I am Bryan Pierce. I am here now. I'm here now. I'm here now.* He repeated the mantra for a full minute until he regained control.

By the time Linz returned, he had composed himself and was standing in front of a dramatic framed puzzle that took up the entire back wall. A little plaque underneath it read: "LIFE: The Great Challenge by Royce B. McClure. World's largest puzzle, twenty-four thousand pieces." The puzzle was a whimsical composite of an ocean surrounded by wildlife, sailboats, and hot-air balloons, all under the Milky Way. It made him smile.

He took a deep breath and turned around. She handed him his coffee.

Bryan murmured thanks as he tried to hold all of the memories swirling in his mind at bay. He could now recognize Linz from over two dozen dreams and counting. He had never had this happen with any one person before. But even if he could take an eraser and wipe away all those memories, his pulse would still be racing. There was something about her being that electrified him.

He moved on to study the apartment's one remaining eccentricity, an indoor sand garden that took up one full corner of the living room.

Linz studied him as he stood there in silence.

"You rake patterns in the sand," he said finally, marveling at the beautiful symbol she had drawn. He resisted the urge to touch it.

She nodded, looking embarrassed. "I got the inspiration for it watching a travel show about a garden in Kyoto. The next weekend I went to Home Depot and bought everything." She took the rake and erased the design as if it were too private for him to see. "Every grain and pebble had to move with me from California."

Bryan could hear the nervousness in her voice. She was uncomfortable. Was he really just a stranger to her? He continued his tour around the room, taking the space in, trying to understand her as much as he could. "Puzzles, stars, and sand gardens," he murmured. "No chessboard?"

"In the closet."

"And Bach," he offered. The violin continued to softly fill the room.

"This is my favorite concerto." She watched him move to finger the puzzle pieces covering the dining table. It was a puzzle of the *Mona Lisa*. "They're kind of an addiction. Sometimes I frame favorites and hang them on the wall." She gestured to the living room. "Do you like puzzles?"

She was trying to seem relaxed, but Bryan could hear the stress in her voice. She was regretting this meeting. He looked around the room again and took it all in. Her home was like a fascinating kaleidoscope offering a glimpse of her inner self. And yet it also felt . . . lonely. *She never has anyone here,* he thought. And yet, she wanted him to come. A rush of emotions filled him. He picked up one puzzle piece from the hundreds spread out on the table and placed it in the correct spot.

Linz gave him a perplexed look. "How did you do that?"

"Do what?"

"Know where the piece fit. You hardly looked at it."

He put his hands in his pockets again. "I looked at it."

"You have a photographic memory." She said it like an accusation.

"What makes you say that?"

With a raised eyebrow, she picked up several puzzle pieces from the stack and put them into place. With a little smile, Bryan watched her hands and accepted the challenge. He picked up three pieces from the stack and placed them. She took three more. He took four.

Soon they were hunched over the table, battling over who could connect the pieces faster. Bryan found the task a soothing distraction.

"Why did you sign the painting Origenes Adamantius?" she finally asked.

At first Bryan didn't answer. "Why do you think Origenes Adamantius was the man's name?"

Linz gave him a searching look. "Because it was. Wasn't it?"

"Yes, but how do you know that?" he insisted.

"From a dream I had."

Bryan glanced up at her. "What was the dream?"

She looked away, focusing on the puzzle, and for a moment she didn't say anything. Bryan could tell how hard all of this was for her. She seemed very private. But then she began to speak. "I've had it over and over since I was a child. It's always the same. In the dream I am this . . . woman. . . ." She said the words in a slow detached fashion. "From ancient Rome. There's a huge trial, a religious persecution. I was one of thousands who were burned. And it's just like your painting, every detail . . . the bird, the child crying, the dress she was wearing, the cross in my hand—her hand. He had given it to her."

"The priest. Origenes." Bryan watched her thumb absently trace a pattern on her index finger, knowing that if she did it long enough the circle would change into a figure eight.

Linz nodded. Her voice wavered. "The guards tied her to a post and set her on fire. The priest was forced to stand there and watch as punishment. I can tell he wanted to save her, but he couldn't." Her words trailed into a whisper, "Just before I wake up, I feel my feet burning."

Bryan fought back a surge of grief. He couldn't speak.

She misinterpreted his silence as disbelief and added, "I know it sounds crazy. My father took me to therapist after therapist. By the time I was a teenager, the dream had become less frequent and eventually went away. Then I saw your painting."

Instead of responding, Bryan began to place the remaining puzzle pieces with unbelievable speed.

Linz watched his hands work with a rapt expression on her face and prompted him again, "Where did you come up with the idea for the painting? Did Penelope mention it to you?"

"No." He placed several more pieces.

Linz waited, asking him again. "Why did you sign the painting Origenes Adamantius?" She tried to lighten the mood by adding, "And don't you dare say serendipity."

Bryan wasn't sure how to respond. Right now, she wouldn't believe any explanation he could offer. So he settled for, "It's complicated."

Linz put the final piece into the corner of Mona Lisa's mouth and sat back, folding her arms. "I like complicated."

They held each other's gaze, and a current passed between them.

"Sorry, I have to go." He stood up abruptly. "Thanks for the puzzle."

He reached out with his finger and touched her hand on the table. It was the smallest stroke, the slightest caress. By the time Linz registered what he had done, his hand was gone and Bryan was almost to the door.

He held his breath, terrified that a vision might take hold of him any minute. He had stayed longer than he should have, and could feel a recall bearing down on his consciousness like a wave. Only minutes remained before it crashed.

"Wait!" Linz stood up, looking flustered. "Derek said the painting was the only one that wasn't for sale. I'd be willing to pay double what you'd want. Money isn't a problem."

Bryan tried to focus on her but his vision was beginning to blur. He shook his head and backed away in a blind daze. In two steps, he was out the door.

He hurried outside and staggered toward his car. Fumbling for his keys, he got into his SUV, locked the doors, and lay down in the back. The last thing he remembered thinking was that he was glad he had bought a car with tinted windows.

A low moan escaped his mouth as his mind dilated, allowing in another time and place.

NINE

Michael Backer's eyes fluttered as he regained consciousness. He was lying on a padded table in a dim laboratory chamber filled with cutting-edge technology. Electronic equipment hummed in the background and a helmet-like device with electrodes attached to it covered his head, busy recording all the neural oscillations and electrical activity going on in his brain.

Three scientists observed him through a glass wall. Finn Rigby, the youngest of the trio, watched the EEG monitor and checked his watch for the tenth time, while fellow team member Diana Backer hovered next to him, reading several printouts. She looked tired. "Someone want to remind me why we're doing this?"

"Because your husband is crazy," answered the third member of the group. Conrad Jacobs took off his horn-rimmed eyeglasses and rubbed the bridge of his nose. He was an East Coast intellectual who was perpetually disheveled, with food-stained clothes and a case of serious bed head. "People, I'm fried. This is going nowhere. I suggest we go home, get some sleep, and get back to real science tomorrow." He stood up to leave just as Michael began to speak from inside the chamber.

Everyone strained to listen. "What's he saying?" Diana motioned to the volume control for the laboratory's microphone. "Turn it up."

Finn turned a knob on the instrument panel and brought Michael's voice into the room. The EEG reading went ballistic as Michael's brainwave patterns spiked.

Diana closed her eyes to hear the words better. "What the hell is he speaking, Latin?"

Conrad sat back down. He wasn't going anywhere now. "No. Greek."

Finn looked over at them. "Mike knows Greek?"

Diana shook her head.

Conrad snapped his fingers twice. "Hey, Dixie, you recording this?"

Finn scowled. Conrad had a knack for getting under people's skin. Finn was a gentleman, born and raised in South Texas. He had all the manners that straitlaced churchgoing parents could instill, but Conrad's condescension rubbed everyone the wrong way.

Finn exaggerated his Southern drawl. "Never crossed my mind, Yankee Doodle."

Conrad ignored the jibe as he listened to Michael ramble in fluent Greek for close to ten minutes.

Finn whistled as the EEG readings went off the charts. "Shit on me."

"Not as eloquent, but precisely my thought." Conrad folded his arms, his face set in a deep frown. "This is implausible, people. Anyone here fluent in Greek?"

Diana shook her head. "No, but somehow he is."

Michael's words grew softer until they faded to silence. The team waited to see if he would speak again. But Michael remained immobile, apparently still asleep.

In reality Michael had been awake, trying to reconcile what had just happened to him. But he couldn't come to terms with it. His panic rose and he sat up, yanking the electrodes off his head.

Diana hurried in and brought up the lights. "Hon? You okay? What the hell just happened?"

Michael took several deep breaths as he prepared to lie to his wife for the first time. "What do you mean? What happened?"

"You were speaking in Greek just now."

"Greek?"

"We recorded it."

He looked away, disconcerted . . . that complicated matters. He remembered speaking Greek in his dream, but he hadn't realized he had spoken aloud. He also remembered speaking Latin and Hebrew. Dizzy, he closed his eyes. Diana reached out to support him.

Finn spoke into the microphone. He and Conrad were still behind the glass wall in the control room. "You okay in there, chief?"

Conrad leaned in and added, "Mike, can you describe what happened?"

Everyone waited for an answer. "Sorry, it's all kind of disjointed." Michael could feel their disappointment.

Diana tried to buoy the group. "Everyone, it's late. Let's give him time."

She continued to talk but Michael wasn't listening—instead he was riveted by her eyes. How could he explain his certainty that she had been the woman he had just witnessed being burned alive in ancient Rome? The memory still fresh in his mind, he walked out before anyone could see him cry.

It was four-thirty a.m. and only six cars sat in Boston's Neurological Institute's parking lot. Diana got behind the driver's seat of an old Jeep Cherokee. Michael climbed in beside her and closed his eyes. After a few tries, the car started and they pulled out.

The drive home to their apartment in Charleston took ten minutes. Michael felt the car come to a stop.

"Hon? We're here," Diana said softly, keys in hand.

He appreciated her not grilling him on the way home but could tell she was brimming with questions.

She led him up the stairs, unlocked the door to their apartment, and disappeared into the bedroom. Michael sat on the couch and listened to her move about as she changed. He stared at the small living room. Everything looked the same but different.

A tiny one bedroom, the place had been perfect while they

were in med school—the rent was cheap—so they had stayed even after they had gotten married. They were currently channeling all their funds into their research, with the hope that it would pay off down the road. Michael wasn't sure if what happened to him tonight was their biggest breakthrough or a brutal end to their study.

Diana came out in her nightgown, her face scrubbed and her hair in a ponytail. It made her look sixteen instead of forty, and Michael gave a small smile. It reminded him of an old gymnastics picture he had seen of her in high school, poised on the balance beam—head gymnast, she liked to remind him. Petite and athletic, she still had a nymph-like air about her, coupled with a look of immense concentration and determination to tackle any obstacle. Right now, the obstacle happened to be him.

She sat on the chair instead of the couch, and crossed her arms. "Are we going to talk about why you lied?"

Michael remained silent.

"I know you remember what happened in there."

"I need some time."

"For what? Shutting us out of our own study?"

Michael didn't want to do this now. "I'm not shutting you out," he insisted and went to the kitchen to get a glass of water. The apartment was so small they were still in the same room, but she followed him anyway.

"We sanctioned this. You can't have a reaction and keep it to yourself. This isn't just about you." She pointed her finger at his chest to punctuate the point.

"I know that. Don't poke me."

"I didn't poke you," she snapped.

"Yes, you did," he yelled back.

"I can't believe you're trying to change the subject."

"I'm not! I said I can't talk about it yet. Can you please accept that and let it go?"

"How can you tell me to just let it go? You were speaking Greek! I'm pretty sure that's not a normal side effect!"

"Yes, I'm aware of that!" He drank the water and spit it out. For some reason he could only taste the chlorine, fluoride, and heavy metals.

"What's wrong?" she asked, her concern overriding her anger. She took the glass and smelled it.

"This tastes horrible." Then he realized his perception of how water should taste had changed now that he had something to compare it to—pure water from the third century.

Diana stormed over to the liquor cabinet. "How about a real drink?"

Michael debated. A stiff one might help. "No, then I can't drive."

"Where are you going?" Her back was to him. He could hear the hurt and bafflement in her voice.

He wanted to apologize to her—he knew he should—but instead he said, "I need a library."

"At five a.m.?" Diana abandoned the drinks and sat on the couch, putting her head in her hands. "I knew this was a mistake. I can't believe you talked me into letting you take it. Everything was on track. This could derail the study, our grant . . . everything."

"Diana, you have to trust me." Michael couldn't stop his voice rising again. "I will tell you everything, but not tonight."

"Well guess what?" She glared at him. "It's morning."

Feeling helpless, Michael gently shook his head no.

"Honey, I'm scared," she pleaded with him. "Something happened to you. Ever since you took Renovo and woke up on that table, it's like you're not even here. Look at yourself in the mirror. What the hell happened?"

Michael turned away from her, unable to deal with this right now. He could count on one hand the number of times they had fought in their six years together. She was his partner in everything and he had never kept her in the dark before. He grabbed the keys.

His voice sounded far away, even to his own ears. "I can't do this tonight. You're not helping me." He left before she could respond.

He got into the car. The first thing he did was adjust the rearview mirror so he could see his reflection. Diana had not been imagining things. Something was different. Outwardly, he still looked the same—the same Roman features, the same thick, black hair peppered with gray, the same five o'clock shadow he could never seem to lose. But there was a barely perceptible change within his eyes. Of course Diana had seen it. She knew him better than anyone.

He readjusted the mirror and drove, trying to kill the guilt he felt for shutting out his wife. She would forgive him later, once he explained, but for now he needed solitude to sort out the chaos in his head and prove that what existed in his mind was not some elaborate delusion triggered by the drug. He needed books.

Checking the time, he knew the Research Services Desk at Harvard's Lamont Library wasn't open yet. He would have to wait. Driving aimlessly, he saw St. Francis de Sales up ahead and pulled over. Michael had driven past the church countless times but had never felt the urge to go inside, until now.

He found the doors unlocked, inviting those in need of quiet reflection before the six-thirty mass inside. He walked in and was relieved to find no one else in sight.

As he sat on a pew, the enormity of it all hit him: his team had just created a super drug that made LSD seem like baby aspirin, he had just relived the life of a priest in third-century Rome, and he was not sure if what he had gone through was a series of hallucinations or actual memories.

All he knew was that the dream had felt as real as life and would bring ramifications. In one day, another man's experiences had been added to his—a man who had lived over eighteen hundred years ago. Michael also couldn't ignore the feeling that he had recovered a piece of himself he hadn't even known was missing.

The scientist within him could not accept those findings. He wasn't sure how to even begin to form a hypothesis, let alone how to analyze the data.

He found himself kneeling and closed his eyes. The Act of Love prayer came to his lips of its own accord. "*Domine Deus, amo te super omni et proximum meum propter te, quia tu es summum, infinitum et perfectissimum bonum, omni dilectione dignum. In hac caritate vivere et mori statuo. Amen.*"

As he spoke, he listened to the Latin, simultaneously translating the words in his mind: *O Lord God, I love you above all things and I love my neighbor for your sake because you are the highest, infinite, and perfect good, worthy of all my love. In this love I intend to live and die. Amen.*

The prayer sounded alien to him, and he wondered how he, a declared atheist, could have internalized these beliefs. But his spirit embraced the words and the emotions they inspired, making him forget the question. He felt tears well in his eyes, and despite himself, he cried without shame.

Soon the sounds of parishioners intruded on his thoughts as they began to file in for mass. The curtain at the altar parted and an elderly priest came out from behind, busy preparing the table. He gave Michael an inquisitive look. It was obvious he had been listening.

Michael hurried to the exit, wanting nothing more than to avoid people. Outside, he got back in his car and stared at the church. *What in the hell was that about?*

Without warning, he felt an urgent need to sleep. The library would have to wait.

He locked his doors, leaned back in his seat, and within moments sank into blissful oblivion.

TEN

Bryan opened his eyes and stared at the ceiling of his car, still feeling himself fall asleep as Michael Backer. His visions had never brought such clarity before.

He was Michael Backer.

Bryan sat up and laughed at the irony of it: he no longer thought he was crazy because he believed he was a forty-year-old neuroscientist from the eighties. But somehow it made perfect sense. Although he still had a thousand questions—to begin with, who the hell were these people and what had happened to them?

He closed his eyes and tried to recall more, frustrated that he had only remembered a small part of Michael's life. This man was the key to everything, just as he felt certain that Linz had been Diana, Michael's wife.

Bryan abandoned his attempt to retrieve more memories and checked his watch. He had been in Linz's parking lot for over nine hours. Their meeting this morning felt like a lifetime ago. He grabbed his cell phone and called her.

"Hello?" Linz answered, between bites of pizza as she worked on her computer.

"Linz? This is Bryan, from this morning."

She sat up in disbelief.

"I was wondering if we could meet again?"

Linz was speechless. He literally ran out the door this morning and now he wanted to meet. This man was an utter enigma. And one thing Linz couldn't resist was a puzzle. "Um, when?"

"Now, I'm outside."

"You're here?" she squeaked. She'd just changed into her pajamas. Linz rushed to peek out the window and was able to see him on the street.

He pressed on. "It's important."

"What's important?"

"Can I come up?" he asked.

"No." She knew she sounded irritated, but she couldn't help it. He ran out on her, dammit. "Just tell me over the phone. I'm busy with work."

"I can't. I need to see you," he insisted.

Linz shook her head at herself. She was actually deliberating whether she should see him—because she desperately wanted to. She hadn't stopped thinking of him all day.

"Linz. Please." He said softly, his voice insanely intimate.

That did it. She was in big trouble. "Well, there's a bar down the street called The Corner," she offered, hating how flustered she sounded. She had to get a grip on herself. "I'll meet you there in twenty minutes."

She hung up and rushed to the bedroom to change. Debating on a little black dress in the mirror, she rolled her eyes at herself and settled for jeans.

The Corner was a quaint neighborhood pub with dim lighting, leather booths, and three dartboards along the back wall. Bryan sat in the far corner with a vodka shot and kept his eyes on the door.

Linz walked in. She scanned the bar and found him. When they saw each other, Bryan's chest constricted, making it hard for him to breathe. New memories threatened to take hold of him. He closed his eyes and tried to focus. *Stay here. Stay. Here. I am here now. I am here now.*

"Bryan?"

Bryan opened his eyes to see her staring down at him with a frown on her face, and he couldn't help but laugh.

"Something funny?" she asked.

"My life." He gestured, "Please."

She sat across from him and put her laptop on the table.

To Bryan, the intimate booth became even smaller. He stared at the tattoo circling her arm, seeing it for the first time. "That looks like the armband from the museum," he commented. It also made her look fierce.

Her eyes flashed in surprise at his observation.

"I like it," he said simply, feeling her size him up.

"So do you normally show up at people's doorsteps like this?" she asked. Her laptop beeped.

"Do you normally bring a computer everywhere with you?"

"I was in the middle of scanning a program when you called. It needs babysitting." She typed in a quick command. "This'll just take a second."

Bryan waited, content to watch her. He had so many memories of her brimming up inside of him, but instead of dwelling on them, he forced his mind to find the most socially acceptable question he could possibly ask. "What do you do?"

Linz focused on the monitor as her hands flew across the keyboard. "Give you a hint." She motioned to her tattoo.

Bryan wasn't sure what she was getting at. He took a guess. "A spiral?"

"A double helix."

He choked on his drink. "You're a scientist?"

"Geneticist." Her computer beeped again. "I decipher code to determine how the brain makes memories." She saw the expression on his face. "Your disbelief is noted."

"No, it's not that. I . . ." he floundered, grappling with the impossibility of it. What could he say?

Just then a gum-smacking waitress came over to take their order. "What'll it be, kiddos?"

Linz debated. "I'll have a glass of the claret."

Bryan tapped his glass. "Another Stoli."

"You got it." The waitress sashayed off.

Linz typed one more command. Bryan studied her fingers. *She has Katarina's hands.*

Her computer beeped in response and she turned to Bryan, giving him her undivided attention. "So. What did you want to talk to me about?"

Bryan didn't know where to start. He saw the hurt lurking in her eyes and realized she needed an apology. "First off, I'm sorry I ran out on you this morning. I'm not good with people."

"No kidding."

He ignored the jibe. "I don't talk about myself, ever, but you deserve an explanation." He took a deep breath, about to go out on a limb. "I did the painting after a dream I had. Well, kind of a dream." He frowned. How to explain it? "Sometimes, I wake up, and there's the canvas—done. It's not painting. I don't know what it is. Most of the time, I don't even remember doing them."

He didn't go into the fact that the paintings had been a coping mechanism for years now, or that he had started painting when he was a young teenager at the height of his attacks. He called them attacks because that was what the dreams felt like, battering the wall of his consciousness, until sometimes he didn't know reality from the dream. He had other names for them as well: visions, recalls, episodes, foreign memories. But no matter what words he used, it was all the same.

Linz stared at him, her eyebrows raised in disbelief. Bryan wondered if she realized he was telling her something no one else knew.

She prompted, "And in the dream?"

"A priest named Origenes watched his dearest friend and most loyal follower be executed. Her name was Juliana."

"How do you know that?" Her eyes widened with shock. "How do you know her name? I never told you that. Why didn't you say this before?"

He could see her working herself up, and he hadn't even gotten started. "You know, I'm sorry. This was a bad idea."

She touched his arm in apology. "Wait. I'm not accusing you. I just find this a little hard to believe. People don't share the same dream."

Her hand sent a quiver down his body. He moved his arm away, severing the connection. "Maybe people share the same dreams all the time and just don't know it. If you hadn't gone to my opening, we wouldn't be having this conversation."

Linz sat back and chewed on her lip. "In my dream the priest said something to her when she died. What about yours?"

Bryan nodded with surprise and his chest constricted again. Origenes had never known if Juliana had heard him call out to her before she died—but she had.

Linz took a napkin and wrote on it, folded it up, and handed him the pen. "Write it down."

Bryan did, and they exchanged napkins like contraband. He didn't bother opening hers. He knew the same three words were written on each of them and that they were the words Origenes had called out right before the flames had devoured Juliana's body.

Bryan searched her face, eager to see how she would react. "He said, 'Go to God.'"

Linz stared at the napkin in her hands. "This is unbelievable."

Bryan took an even bigger gamble and asked a question—in Greek. *"Do you speak Greek?"*

"No, I don't speak Greek." Then she froze.

I knew it. Bryan sat back, amazed. *"You do speak Greek."*

"Trust me, I think I'd know if I . . ." She trailed off. The waitress hovered with their drinks, listening to Bryan reproach Linz in Greek.

"You understand me."

Linz couldn't answer. She was dumbstruck.

Bryan insisted, *"You do. I can't believe it."*

The waitress plopped their drinks down. "One wine, one Stoli."

Utterly perplexed, Linz looked up at the woman. "Did you understand anything he just said?"

"Not a clue, honey." The waitress popped her bubble at them and left.

Linz nodded and took a big drink from her glass. Bryan remained quiet, giving her a moment to process everything.

He switched to English. "See?" he said gently. "You understand me. You understand what I'm saying."

"But that isn't possible. I don't speak Greek." She reached for her drink again.

"I didn't either. Until I had our dream. They spoke in Greek."

Linz shook her head. "But they were two separate dreams by two separate people. And mine was in English."

Bryan placed their two cocktail napkins side by side to make his point. "Maybe you just remembered it in English."

"It was in English."

"*Was it?*" he asked again in Greek.

"Would you stop? A person just can't become fluent in another language at a bar!" She put her head in her hands.

"I think you've been fluent for a long time and didn't know it." Bryan reached out and held her other hand to comfort her. "The same thing happened to me."

Linz's eyes grew bright, emotions churning inside her. She gently tugged her hand away and stood up, finishing her wine in one gulp. "Let's go. I need to see something in Greek."

❦

They took a cab to the Central Library in Copley Square. Linz stood at a bookshelf labeled "Languages–Greek," and read *Zorba the Greek* by Nikos Kazantzakis. Bryan pretended to read it over her shoulder, but in reality he was distracted by her scent. Strange, how memories could have their own fragrance.

Linz turned to him and pointed at the page, shouting like an excited kid, "Would you look at this?"

Bryan startled with a laugh and leaned close to whisper in her ear. "You're yelling."

"I'm not yell—" She looked around, realizing people had begun to stare, and dropped her voice. "How can you be so calm?"

"Because this isn't new for me."

Linz grabbed a handful of books and headed to a reading table.

"Well it is to me. Do you enjoy disrupting my world? I share dreams with strangers. Now I understand Greek. What else?"

"Well . . ." Bryan hesitated. Maybe now was not the time to lay more on her. He didn't want her to implode at a public library.

"How in the world did you know I'd understand Greek?"

Bryan wasn't sure how to answer. "I don't know. A hunch?"

Linz got an odd look on her face. "What if . . . ?" She went to the library computer and typed in a search, mumbling to herself. "I can't believe I never thought to look." She backed away in shock. "Wow."

Bryan took her place at the monitor and saw the search results. "Whoa," he agreed.

He followed Linz to the Theology Section and watched as she searched the rows until she found what she was looking for.

"Guess we didn't have a hunch about this," she said, showing him the title: *Origenes Adamantius, His Life and Times.* "The priest really existed."

Bryan kept silent as he studied the rows of books. He already knew Origenes had lived. He also knew all the priest's works by heart, in their original language, but it was always interesting to hear what history had to say.

Linz gathered more books. With Bryan's help, they hailed a cab and headed back to her place. Neither said a word in the car. The windows were down, and the Turkish cabdriver had a classical song from his homeland playing. Bryan turned his face to embrace the wind, marveling at how luminous Boston appeared at night. Finally, he had found someone who could possibly understand his world, and yet he hesitated to reveal it to her. He wanted to hold Linz's hand, to revel in their connection. But he knew that she was still reeling from their discoveries. Even Bryan was having trouble grasping her ability to speak Greek, that this was something she shared with him. He had no idea what it meant, or where they should go from here.

Perhaps they could start with dinner and movie, or another battle at chess. Bryan chuckled at the thought.

"What?" Linz looked over at him.

"Just thinking about the future," he said. She looked away quickly and he smiled to himself, beginning to grow accustomed to her reserve. He found it endearing, and a challenge. They were more alike than she knew. One day, he hoped, she would let him in.

When they arrived at her place, Linz had mixed feelings. Part of her just wanted to be alone, to forget this whole evening, to forget the Greek swimming in her head, to forget Bryan's relentless gaze. Maybe she liked it better before when he wouldn't meet her eyes because now he was staring at her like he knew her thoughts. She looked away and grimaced at the stack of library books. . . . What the hell was she doing with all of these books?

Linz paid for the cab. "Care for some light reading?" she asked Bryan. She tried to pass it off as a joke but failed.

With a silent yes, Bryan took the books and got out, letting her lead the way.

When she opened the door, Bryan went to sit on the floor and piled all the books on the coffee table. "I think you got all of them," he teased and picked one up from the top of the stack and began to leaf through it.

Linz studied him again. There was something about his startling blue eyes, his disheveled hair. They hadn't even known each other for forty-eight hours, but it didn't matter. She was sure a connection existed. She could feel it, although the logical side of her brain rebelled at the thought.

He glanced up at her and smiled, and when she replied her voice sounded faint. "I'll just go get us some wine."

She escaped to the kitchen and cracked open a bottle. In her mind, she began to make a crazy plan. She would seduce him tonight and they would have sex. She would allow herself one uninhibited "night with the eccentric artist." It would be a first on all fronts but at this point Linz didn't care. She needed to get him out of her system so she could get back to real life.

Her last fling had been two years ago with a fellow student at Stanford, a biochemist named Greg who had been nice, safe, and

boring. She had called it quits when checking the spectrometer
had become more stimulating than a romantic tryst. Before Greg
it had been Todd, the prequel to nice, safe, and boring. Both were
good guys with four-letter names, friends who had morphed into
something else for a time. Linz had tried to convince herself that
she felt more for them than she did, and went along with being a
couple until they tried to pour cement into the idea. Then she would
end it. The truth was she preferred solitude. Her work had always
been her passion. And having a one-night stand with Bryan would
not interrupt her life at all.

Feeling more in control, she returned to the living room with
the wine. Bryan was still immersed in the book.

"Anything?" she asked, sitting a few feet away from him.

"Origenes lived in the third century. He was one of the church's
most controversial teachers, considered a scholar of his time." He
handed the book to her and grabbed another, moving away to sit
on the couch. His smile was gone, replaced by a solemn, strained
look.

Linz grimaced to herself. So much for the grand plan. Now he
was acting like they were at a funeral. With a sigh of resignation,
she opened a book and began to read.

An hour later, Linz and Bryan had both skimmed the majority of
the books and the bottle of wine was gone. Reading about Origenes' life, Bryan had grown angry—at what history had gotten
wrong, at what had been left out, at the memories he was stuck
with forever. After a while he had stopped reading, only pretending to by turning the pages.

"He believed in reincarnation," Linz noted as she scanned the
text. "A doctrine the Church struck down in 553 AD, three hundred years after his death." She looked up at Bryan with surprise.
"So reincarnation was once a Christian belief?"

Bryan hedged. "He taught it, but who knows."

"It says here he was imprisoned and burned at the stake."

"No," he corrected, unable to stop the edge in his voice. "He was tortured, pilloried, and bound by his limbs to a block for three days. He died a week later from the injuries." He stood up and wandered over to Linz's sand garden. "The man who ordered his death was named Septimus. He had a certain hatred for all Christians, but despised Origenes the most. The priest's end was . . . savage."

"Septimus," Linz whispered with a shudder. "Yes, that was his name." She sat still for a long time, trying to process this new information. "You remember his death like I did hers."

He kept his back to her, staring at her garden and nodded to the rake. "May I?" At her consent, he took off his shoes and stepped into the sand, talking while he drew. "When I was a little kid, I had vivid dreams . . . nightmares. I sleepwalked, talked . . . even had narcolepsy for a while. Then, when I was seven my brain flipped a switch and I recalled an entire lifetime."

Linz looked astounded. "You remembered his entire life?"

Bryan nodded, letting her assume he meant Origenes. He didn't tell her that it had been Abu Ja'far Muhammad ibn Jarir al-Tabari, a Persian historian who was born in the ninth century. A scholar of unequaled acumen, Tabari wrote *The History of the Prophets and Kings*, a detailed account of Muslim and Middle Eastern history spanning the time of Muhammad to the present. Tabari then went on to write *The Commentary of the Qur'an*, which he had memorized at the age of seven. Now, Bryan had the Qur'an memorized too.

It was quite a heavy load for a child to carry—when Bryan awoke his mind was filled with every memory Tabari had ever had, transmuting an innocent boy's thoughts into the deep and hard-earned wisdom of an eighty-five-year-old scholar. Tabari was only the first of many visions as his mind stretched its seams beyond any normal pattern.

Bryan gave a twisted smile. "I stayed home 'sick' for two weeks. It took me six months to realize I was fluent in another language. My life changed, to say the least."

"What about your parents?" she asked with a frown.

"They didn't know how to handle the problem." Bryan added,

"It didn't help that my mother is a psychiatrist. She took it as a personal offense that *her son* had issues—major issues—and dragged me to countless doctors. No one understood what was happening. When I was sixteen I finally convinced everyone that the visions had stopped."

"So . . . what are we talking here, reincarnation?" Linz had moved to the edge of the sand garden.

"I don't know," he said softly, taking her hand. "What do you think?" He led her into the garden, so that she stood with him.

Linz looked down their joined fingers. "I think you're doing this to me."

Bryan leaned toward her. "You're doing it to me too."

When the kiss happened, it felt inevitable. Every nerve ending in Bryan's body fired. He pulled her against him and they sank into the sand, his body covering hers. She surprised him by wrapping her legs around him and pulling him toward her.

Bryan nuzzled her neck as his hands explored her body, remembering all of the times they had been together in the past. Now those memories were devouring the present, threatening to take him over the edge. Linz guided his head back up and kissed him deeply, their passion meeting—until Bryan's head jerked back in pain.

Startled, she opened her eyes and pulled away to see his face. "What is it?"

With their bodies pressed together, he couldn't think, much less talk. "I just . . . my head . . . I get migraines sometimes."

"Can I get you some aspirin?" she asked, kissing his neck.

Bryan shuddered, about to lose control. He could not suffer a recall in front of her. "I need to go. I'm sorry." He slid off her and hurried to the door.

Linz sat up. "Are you sure you don't need—" But it was too late. He was gone.

Linz looked at herself, half undressed and covered in sand. Embarrassment crept in as she fixed her shirt. She had never been so wild and abandoned with anyone before.

Feeling a little dazed, she moved to sit at her dining table. The *Mona Lisa* puzzle stared back, mocking her. Only twelve hours had passed since she and Bryan had finished it. He seemed to have a habit of running out on her.

"What are you smiling at?" Linz grumbled and scrunched the puzzle back up into thousands of pieces. She looked at the mess and felt no satisfaction. Today had been the strangest day of her life.

ELEVEN

Michael was growing weary of defending himself. "Nothing has been compromised. If anything, we're closer now than we ever thought possible."

"Closer to what?" Conrad's voice rose as he waved his arms in frustration. "Losing our grant? Let's just tell the NIA that you can recite the Hexapla in ancient Greek after popping our pill and see how that flies."

Michael looked around, relieved that everyone else was too far away to hear their conversation. He and Conrad, along with Finn and Diana, were sequestered in a booth in a back corner and not many customers were around. In fact, the sprawling Old New England–style restaurant looked deserted.

They had come at an off-hour. Four elderly couples sat together near the front, eating Doc's famous clam chowder. Michael knew they were regulars who stopped by every Friday at four before a senior dance class nearby. A few tourists straggled in, taking shelter from the nipping wind outside, and sat down to enjoy Irish coffees at the bar.

Finn drummed two of his fingers on the table, something he did whenever he was deep in thought. He looked more like a cross between a surfer and a cowboy than a scientist, and at Harvard he had broken almost every girl's heart with his green eyes, long blond hair, and playful charisma. He finished his beer, gave a monstrous burp, and waited for the others' groans to subside before announcing, "I think we all should try it."

"What a great suggestion, Dixie. Sterling scientific process we've got going." Conrad raised his beer in mock solidarity.

Finn slammed down his glass. "I am tired of your holier-than-thou bullshit, Doodle Dick."

"And maybe I'm not ready to throw away my career for a bunch of hallucinations. The sixties are over, people, get a grip."

"Guys, please." Diana touched Finn's arm. "Finn, I actually agree with you. I say we all try it and see what happens."

Finn gave Diana a silent nod of agreement, which did not surprise Michael. They had been close friends for years. Both from small rural towns—Diana from Wyoming and Finn from Texas—they had felt an immediate affinity since the day they arrived at Harvard. Both shared a daredevil streak, and within a week of meeting they had talked each other into going hang gliding in the Berkshires. Michael had known they would both be more than willing to jump into the abyss with him.

He shook his head. "I don't think it's a good idea."

Diana pounced. "Why? You were so quick to assure us it was harmless when it was just you."

Michael had not told any of them the full truth yet, not even Diana. It was now or never. "I can't just recite the Hexapla. I remember writing it." There was a pregnant pause—everyone was speechless.

Conrad looked predatory. "Care to elaborate, Mike?"

"Yes, please do." Diana sat back and cocked her head to the side. Michael knew that look. He would have hell to pay later.

"I'm sorry. I needed time to process everything before I could explain." He took a deep breath. "I experienced a series of visions . . . It felt like I lived the life of a priest in third-century Rome."

The team was silent. Finn found his voice first. "You're saying you recalled the memories of a Roman priest?"

Conrad took off his eyeglasses and rubbed the bridge of his nose. "And now you think you're him? Can I get communion?"

"No, I don't think I'm him," Michael said, measuring his words carefully. "But the fact is I experienced the lifetime of someone named Origenes Adamantius. The man wrote thousands of works, including comparative studies of various translations of the Old Testament. I've never even picked up a Bible, but now I could be a scholar of several versions. This is not my imagination," he stressed. "I went to the library. I remember everything just as he wrote it."

No one spoke for a long minute. The only sound was Finn drumming his fingers on the table. He broke the silence first, "Chief, we need to set up tests for you and record the hell out of this."

Diana gave Michael's arm a little pinch. "Ow." He rubbed his skin.

"Quit holding back," she threatened.

Michael smiled. She knew him so well. There was nothing to do but drop the next bomb. "I'm now fluent in several languages."

Conrad finished his beer in one gulp. "Can you fly too, Superman?"

Michael couldn't help but laugh at that, and he felt some of his tension release. It was true that he did feel a strange new power and wisdom. No one else on Earth possessed the firsthand knowledge of what it was like to live in ancient Rome. "I know it sounds crazy, but I can read, write, and speak ancient Greek, Latin, and Hebrew. I also know some Egyptian."

Everyone struggled to digest this. Diana finally said, "Are we talking past life recall?"

Michael shook his head. "I don't know. But it was an episodic, semantic, and emotional experience. Long-term memory access is dependent on new proteins. Right now I'm getting huge amounts, plus additional synaptic firepower. What if the drug enabled new pathways and I retrieved some kind of subliminal memory?"

"Then there could be more memories—more lives." Diana sounded concerned.

Conrad added, "Like a schizophrenic."

Michael glared at Conrad, trying to keep his frustration in check. "Whatever it is, we can't shy away from what I experienced. I think our best course of action is to wait several weeks before anyone else takes it. Until we know the full extent of my reaction." Diana reached out and gave his hand a squeeze, and he knew he had been forgiven.

Finn leaned forward. "I disagree, chief. This could be the biggest breakthrough since the discovery of DNA. We need to forge ahead."

Conrad scoffed, but Michael ignored it. "We will, believe me. I just think we need to forge cautiously. Two weeks is all I'm asking."

Finn signaled the bartender, Patty, for another round. "It's all you're getting."

Conrad studied Michael like a specimen under a microscope. "You can really speak all those languages?"

Michael tried to lighten the mood. "Worried I'm smarter than you now?"

Just then Doc came over with another pitcher. "You guys win the Nobel Prize or something? You haven't drunk this much since you got that grant."

Finn raised his glass. "We're having a breakthrough."

Conrad mumbled, "Or something."

"How about four clam chowders and a basket of bread?"

Diana put her hand on her stomach. "Doc, you're our hero."

Doc was always trying to feed them on the house. His restaurant had been a second home since he had opened it. He and Michael had been roommates before Diana had come into the picture. The two men had known each other since childhood and had been friends growing up in a suburb outside of Chicago. When Michael moved to Boston to complete his graduate degree at Harvard, Doc had just finished culinary school and came out to visit. He had loved Boston so much that he had stayed and gotten a job at one of the city's top restaurants, quickly rising in the ranks to executive chef. Later, with his family's help, he had opened up his own restaurant: Doc's Waterfront Bar & Grill.

Doc was still hovering at the table, which was unusual. He bent toward Michael. "Captain? Can I talk to you for a second?" He motioned toward his office.

"Sure." Michael stood up, glad to have a break from the table. He followed Doc to the back, wondering what was up.

They went into his tiny hole of an office and Doc shut the door. "I'm glad you're here. I was hoping you'd come up for air."

"I've been busy with the project," Michael said. Doc had a point, though—it had been a while.

"Well, it's good to see you."

Michael raised his eyebrows at Doc's formal air. "You too, buddy. What's on your mind?"

"Well . . ." Doc sat, looking a little lost.

Michael waited for Doc to gather his thoughts, but he couldn't. "Doc, please just spit it out. I've had a rough couple of days."

"It's about Barbara . . ." Doc finally blurted. "Barbara and me."

"You don't need to tell me—"

"—No, I want to tell you. I want to be the one to tell you."

Michael forced himself to remain quiet. He loved Doc like a brother but Doc had fallen for the girl Michael had dated before Diana and was convinced this would ruin their friendship. Michael had tried to assure him that it had been casual—over before it even began. His relationship with Barbara had barely amounted to a month of dinners and movies, and a few kisses outside her dorm. She was a psych major, the kind who wanted to analyze every thought and feeling anyone had ever had in order to earn her PhD. Michael had no idea why he had dated her in the first place and had all but wiped their short-lived relationship from his mind, but Doc still felt like he had to treat the whole situation with kid gloves.

"Things are getting serious. I think I'm going to ask her to marry me."

Doc waited for a reaction. Michael was tempted to tell his buddy he needed a sanity check. Instead he did his best to feign excitement. "Great. Congratulations."

"Mikey."

Michael laughed and said, "No, I'm serious. I'm happy for you two. You didn't have to tell me like this."

Doc fiddled with a pen. "I just didn't want you to hear it from anyone else."

"Listen, my feelings about you and Barbara getting together haven't changed. I don't mind! Got it, knucklehead?"

"There's one more thing. About the wedding . . ."

"You were my best man—I don't expect to be yours. I won't

even be offended if I'm not invited to the wedding. Okay? So stop worrying. Please."

Doc nodded and tried to hide it as he wiped the hint of a tear from his eye. Michael had read him right. "Come here, buddy. Congratulations." Michael gave him a hug and joked, "Think you can talk her into naming a boy after me?"

"I suggest that and I'll be living on your sofa forever."

Bryan opened his eyes and a thousand thoughts flooded his head. Michael Backer had been his father's best friend. Doc had even been in his wedding. Which meant . . .

Barbara. Holy Christ, Bryan had dated his mother—and dumped her. He felt ill.

He tried to sit up but his back protested. He had to quit passing out in his car. As he climbed into the driver's seat, he looked back at Linz's building and fought the urge to call her. He wanted to tell her everything, to have her remember it. For her not to possess these memories along with him felt close to physical pain.

With that thought a new fear engulfed him. *What if she never remembers?* No, he couldn't think that way. The fact that her subconscious had reproduced a piece of Juliana's life meant Diana must have taken Renovo too, and if she had, then it was possible she would remember more, like him.

Bryan was frustrated by his inability to recall Michael's life in its entirety. And he was afraid that perhaps he never would. Only fragments were coming, and he knew he needed a tidal wave of memories to understand it all. Michael had only been forty in 1982. If these dreams were memories of a past life, then he had died young—along with Diana. What had happened to them? To their research? To Finn and Conrad?

The questions bombarded him. As he drove home, his mind sifted through what he had learned tonight, but he found no answers. He only knew Michael had remembered Origenes as well,

and whatever drug Michael had taken had somehow formed a
bridge between their lives.

Bryan glanced at the clock on the dash—two a.m., too late to go
to his parents' house. He would question his father about Michael
tomorrow. The Internet would have to do for now.

When he arrived home, he fired up his laptop and made coffee,
but instead of sitting at his computer, he found himself wandering
over to his studio, drawn to a blank canvas. Without hesitation, he
put fresh paint on his palette and picked up a brush, overcome by
an urge to paint Diana.

He painted her on the beach at Nantucket, with the sun on the
horizon. She and Michael had rented a little bungalow for the
weekend, and Bryan captured her expression at the exact moment
when Michael had asked her to marry him. She stood in the ocean,
laughing, her arms opened wide as she embraced the wind.

Bryan stared at the canvas and whispered, "What happened
to us?"

He was afraid to find out, but he had to. He put down the brush
and abandoned the portrait. His computer was already on, and he
knew the Internet was waiting with answers. He typed in the
name Michael Backer and stared at the links as they started to pop
up. He clicked on one: "First grant given by the National Institute
of Aging for a study on memory enhancement." An article appeared, along with a photo of Diana, Michael, Conrad, and Finn,
looking fresh out of med school and ready to take on the world.

Bryan skimmed the article and clicked on another. His heart
stopped when he read the headline. "NIA Neuroscientists Perish
in Lab Explosion."

He forced himself to read it. Michael and Diana had died in the
lab. Bryan sat back, stunned. That was impossible. He continued
reading. "Finn Rigby, the one survivor, was pulled from the flames
by firefighters."

The article was dated March 10, 1982. Bryan reread it again and
again. Michael and Diana had died, and Finn survived. But where
was Conrad in all of this?

He typed Conrad's name and National Institute of Aging into the search engine and came up with twenty times more hits. He clicked on a link, scrolled down, and saw Conrad's picture with the caption: "Conrad Jacobs leaves NIA to form Medicor Industries."

Bryan clicked on the corporate Web site. It appeared to be a global company with operations around the world. Conrad had come a long way in thirty years. Bryan studied Medicor's corporate logo for a moment. It was the symbol of a pyramid, with a DNA strand running up through its center and a phoenix resting on top.

He would need to track down Conrad and Finn at some point, but he couldn't just show up at their doors—at least not until he had more answers. Right now, he needed to figure out how he was going to talk to his father about any of this.

TWELVE

Off the 128 Beltway, within a cluster of skyscrapers, one building stood apart from the rest like a towering pinnacle: Medicor Industries, one of the world's largest pharmaceutical companies.

Mozart's Haydn Quartet emanated from Linz's car as she pulled up to the entrance of the parking lot. She flashed her badge and ignored the look on the security guard's face when he saw her name. She was used to getting these reactions.

As she started to park, she glanced at her watch and swore. She was late. There wasn't even time to stop by the lab. She tied her hair in a knot, and slipped on her lab coat as she entered the building. On her way to the top floor, she fished fake eyeglasses from her purse and put them on. When she stepped out, she looked more like the scientist she claimed to be.

She power walked through the hallway, smiling hello to assistants and secretaries as she whizzed by, all the while wondering how in the world she was going to sneak into the conference room unnoticed. Distracted, she collided with an intern carrying a tray of coffee. A caramel macchiato found a new home all over her lab coat.

"Oh my God, I'm so sorry!" The poor intern looked ready to cry, as she grabbed a bunch of napkins and began blotting up the mess.

Linz stopped her from spreading sticky macchiato foam onto her clean shirt underneath. "It's okay. I'll live."

She took off the jacket, and went back to just wearing a not-so-professional T-shirt. Something told her the cute little monster yelling "Hey! Spare Some DNA?" wasn't going to fly.

The intern was too impressed with Linz's tattoo to notice. "Cool. I love that. Is that a DNA strand?"

Linz nodded, about to go in. "Could I leave my coat with you?" She opened the doors. Everyone was about to meet the real her—monster, tattoo, and all.

The conference room was packed with board members and project directors. Everyone was sitting around an enormous glass table, listening to the new director of Medicor's Genome Project, Dr. Parker, give a presentation. Linz still felt annoyed with herself even though she was only a few minutes late. It was the company's quarterly meeting and the first she'd attended since she had arrived. Talk about a stellar first impression. She took a seat and ignored the inquisitive look from her father, who was seated at the far end of the table.

Dr. Parker was a frail, cerebral-looking man in his late sixties who spoke with an earnestness that made him seem more charismatic than he was. Linz pretended to listen while her thoughts drifted.

So much had happened since the art opening: She had met someone who shared her dream—literally—and she had discovered that she spoke Greek. In her heart, she also knew she had met someone who could change her life if she let him—and if he would stop running out on her. Two days had passed since their strange night together and she hadn't been able to get him out of her mind. She couldn't focus on work; her concentration had splintered. He had taken up residence inside her brain, occupying her every thought. Had they really been Origenes and Juliana? What did that mean?

Life itself had suddenly become the puzzle. But at the end of the day, she was still a scientist who dealt with bodies of facts confirmed by evidence, observation, and experiments—and he was an artist who painted dreams. They lived at opposite ends of a spectrum. Two lives had never seemed so far apart.

Her father was speaking now. Linz forced her attention back to the room.

"I think you'll all agree our Genome Project is on the fast track with Dr. Parker at the helm. I'd also like you all to welcome my daughter, Lindsey, to the Genetics Department. We were lucky to entice her away from Stanford. She and her team are making great strides with her plasticity study."

With all eyes on her, Linz gave a warm smile even as she cringed inwardly. Did her dad really have to introduce her as Lindsey?

"I think her accomplishments speak for themselves. The results of her research can only be called revolutionary. She has won the National Academy of Sciences Troland Research Award and the Society for Neuroscience Young Investigator Award for discovering one of the first plasticity gene receptors in the brain. Lindsey, do you have anything to add?"

Why didn't he go ahead and tell them her GPA while he was at it? Linz couldn't help the scowl on her face, annoyed at her father's blatant display of pride. Feeling like a kid on the first day of school, she stood up and launched into an overview of her study.

"To understand the brain's mechanisms, we need to identify genes, their functions, and the proteins they encode. Our ultimate goal is to decode all three hundred sixty-two genes and their receptors, which control the brain's ability to create and retain memories. Once we identify the function of each gene—its characteristics— then we can define it. For example, a candidate plasticity gene I've just targeted has been shown to slow a cell's apoptosis. We need to figure out what triggers it, what causes it to construct and deconstruct, and how these events can be controlled. We're also looking at synaptic structures and their dynamics using several methods."

Linz knew she sounded like she was on automatic pilot, but she couldn't summon the energy necessary to engage the room. She decided to wrap things up more quickly than she'd planned to spare everyone, including herself, the pain.

"Once we have that knowledge in hand, our ability to heal any brain disorder will be unlimited. We have a long road ahead of us, but I am confident we will achieve success. Thank you."

She sat back down. Her father shot her a questioning look. She was rarely ever off her game.

The meeting adjourned and when the last suit had left, Linz stayed behind to face the music. Her father shook his head. "What happened? You made Dr. Parker seem downright entertaining. I didn't think that was possible."

"Sorry, I know I underwhelmed," she admitted. "But don't think I didn't notice that you called me Lindsey. What happened to Dr.? Or even Linz? That introduction was beyond embarrassing. We talked about this. I don't want anyone to think I'm program director because of you."

"No one thinks that. Hell, they've all seen your résumé."

She shot him a warning look.

He held up his hands in mock surrender. "Fine. From now on it's Dr. Linz, no relation. I promise."

Linz rolled her eyes at his attempt at a joke. He pressed a button and the conference room wall slid open to reveal his private office. It was the size of a large hotel suite. In the far corner, nine flat-screen TVs were mounted on the wall, each continuously broadcasting news from a different country. A sleek leather sofa sat just far enough away to allow perfect viewing, and behind that there was a bar fully stocked with every fine liquor imaginable to accommodate international visitors.

The most dramatic aspect of the room was a magnificent life-sized sculpture of Atlas holding up the world on the back of his shoulders. The sculptor had captured every strained muscle of Atlas struggling to lift a spiraling strand of DNA toward the heavens with his free hand. Linz remembered when her father had commissioned that sculpture. She was sixteen and it had been the inspiration behind her tattoo.

Her father headed to his desk, walking past a wall of windows that offered an all-encompassing view of Boston. Linz took a seat, admiring an unusual antique chair from sixteenth-century France for the umpteenth time. She was always struck by how palatial his office seemed. Her father definitely knew how to make an impression, and the same could be said of the way he presented himself. If anything, he had grown more handsome and commanding over time. Linz remembered seeing old photos of him that had been taken before she'd been born and giggling at the scruffy nerd who had been captured on film.

She watched him sift through the paperwork on his desk and asked him, "Did you have your checkup with Dr. Alban?"

He playfully tapped his chest. "Ticking just fine. The pacemaker got a new battery and an oil change."

"Oh you're funny."

"I heard you turned your office into a rec room," he said while signing several letters. "No doubt a maneuver to instill camaraderie among your troops."

"We needed a lounge."

"Give it time. This isn't a university. You will get special treatment."

"I know." Linz rubbed her forehead. The past few nights of restless sleep were beginning to take their toll.

Her father looked up and put down his pen. "Okay out with it, Stormy Weather."

She gave him a weak smile. Stormy Weather had been her nickname since childhood—it was what her father called her whenever she had something on her mind. She resisted the urge to share everything with him and asked, "Do you think two people can have the same dream?"

"The same dream?"

"I went to Penelope and Derek's gallery and saw a painting identical to my dream."

He looked speechless for a moment. "Of the woman and the priest?"

Linz saw his alarm and immediately regretted bringing it up. She loved her father, but he had a tendency to be overprotective. She tried to play it down. "He signed the painting with the priest's name and it turns out the guy actually existed. It was just interesting, that's all."

"Really." He took off his reading glasses and rubbed the bridge of his nose. "That is something."

"I know. It was all kind of weird. But it's not a big deal." Hopefully he would let it drop and not get all worked up. What had she been thinking, telling him? Now he'd fixate on it.

"Well, I would put it out of your mind. Sometimes life throws strange coincidences at us. You stopped having that dream a long time ago."

"I know. It's nothing." She could feel the worry emanating from him, and she pretended to check her watch. "Sorry, I have a meeting. I'm fine, really. Let's just forget it."

She gave him a quick peck on the cheek and escaped the office, unable to stop the sinking feeling that she shouldn't have said anything.

THIRTEEN

Bryan pulled into his parents' driveway, relieved to see his mother's car was missing.

Not bothering to try the front door, he went around back where he could hear his father talking to the plants. He smiled. Doc had gardened for as long as he could remember and over time he had transformed the backyard into a miniature organic farm. Everything he grew ended up at the restaurant.

"Am I interrupting a private conversation?"

Doc's face lit up when he saw him. "Just coaxing my brussels sprouts along. They need extra love. Want to get your hands dirty?" He held out a bucket. "Pull up my Purple Majesties over there?"

Bryan took the bucket and went over to the plot. His father had once taught him that all potatoes were originally from South America and that there were over three thousand varieties. Doc was both a scientist and an artist when it came to food. He knew where everything came from and how to make it delicious. He possessed a true gift and Bryan had always admired him for it—especially since he only knew how to microwave frozen dinners.

They worked for a long time in comfortable silence, as they had a tendency to do. Bryan had always felt connected to his father. It made him wonder if people chose the lives they were born into. The relationships in his life seemed far from random.

Doc studied him. "You look different."

"Not hungover today."

Doc grimaced. "I am still recovering from that vodka you forced down my throat."

"Hey, I paid for your cab."

"*Danke*. How's the painting going?"

Bryan thought of Diana's portrait drying in his studio and wondered what his father would think if he could see it. "It's going," he said cryptically.

Doc held up an enormous string of sprouts. "Oh, these are beauties." He placed them in his basket. "Did you sell all your paintings?"

Bryan shook his head. "No clue." Derek and Penelope communicated with him by e-mail, and he hadn't checked his in ages.

"Well, I know you sold at least one."

Bryan stopped digging. "Dad, I told you guys not to buy anything. You're welcome to it for free."

"Your mother wanted to. She fell in love with that Versailles painting."

Now that was interesting. But of course she would. The Versailles painting had been done after he remembered Louis Le Vau's life, the first architect to Louis XIV, King of France. A brilliant innovator, Le Vau's expertise in visual grandeur had left an everlasting mark on the country. During Louis XIV's long and prosperous reign, Le Vau envisioned the Vaux-le-Vicomte château and La Salpêtrière hospital, rebuilt the Louvre, designed the Collège des Quatre Nations, and transformed Versailles into the magnificent palace it is today.

Bryan had dreamed Le Vau's life when he was seventeen—the year before he had left home. The next morning he had come downstairs for breakfast and hadn't said a word, trying to assimilate the memories. His mother had taken offense at his silence, which had resulted in their worst fight ever. In his anger, Bryan had struggled to speak in English. He could still remember the moment when he glared at her and recognized the spirit of Françoise d'Aubigné, Marquise de Maintenon, Louis XIV's second wife. The most educated woman in court and the widow of a renowned poet, she had caught King Louis's eye and replaced his then-mistress. When the queen died, Louis married her in secret and she wielded great influence over her husband. Although she was never officially titled, she liked to have a hand in all things pertaining to the crown, and Le Vau resented her involvement in his work. Bryan had thought then how fitting that his mother had once been a virtual queen, and he was not surprised to hear that she had a connection to the Versailles painting now.

Doc gave a rueful smile. "She said she wants to redecorate the living room so she can hang it there. Thanks a lot."

"Anytime." Bryan dug up more potatoes. The bucket was almost full. He decided to take the plunge. "I just got asked to be best man in a friend's wedding."

Doc looked up. "Really? Best man?"

Bryan kept his face averted, afraid that his father would see the lie. "Another painter from my days in Europe . . ." he explained. "Anyway, I was wondering what does a best man do? Have you ever been one?" Bryan stole a glance at his father and immediately felt guilty when he saw the sadness in his face.

"Yeah, once. An old buddy of mine who's no longer around."

Bryan kept digging, trying to sound casual. He had to maneuver this just right to get what he wanted. "What do you mean not around?"

A long moment passed. Bryan wasn't sure if his dad would answer. "He and his wife passed away before you were born."

"That's horrible. How did they die? Car accident?" Bryan cringed inside but he knew he couldn't stop now.

"No, no. Terrible accident at work, some kind of gas explosion. I don't know the details. It's still hard to believe they're gone."

"How come you've never talked about them before?"

"It's complicated. Your mother knew them too."

Damn right it's complicated, he thought. But Bryan held back.

"I still have their things in storage at the restaurant. Guess it's about time to get rid of it all."

Bryan dropped his shovel in astonishment and blurted out. "You have their things?" He quickly picked the shovel back up again, praying his father wouldn't notice his odd reaction.

But Doc seemed distracted. He looked around as if worried Barbara might hear. "Mike and I were roommates before he and Diana got engaged. I had a key to their apartment. After they died, the landlord was going to throw everything away—Mike didn't have any family, and Diana's parents were getting on and couldn't fly out to handle it all. They didn't want anything and I couldn't bring myself to throw it away, so I stored it."

He'd kept their things. Bryan's heart leapt, and he fought back the urge to embrace his father. Without a doubt he knew he had chosen to be his son. Michael's best friend and protector—Doc had subconsciously known what to do.

"I don't know why I kept it all as long as I did. I was about to clear it out last year, just get rid of it. Lou Lou's been all over my case to turn the storage room into her office. Promised I'd start working on it soon, but my back still isn't a hundred percent."

Bryan had forgotten that his father had injured his back on a hiking trip. Doc had been a serious hiker all his life, tackled just about every ambitious trail in the U.S., Canada, and Mexico and never had hurt himself. Ever. What were the odds?

Bryan hurried to offer up his help. "I can clean out the storage room for you." Doc's eyes grew so round that Bryan couldn't help but laugh. "I'm serious. You shouldn't be lifting anything yet and I have the time." Even as he said it, Bryan felt a little ashamed at his selfish motives—he could tell that his father was touched by the offer.

"You sure? It's over two dozen boxes covered in dust and Lord knows what else."

Bryan held back his excitement. "It'll give me a little break from the studio. I need it."

Doc reached into his pocket. "Here's my keys. I've got another set." He hesitated. "Just don't tell your mother about it."

As if on cue, they heard her car pull into the drive. Bryan pocketed the keys and handed over the potato bucket. "I'll go say hi." He couldn't avoid her forever.

Barbara came in the back door carrying several bags. "Bryan? You here?" She turned the corner and saw him at the kitchen sink washing his hands. "This is a surprise. I thought you were avoiding us."

Bryan grimaced to himself. "Sorry, I've been meaning to call you back." He wiped his hands on the nearest towel and turned around. "It's been a crazy week."

Barbara busied herself putting groceries away. "Well, we came to your art opening. You weren't there."

Bryan watched his mother whiz around the kitchen like a dynamo. *She looked . . . good.* He cringed at the thought but could see why Michael had attempted to date her. Barbara was an attractive woman. Now approaching sixty, she took excellent care of herself and looked at least ten years younger.

But she was also a difficult person—too caught up in her own head, cross-examining everything all the time. It was wearying. Throughout his childhood she had been obsessed with curing him and had shipped him off to institution after institution, allowing psychiatrists, neuroscientists, and sleep therapists to become his surrogate parents. The one person he had yearned for had rarely been there, and when she was, she was always in doctor mode, studying him and quizzing him. Over time, his longing had turned to anger and then the anger had faded to distance, until they didn't even know how to have a conversation anymore. A mother was supposed to know her child better than anyone and she didn't know him at all.

Now that he was older, he could look back on her actions with a glimmer of understanding, though the child in him still hadn't forgiven her. When he had returned to Boston he had thought they could try again, maybe even start over. But now he had Michael's memories to contend with. And they definitely didn't help.

Barbara busied herself by chopping salad ingredients. "I found the most amazing antique the other day," she said, motioning to the bag by the door. On weekends she rummaged around flea markets with her girlfriends, looking for antiques. It was a longtime hobby.

Bryan was not surprised that she didn't comment on his paintings. She hated to compliment or give praise; the tendency was not
in her nature. Still, it stung a little. If Doc hadn't mentioned that she
had fallen in love with the Versailles, Bryan wouldn't have known
she'd bought it. She was such a different person with his father.
Bryan had always felt like the odd one out, despite the dreams, and
now it made sense.

"Something funny?"

Bryan snapped back to the present. "Sorry, what?"

"You had this little smile."

"That not allowed?"

Barbara ignored his remark and went to work peeling a carrot.
"Are you all settled in? I'd love to see the new place."

"It's just a loft where I work. There's nothing to see."

"You could at least have us over for dinner. You live like a hermit."

Bryan crossed his arms. "Because I paint."

"That doesn't mean you have to keep yourself isolated. It's not
healthy."

"Ah Jesus, here we go."

She turned around and put her hands on her hips. "Don't get
defensive. I just worry about you. You look like hell. I've seen street
bums who dress better. Are you even eating?"

Bryan stole the carrot from her cutting board and took a big bite
to make a point. Barbara kept talking. He tuned her out and wandered over to the counter by the back door and peeked inside the
bag from the flea market. What he saw inside flabbergasted him.
He carefully lifted the object out and set it on the counter. "You
bought a clock?"

"Yes. Don't change the subject. Do you see what I'm trying
to say?"

"Oh, I see what you're trying to say, Barbara. I just don't have to
agree with it."

The color drained from Barbara's face, and Bryan realized he
had just spoken to her as Michael. It was something he had said to
her verbatim during their last fight.

"The way you said my name just now . . ." she was clearly battling a ghost. "Since when am I Barbara? I thought my title was Mom."

Bryan turned back to the clock and began to fiddle with it. Neither spoke for several minutes.

"It doesn't work," she announced unnecessarily. "But it was so beautiful I had to buy it. The man said it was French and very old."

Bryan opened the back to look inside at the mechanism that made it tick. "It is old, but it's not French. It's Dutch."

"How do you know that?"

Because I built it in the seventeenth century. How the hell his mother found it at a flea market was beyond him. But she had done that all his life: found objects he could identify from his past. It was one of her talents.

In this particular lifetime, Bryan had been Christiaan Huygens. His father, Constantijn, was a poet and composer—friend to Descartes, Rembrandt, and many others. Christiaan's mother had died when he was eleven after giving birth to his sister, and his father had never recovered from the loss. Constantijn hadn't known how to relate to his children, and when Descartes recognized Christiaan's budding genius, he suggested that Christiaan be sent to school in Leiden.

Christiaan excelled and he soon surpassed his teachers. He wrote the first book on probability theory and hypothesized a law of motion, which Isaac Newton would later reformulate. His quest to understand mechanics led him into every field . . . mathematics, physics, astronomy. He proposed that light was made of waves and discovered centrifugal force. A master in optics, he also created a refracting telescope, which he used to speculate that Saturn had rings and to detect its first moon, Titan.

But Christiaan's greatest passion was time. And when he designed the pendulum clock, the most precise timekeeper of its day, he helped the world to capture it.

Christiaan had sent the clock that Bryan was holding to his father as a gift just before the old man died. Bryan still couldn't believe that Barbara had found it. Had she been Constantijn? *No . . .*

she couldn't be. He forced himself to focus and he stared deep into her eyes, actively seeking the recognition.

Attempting to place a person in the past was something he generally tried to avoid, but in moments like these he couldn't resist the impulse. He had learned how to recognize someone's spirit by honing his thoughts in on them and connecting with them through their eyes. On a rare occasion a recognition would come without his trying, especially if he was angry or upset, but usually it took immense concentration. Barbara stared back at him with her eyebrows raised, clearly baffled by the silent exchange.

And then he saw it—Constantijn's spirit shimmering in her eyes. Bryan turned away, disconcerted. Rarely did he recognize a soul that had crossed over to the opposite sex. This was also the first time he had envisioned his mother as a man and the idea felt alien to him. But still, to recognize Constantijn within her, and as he held Christiaan's clock . . . His anger melted, and he swallowed the lump in his throat. "If you'd like, I can fix it for you."

"That's right, I forgot you went through a watchmaking phase." She shook her head at the memory. "I'll never forget when I came home and found you with all our clocks and wristwatches in pieces on the table."

Bryan remembered it too. That had been right after he had recalled Christiaan's life. He had rebuilt clocks every day for months, explaining it away as a new hobby. And he hid his new fluency in Dutch and French—although he did allow himself to get As in math from then on out.

He tried to make a joke of it. "Hey, I put them back together."

"That's true."

They smiled at each other as Bryan placed the clock back in her flea market bag.

Barbara asked, "Are you going to stay for dinner?"

"Sorry. I've got plans." He saw her disappointment and added, "We'll do it soon, though. Promise."

"At least have some of your birthday cake. Your father's been eating it all."

"That's okay, thanks." He picked up the bag and left before she could say anything else that might get him to stay.

Bryan drove down the street, parked his car, and pulled out the clock. He sat for a long time hugging it to him, filled with a yearning that always came when he handled something that had once been his. He closed his eyes and let the feeling wash over him. How he would love to go home and fix the clock, to lose himself in Christiian's world, but that would be a distraction. Doc's keys sat heavy in his pocket, and he knew answers lay locked away in Michael and Diana's things. He only wished that Linz could help him go through them.

Linz. He needed to help her remember. Juliana or Diana—at this point it didn't matter. She just needed to start remembering something. His thoughts landed on the painting. Before he went to clean out the storage shed, he had to get it.

FOURTEEN

Linz rode the elevator down to the tenth floor. It was one of five housing genetic research. Her lab was at the end of the hall, and she couldn't have designed a better workspace. Everything was state of the art—no expense had been spared. Boston was the epicenter of Medicor and it showed.

Even though the biomedical industry was witnessing a decline in research and development, the pharmaceutical market projected it would grow at a rate of over eight percent a year due to an aging global population. Linz believed that her father's vision and tenacity had kept Medicor on top, boasting the largest development portfolio in a shrinking pond. Not only were they responsible for a huge percentage of the country's pharmaceutical research, but they also invested in other labs across the globe, helping to keep them afloat.

Growing up, she had played on the floor of her father's office with her toy microscope and sat beside him on planes as they flew off to conferences around the world. Her unusual childhood had helped to shape who she was, giving her a love for science and the ambition to become a pioneer in her own right.

In college, she had reached a crossroads where she had to decide what path in science she would take. The human brain had always fascinated her the most because she had often wondered if her own mind was abnormal. The recurring nightmare of the woman in ancient Rome had always felt more like a memory to her and this conviction had galvanized her to try to understand where it had come from. Specializing in neuropathology and genetics had seemed only natural. In many ways the tangible findings and detective work were a comfort, and she believed that it would be possible for her to fully understand how the brain created memories within her lifetime. It was a belief that gave her extraordinary drive.

These last several months had been encouraging, especially now that the lab was up and running. When Linz had come aboard, she had absorbed a small staff from a project that had been terminated after the lead scientist had retired. Steve, Maggie, and Neil were all hungry, just out of grad school and ready to make their mark. At first they had been intimidated by the idea of working for her—the CEO's daughter—but Linz quickly won them over and the initial awkwardness hadn't lasted long.

Linz ducked into the employee kitchen and found Steve making coffee. He was the youngest in the group and had a crush on her as obvious as a neon sign. She tried hard not to notice. "Hey, where is everybody?" she asked him.

Steve started and turned around, eyes wide behind his John Lennon glasses. "Doughnut bonanza down in Patents."

Linz thought he could use a few doughnuts. The poor guy gave skinny jeans a whole new meaning. She wished he would stop staring at her.

"I put your mail on your desk and I got your favorite coffee, Kona." He showed her the bag of beans as proof. "I just made some now."

Linz poured herself a cup. "Thanks. Can you do me a favor?"

"Anything." He held out a sugar pack and stir stick.

"Research phonetic studies documenting unexplained cognizance of a foreign language."

"Unexplained cognizance? Can that happen?"

"I think so." She was about to leave, when she turned around with an afterthought. "This is a little off the wall, but do you believe in reincarnation?"

"Well . . ." His Adam's apple bobbed up and down as he swallowed. "I think, um," he gulped again. "You know . . . that you meet certain people you feel this, um, intense connection to . . . and maybe it means something?"

"Er . . . right." *That was not helpful.* Linz saluted him with her mug. "Thanks for the coffee." As she turned away, she caught Steve putting his finger to his head and pulling an imaginary trigger. She smiled and closed the door.

She walked along the long glass hallway and peered into the various labs as she made her way to her own lab, slowing to admire Cyclops, the heart and soul of the Genome Project. Its long robotic arms took slide samples from endless rows of drawers against the wall with surgical precision. It was an omnipotent octopus of technology that generated matches to potential gene fragments with lightning speed, providing answers in seconds.

Dr. Parker saw Linz pass and smiled, waving as if they were old friends. Linz was surprised by the warmth of his greeting—she had only met him this morning at the board meeting. She gave a quick wave back and continued down the hall, entering her lab at the same time as Maggie and Neil.

Maggie had magenta hair, two nose rings, and could make a lab coat look cool. She was also brilliant and worked with Linz on genetic screening and sequencing. Neil managed all the programming and was a serious computer jock who could barely squeeze his large gut into his chair. Linz didn't know how she had ever lived without him. In the space of three months, he had written new software to track all the data results they had generated. He was so ingenious that she suspected he just might be a computer hacker on the side—when he wasn't attending gaming conventions.

"Neil, the scavenger program you wrote is kicking serious ass."

"All my programs kick serious ass. Why do you think I always wear this?" He pointed to the faded Bruce Lee T-shirt under his lab coat.

Maggie snorted. "Because you don't do laundry."

Linz chuckled and headed to her desk, trying to ignore the Greek books piled next to her computer. She had brought several in to work, thinking she would read them at lunch. Now she was beginning to question her sanity. They were nothing but a screaming distraction. She checked her cell phone again, hoping Bryan had tried to get in touch.

Maggie followed her over. "Your father called to remind you about the company party on Sunday. You going?"

"Yep, planning on it."

Maggie perched on the edge of her desk. "Bringing anyone?"

Linz considered the idea. In an ideal world she would have invited Bryan, if they could just have one normal meeting together. Instead, their encounters had been surreal, and the last one had been flat-out unbelievable. He had left her sprawled in the sand garden and then he hadn't even called her later to apologize. The more she thought about it, the more she began to seethe. If he did call, she would let it go to voice mail. She didn't want to talk to him.

Maggie was waiting for an answer and growing more excited by the second. "Oh my God, you met someone."

Linz sighed. What could she say? Technically, yes. But she and Bryan defied normal.

Maggie gushed, "You totally met someone. Say no more." Turning to leave, she noticed all the books. "Wow, you know Greek?"

Linz nodded, glowering at the incriminating evidence. "A little," she admitted and shoved the books into her bottom desk drawer. She forced Bryan from her thoughts and got back to work.

When Linz arrived home ten hours later, all thought of work fled her mind. A wrapped canvas was propped against the door with a little card taped to the top: *A gift to a fellow dreamer. Call me.*

Linz unwrapped the painting in disbelief and brought her hands to her face with a gasp. It was too much. Reaching out to touch the canvas, not caring that she was still in the hall, she sank to the floor and began to cry.

It was the painting of Origenes and Juliana. Bryan had given it to her.

The last box was marked "wedding," and a photo album rested on top. Underneath were stacks of Super 8 film and an old projector.

Without hesitation, Bryan sat on the storage room floor and took the photo album out.

The first picture reached out and stole his heart. Michael was holding Diana in his arms as her wedding dress trailed to the ground, forming a pond of frilly lace. Bryan smiled, remembering how she had worn her mother's gown because they couldn't afford a new one. It was originally three sizes too big, and the seamstress who had altered it had messed up twice before producing something wearable. Next to the beaming couple, Doc, Conrad, and Finn stood in seventies tuxedos alongside Diana's bridesmaids. Everyone made funny faces at the camera.

Bryan stared at the portrait, captivated by the joy it contained, and the question played in his mind like a broken record.

What went wrong?

FIFTEEN

Lord Asano, Daimyo of the Province of Ako, woke with a start, knowing he must have been dreaming. He had been standing on top of a mountain, with clouds swirling around his feet. In the mist a woman was seated on top of a boulder, still as stone.

At first Asano had thought the woman was a statue of a strange goddess, but when he moved closer, he saw her breathing. She was the most exotic creature he had ever seen, and she reminded him of a portrait that a Dutch trader had once shown him from his travels to a place called Egypt. Her long black hair had been plated into braids that cascaded over her shoulders, and her eyes were decoratively lined in black kohl and emerald powder. Gold and precious jewels adorned her body, holding an intricately knotted robe in place that shimmered like a blue Akoya pearl.

Asano had hesitated to speak. The luminous stranger appeared to be in deep meditation, but then she had opened her eyes and said, "Yes, I see you too."

Then Asano had awoken.

This was not the first night during Lord Asano's stay in Edo that had brought poor sleep and strange dreams. He hated the city and his obligation to attend the Shogun's court. Today would be his last for the year, and then he and his wife could return home to their castle at Ako. He just needed to make it through the ceremony.

The thought brought on a surge of anxiety. Under normal circumstances, Asano would only observe the pomp at court, but his name had been drawn to be the Shogun's official representative at the reception for the Emperors' envoys. The Emperor's ministers rarely visited, so it was crucial that everything be perfect.

Asano had tried to excuse himself from the assigned duty, implying that he was a simple country lord who knew nothing of the ways of court. The truth was that he was a private man who could not shoulder the mental burden of having to perform duties in such a severely formal ceremony. He was also currently unwell and suffering from a cold, his third in as many months. But the court had denied his request and placed him under the tutelage of Lord Kira, the Shogun's Master of Ceremonies—and a man Asano despised. To Asano, the bribe-taking bureaucrat embodied everything wrong with the decadence that was drowning Edo.

Lord Kira expected Asano to pay him for his guidance, which Asano had no intention of doing. Even though Asano was only a young lord of thirty-five, he still adhered to the old ways and lived by a samurai's code of honor. He knew Kira was already well paid by the court, and he would not give in. The animosity between the two men had reached a boiling point, and as the hour of the reception drew near, Asano grew more nervous about his decision. Kira had the power to make him look like a fool.

The morning light crept into the room, scattering Asano's thoughts. He might as well get up and begin the painstaking process of putting on his ceremonial robes. It would make the day's end seem closer.

Once dressed, he took his palanquin to the castle. He sat enclosed within the ornate litter's small box, which was hanging from a long pole that was carried by four men—two in the front and two in the back. A man walked in front of them, proudly holding a banner with the clan's *kamon*. The crest on the flag was the only way anyone could discern which lord was inside.

Asano could barely tolerate the suffocating space with all the jostling. His head was throbbing and his stomach felt hollow. Maneuvering through the market was always an annoyance—to both the lord and the people of Edo. Whenever a lord's entourage went past, everyone on the street—merchants, farmers, and beggars alike—had to stop, drop to their knees, and bow. They were not even allowed to lift their eyes to watch the procession.

Even with his passage cleared, it still took all morning to reach the Shogun's castle. When he arrived at the inner sanctuary, Asano exited the palanquin with relief and made his way to the Hall of the Thousand Mats. He greeted the other lords who had arrived early. They were all forced participants. Everyone but Asano had paid Kira to enlist his help in getting through today's spectacle, and they all gave him calculated looks, wondering how the young, handsome lord would fare.

Lord Kira entered in all his glory, adorned in ceremonial robes that outshined them all. He smiled at the lords, showing blackened teeth.

Ohaguro, staining one's teeth, was a fashion originally reserved for married women with children, or geisha, but had become quite popular with some noblemen and those in upper society. The effect was obtained by melting metal in a vinegar base and then adding Chinese sumac powder. The tannins in the powder would turn the foul-smelling brown liquid into a black viscous lacquer. One had to paint the teeth every few days to maintain the effect, and Asano found it repulsive—another symbol of the vanity and corruption eating away at the court. He stared at Kira and thought it made the old man look like a lizard with a diseased mouth. He made no effort to hide his disgust and turned away, making sure Kira noted the snub.

Asano went to stand by the door, where a servant entered and approached him. "Forgive me, Lord, but my master asked me to inquire about the starting time of the ceremony?"

Before Asano could answer, Kira interjected in a voice loud enough for the entire room to hear. "Don't ask that one, his ignorance is even greater than yours."

A hush fell over the hall. Asano could not believe his ears. To add further insult, Kira moved toward him and whispered. "You see, young lord, I can make your life quite miserable. But I am still willing to help an Ako-inbred country monkey like yourself."

At Kira's words, unbounded rage overcame Asano and he drew his sword.

Everyone gasped in shock. Such an act inside the Shogun's castle equaled treason and was punishable by death, and Asano's rational mind screamed at him to stop—to kill this man would destroy his clan and his name. Kira wanted nothing more than to witness his ruin. By drawing his sword, Asano had granted his wish.

Reason deserted him. He raised the sword high into the air and with a shaking arm brought it down on Kira's head. Shogun Tsunayoshi entered the hall just as the blade struck. The sword glanced off of Kira's forehead, drawing blood, and Kira fell to the ground. A great commotion erupted as attendants rushed to help the victim. Everyone could see that the cut was not deep—that Asano hadn't had the strength to kill him. Kira would live.

Asano blindly raised his sword to strike again, but the other lords and their assistants rushed him and they held him back as they screamed for help from the guards outside.

Shogun Tsunayoshi backed away in horror. Asano's sword was wrenched away from him, and now that it was gone, his sanity returned. His head was pounding; he couldn't think. He could only stand there frozen, held back by the arms of his fellow lords. What had just happened?

The Shogun's *Rojyu*, his second-in-command, roared. "You disrespect the Shogun's house! His laws!"

Asano dropped to his knees and bowed low in deep remorse.

No one spoke. Seventeen years ago, the Shogun's prime minister had been struck down in this very room. Rumors of the Shogun's involvement had surrounded the assassination, so he took Asano's actions as a personal offense.

Asano remained kneeling, his forehead touching the floor. "I beg forgiveness. There is no excuse for what I have done."

The Shogun did not acknowledge his plea and stormed toward the door. The Rojyu followed as he bellowed, "The ceremony is ruined. Send everyone home!"

Stripped of his swords, Asano remained on his knees with a rigid back for hours, waiting for his captors to decide what to do. He tried to make sense of his absolute loss of control. Did he hate one man so much that he would throw away his life? He found no answer, only anguish.

A troupe of guards arrived to secrete him away from the castle to Lord Tamura's mansion, where Asano would await his sentence. Once there, he was allowed to write his wife a letter. He described the day's occurrence and could only hope that she would pass his message on to his head *kerai* and chief retainer, Oishi Kuranosuke Yoshio, whom he trusted more than his own brother. The fate of his house now rested in Oishi's hands, and Asano prayed that his kerai would somehow help to repair the damage he had inflicted.

Just as he finished the letter, the Shogun's officer arrived to deliver the sentence. The Shogun's decision had come more rapidly than usual. His envoy read it aloud: "By the command of Shogun Tsunayoshi, Lord Asano is to commit seppuku on this day."

Asano was stunned. He had prepared himself for the possibility of a death sentence, but for it to come so quickly was inconceivable for a lord of his standing. He would have no time to put his house in order.

"The Lady Asano is to suffer permanent exile, and all the property belonging to the Asano clan will be put under the Shogun's protection."

Every word was a venomous sting. All three hundred samurai under the House of Asano and their families would be stripped of their homes, their livelihood. Asano forced himself to focus on what the envoy was saying. The worst had been saved for last.

". . . The Asano name and its lineage will be struck from the Book of Records."

On hearing those words, Asano felt the odd bodily sensation of drifting—the anchor to his world had just been cut away. His clan's entire history was to be forgotten. Only in one way had the Shogun demonstrated mercy: by granting Asano the privilege to die with honor by seppuku.

Seppuku was the ultimate test and sacrifice a samurai could make, and it gave Asano the chance to atone for his actions. Like many others, he believed that if his karma had brought him to the brink of death, it was better to die by his own hand, so that it would not follow him into the next life.

The Shogun's men led Asano into the garden, where several layers of white cotton cloth had been laid. A small stand holding a dagger had been placed in its center. His Second, his *Kaishakunin*, stood at stoic attention behind him with a sword, prepared to sever his head at the end.

Lord Asano had now changed into a ceremonial white kimono. He took the proper stance and sat on his heels. As part of the ritual suicide, he picked up the sake cup from the wooden table and drank it in four sips. Then he wrote his death poem on a sheet of *washi*, paper made from mulberry leaves. He did not know what to write but somehow, his brush moved across the page.

> *Wind makes the flower fall*
> *I too am falling*
> *Not knowing what to do*
> *With the Remaining Spring*

It would be remembered as a poor death poem, he thought, and he felt ashamed. He slipped off his outer garment and tucked the sleeves under his knees. He grasped the cold dagger in his hands and thought about his dream of the strange Egyptian woman upon the mountain. Had she known this day would be his last?

As he prepared to end his life, Asano remembered the rest of what she had said to him.

"*Between the beginning and the end, this life is but one moment.*"

Asano grabbed onto her words as the blade pierced his skin. He did not feel the Second's sword on his neck.

He was already gone.

SIXTEEN

The memories come without warning. This is the second time this week I have suffered a recall. Today, I was working in my office when my sight began to blur and the dream took me. I have stopped the medication, but that hasn't slowed the visions. It is as if Renovo has opened Pandora's box.

I have shared what I have recalled with the team, but only to a certain point, and have taken to locking myself in this office, searching for some kind of answer. My mind keeps going back to the Egyptian woman in Asano's dream. I have seen her appear in the dreams of other lives I have recalled as well, and I cannot help but feel she is a key to understanding all of this. Who is she? A goddess? An ancient priestess? A traveler from another time and place with a message for a dying man?

None of this makes sense and I am afraid to voice these thoughts. I have limited my interactions with the team to the tests Finn is conducting. I have even sworn to keep Diana away until I can sort out what is happening.

I am now fluent in over ten languages and have knowledge of historical events and written texts that cannot be found in books. It is a persuasive argument for reincarnation to be sure, but the scientist in me is still not convinced these are memories of past lives. Even so, it is hard to deny these recollections feel like my own.

Now I have relived the life of a Japanese lord from the seventeenth century. I first heard about Lord Asano years ago when I took an Asian Studies course as an elective my freshman year of college. My professor, Mr. Yamamoto, loved to entertain us with stories from his homeland. The account of Lord Asano's death and the bloodshed that followed became one of the greatest sagas of Japan.

His tale gripped me, but I told myself I was no more enthralled than any other student. Strange to think I might have been the one who caused the story.

Diana played an instrumental part too. Just as she did in Pushkin's life. I am certain she was my wife, Natalia. Natalia who had raged about how she wanted to be a man in order to avenge her husband's death. When I look into Diana's eyes, I cannot help but feel that she did come back as a man in the next life. And what a war she waged.

I don't know what will happen when Diana remembers her life in Japan, but I pray she never will. The whole team has taken Renovo now. God help us.

Bryan put the journal down. He couldn't bring himself to read anymore.

He was sitting on his living room floor. Michael and Diana's boxes littered the space. Earlier at the restaurant, after going through the wedding album, he had hurried home to open the rest of the boxes. He had found Michael's journal almost immediately and had been reading for hours.

Bryan had remembered Lord Asano Naganori's life ten years ago and had spent months afterward painting it—he had even attempted to paint Asano's dream. He went to the storage closet and pulled out the life-size portrait of the Egyptian woman. Her face was uplifted to the sky, her feline eyes half open. She was shrouded in the mountain's mist—Bryan had been unable to get her features right and had used the mist to his advantage. But she was still exquisite, and the portrait gave him goose bumps every time he saw it. No one had ever seen this painting.

He wondered if he should show it to Linz the next time he saw her, knowing he would see her soon, even though they hadn't spoken since the night of the library. He had wanted to give her space to come to terms with all that she had discovered. And he was also hoping she would forgive him for his quick departure. At some point he would have to explain his problem. He could just imagine it: *You see, I have this habit of reliving lifetimes when I'm with you.*

That conversation would be a winner. With a sigh, he put the Egyptian woman back in the closet. Maybe Linz shouldn't see this yet.

◂◦▸

Linz sat on the couch and stared at the painting for a long time. The image loomed larger than life, its violence captured in incredible detail. She felt a powerful urge to destroy the canvas, but she knew she could never live with herself if she did. For a moment she had thought about returning it to Bryan, but she didn't want anyone else to look at it either. Finding a temporary solution, she got up and put it in her closet and then sat on the floor with her head in her hands, feeling emotionally drained.

She had broken down when she saw the painting outside her door, and it had taken her hours to calm down. She hadn't cried like that in years. Seeing the painting had brought back all the memories she had tried so hard to suppress. As a child she had remembered so much more about Juliana than her death—vague feelings and experiences she couldn't explain that she had never talked to anyone about. Growing up, forgetting the vivid terror of Juliana's death had seemed most important; all the other memories were gentle and nonthreatening in comparison, like a soft image out of focus. But now that she was older, maybe it was time to revisit them. Because when Linz opened her heart and let go of her fear, her sense of self became eclipsed by the feeling that this Juliana was a part of her. Perhaps it was the same for Bryan.

Bryan. She needed to hear his voice. She called him without giving her impulse a second thought.

The phone rang. A man with a European accent answered, *"Hallo?"*

Linz hesitated. "Hello, yes, is Bryan there?"

"Wie noemt alstublieft?"

The voice sounded similar to Bryan's yet different. She must have misdialed. But instead of hanging up she asked, "Bryan, is that you?"

"Ik ben Christiaan. Goede dag."

Bryan hung up the phone and got back to work. His mind had shut down after he'd read the journal, and when he saw Christiaan's clock, he had gotten out his old toolbox and begun to take it apart.

He had promised his mother he would fix it, and the task of disassembling the gears had calmed him. He quickly pinpointed the problem: the escapement mechanism had rusted and the screws were bad. With great care, he had cleaned every piece, losing himself in the work until he was no longer spinning out of control and the life in ancient Japan had receded into the back of his mind.

The intrusive ticking of the restored clock brought him back to reality. Bryan blinked and looked around at Michael and Diana's boxes. The past had weighed on Bryan all his life, and now it was as if the answers were arriving on a baggage carousel that was moving too fast. He lay back on the floor and stared at the ceiling.

The phone rang. He reached for it. "Hello?"

"Bryan? Hi, it's Linz."

His body relaxed at the sound of her voice. She had no idea of her effect on him. His tone became intimate. "Hey, I was hoping you'd call."

She hesitated. "I actually did before, but some foreign guy answered. He sounded German or something. I couldn't tell."

Bryan sat up in surprise. He didn't remember her calling. He must have answered the phone in Dutch while he was lost in Christiaan's thoughts.

"I thought I got the number right, and it sounded like your voice . . ."

Bryan waited, hoping she would let it drop so that he wouldn't have to explain. Things were strange enough between them as it was.

"I was calling to thank you for the painting," she continued. Her voice sounded thick with emotion.

He couldn't believe he had only left it on her doorstep this morning. It seemed like weeks ago—so much had happened since. "I wanted you to have it."

"I'd like to pay for it," she said tentatively.

"No. It's a gift."

"I still want to."

"It's a gift. I insist."

Linz was silent for a moment. "Thank you."

Neither said a word for a minute, just listened to the sound of each other breathing. Bryan wanted to hang up the phone and drive over there. He needed to see her soon.

Linz started talking again. She sounded nervous. "So I've been reading some more of those library books. I still can't figure out our dream. I mean, why ancient Rome? Why not some other time?"

Bryan looked around at all his paintings. She had no idea. She was still stuck on that one life. Then it occurred to him, maybe if she saw everything in his studio she would remember more. "Come over tomorrow night?" he offered. "I'll make dinner."

He could detect a hint of a smile in her voice when she asked, "What time?"

SEVENTEEN

"You slept with him?" Derek yelped.

"I didn't sleep with him. I said I attacked him in my sand garden." Linz was beginning to question her impulse to drop by the gallery for a little girl talk. Even though they had sequestered themselves in the back room, she hoped no one else could hear their conversation.

Penelope gave her a look and went for the leftover chardonnay in the fridge.

Linz tried to defend herself. "It just happened. There's this bizarre, intense chemistry between us." Intense was putting it mildly. She blushed at the thought of their last meeting.

Penelope handed her a glass. "The guy is a freak of nature, an artistic genius. I'll grant you he's sexy, but my God, can he even talk?"

"Of course he can talk!" Linz knew she sounded defensive. So what if he was a little eccentric. So was she.

Derek rolled his eyes. "Fine, he talks to you. We get it. So how was the hanky-spanky?"

Linz shook her head and laughed. "Derek, come on."

"What? Let us ride the roller coaster with you. I haven't had sex in a year and Penel's about to become a lesbian."

Penelope gave him a withering look and sat next to Linz. "Okay, let's do a reality check. First, he's not your type. Trust me."

Derek agreed. "Yeah, wasn't your last boyfriend some bald, fat accountant named Todd?"

Penelope reminded him, "You're forgetting about Greg."

Derek snorted, "Honey, I think we've all forgotten about Greg."

Linz had to laugh at that. "Todd wasn't fat. And he was a financial consultant."

"And you took his DNA sample before you had sex with him. What's up with that?" Derek snickered.

Linz turned to Penelope. "You told him?"

Penelope looked sheepish. "Oops."

"Look, I know you guys are right," Linz admitted. They weren't saying anything she hadn't already told herself. "He's just so in my head. I can't stop thinking about him."

Derek gave a dramatic sigh. "Well at least you have this dream connection going. My relationships are so god damn shallow."

Linz grimaced. She couldn't believe she was going to ask this again. "Do either of you believe in reincarnation?"

Penelope held up her hand. "If you say soulmates I'm going to puke."

"Here, here." Derek clinked his glass in solidarity with Penelope. "Honey, past lives are an excuse for people who are unhappy with their own. Can we get back to the sandbox?"

"No. What do you know about him though? His background."

Derek said, "Darling, we're not a credit check."

"Linz." Penelope put her hand on Linz's like a concerned parent.

"Relax, it's just dinner," she assured them. "It's not like we're getting married."

Michael and Diana's wedding portrait sat on a storage box, watching Linz and Bryan eat.

Linz motioned to the boxes. "Are you moving in or out?"

"Neither, I was cleaning out an old storage room." Bryan left it at that.

Linz examined the space. The enormous loft was divided into two areas. She assumed his studio sat on the other side of the Japanese silk screens. The sofa and dining table were the only indications that someone lived there.

She glanced again at the wedding portrait. Something about it made her uneasy. "Are they your parents?"

"No. Does the word 'Renovo' mean anything to you?" Bryan asked.

"Sounds like an awful name for an Italian car. Why?"

"Do you dream when you're awake?"

Linz put down her fork. Between Bryan's searing gaze and the stares of the couple in the wedding portrait, she was losing her appetite. "You know, we have the weirdest conversations. I feel like everything's happening backward. We hardly know each other."

Bryan searched her eyes. "We know each other."

Linz looked away. "I mean conventionally. I don't even know where you're from. If you have any brothers or sisters, those things."

"Words."

Linz swirled her wine, watching it spin. "I like words. It's called communicating."

"Okay. I was born in Boston. No brothers or sisters."

Linz laughed. "That's it? What about your parents? School? Jobs?"

"Parents both live in Boston. Dad's a chef. Mom's a shrink. Never went to college. Barely graduated high school."

She found herself defending him. "You're quite talented. Were you always into art growing up?"

"Hardly. I couldn't even hold a paintbrush."

She was surprised to hear that. "When did you start studying?"

"I've never studied."

It took Linz a second to process what he was saying. "You're telling me you've never taken an art class?"

Bryan looked at her. She could tell he was making an important decision. "When I was thirteen," he said, "I had a dream I was a painter." He took a deep breath and added, "After that I could paint."

She waited for him to say more, but he didn't. "So you could paint, just like that." She snapped her fingers.

"Like you can speak Greek, just like that." He snapped his fingers back.

Neither spoke until Bryan broke the silence. "You wanted to know."

"Does anyone else know about this?"

He shook his head. "No. Just you."

Linz could feel herself getting emotional and had no idea why. "What was the dream?"

"Not what, who."

He got up and disappeared behind the screens, and returned a moment later with a portrait of an old man with a turban on his head. "Meet Jan Van Eyck. He was the painter, not me."

Linz studied the painting and noted the signature at the bottom: *Johes De Eyck Me Fecit Ano MCCCC.33.21 Octobris.* On the top of the frame he had painted in Greek-looking letters *ALC IXH XAN.* The inscription almost looked carved.

"What does it say?"

Bryan translated, "Jan Van Eyck made me on October 21, 1433."

"And what does this mean?" she asked, pointing to the three words at the top.

" 'As I Can.' " Bryan smiled as if remembering something private. "He signed a lot of paintings with that motto."

"As I can," Linz murmured, looking at the portrait. There was something mysterious about Jan's gaze.

"It's the first painting I ever did. I was upstairs in my room and I felt an episode coming on. When I woke up, this painting was done, staring back at me."

"You painted that while you were dreaming?"

"I remembered Jan painting it. I must have re-created it as I was reliving the memory."

"And you just happened to have oil paints lying around?" Linz couldn't keep the disbelief from her voice.

Bryan laughed. "My mother had bought me a set of paints and canvas boards earlier that week, after she had read about the power of art therapy. She thought it would help." Bryan grew quiet. "For a while, I convinced myself that on some kind of subconscious or maternal level, she had known I would need them." He gave a rueful shake of his head.

"So you've been able to paint ever since," Linz said, still not quite able to wrap her mind around what he was saying.

"Ever since." Bryan propped the painting against the wall and sat back down. "You're the first person to see how it all began." He swirled his own glass of wine around and murmured, "Your turn."

Linz watched his hands, noting all the calluses and faint shadows of paint stains. She couldn't imagine waking up one day and being able to paint like a master. Her brain tried to compute how that was possible—something she had found herself doing more than once since she had met him.

Still thinking about his confession, she launched into her own history and realized Bryan was right—all this was unnecessary. They were well beyond small talk, but she continued to explain herself to him anyway. "I'm from Boston too. You already know about my mother. She and my brother died in a car accident." Before he could say anything, she rushed on. "I don't remember them. I grew up with just my dad. Got into science. Lots and lots of never-ending school, first Harvard and then Stanford. I moved back here after finishing my PhD."

"What made you decide to become a neurogeneticist?" he asked.

No one had ever asked her that question, but the answer came easily. "Because genes are the most beautiful puzzle I've ever encountered. And I solve puzzles."

She glanced up and they both grew quiet. Bryan reached out and took her hand, whispering, "What do you see when you look in my eyes?"

The question made her chest constrict. "That's a strange question," she said.

Bryan pulled his hand away and stood up to clear the table.

Linz saw the closed look on his face and tried to repair the moment. "That was delicious." In fact it was the most delectable meal she had eaten in a long time. He had served Greek food. She had tried not to read too much into his choice of cuisine and stuffed herself with dolmas, hummus, spanakopita, and decadent pistachio pasta. She assumed he had ordered it from some swank restaurant, but the last thing she wanted to do now was ask in case he might bring out a painting of some famous Greek chef. "Can I help?" she offered.

"That's okay. I got it." His voice held a hint of frustration.

She watched him stack their plates, unsure if this was a signal that the evening should come to an end. Although now that she had seen the Van Eyck, she was eager to see the rest of his work, but she felt nervous about asking. "Do you mind . . . if I take a peek at your studio?"

He hesitated only a fraction of a second. "No, I'd like you to," he said, before disappearing into the kitchen with the plates.

Left alone, Linz got up and approached the Japanese silk screens, thinking again about how exquisite they were. But the thought fled her mind when she stepped around the partition. Over a hundred paintings on the walls greeted her, ranging in size from modest portraits to grand canvases.

She sensed a great energy in the room, bombarding her psyche—every image stirred her to life. This silent audience broke her heart, made her want to weep, to laugh, to even scream. She loved every single painting—was moved by their beauty, their tragedy.

She was unaware of her feet moving; she needed to look at them all. But there were too many to take in. She stopped at a painting that was propped against the wall in the corner, and crouched to get a closer look.

Bryan came in and hovered behind her. Without turning around, she asked, "Who is she? This is the woman from the wedding photo."

"Her name was Diana Backer."

Linz glanced up at him and saw the question in his eyes.

"Do you recognize her?" he asked.

"No. Should I?"

"She was a friend of my father's who died before I was born. I found her picture last night."

Linz tried to make sense of what he was saying. "You saw her picture after you had already done the painting? So when did you do this?"

"The night we met. You inspired it."

His meaning was clear. She stood up. "Oh, no. Don't bring another dead person into the equation."

"It's not an equation. It's a feeling."

Linz was at a loss. She pretended to glance at her watch. "You know, it's getting late. I should go. Thanks for a lovely dinner." She knew she sounded a bit formal, but she couldn't help it. She didn't know how to deal with this.

"Just hear me out for a second. Look at Diana's painting again. Please."

"No, I should go." Linz made it to the door but then turned around. Bryan looked completely shattered. So she ignored every rational thought running through her head and put down her purse and stayed.

They sat quietly on the floor in front of Diana's portrait. Linz checked her watch again. The minutes felt like hours. "I don't know, Bryan. I'm tired." *And this is crazy.*

"Don't give up. What do you feel?"

"What do you want me to feel? The same way I felt about the other painting? Well I don't."

"Why can't you see it?" Bryan was getting frustrated. "You're not trying hard enough."

"How can I? I've never dreamed about this woman," she stressed.

"Well I have, more than once. I . . . ." He trailed off. Suddenly the zipper on his sweatshirt seemed to fascinate him.

"You what?" she prompted, not sure she wanted to know.

"I was her husband. We were married."

Linz couldn't help the nervous laughter bubbling up inside. That sounded like a proposal. "Okay, I think we should stop there. Thanks again for dinner." She gathered her things and started to head toward the door, intent on leaving this time.

He followed her. "Don't run away. You feel something. I can see it."

Linz didn't know what she felt anymore. She hadn't been prepared for this new turn of events. "Bryan, I really have to go." She opened the door and turned to look at him.

Bryan tucked away a stray hair dangling by her cheek, as if he'd been doing it for years. "All right, but that doesn't mean I won't think about you."

He was making this very difficult. "Just please don't bring any more paintings into this relationship," she pleaded, kissing him softly. His lips fit hers perfectly. "Good night," she whispered.

"Tomorrow's Friday. Are we still going to play?" he asked.

"So you can gloat?" she teased.

Bryan leaned against the door and watched her head to the elevator. "You know we're going to play tomorrow."

She couldn't help but laugh at that and waved without turning back.

The first thing Linz did when she got home was get online and look up Jan Van Eyck. A Flemish painter who lived in the fourteen hundreds, he had obtained fame in his lifetime as one of the best artists of the century. Historians called him the Father of Oil Painting.

She scrolled through his works and stopped at a painting titled *Portrait of a Man in a Turban* with a notation in italics that said, *"possibly a self-portrait."* She was shocked. Bryan had shown her the exact same painting tonight. They were identical, right down to the subject's enigmatic gaze.

She studied the picture on the screen, unable to comprehend the fact that Bryan had dreamed about this man, painted his self-portrait, and acquired his artistic mastery—at the age of thirteen.

Linz clicked on every one of Van Eyck's paintings . . . his style felt quite similar to Bryan's, though the subject matter varied dramatically. She would love to compare Bryan's portrait to the original up close. She had a feeling they would be hard to tell apart.

Glancing at the clock, she saw that it was well after midnight. She knew she should go to sleep, but she felt restless and reached for the book by her nightstand: Aristotle's *First Philosophy*, later translated into Latin and coined *Metaphysics*. She had been reading the original version in ancient Greek every night instead of raking in her sand garden.

She also had been reading the treatises and dialogues of Aristotle's mentor Plato, who had written much about his own mentor Socrates. In college she had taken a philosophy class and honestly had been a bit bored by their interpretations of consciousness and the purpose of life. But now that she could understand their native language, the trinity of philosophers who had created the foundation of Western thought had never felt more accessible.

According to Plato, Socrates believed all knowledge came from a divine state, but humans had forgotten it. Most lived in a cave of ignorance, but one could become enlightened by climbing out of the darkness and understanding the divide between the spiritual and material planes.

Had Linz tapped into some divine state, or was she still in a cave, preferring its dark solace to whatever waited for her outside?

Her eyelids drooped and the Greek symbols started to swim as sleep enveloped her. Her last thought before she sank into a wave of oblivion was that she would go to Harvard Square tomorrow. She had to see Bryan again.

EIGHTEEN

Diana has remembered a lifetime from the early fourteen hundreds—a Flemish woman, Margaret Van Eyck, who was married to the painter Jan Van Eyck. She insists that Van Eyck was me, though I have no memory of him. She also woke fluent in Dutch.

Finn has had several recalls, the first an aboriginal boy from Australia. The boy died young from drowning, and Finn has had a difficult time assimilating the memory. He is also complaining of migraines and sensitivity to light and has started wearing sunglasses. Yesterday Diana teased him, telling him he looked like a hungover rock star, and he bit her head off. Even their friendship is feeling the strain of what's been happening. Conrad is the only one who has not been affected by the drug, and he doesn't understand the challenges of trying to assimilate someone else's life while living your own. I don't think he would even be taking Renovo if it weren't for the fact that I know so many languages.

Both Finn and Diana think we should include our experiences in the clinical trial, but Conrad remains adamantly against it. He thinks our careers will be destroyed if we divulge what we are doing. I understand both sides. I just need more time to decide the best course of action.

In the meantime, I've become obsessed with reading about the history of ancient Egypt and its rulers, hoping to learn something about the Egyptian woman. She has the bearing of a leader, and I can't help but think she had been of noble birth. Perhaps she was some sort of a princess, if she even existed at all.

I do not know if the memories I am reliving are real, so the legitimacy of these people's dreams is even more doubtful. But whatever the answer, this woman is becoming a constant in the equation. She visited both Lord Asano and Alexander Pushkin near the end of their lives. Were their minds more receptive to her at the time of their deaths?

I admit that I've been waiting for her to materialize in my own dreams. Lately, I have begun to wonder if my death is near.

NINETEEN

The chess pieces moved themselves. Linz had given up focusing on the game and was trying to let her hand make spontaneous plays. It was the only way she could beat him.

They had been playing for hours now, and she was mentally exhausted. Each game was more like several, with multiple paths that a player could choose from, and she had yet to penetrate Bryan's "brainbox" and grasp his strategy.

"How are you so good?" she asked him, resigned to the fact that he would continue to win.

He gave her a sheepish look and shrugged.

She suddenly stopped playing. Her mouth became an O. "Because of a dream?" she asked, and then quickly added, "Don't answer that."

They played in silence for a bit until he spoke. "You know, I want to apologize for last night . . . making you sit and stare at that painting."

"That's nice of you," she said, a bit sardonically. "So no more forcing me to stare at paintings and imagine that they're me?"

"Promise." He flashed her an innocent smile and made his move. "Checkmate."

She studied the board. He was still six moves ahead from taking her king, but it was clear he would win. "Okay. That was humiliating. I think I'm done for the day."

"I'll buy you dinner to make up for it."

"Thanks but I've got plans." She saw his crestfallen look. "The symphony," she added.

"A date?"

"With myself." She admitted, trying not to be embarrassed. "I go alone."

"You go alone to the symphony?" He looked at her like she had just sprouted an extra head.

"I love it." Linz knew she probably sounded a bit odd, or even worse, lonely. But it had always felt natural to go alone. In fact, she had gotten into the habit of buying a season subscription for not one but three seats just so she could sit by herself.

In reality, so many things felt natural for her to do alone that Linz sometimes wondered if she were emotionally stunted. Maybe if her mother had been there for her when she was growing up, she could have helped her come out of her shell. Or maybe not. She had always been introverted. She hated small talk, and she rarely let loose or did anything that could be remotely categorized as silly.

She had brought a date to the symphony once, and it had been a complete disaster. The guy had wanted to hold hands, caress her shoulder, and whisper in her ear, when all she wanted to do was close her eyes and listen to the music. She had sworn she would never bring anyone again.

"I love music too," Bryan said. "All kinds of music," he added, and surprised her by pulling out a small wooden pan flute from his pocket.

She laughed.

"What?" Bryan asked, pretending to look offended.

"You just carry that thing around?"

He shrugged, a bit shyly. "For special occasions."

She hesitated, not wanting to dwell on what that could mean. "It's beautiful," she said, touching it. "What's it made of?"

"Cane. From Asia." His expression made it seem like there was a story behind it.

"Can you play?" she asked, a strange sense of anticipation building inside of her.

"Yes, but only for you," he said and brought the flute to his lips.

He stunned her completely by launching into an exquisite song. The notes swirled and changed with incredible speed as the flute sang. Pedestrians gathered to listen, and other chess players stopped their games. But Bryan didn't seem to notice.

Linz could feel goose bumps on her arms, and she told herself it was from the wind. Everyone clapped when Bryan finally stopped playing. He stood up and gave a bow. Someone offered him money, but he shook his head and sat back down.

"That was amazing," she gushed.

"Thank you." He gave her a fleeting smile, but his eyes suddenly seemed wistful.

She found herself offering, "You know, you can come to the symphony with me if you want to."

"I'd love to," Bryan said as he put the flute away.

She watched it disappear back into his pocket and wondered what other surprises he had in store.

Their seats were on the first balcony toward the left side, where they could see the conductor's face. Linz had been eagerly anticipating tonight's performance: Anne Akiko Meyers was going to be the guest violinist and would be playing her famous *Vieuxtemps* Guarneri del Gesù violin, one of the most treasured in the world.

"It's reportedly worth over eighteen million dollars," Linz explained to Bryan while they waited for the concert to start. "An anonymous buyer purchased it and granted her lifetime use as a gift."

Bryan looked suitably impressed. "So it's like a Stradivarius?"

"Yes and no." She hedged his question. "You see, Stradivari and Guarneri were both from Cremona. They lived at the same time, only Stradivari was highly successful and died at ninety-three, which is pretty incredible considering it was the seventeen hundreds." Bryan nodded, encouraging her to go on. "He made countless violins for rich and powerful patrons. But Guarneri . . . he died when he was only forty-six. He worked alone and had humbler clients. Still, his violins—they're each called a 'del Gesù'—definitely rival Stradivari's." Linz knew she was rambling but she couldn't stop. "It was Paganini who kept Guarneri from being lost to history. He was given a del Gesù and after that he wouldn't play anything else. He called it his Canon."

"Sounds like you like Guarneri more."

Now that she thought about it, it was true that Guarneri held a more romantic appeal to her. She shrugged. "Stradivari and Guarneri were both geniuses. The world has never seen anyone else like them."

Bryan teased. "So I take it you like the violin?"

She playfully rolled her eyes.

The lights dimmed, and as the concert began, Bryan grew still. He didn't reach for her hand in the dark or try to distract her. He was riveted.

The orchestra looked majestic and when Anne Akiko Meyers took the stage everyone burst into applause. The *Vieuxtemps* gleamed in the light, emanating an energy all its own. Even though it was over three hundred years old, the instrument had remained unblemished by time—it was as perfect as the day Guarneri carved it.

Soaring music filled the hall. Tucked under the chin of a master, the violin shared the stories of every hand who had played her.

Linz felt a quiver run through her body as the sound swept her away, and she forgot that Bryan was even there until just before the intermission. When she looked over at him, she could see a hint of tears in his eyes. And in that moment he stole her heart.

After the symphony, they were both quiet as they strolled down Massachusetts Avenue toward the St. Botolph neighborhood. The concert had affected Bryan more than he had expected.

"I can see why you go alone," he finally said. "Thank you for letting me tag along." Bryan reached out and took her hand, neither needed to say a word.

They meandered through the historic neighborhood until they reached Back Bay. He escorted her to her door and stood there, reluctant to go.

Something had happened tonight that had changed everything.

It was as if Guarneri's *Vieuxtemps* had put them in tune with each other.

"Do you want to come in?" she asked.

"Yes. But I won't." He took her hand and brought it to his chest. Somehow this was more intimate than a kiss.

"I'm glad you liked the symphony." She sounded breathless.

He finally let go of her and stepped away. "Sweet dreams."

She nodded, giving him a little smile, and unlocked the door and stepped inside.

Bryan walked home slowly, his heart full, and he hummed a quiet tune along the way—it was the melody Guarneri often sang to himself in his workroom when he was happy.

TWENTY

After the symphony, Bryan had come home and finished going through the storage boxes, unpacked Michael and Diana's Super 8 home movies and watched them on their projector all night long. The celluloid was almost better than the dreams: it captured their world.

He lost count of how many times he had viewed the wedding reel. Like an addict, he rewound it again and again, drawing the blinds and shutting out the sunrise to see the image projected on the wall.

The phone rang just as Diana was walking down the aisle. Bryan felt goose bumps cover his arms as he answered the phone. "Linz?"

"How did you know it was me?" she asked, laughing.

"Wild guess."

"What are you doing right now?"

Bryan could hear one of Beethoven's Late String Quartets playing in the background. "Watching home movies."

"You have home movies?" She sounded surprised. When he didn't answer, she hurried on, "So I can't believe I'm asking this, but would you like to go to a party with me tomorrow night? My company is having their annual shindig, free food, dancing . . ."

Bryan smiled. She sounded like a high schooler pitching the prom. He watched Michael and Diana kiss. The wedding party clapped as they left the chapel, now husband and wife.

"Bryan, you there?"

The film ended. "Yes. I'd love to, yes."

"Great. It's kind of formal, so suit and tie if you have one. I'll pick you up at six. Gotta go."

She hung up before he could say anything more. Bryan played back the conversation in his head and frowned. "Suit and tie."

He rummaged through Michael's old clothes, dusted off a suit jacket, and tried it on. Linz had never seen him dressed up and he wanted to impress her. He went to the bathroom and looked at himself in the mirror with a critical eye. Diana had always loved this suit.

The only problem now was that he had thirty-four hours to kill until he saw Linz again—practically an eternity. He thought about the portrait of the Egyptian queen he had put back in the closet. He got it out again, and for the first time ever, he hung it on the wall of his studio. Maybe returning to the Great Pyramid exhibit would shed some light on her. Michael clearly had shared his fascination. He could even go today.

But the first order of business was to take Michael's suit to the cleaners. The musty smell nauseated him.

Twelve hours later, Bryan sat up in bed, relieved to discover that his migraine had finally receded to a dull throb. He thought about how his plans had gone totally awry and grimaced.

Within minutes of his arrival at the museum, a jackhammer had starred pounding in his head. Even the exhibit's dim lights were difficult to bear, and he had staggered out of the building in serious agony and hailed a cab home. He took four aspirin and crawled into bed, pulling the blanket over his eyes, unable to move. Then he slept, dreaming of nothing as his body tried to right itself.

Thankfully, now he could function again, but barely. Slowly, he slid out of bed, afraid that the slightest movement might bring back the migraine. He gingerly made tea and microwaved the leftover Greek takeout after realizing it had been a while since he had eaten. Maybe that's what had caused it.

Moving over to his computer, he figured he could at least research Conrad and Finn, but he kept a bottle of aspirin nearby just in case. He still wanted to pay them a visit at some point, though he was unsure if he should take Linz. Maybe meeting her old team would trigger a recall for her. It was worth a try.

Part of him felt guilty that he wanted her to suffer the same pain of remembering, but he also couldn't stop the feeling that it was imperative she did. It was apparent that the Renovo experiment was still very much alive, and he needed Linz to remember Diana's life if he had any hope of understanding his own. Somehow, Michael and Diana had altered the chemistry of their brains and the effects had carried over into this lifetime—it was the only explanation that Bryan could come up with. By taking the drug, they had opened their minds and their minds had stayed open.

Bryan was obviously more affected than Linz was—he remembered multiple lives and countless languages. But then Michael had taken larger doses of Renovo and for a much longer period. Linz's recollection of Juliana's death and her willingness to acknowledge that she could, in fact, speak Greek were steps in the right direction. Now Bryan was gripped by a new urgency to pick up the pieces and move forward.

The next morning it hit her—she was taking Bryan to a company function, and she needed help. In a panic, Linz called Derek, who then called the owner of the most exclusive salon in Boston. She managed to squeeze her in for a haircut, manicure, pedicure, and makeup.

Linz was a little embarrassed by all the pampering, but when she looked at herself in the mirror, she had to admit she'd been transformed.

Of course, the new look required a new outfit. Her old black cocktail dress wouldn't do. Glancing at her watch, she saw that she had a few hours before she needed to pick up Bryan, so she headed to Copley Mall, planning to just cut the tag on whatever she bought and wear it out of the store. *I'm acting like a lovesick teenager.*

Linz couldn't help but laugh at the thought of it, amazed at herself—she had never acted like one when she was younger.

An hour and a half later, she slid behind the wheel in a siren-red Nina Ricci dress and a pair of sexy Manolos. She didn't want to overthink tonight, but she also had never made this much of an effort to impress a man before. But Bryan was changing her. When he was around anything seemed possible; nothing felt certain.

She saw him waiting outside his building, looking quite the artist in a funky suit and tie straight from the seventies. The pea-green color collided with her red dress like a train wreck, making her wish she had chosen a more conservative black. She began to get the feeling that tonight wasn't going to go well.

She pulled the car up beside him and Bryan hopped in. He looked stunned.

"I had my hair done," she said, turning her head self-consciously. Bryan continued to stare. "It's a new dress." Linz wished he would say something so she could stop making this stupid commentary.

"Are we in park?" he finally asked her.

"You mean the car?"

Not waiting for an answer, Bryan reached over and pulled her onto his lap. He kissed her. Linz's dress rode up as she turned to fully face him.

The kiss went on until a horn blared behind them. They broke apart, both breathing heavily.

Bryan whispered, "Why don't we forget the party and go to your place?"

Another honk sounded and the car finally drove around them. Linz closed her eyes, trying to gain some self-control. "I can't. I need to make an appearance first. It's my work."

Bryan let go of her and leaned back in his seat, looking tortured. "Okay, let's go."

Linz climbed back over to the driver's seat, already regretting her decision. She drove to Belmont Hills on autopilot. They kept their conversation limited.

"So what have you been up to?" Bryan asked.

"Oh you know. Stuff. What about you?"

"Stuff."

They rode the rest of the way in silence. Linz glanced down at her fake nail tips and grimaced. She could not wait to get home and rip them off.

Bryan stared out his window at Belmont's gated mansions. They looked more Beverly Hills than Boston.

Linz finally turned into a long driveway. Valets stood at the end, waiting to whisk the car away. Bryan took in the enormous French classical château and whistled. It was nestled in its own little forest. "Who lives *here*?"

Linz hesitated. "My dad." She got out, leaving him flummoxed. "This is your house?"

She threw him a look. "I moved out in college."

He followed her toward the front door. "What are you, royalty?"

"Crowned princess of the pharmaceutical industry." She hooked her arm through his. "Party's this way."

Linz usually loathed revealing to people just how much wealth she came from, especially in a dating situation—not that she dated often. Medicor was the largest privately owned pharmaceutical company in the world, and she was happy to let her share sit in various accounts and accumulate interest. One day she would need it all when she opened her own research institute, but in the meantime she preferred her low profile.

For the first time, she didn't care if Bryan knew. She felt liberated by the fact that their relationship existed beyond material things. Growing up, she had been cocooned in a bubble filled with science and academia. It had been a hard decision to trade in her anonymity and go to work for her father. Many saw it as a public grooming for her to take over the company when he stepped down. In reality, she couldn't have cared less about running Medicor. Her research was her primary passion—strange how she had thought about neither since she met Bryan.

They heard the music before they saw the band. With Bryan's

arm in hers, they walked toward a large, tented dance floor with a stage that had been erected between the pool and the tennis court. Two dozen round tables filled the yard. Each one was decorated with ivory damask linens and vintage French vases filled with long-stemmed red roses to complement the black china. Two champagne fountains, along with an impressive ice sculpture, finished off the dramatic presentation. There were at least three hundred guests there to appreciate the effort.

Linz spotted her project team sitting together at a nearby table and led Bryan over. Everyone's attention was turned to the stage, where Conrad Jacobs was giving a speech.

"In med school, an old professor of mine used to say that being a scientist doesn't require eyeglasses and a lab coat. I'm glad to see you all left yours at home." He waited for the laughter to die down.

Bryan sat in the closest chair before he collapsed. He could no longer feel his legs. There stood Conrad, the person he had been researching. Bryan noted how little Michael's old colleague had aged—he looked the same aside from the distinguished gray along his temples and a more confident air.

Then Bryan realized something else. He leaned over to Linz with an incredulous whisper. "Is that your father?"

Without looking at him, she nodded yes. She was too busy listening to the speech to notice his reaction.

"I was living on a shoestring, struggling to get by on a government grant when I discovered I could make a difference, and Medicor was the result of that vision. We've come a long way in thirty years. Now Medicor is a global enterprise with research facilities around the world. And everyone here tonight has made us who we are today. Leaders. Dreamers. Healers."

Bryan felt like he had been transported to another planet. Conrad now lived like a king in a castle, and was surrounded by hundreds of employees listening to his every word like gospel. So much had changed in thirty years. Even more mind-blowing was the fact that Linz was his daughter.

". . . scientists at the top of our fields, striving to go over and above our imaginations. Medicor means 'to cure' in Latin and that remains our mission. Tonight we celebrate our drive to achieve it. Please enjoy."

The speech was followed by strong applause. Bryan looked at Linz, disconcerted by the pride and love shining in her eyes. Tonight would not be the night to ask her about her father.

He also hadn't failed to notice all the curious looks he was getting from her coworkers. Steve gave Bryan an appraising glare and leaned toward Linz. "I researched 'unexplained phonetic cognizance,'" he shouted across the table. "I couldn't find any cases."

"Thanks, Steve." Linz shot Bryan a rueful glance. "Steve, Neil, Maggie, this is Bryan, a friend."

The jazz band began playing Louis Armstrong's "What a Wonderful World." Bryan saw Conrad signaling Linz, and she stood, looking apologetic. "I'll be right back."

She left Bryan alone to fend for himself. Steve was growing less cordial by the second. "How long have you guys been dating? Did you meet online?"

Maggie kicked Steve under the table and smiled at Bryan. "Sorry, he's not used to social interaction."

Neil joined the conversation, a chicken satay in each hand. "So what do you research, bro?"

"Research?" Bryan watched Conrad and Linz step out onto the dance floor.

Steve crossed his arms. "Yeah. What's your specialty?"

Bryan turned back, realizing they all assumed he was a scientist. "Oils. Excuse me." He stood up and set off toward the house. Now that he knew it belonged to Conrad, he couldn't contain his curiosity. He left everyone scratching their heads.

"Oils? That bioengineering?" Neil reached over to Steve's plate and stole his shrimp brochette. "And what's with the suit? Is retro back in?"

Maggie rolled her eyes. "Like you would know. I think he's hot."

On the dance floor, Linz followed her father's lead. She was used to dancing with him at functions.

"Nice speech."

Conrad spun her around. "Does that mean, Dr. Jacobs, that I can start calling you Lindsey again in public?"

"Fine, I overreacted at the meeting." Linz glanced back at the table. Bryan hadn't lasted long. She watched him disappear inside and felt guilty for leaving him.

Conrad noticed him too. "Who's the suit?"

"The artist I was telling you about."

Conrad faltered with his next step. "You brought him here?"

Linz laughed at the astonishment on his face. "Watch your feet, twinkle toes. It's just a date."

Bryan wandered through the main hallway, his architectural eye taking in the curving colonnade and sweeping pavilion. Earlier, when they had come up the drive, he had been astounded to recognize a design Louis Le Vau had studied on paper hundreds of years ago.

The house clearly resembled one of the scrapped plans for the East Wing of the Louvre. Bryan remembered the debacle like it was yesterday. Le Vau had already remodeled most of the Louvre but had been unable to finish it after he had been fired by Jean-Baptiste Colbert, advisor to Louis XIV. A train of architects had stood in line to attempt to remodel the wing, including the most influential architect of the French Renaissance: Francois Mansart. An utter perfectionist, Mansart often tore down partially completed projects and began again. He had drawn up several brilliant plans for the wing, but Colbert had released him as well. Le Vau had seen the plans because he had remained on the Louvre's building committee. Bryan would have recognized Mansart's original design anywhere. He wondered how Conrad had gotten his hands on it.

Bryan passed under a Roman arch and ended up in a formal living room where several photographs were displayed on a Grecian table next to a grand piano. Most were of Linz. One photo showed her winning the World Junior Chess Championship. Bryan picked it up and smiled. Toward the back, he noticed a small photo of the entire family taken when Linz had been a baby. The woman holding her could only have been her mother. She and Linz shared the same beauty. Conrad and his wife must have met after Michael's death—Bryan didn't recognize her. Linz's brother looked to be about two or three in the picture, his face oddly solemn. It was the only photo of her mother and brother in sight. Perhaps grief kept the others locked away.

He picked up another photo of Linz as a young girl. Dressed in a ballet costume, she stood on pointe, her other leg extended high in the air. Her face had a calm, focused look, as if striking such perfect balance came effortlessly to her. Bryan wasn't surprised. Balance had always been one of her strongest attributes. It had been one of the first things he had noticed when he had met her this time—her carriage, her poise. There were other qualities that she also had unknowingly carried with her: the way she tilted her head slightly to the right when she was contemplating something, the unblinking focus of her eyes at times, and the way her thumb performed a circular pattern on the tip of her index finger when she was truly deep in thought.

Bryan looked around the room and noticed another door leading away from the living room. He glanced back to make sure no one was watching and entered.

On the other side was an enormous gallery housing an antique collection that would rival any museum's. Bryan took a few steps inside and stopped.

Coming into this room had been a mistake. These were relics from his own memories. His eyes darted around in panic as the fingers of the past started to wrap themselves around his neck, choking him.

Before he could turn around and escape, he saw a tall glass case in the center of the room displaying a small item. He walked toward it in astonishment, his chest heavy, and he felt the room collapse as the weight of a vision propelled him to another time and place.

TWENTY-ONE

The wind hid Odin's breath—Bjarni knew only a god could have conjured such a storm. He dropped sail to slow his speed, but the gales continued to push him off course. The ocean waged its war against his ship for a second day until Bjarni began to believe it wasn't Odin, but Hel herself from the Underworld, raising her hands within the waves in an attempt to capsize them. He would never reach Greenland.

Bjarni prayed once more to Njord, God of the Sea and protector of all sailors, to keep them from her clutches. He gripped the *vegvísir* tighter in his palm and felt the stone grow warm in his hand.

A magical charm, the vegvísir was said to keep anyone from losing his way on the roughest seas. Bjarni looked down at the stone's rune-like symbol, its ornate lines stretching in all four directions, cross-points perfectly carved, and had to believe it would. Garnissa had made it for him when she realized he would return home and find her gone.

Every winter Bjarni went back to Iceland to stay with his father, Herjólfr, at Eyrarbakki until the weather cleared. Bjarni was one of the best traders in the land, and he had accumulated his wealth over the years for one purpose—to build the finest longhouse for Garnissa and obtain good farmland. He had been planning to settle the agreement with her father for her hand. But when he had arrived, he had not even begun to unload his cargo when his old friend Guid had come running to deliver the news.

"Your father's gone—Garnissa too with her family," Guid had said.

A swift panic rose within Bjarni and he had fought to hide it. "Gone?"

"They all joined Erik the Red to sail for the new land he's discovered."

"Erik's returned?" Bjarni frowned. Erik had been banished from Iceland for the past three years. He had killed two of his neighbors in a dispute over pasture lands. Before the controversy, Erik had been a good friend of Bjarni's father and Bjarni had grown up playing with Erik's sons, Thorvald, Thorskeinn, and Leif, often getting into mischief with them.

Usually the boys preferred to be caught and punished by Bjarni's father, who was much more soft-spoken in comparison to Erik, who had a temper to match his flaming red hair. Even when he was a child, to Bjarni, Erik had been the strongest, most intimidating man he had ever met. He possessed the spirit of a true leader, charismatic and bold, and he hated fools. It did not surprise Bjarni to hear now that Erik had returned and been able to persuade most of the village to follow him to a new land where he would be Chieftain.

"He's calling this grand new frontier Greenland," Guid said with a hint of skepticism. "People left their farms and took their trade."

"How many ships?" Bjarni asked, unable to believe Garnissa and his father had gone without him.

"Twenty-five. They left late spring to settle well before winter."

Twenty-five ships meant hundreds of people. Bjarni said nothing, his thoughts racing ahead as he weighed his options.

"Garnissa asked me to give you this." Guid handed Bjarni a small object wrapped in hide.

Bjarni had opened the bundle to find the vegvísir, and his heart had quickened when he saw the stone's intricate design. He would have recognized Garnissa's hand anywhere—she was the finest carver in the village next to her mother. Leaving the gods' compass with Guid had been the best message she could have sent: *Come and find me.*

Without question, Bjarni had decided to continue on to Erik the Red's new land—a brash move considering winter was almost upon them and he did not know the way, nor would they be traveling with the support of other boats. And to make matters worse, he had twenty crewmen eager for land.

Keeping his face expressionless, Bjarni had tucked the stone into his belt. His crew could not know that he was trying to beat winter to Greenland because of a woman. The men would have taken their cargo and refused to sail.

Bjarni had gathered them on shore and looked each one of them in the eye. "Accompany me to this new paradise and see what you will gain. I promise a land of plenty as Erik's described it, with boundless edibles and wildlife. The markets in Iceland have been slowly dying for years, the land overharvested . . . we are all restless for something better. Greenland promises a new beginning for those of us who are willing to grasp it. Come with me." The men had grumbled but were game to follow him, and they had left port that same day.

Now they were lost at sea.

Bjarni did not believe in the magic of the Old Ways as Garnissa did, but he held on to the belief that her vegvísir would help him find his way. After two days of ceaseless battle with the storm, the crew was exhausted, sleep-deprived, and weary from bailing water to keep the ship afloat. Bjarni gripped the stone tighter. He was not ready to die just yet.

He yelled out over the wind, "Secure the spare sail to the mooring line! We'll pitch it aft and make a *droug!*" Perhaps a crazy move in such a storm, but he saw no other choice.

All accomplished seamen, the men took action, knowing it was their captain's final attempt to gain some control of the boat. They managed to lose speed but continued to sail on blindly.

Bjarni fought the wind to reach the tiller and relieved Olvir to man it himself. If any *knarr* could survive Odin's storm it would be the *Gata*. He had built the boat with his own hands ten years ago, guided by his eldest uncle, the finest shipbuilder in all of Iceland. The trees had been carefully chosen from his father's land

and blessed by his mother. And when he and his uncle had split the first piece of wood for the helm, Bjarni had not looked away but had chosen to see the boat's fate. Few men did.

"Look, boy. The wood split even and true," his uncle announced, slapping his back in celebration. "I swear by the gods this boat will not shipwreck you."

His mother had cried while the men laughed in relief. Bjarni bent down and picked up the two pieces, fitting them together perfectly.

"She will never fail you," his uncle said solemnly. "Remember that." And then the old man had walked off to build it.

The ship's name had come to Bjarni on the morning it was ready to meet water—the *Gata*, which meant the road. His ship would be a road through the sea, and no vessel would travel it better.

True to his uncle's words, the *Gata* did not fail him but rode out the storm until its fury broke on the third day, leaving only fog behind. Bjarni raised the sail to catch what wind he could and took out his sunstone to find the sun's position. But even his treasured crystal could not help him. That night Polaris—the North Star—and its two pointer stars remained hidden as well. Odin was not through with him yet.

The *Gata* sailed for two more days. Fortunately, the crew had plenty of casks of fresh water and dried food for the journey, and the men took the time to rest. Only Tarr was discontent.

This was Bjarni's first voyage with the man, and he had begun to question his decision to allow him passage, but he had been in need of an extra hand. Olvir had vouched for the stranger, though not with any conviction—Tarr had been a raider most of his life and bore the hardness of it in his eyes. Bjarni had heard tales of raiders since he was a child, of looting and murdering on foreign lands—how men skirted coasts and swiftly attacked sleepy villages, leaving behind only burned buildings and sorrow.

Tarr looked as if he could tell such stories. His skin was marred with scars from battle-axes and arrows, more so than most. He had paid for his passage on the *Gata* with *wadmal* and coin like the other men, but Bjarni could not help but feel that the moment his back was turned, Tarr's knife would appear to rob him of both. It would be a hard fight if it came to pass—the men were both of equal height with strong builds, though the similarities between them ended there. Tarr was dark-haired to Bjarni's blond, and where Bjarni's eyes were warm and green like a forest in summer, Tarr's were the palest blue ice and hid the same coldness.

Bjarni had caught Tarr watching him more than once. He had never disliked any man without good reason, but he disliked Tarr and did his best to ignore him.

On the fourth day, the fog lifted. Bjarni heard the birds first and then saw the coastland.

Olvir joined him portside. "Have we found it?"

Bjarni studied the land and shook his head. "It's not Greenland. There are no glaciers, and look at the trees." Rich forest stretched as far as they could see. Bjarni had heard every seafaring story and knew this was undiscovered land. Excitement filled him and he almost called out to change course and head for shore. He could claim this land—he could be as famous as Erik the Red. He could—but then he stopped. Going ashore carried too many risks, risks that increased the chances that he would never see Garnissa again. He would rather die than take them.

"We should go to shore," Tarr said, coming to join them.

Bjarni shook his head firmly. "Then we'll never beat winter to Greenland." He could not let Tarr or any of the men know he was resisting the same urge.

"This could be our own Greenland," Tarr countered, raising his voice so all could hear him. "Our own frontier. Unspoiled land with untold riches waiting."

Bjarni turned to Tarr, standing his ground. "Then build your own boat, gather your own crew and return." He met the gaze of all the men. "We go to Greenland."

Tarr's hand snaked out and grabbed Bjarni's, turning it over to expose the vegvísir. "Does a woman wait for you there?" He sneered. "Is that why your manhood's missing?"

Several men snickered. Bjarni jerked his hand away, refusing to be baited. "Olvir, man the tiller," he ordered, and headed toward the bow. He took out his sunstone again and this time he located the sun behind the clouds. Testing the wind and seeing that they had gone too far west, he directed Olvir to steer a new course.

As he watched the new land retreat into the distance, doubt tugged at him. Was he doing the right thing? In any other circumstance he would have stopped. How he wanted to stop—but he couldn't. He tried to assure himself that perhaps one day he would return with Garnissa beside him.

As if the three fates were tempting his steadfastness, the next morning Bjarni sighted more land with the same forested terrain. Once again Tarr tried to sway him. "The fates are smiling on us, Bjarni, don't be a fool. These are undiscovered lands. We would be the first to settle upon them."

Everyone gathered around, their excited eyes turned to shore as they listened to Tarr carry on. Again Bjarni resisted the urge, reminding himself that if he stopped now, they would never reach Greenland—he would never see Garnissa. The fates were not smiling upon them. This was a test. Who knew what this new frontier held or if they would have enough provisions to last the winter. Everything in his bones told him to reach Greenland before it became frozen in ice.

"We continue on," Bjarni said, as he stared Tarr down.

Tarr went for his dagger, but Bjarni grabbed him first. The men jerked and twisted, each trying to pin the other to the deck. Tarr pulled one of his arms free and punched Bjarni full in the face. Bjarni staggered backward and hit the side of the boat, holding on to it.

The crew gave them a wide berth. No one would interrupt this fight, no matter how much they wanted to sway the outcome. A man's battle was his own.

Bjarni wiped the blood from his nose and tried to clear his head. He took his best stance, relaxing his arms and legs. Tarr may have had more experience with a sword, but Bjarni was by far the superior wrestler. Using all his skill, he advanced quickly, feigned right and went for Tarr's inside leg. Before he knew it, Bjarni had him in a headlock and was jabbing at Tarr's face with his fist.

Tarr stood up with a roar, taking Bjarni with him, and threw him over his head. Bjarni hit the deck hard and he struggled to stand up. The two faced each other. Blood dripped from Tarr's chin, and he bared his teeth like a feral beast from Hel's den. The boat rocked and swayed, as if trying to knock both men off balance. Tarr staggered forward, but Bjarni remained sure-footed and confident, letting Tarr come at him. With perfect timing, Bjarni took Tarr's body and twisted him into the air, using his own momentum to throw him down. He had practiced the move a hundred times in his youth, and Bjarni would not be beaten aboard his own ship.

Tarr strained with all his might, but Bjarni had him pinned. He humiliated Tarr further by ordering Hugi, his biggest and most loyal man, to take Tarr's weapons.

"Throw them overboard," Bjarni commanded.

Hugi saw the murderous gleam in Tarr's eyes and hesitated.

"It's either him or the weapons," Bjarni said.

Hugi threw everything into the sea and motioned for the men to disband and leave the captain to deal with the usurper.

Bjarni kept Tarr pinned to the deck. "Now you maggot-ridden fool," Bjarni said softly, "I can either tie you up until we reach Greenland or release you. But try to strike at me again and I will kill you."

Seething, Tarr gave a curt nod of consent and Bjarni let him go.

Tarr stood up. "Bjarni Herjólfsson." He spat his name on the ground. "You will regret this day and remember me when you die."

That was the only thing Tarr said to him for the rest of the journey. Bjarni tried to shake off his sense of unease, but when he woke the next day, Garnissa's vegvísir was missing from his belt. He knew Tarr had stolen it and prayed to Forseti, keeper of peace and justice, to guide him. To accuse Tarr would result in a fight to the death, and that was exactly what the raider wanted. So instead

Bjarni went about his business with the ship, sailing the rest of the way without trouble until he reached his father's port.

True to Erik the Red's tale, the lands were rich for farming and nestled right among the glaciers. The settlers all gathered to greet them. Bjarni's father, Herjólfr, stood beaming at the front.

"I expected you to come to us next summer, boy," he called out laughing. "How did you find your way?"

"With some help," Bjarni said, walking to greet him. His eyes scanned the crowd and easily found Garnissa. Her long tresses fluttered in the wind along with the colorful ribbons adorning her red and blue skirts. Her hair was pale gold and her eyes were a mixture of green and blue like the sea. They twinkled back at him— she knew he spoke of her.

Everyone crowded around the newcomers, enlivened by their arrival and ready to trade whatever wares the *Gata* had brought. The crew began to unload the cargo, and Bjarni followed his father to his newly constructed longhouse nestled on a nice patch of clearing. He wanted to soak in the bathhouse and change out of his filthy tunic before seeing Garnissa that evening.

Whenever a new ship came to port, it was tradition for the village to gather around the fire at dusk. They would often look for any reason to congregate and drink strong mead, tell stories and riddles, and sing the songs of old. Tonight was no different.

When Bjarni arrived at the bonfire, Ulfied, his burly shiphand, was in the midst of telling the story of the new lands they had sighted. Bjarni suffered many a joke for his decision not to stop. Soon drunken men were performing skits, pretending to be a daft captain unable to steer his ship. Bjarni took all of it with good humor, purposefully ignoring Tarr's murderous gaze. He became grateful when one of the elders, Aldar, began to entertain the rowdy group with a poem.

"One day," Aldar began, taking care to meet the eyes of every child sitting around the fire, "Odin's ravens, Huginn and Muninn— seers of all thought and memory—swooped down and stole the threads from the three fates, the *Norns*. Now, we all know who the three fates were."

A chorus of children yelled out their names, "Urd! Verdani! Skuld!"

"Yes!" Aldar hissed, sounding like a sorcerer himself. "Weavers of the past, present, and future. Now, because of the birds' trickery the Norns could no longer spin the tapestry of life and time itself was in danger of being lost."

Bjarni tried not to laugh at the wide-eyed children, enthralled by the old poet's tale. Aldar had been a *skald* at Norway's royal court as a young man and could launch into a perfectly metered story on a whim. Bjarni hoped that some day his own son would be able to sit at Aldar's feet as he had and hear the poet conjure up worlds as real as their own.

Bjarni met Garnissa's eyes, and she left the fire discreetly. He was not pleased to see Tarr's gaze on her as well. It seemed that she had caught his attention. Bjarni locked eyes with him and followed Garnissa, marking her as his own. Tarr might have a grudge against Bjarni, but he would not let Tarr's shadow fall on her.

Leaving quietly, Bjarni made his way to the river to meet her. Finally they were able to be alone.

"Welcome to Greenland, o fearless explorer of new lands," she teased, yelping as Bjarni swooped her up in his arms.

"Would you have had me on another shore without you?" he asked, nuzzling her neck.

"Never," she said, bringing his face back up to hers to kiss him fully. "I'm glad you didn't stop."

"My refusal has made me enemies," Bjarni admitted.

"The raider," she nodded. "He's a mean one."

"Promise me you'll give him a wide berth until he's gone after winter."

"And will you be gone after winter too?" She held his hand.

"No. Greenland is my home now. With my wife and sons."

"Sons?" She laughed, her eyes shining. "And where are these sons?"

Bjarni took her in his arms. "Waiting for us."

Skuld, future's fate, had shown him his path long ago. He was certain Garnissa felt it too, perhaps even more clearly.

"You're looking quite pleased," he teased her. "Have you been casting runes?"

She nodded happily, a little smile on her face.

"You've no need to. I am yours, Garnissa. Always." He embraced her tightly.

They lay down on the grass, wrapped in each other's arms, and listened to the merriment from the bonfire. The night was cool, signaling winter would soon arrive. Bjarni's eyes grew heavy as the laughter lulled him to sleep.

He knew not how long he slept, his body a still stone upon the earth. The mist began to grow colder, sharper, like stinging nettles coming on the wind to find him, and he awoke.

He heard rustling and forced his eyes open to find a woman staring down at him. She had long, raven black hair that was woven into a crown of braids, a queen's crown. Her arms and neck were adorned with heavy bands of gold encrusted with priceless gems. Bjarni could not speak. She was the goddess Freyja surely.

She bowed her head and acknowledged him. "You are dying, Bjarni Herjólfsson. As am I."

Bjarni woke from the dream to a world of snow and ice. He was lying by the same river where he had asked Garnissa to marry him thirteen years ago, only now his body was naked, exposed mercilessly to the elements and shivering with cold. He knew he would be dead before nightfall, as he had planned.

The goddess who had visited him must have been a *fylgje*, a follower, who showed themselves in dreams at the time of a person's death. He had felt a sense of kinship upon seeing her.

Where she had stood, a niviarsiaq flower now grew, struggling to bloom despite the frost. It made him think of Garnissa, and tears rolled from his eyes, freezing on his cheeks before they could fall.

She had been missing for months now—taken the same day their son had been murdered.

Bjarni had returned home from his fields to find Anssonno lying dead on the doorstep, his neck slit open like a hunted animal's. Inside, the longhouse was marked with signs of a dreadful fight, and the weapons Bjarni kept hung by the door were strewn across the bloodied floor. Garnissa was gone.

The villagers had searched the area for days, but Bjarni knew she would not be found. The intruder had left behind something Bjarni had thought he would never see again—Garnissa's vegvísir. His eyes had settled on it as he had cradled his son's lifeless body. It was lying in the doorway on top of Garnissa's *hustrulinet*, the lovely white headdress she wore over her hair. When Bjarni saw the vegvísir and headdress together, he knew that Tarr had taken her and that he would never see his wife again.

There had been talk of a raider's ship being spotted up the coast two days before. It had been well over a decade since Bjarni had last seen Tarr, and he had thought him gone from his life. But Tarr must have remained intent on taking his revenge. And Bjarni could now see that Tarr had not plotted to kill him, but had waited to destroy everything he loved.

When Bjarni realized that Tarr was the one who had taken her, he—along with Garnissa's brothers—had set out in the *Gata*, searching for any sign of the raider. But they had no success, and for months he had sunk into the darkest despair.

It was in such a state that his old friend, Leif Erikson, had found him. One of Erik the Red's sons, Leif had been living for many years in Norway at the royal court. Bjarni had not seen him since their youth. Leif had finally come to Greenland to see the settlement for himself and bring priests of a new religion called Christianity that had been gaining popularity in the south. They were already busy building a chapel and visiting all the settlers to invite them to attend.

Leif had come to Bjarni's longhouse to pay his respects. The loss of Garnissa and Anssonno were still the talk of the village.

"Would you not see one of the priests?" Leif had asked him gently. "Perhaps it would help bring you peace."

Bjarni looked at him with eyes red from too many tears and too little sleep. "If I went to Odin, ruler of Alsgard, or to your new god, and asked them why Garnissa had been taken, why my son had been killed, I wager neither would have an answer."

Leif did not press the point and nodded solemnly. They drank mead by the fire, and Bjarni turned the subject to Leif's plans.

"I had not given it much thought beyond reaching Greenland," Leif admitted.

"Have you need of a ship?" Bjarni asked.

Leif looked at him in question.

"I am to sell the *Gata*. I do not need it anymore."

"But she is yours."

"I would give her to you," Bjarni said. "And rest easy knowing that she was out on the sea with you as her captain."

Leif was speechless. A ship as fine as Bjarni's would change everything.

"I have but one request," Bjarni said.

"Anything."

"Find the land I sighted. I will tell you the way."

Leif nodded with excitement. Everyone had heard the stories of Bjarni's discovery, but he had never told anyone how to find it. Bjarni had always hoped that one day he would give his son the *Gata* and let him explore the new land. How many times had he contemplated packing up their belongings and taking Garnissa and Anssonno there while they were still young? If he had, Tarr would never have known how to find them. Instead every dream died the day Anssonno had been murdered. Now Bjarni only wanted to follow his son to the grave.

"Take this." He placed Garnissa's vegvísir in Leif's hand. "It was made by my wife." He swallowed, forcing himself to continue. "It will help you find your way."

"You do me a great honor, Bjarni Herjólfsson." Leif bowed his head and pocketed the vegvísir. "I will find your land." He swore a solemn oath and they finished their mead in silence.

As Bjarni lay on the snow, he wondered where Leif was. Their talk had only been last spring and yet now it seemed like years ago. Bjarni had made the decision to end his life as he had watched the *Gata* set sail without him, with another captain holding Garnissa's compass. In the weeks that had followed, he had given away the remainder of his possessions and cleared out his house—then he waited.

On the morning of what would have been Anssonno's thirteenth birthday, during a full winter storm, Bjarni had stripped off his clothes and walked to the river to die.

He stared up at the bleak sky and thought of *Yggdrasill*, the tree that towered over all the nine worlds. At its root was the well of highest wisdom, which the giant Mimir guarded with his life. Odin had even sacrificed an eye to have a drink from the well in order to obtain infinite knowledge. Bjarni would have bartered every bone in his body to have one drop of that same wisdom before he died—to know if Garnissa was still alive. Was she in pain? What had Tarr done to her? And was Anssonno in Valhalla, the place where the bravest warriors went when they died? Bjarni knew he must be, because his son would never have let his mother be taken without putting up the fiercest fight. Anssonno had battled for her with his life and lost.

The night of their wedding, Garnissa had dreamed of their son in Valhalla. The dreams that a bride had on the first night of her marriage were considered to be prophetic—foretelling the number of children the couple would have, along with their destiny. It had taken her years to tell Bjarni about her vision. Seeing their son in Valhalla had terrified her, and made her quite protective of Anssonno after he was born. She had always believed they would only have one child, even though they had tried for many years to have more.

Bjarni sobbed and drew his last breaths in with the cold. This death would not allow him entry into Valhalla—Anssonno was lost to him. Images of his son and Garnissa filled him, and Bjarni begged the snowstorm to take his life. He could not live another moment imagining their pain.

As he closed his eyes, he saw a rainbow extending from the

horizon and into the clouds, and he knew it was *Bifrost*. Odin was showing him the sacred bridge from Asgard to Middle Earth, as if to say that his journey was not yet over. Weary, Bjarni took his last breath and wished he had Garnissa's vegvísir to help him find his way.

TWENTY-TWO

Michael woke up on his office floor, his body shivering. He tried to call out for help, but his voice sounded like the cry of a wounded animal.

Diana came rushing into the office. "My God, what happened?"

But her words had no meaning to Michael. He was consumed by Bjarni's pain.

She knelt beside him. Finn and Conrad hovered in the doorway, looking unsure about what they should do. Diana tried again. "Michael—listen to my voice. You just had a recall. Come back."

Michael saw her face and began to sob. "Garnissa?" He sat up and held her in a fierce embrace, "Garnissa." He could not stop the pain rising within him, as he gasped for breath and tried to explain what had happened to her and their son.

"Get me a blanket!" Diana shouted over him to Conrad and Finn. "Hurry!"

Finn ran to the closet and returned with one they used for the sofa. Diana wrapped it around Michael and began rubbing his body, trying to warm him as he rambled on.

Conrad watched in fascination and whispered to Finn, "What language is he speaking?"

Finn was staring at Michael in shock. "Old Norse."

Diana kept working to warm Michael's body and repeated the same thing again and again in an attempt to calm him. "Shhhh. It's me. Diana. I'm right here."

But Michael could see Garnissa's spirit shining in her and it only made him cry harder. His body was racked with cold—Greenland's winter still clutched at his mind. He forced himself to take several deep breaths and struggled to assimilate the memories.

Looking around in a daze, he saw the overturned chair and the files scattered on the floor. He must have passed out. He closed his eyes and tried to focus on feeling warm. The chill was just a memory.

Diana reached out for his hands and held them in hers. "What happened? Who were you?"

"Bjarni Herjólfsson." He struggled to put his answer into English. "A Viking trader from Iceland."

Diana's mouth dropped open. Finn, still looking stunned, sat down in the nearest chair.

Conrad was the only one laughing. "Jesus, now you're a Viking?"

"Conrad, please." Diana glared at him.

But Conrad continued to taunt him. "Did you sail the seas, terrorizing villagers with Thor's hammer?"

Finn looked ready to implode. "Hey Yankee Doodle ass wipe, shut up."

"Why? Because I'm the only one not going psycho around here?"

Diana ignored them both. "Who was Garnissa?" she asked Michael.

"Here we go again." Conrad leaned against the doorframe and crossed his arms. "The lovebirds through time. Can't you see you're creating a neurotic fantasy? None of this is real."

Finn jumped up. "Just because you can't remember anything, don't belittle what's going on with the rest of us." He pinned Conrad against the wall with one hand, their faces inches apart.

But Conrad didn't back down. "Take a look at yourself in the mirror, Finn—those sunglasses are ridiculous. And try taking a shower too, you stink."

Finn grew rigid as he stared into Conrad's eyes. His grip tightened on Conrad's neck, choking him. Conrad held his breath, refusing to cower.

Diana grabbed Finn's arm. "Finn! Stop! He can't breathe."

Finn squeezed harder, ignoring Diana's screams.

Michael sat up. "Finn! That's enough! Let him go!"

Finn finally released him and Conrad bent over, wheezing.

"Are you okay?" Diana rushed over to Conrad.

Conrad backed away, looking at all of them with disgust. "I need a break from you people." And he left.

Finn sat down again. "Sorry, I . . ." He hugged himself.

Diana went over and knelt beside him. "What is it? Talk to me."

Finn started shaking and broke down. "He's lying. The bastard's lying."

"What are you talking about?" Diana tried to get him to look at her, but he wouldn't. "Please, tell me. What's going on?"

"It's all fucked up. I can't . . . I'm sorry." Finn got up and ran out of the room without another word.

Diana put her hand over her mouth, looking ready to cry herself. Michael reached out for her. He was still shaking from phantom hypothermia.

"You need a doctor," she said.

"I'll be fine." His tone was final.

They stared at each other for a long moment. "What the hell is happening to us?" she whispered.

Michael couldn't answer at first. "We'll be okay," he finally said, willing himself to believe it as he tried to reassure her. "I'm all right now."

"And Finn?"

"Finn will be too," he said, with more conviction than he felt. "We're all just tired."

"I've never seen him like that."

"We'll go see him in the morning." He tried to stand, surprised at how weak he felt. He just wanted to go home and crawl into his bed and hold Diana in his arms. Losing her was still fresh in his mind.

Diana drove them home, understanding his need for silence. Michael kept his eyes closed the whole time. It took all his strength to get out of the car. His feet were lead weights as he climbed the stairs. Diana followed, her hand on his back for support. She unlocked the door for them and went inside.

Michael collapsed on the bed and listened to her as she brushed her teeth and got ready for bed.

"You know what's most frustrating?" she said. "You're being deluged with all of these memories, and so far I've remembered a Dutch woman who had babies and watched her husband paint all her life. The only thing I can do now is go to a convention in the Netherlands and not need a translator."

She crawled under the covers. Michael pulled her into his arms. There were several things he hoped she never remembered, like being burned alive in ancient Rome or her life in feudal Japan. And he never, ever wanted her to remember Garnissa. He couldn't even begin to imagine what her fate had been in Tarr's hands.

He turned off the light and felt her relax against him.

"Can you tell me about them? Bjarni and Garnissa?"

Michael stared into the darkness, unsure of how much he should share. "Bjarni first saw her at this thing we called the 'Great Assembly.'"

Michael caught himself slipping into first person and focused on trying to stay detached from Bjarni. Diana either didn't notice or was too tired to comment.

He continued. "All the tradesmen would bring their eligible daughters to cook at their booths and show off their housekeeping skills. Garnissa was the best— Ouch."

Diana pinched his side. Her eyes were still closed, but a smile was on her face. "Give me a break. The best cooker?"

"What? She was."

"Okay, He-Man. Was she pretty?"

Michael thought about it. "Not by today's standards."

He grabbed her hand to stop her from pinching him again and chuckled. One thing Michael had begun to see with these memories was how beauty was not fixed, but always changing, determined by a trinity of time, place, and perception. "What I mean is that female Vikings were a bit more masculine." He tried to imagine all the women in the village and struggled to accurately describe what he saw. "They had broader noses, smaller eyes—or perhaps they were just more inset—and their bodies had stronger builds. It was a different kind of beauty."

"Okay, strong Viking women. Got it."

Michael laughed. "Bjarni swore on seeing her that she would be his wife. Usually marriage was a business contract between families, but Bjarni had been struck by *inn mátki munr.*"

"Inn ma-what?" She yawned, tucking her hands under the covers.

"The mighty passion," Michael said with a soft voice.

In response, Diana gave him a tender kiss where her head was resting, just below his neck.

"And so he worked toward securing a *handsal*, a formal agreement with her father. At the time, eight ounces of silver was the minimum bride-price. Bjarni paid double in gold, plus a horse, a cow, and swords for every brother—"

She pinched him again, harder this time.

"Ouch! Stop pinching me. I'm just telling you like it was."

"But I can hear your smug smile." She opened one eye and peeked at him. "A horse and a cow?"

He rolled his eyes back at her and continued. "The *morgen-gifu*—the gift he gave her the morning after their wedding—was the most generous in all of Greenland." Bjarni had given Garnissa clothing and jewelry that he had purchased through his trades, as well as livestock and the land he built their longhouse on, to ensure that she and their future children would have security after he was gone. Michael fought to keep his voice steady.

"They married during their first year in Greenland and stayed with Bjarni's father, Herjólfr, until they could build their own home. Garnissa became pregnant the next summer with their son, Anssonno."

"That's a beautiful name," Diana said, and snuggled closer to him.

Michael nodded, his mind full with the memory of their son. "He was a beautiful boy. They had a good life, up until the end." Michael didn't tell her that the end had come too soon, and with incredible violence. Instead he pictured their farm as if it were projected on his bedroom wall—he only wanted to see the laughter and love.

Anssonno had been the light of his life, asking endless questions about the world. He had been at Bjarni's side when his own father, Herjólfr, had died and helped him to shoulder his grief, as only a son could. And, growing up, Anssonno had sat by the fire at Aldar's feet, just as Bjarni had hoped he would, and heard the old poet's stories.

The thought brought back the bitter knife that had killed his son and stabbed Michael's heart once more. Anssonno was dead.

He stroked Diana's arm in the dark, the movement lulling her to sleep.

"What happened that made you so sad?" Diana murmured.

Michael shook his head, unable to speak the words.

"I'm sorry," she said, and drifted off.

Michael felt an unchecked tear slip down his cheek. He did not want to cry again—he feared he would never stop.

Instead he recited the words silently in his head, *I am here now. I'm here now. I'm here now, I'm here now* while he listened to Diana's breathing deepen. Waiting until he felt sure she was asleep, he took his journal out of the nightstand and began to write.

DAY 25—MARCH 2, 1982

I feel like Tarr is near me, along with d'Anthès and Kira. Are they the same man? If these are truly past life memories and my instincts are correct, one soul has tried to destroy me across time. Perhaps I'm being paranoid, but I cannot ignore the feeling. It lives in my bones.

I am beginning to see a pattern and I find myself wondering if the laws of karma exist. Are souls destined to love or hate the same souls again and again? Or can we achieve some kind of resolution or enlightenment?

If a tragedy is destined to be repeated, we need to figure out how to break the cycle. Until we do, I have to trust this gut feeling. The malevolence that has shadowed so many of my lives is coming for me again.

TWENTY-THREE

"There you are." Linz's voice jolted Bryan back to the present.

Bryan was still standing in Conrad's antique gallery. Within the span of a few minutes, he had just recalled moments of two lifetimes that were nearly a thousand years apart. They were the quickest visions he had ever experienced—it had felt like an electric shock.

He stared at the stone trapped in the glass case and his eyesight blurred. *Conrad had Garnissa's vegvísir. How?* He tried to focus on Linz and saw Conrad standing next to her, and again he felt the chill of Bjarni's death. Now he wasn't sure if it would be wise to expose his identity to Conrad. Maybe the explosion hadn't been an accident—maybe Michael's fear had come to pass. Bryan felt light-headed, like his legs were about to buckle.

Linz saw the look on his face and rushed to his side. "Hey, are you okay?"

Bryan couldn't take his eyes off the vegvísir under the glass case. "I'm not feeling well. I have to go."

He staggered toward the door. Once he'd exited the room, the spinning subsided but he was still nauseous.

Linz put her arm around him for support. "I'll take you home."

"No, I'll get a cab. I don't want you to have to leave the party."

Conrad stepped forward. There was a hint of impatience in his voice. "I take it you're Bryan."

"Sorry, Dad, I'm being rude. It's just he . . . Bryan, this is my father."

Bryan was unable to look Conrad in the eye. He was going to be sick.

"I hear interesting things about you, Bryan. Perhaps we'll meet again when you're more yourself." He gave Linz a tender kiss on the forehead. "Drive safe, I'll see you at the office." He left them and went to talk to a few guests who had wandered into the foyer.

Linz touched Bryan's forehead. "God, your skin is like ice. Let's go."

Conrad watched them holding hands as they headed out the front door.

Neither spoke much on the drive to Bryan's apartment. He kept his eyes closed and hugged his body, trying to control the shivering.

Like Michael, he now had Bjarni Herjólfsson's entire life in his mind. He remembered Bjarni and Garnissa's time together as if it had just happened. The fight to stay grounded in the present had never been harder.

He took Linz's hand and kissed it, saying something Aldar always said whenever he was about to start a poem, *"From a dream I wake, a bearer of fate . . ."*

Linz glanced over at him in surprise. "What language is that?"

"Old Norse."

She pursed her lips and nodded but didn't pursue the matter. They drove the rest of the way in silence. Linz killed the engine when they arrived at his building. "I'll help you up."

"No. That's okay."

"I'm helping you," she insisted. "You can barely walk." He was too sick to argue. She kept her arm around him as they made their way to the elevator and up to his apartment.

He fumbled as he tried to open the door. "I can take it from here."

"Let me just help you get inside."

Another wave of nausea hit him. Linz took the keys from him and opened the door. He still tried to protest. "Please, just go."

Ignoring his plea, she walked in—and stopped in her tracks. The storage boxes were scattered all over the place, their contents now strewn across the room.

Linz could barely find a place to walk. "What the hell happened?"

Bryan couldn't answer and ran to the bathroom to be sick, leaving her alone to study the disaster. An old Super 8 projector had been set up like Bryan's own *Cinema Paradiso* with film reels stacked around it. A massive collection of neuroscience books was piled on the sofa.

Linz studied the titles with raised eyebrows: *Developmental Neurobiology, Medical Physiology and Biophysics, Subcortical Visual Systems,* and every issue of the *International Journal of Neuroscience* from its first publication in 1970 up until 1982. A pile of papers on the coffee table caught her eye—they were articles printed off the Internet on Medicor and her father. Linz reached for them. *Why did he have these?*

Bryan returned, wiping his face with a towel, and looking a little better. "Sorry about the mess. I was going to . . ." He stopped when he saw what she had found.

Linz stared at him. She was beginning to feel like she didn't know him at all. "What's all this?"

"I can explain. I was just on the Internet researching . . ."

"My father? Why?" she asked. Something strange was going on with Bryan and every fiber of her being told her to leave.

"Wait, don't get the wrong idea. I was researching Michael and Diana Backer, and I found out your father knew them."

"Michael and Diana who?"

Bryan sat down, a look of utter weariness on his face. "The couple from the wedding portrait. Your father knew them. There's an article here with a picture of them together, just let me find it."

Linz now realized that all the boxes belonged to Michael and Diana. "You're going through dead people's things?"

"Not technically," he said, making more of a mess as he dug through the stack of papers. "I know it's here."

Growing more unsettled by the minute, Linz watched Bryan tear the room apart as he looked for the article.

He tried to explain things to her again as he searched. "Your father knew them. Diana and Michael were neuroscientists working with Alzheimer's patients." Linz started to open the door to leave.

"Listen to me," he pleaded, "I didn't even know Conrad Jacobs was your father until tonight." He looked at the Super 8 projector. "The film! He's on the film. Don't go. I can prove it." He found the film he wanted instantly—it was obvious to Linz that he had viewed them all several times.

"My father is on these people's films?"

Bryan threaded the tape through the projector. "These are Michael and Diana's home movies."

"You watched their home movies?" she asked. Now she was beyond unnerved.

"Yes," Bryan admitted, exasperated. "I have to know who these people are, for my own sanity. I can't get them out of my head. It's different than the other times."

"I think it's time we discussed just how many other times there have been," she said, though she wasn't sure she wanted to know. At first, she had been fascinated and amazed by their connection—was even starting to buy into the idea of reincarnation. But Bryan seemed trapped in a dream world, unable to get out, and she didn't know if she wanted to join him there. "I thought we agreed you were going to drop all this stuff about that Diana woman," she reminded him.

"I'm sorry but I can't. Just please sit down and watch the film."

"I don't want to sit down."

"Fine, then stand." He started the projector and turned off the light.

Linz stayed by the door. Diana was projected on the wall, smiling to the camera with her hair in rollers as she got into a waiting car. The next shot jumped to a church, with Diana outside in her wedding dress.

"It's their wedding day," Bryan explained needlessly.

Linz didn't speak. Captivated by the film, she hugged her body in a protective stance as the clicking sounds of the projector ran through the dark.

The film jumped to the altar, where Michael waited with his best man, Doc. Beside him stood two more groomsmen—Conrad and Finn.

"That's my dad," she said, feeling dazed.

"I know." He corrected himself, "I mean I know now."

Conrad moved closer to Michael and Doc. Diana walked up the aisle and took Michael's hand.

Linz watched the entire ceremony, and the silly moments that were captured afterward while the wedding photographer took pictures. Conrad was in every other shot. The film ended as Michael and Diana drove away in their Jeep, decorated with cans that trailed behind the car.

"My father knew those people?" she asked, astounded.

"That's what I've been trying to tell you. I had no idea he was your father. I swear."

She stared at the blank wall where the image had been projected. The whole thing was too bizarre.

"You're shaking." He took her hands.

"No, I—"

"It's okay. Watching them affected me the same way."

"I'm not affected." But even as she said the words, she knew they were a lie. Watching the film had filled her with the most profound ache. She wanted to cry.

She saw how hurt Bryan was by her reaction and tried to make him understand. "Look. I'm normally a logical, methodical person. I don't date artists or talk about past lives or contemplate anything remotely esoteric. I don't want my life turned upside down."

Bryan reached out to touch her arm. "I know all of this seems crazy—especially this whole connection with your father—but don't shut me out. Please, don't be afraid."

"I'm not afraid." Linz stepped away. "But every time I'm with you, the moment I start to get used to things, then it changes and gets weirder. I don't know who these people are. And I don't care. So what if my dad knew them?"

"They were scientists who studied memory and were working on a cure for Alzheimer's," Bryan stressed. "They died in 1982 before we were born."

"And you think we were them."

"Yes." Bryan's eyes were unyielding.

She searched his face, shaking her head sadly. "I'm afraid the ride stops here." She was already regretting the words but she knew they had to be said. "Let's take a break, okay?"

Bryan gave her a little smile and brought her hand to his lips. He kissed the inside of her wrist just as he had the day they met, but he didn't try to stop her from leaving.

TWENTY-FOUR

Linz undressed in the dark. She felt herself sinking into a depression. The emotion felt alien to her and unstoppable. When she had walked into her condo, the place seemed empty and pointless, and for the first time the colorful puzzles on her walls looked silly. As she lay in bed, she stared into the dark at Bryan's painting of Origenes and Juliana that now hung on her wall. She had tried keeping it in her closet, but she knew it belonged in the open. Her dream had been an albatross all her life, and yet it had brought her Bryan. Was that a good thing? She didn't know.

Unable to sleep, she went to her living room and stood in her garden. Enjoying the sand beneath her feet, she took the rake and smoothed the ground, erasing the design she had created two nights ago. Her body relaxed as her hands directed the rake aimlessly, letting it leave fine lines in the sand with its teeth. She worked until she grew sleepy.

When she finished the design and went to bed, she didn't even bother to admire the ornate symbol she had created—a symbol only the most knowledgeable Egyptian scholars in the world would have been able to identify.

Returning from the break room with a third cup of coffee, Linz read the e-mail that had just arrived from her father. As usual, he had kept it short: *Come see me.*

She knew he wanted to discuss the party. Her sudden departure with Bryan the other night had been too strange for her father to let it slide. He would have a hundred questions, coupled with some harsh opinions, but she also had a few of her own—for starters, who were Michael and Diana Backer?

Linz took the elevator up to the top floor, but her father was on the phone.

He waved her in. "I've got five hundred million alone invested in the project. You do the math when we convert to yen." He laughed and switched to flawless Japanese.

Linz looked out the window while she listened to her father's conversation. It had always amazed her that he was fluent in several languages. She had grown up hearing him speak in Japanese, French, and German. Funny how he had never tried to teach any of them to her, and she had never asked him to. What would he think if he knew she was fluent in Greek?

She smiled to herself, imagining the look on his face. Conrad saw her and shot her a questioning look. She indicated that it was nothing and let him finish his call. They had become so attuned to each other over the years that they had developed a way of communicating without words.

Linz had no memory of either her mother or her brother. Her father was her only family. To Conrad's credit, he had never shipped her off to boarding school, but had tried to raise her on his own as best he could. She loved him, although sometimes his protectiveness could become overbearing. In some ways, it bordered on controlling.

She heard him wrap up the call and turned around.

He came over and gave her a hug. "You look tired."

"A little. I wanted to apologize for leaving early . . . and talk to you about a couple of things."

Conrad headed back toward his desk. "Okay, I'm all ears."

"Can you tell me about Michael and Diana Backer?"

Her question had clearly caught him off guard. "Michael and Diana who?"

Linz frowned. It was impossible that he didn't remember them. "Dad, you were in their wedding party."

"Who told you that?"

"Bryan showed me their wedding video."

"The painter from the party?"

"Yes, the painter that you were very rude to."

Conrad sat down. "What's he doing with a film belonging to deceased people he doesn't know?"

"How do you know he doesn't know them? You don't know anything about him."

"Then enlighten me, please." Conrad's voice grew softer and more subdued. He was getting angry, but Linz wasn't happy with the course of the conversation either.

"His father was an old friend of theirs. Why didn't you just say you knew them?"

"His father was an old friend," he repeated. "Which of course makes perfect sense. Why wouldn't he watch their home movies? Then he comes to our house, I catch him snooping around—"

"He wasn't snooping."

"—looking sick. God knows what drugs he's on."

Linz was incredulous. She could not keep her voice from rising. "He's not on drugs!"

"Did you check his medicine cabinet? I'm assuming you watched the film at his place."

"Back up. You've completely got the wrong impression. I just asked if you knew Michael and Diana Backer and you lied."

"I didn't lie."

"Fine, evaded the question."

They glared at each other, having reached an impasse. Conrad finally relented, explaining, "I don't talk about Mike and Diana because it was a long time ago and . . . it's upsetting. We went to school together. They were my best friends, just like Penelope and Derek are to you. What if you tragically lost them?" Linz's anger deflated and she started to feel ashamed. Conrad sighed, continuing, "I can't remember you ever accusing me of lying to you, and I have never criticized the company you keep. What's going on with you?"

Linz tried to get a handle on her thoughts. "I'm sorry. I didn't mean . . . I haven't been getting much sleep."

Conrad's concern overrode his anger. "Are you dreaming again?"

"No. Just a little insomnia."

Conrad's intercom buzzed. "Dr. Jacobs, your eleven o'clock conference call."

Conrad checked his watch in frustration. "Stormy, I don't want to cut this short. Why don't we have dinner tonight? The Bay Tower at eight." He led Linz to the door. "We'll talk more then."

She nodded and fixed her gaze on his tie, recognizing it as one she had given him. "Sorry I upset you. I still want to hear about them though, if you're up to it."

"But why, honey?"

"I can't explain it right now. It's complicated." She gave him a kiss on the cheek and left.

Conrad went back to his desk, looking as if the weight of the world was on his shoulders. Ignoring the flashing light signaling his conference call, he picked up the phone and made another one.

Linz took the elevator back to the tenth floor. As she walked down the long glass corridor to her lab, she saw Dr. Parker through the window of the Genome Department. This time, when he gave her his usual friendly wave, Linz decided to stop. As she entered his lab, he turned to her with excitement, as if they were already in the middle of a conversation. "We have pinpointed the melanoma lineage specific enhancer"—he waved the printout in his hand as he continued—"with clear inducible chromatin looping!"

Linz smiled and went with it. "The wonders of computers."

"Though I'm not quite sure about this Epigenomic analysis," he said, more to himself, and turned away to study a nearby monitor. He had clearly exhausted his social skills. Linz knew other scientists with the same flaw, especially from her father's generation. Luckily she was not similarly afflicted. A thought occurred to her.

"Dr. Parker, did you know Michael and Diana Backer? I believe they were in your field."

He looked up from the monitor, startled that she was still there. "Of course. I met them through your father years ago."

"Because they went to med school together?"

"Yes," he said. "Then Conrad worked for Mike."

Linz nodded as if none of this was news. "Of course."

"He took over their research when he started this company."

Linz nodded again, a sense of surrealism starting to kick in. "What were they working on?"

"A study to help enable memory retrieval in Alzheimer's patients. I was disappointed that it was never published. It was all such a shame."

"Yes, I remember him talking about it. What was the project name again?" Linz prompted.

"I'm not sure if I . . ." Dr. Parker paused a minute. "Ah yes, Renovo."

Linz hid her surprise—that was the same name Bryan had mentioned during dinner. "Right, Renovo."

"Over the years, I've asked your father on several occasions if I could take a peek at the file. But he's always said no. Such a shame, to see their research buried in a coffin."

A shiver ran down Linz's spine. She nodded, unable to speak. Dr. Parker smiled and turned back to his work.

Linz hurried back to her lab, where she found Steve watching a video online. It took her a second to realize it was a video of him on YouTube, doing a bizarre dance-performance piece. The second he noticed her, he killed his monitor, mortified. She pretended not to see. "Steve, can you do me a favor?"

"Anything."

"Get me whatever you can find on a research project named Renovo. Check NIA's databases and our archives."

"What year?"

"1982." The year Medicor was founded—five years before she was born.

Her cell phone rang before Steve could ask her any more questions. It was a number Linz had never seen before—it looked like an international call. She was about to answer when the call dropped. She waited to see if a voice mail would register, but nothing came.

Linz was annoyed. She had hoped it would be Bryan. She knew she should make first contact since she'd been the one to suggest they needed a break, but still she wished he'd ignore her request and call her anyway—or better yet, show up at her door. Linz shook her head, disgusted with herself. *So much for willpower.*

Frustrated, she turned off her phone and threw it in the drawer. Missing him wouldn't accomplish anything. There was work to be done, and it just might help her ignore the feeling that simply wouldn't go away: her life was beginning to fall apart.

TWENTY-FIVE

Bryan hung up the airphone, not sure what he would have said if Linz had answered. He imagined how the conversation might have gone and grimaced. How could he explain his actions without driving her further away?

He had pushed too hard when he had forced her to watch the film. The problem was that Linz remained a stranger to the memories they shared, and the farther down the rabbit hole he went without her, the more she became a stranger to him. The distance between them was growing, and the realization terrified him.

It didn't help that the memories from Bjarni's life threatened to overwhelm him. After Linz had left, Bryan had stared at the ceiling for hours and then headed to the studio to paint.

He had done one painting, but for the first time in his life his art felt like a distraction. An urgency had been building inside him ever since he'd remembered Bjarni's life—there was something in those memories that he needed to find.

Frustrated, Bryan had left his loft to go for a walk. The ghostly history seeping from the nooks and corners of Boston's streets usually managed to calm him and help him connect to a past he knew was alive and breathing. But not that night.

He had walked for hours until he'd looked up and found himself on Commonwealth Street. It was no accident. There, erected in a circular garden, was a life-size bronze statue of Leif Erikson, commemorating his explorations. Leif had found the new land just as Bjarni had instructed him and had created a settlement called

"Vinland," what was now Canada. Some had thought that Leif had explored even farther, reaching Massachusetts hundred of years before the Pilgrims.

Bryan had stared at the statue of his old friend and been filled with a profound feeling of kinship. Leif had done it: he had reached the new land with the *Gata*. When Bryan had looked down at the turquoise ring on his finger, he had known he would not find the answers he sought without taking a leap of faith. Without questioning the impulse, he had gone home and booked a flight to the one place that Bjarni had wanted to go but never did.

Now here he was on a plane. Bryan reclined his chair and stared at the seat in front of him. Was he wrong to leave Linz alone with Conrad? After all, Michael had questioned Conrad's motives and his honesty, and the situation was even more entangled now that he knew Linz was Conrad's daughter. Bryan would have rested easier if Linz were with him. He had even debated trying to talk her into going, but he knew the idea would have sounded insane to her. Things had been easier before, when he was the only one wondering if he was crazy.

He stared at the airphone and tried to ease his anxiety—he should at least leave a message. Picking up the handset, he swiped his credit card again. Dialing the number from memory, he counted the rings, already assuming she wouldn't pick up. "Linz, it's Bryan. Just wanted you to know I'm on my way to Newfoundland . . . Canada . . . to paint. . . . I know it's last minute. Sorry for what happened. Maybe the time apart will be a good breather . . . for you, like you said. Let's talk when I'm back . . . take care."

He hung up, frustrated. His message hadn't conveyed any of the things he'd wanted to say.

The plane started to descend an hour later. Bryan's pulse quickened as he looked out the window. Bjarni's new land lay beneath him.

Linz sat waiting at the Bay Tower Room's best table. She had been there for twenty minutes, sipping a glass of their finest chardonnay.

But the wine, along with the incredible view of Boston's skyline, was wasted on her. She listened to Bryan's voice mail for the third time, kicking herself for missing his call. She couldn't believe that he'd just flown off to Canada. It brought home all of the things she didn't know about him—what if he was seeing someone else on the side? Maybe they were on the plane together or she was waiting for him at the airport. What were Newfoundland girls even like, nature enthusiasts? Linz shook her head at herself, knowing she was being ridiculous, but she couldn't control the jealousy that was welling up inside. She deserved more than a call from an airphone after what they had been through. Why on earth had Bryan dropped everything to go there?

"Sorry I'm late." Her father startled her, planting a kiss on her head before he sat down. "I'm famished." He signaled their customary waiter, who instantly appeared at their table.

"It's a pleasure to see you again, Dr. Jacobs."

"Thank you, Richard. We'll have the lobster bisque, Caesar salad, and the prime rib. Medium-well for the lady. My usual wine."

"Very good, sir." Richard took the menu away and turned to Linz. Conrad gave Linz an expectant smile. She was about to change their order.

Linz didn't even glance at the menu. "Let's make that the sea bass, steam the vegetables, and I suppose we'll let him have the wine."

Their little ritual finished, Richard took her menu and left them alone.

Linz got right to the point. "Why didn't you tell me you worked for Michael Backer?"

Conrad lips thinned to an angry line. He took his time unfolding his napkin, and put it in his lap before he spoke. "Where did you get that information?"

"I spoke with Dr. Parker, who's been trying to convince you to let him look at the Renovo project, and you won't let him. What's going on?"

Conrad leaned forward and lowered his voice. "As far as the NIA's concerned, that project was terminated after the director blew up his lab—killing himself and his wife. I refuse to let my company be associated with an experiment conducted thirty years ago that was just plain bad science. And as my daughter and the next in line to run the company, you should be more discreet about what you discuss with fellow directors."

"I'm sorry, I didn't think—"

"Which you seem to be doing a lot of lately."

Linz couldn't meet his eyes. She had just been scolded like a three-year-old and her father wasn't finished.

"I find it disturbing that all this started when you met your new boyfriend, who seems to be doing nothing short of investigating me—"

"He's not my boyfriend and he's not investigating you—"

"—because the company's worth a fortune," he continued, "and so are you."

"You think he's going to try to blackmail you? That's ridiculous."

"Is it? Anyone on the Internet can find out who we are and what we're worth."

Linz looked away. Bryan had logged his fair share of hours online. And she had seen the results.

Conrad took out a file from his briefcase and put it on the table between them. "I had personnel run a background check on him. It was all done confidentially."

Linz tried to keep her voice down. "Do you want to know how mad I am at you right now?"

"You can be as mad as you like, but did *you* know he grew up in a string of mental institutions?"

"No, he lived with his parents. His mother is a shrink—"

"—who admitted him into every psychiatric hospital on the East Coast," he insisted.

"That's not true." She glanced at the file.

"Your friend is an unstable man. One doctor diagnosed him schizophrenic. Go on, read it." He slid the file toward her.

"I don't want to read it. You don't even know him."

"Do you?" he countered.

Linz rubbed her forehead, feeling another headache settling in.

The whole situation had gotten out of control. "Can we just for-get about Bryan for a minute? I want to know about Michael and Diana. Please."

"Why do you want to know about these people?"

"Just tell me and I will read the file. Okay?"

Conrad shook his head in resignation. He looked weary. "Mi-chael was like a brother to me. Diana was the sister I never had. We became close friends in med school. Renovo was our dream. Losing them, abandoning the study . . . I had to start all over again."

He fought to keep his composure. Linz felt horrible. Why was she pushing him so hard to talk about something so painful?

But she had to know if her connection to Michael and Diana was as real as her connection to Origenes and Juliana. Bryan be-lieved it was, and now she had to decide whether or not to believe him. She just wished her father would stop laying on the guilt.

"Why do I have to bring that pain back to the surface after all this time? Because some painter found a home movie in his father's attic? Can't you understand why I'm upset? Now, I am done with this conversation, and you are never to ask me about them again. Read the file, and you'll understand my concern."

Feeling like a traitor, Linz took the file and put it into her own briefcase. She stood up. "I'm not hungry. Have them cancel my order."

Conrad reached out for her hand, but she pulled away. "I love you, Stormy. I'm just being a father," he said.

"I know." But for the first time in her life, Linz didn't say the words back.

TWENTY-SIX

We visited Finn. He was too distraught to talk at first and stayed in his bed-room. His apartment was shocking, a complete disaster. Dishes were dirty, things were broken. Diana sent me to the store for groceries while she cleaned. The smell of her homemade chicken soup finally brought Finn out.

He wasn't ready to talk about his recalls and said he needed time, which I understand. It doesn't help that his debilitating migraines won't stop. After his third bowl of soup and a second beer, he finally opened up. He had made eye contact with Conrad when he had him pinned against the wall, and he had recognized in him people from his previous lives. He refused to go into detail, but Diana pressed until he told her. My stomach clenched with dread as he said the names: Septimus, Tarr, d'Anthès . . . men who had tried to kill me. I couldn't speak. My body felt hollow. I know Diana felt the same alarm.

Finn believes that Conrad is feigning ignorance to hide his true intentions from us and his identities. I am beginning to agree. If Conrad is lying about not remembering, then we are all in danger. I am going to ask him to leave the group.

To make matters worse, after the visit with Finn, Diana remembered her life as Juliana. It was more traumatic for her than I could have imagined. I have done what I can to comfort her, but she must now learn to live with the unthinkable memory of being burned alive. I can only watch her strug-gle with the pain, and I can't help but feel responsible. If I had never set out on this path, no one would have followed. In hindsight, I've realized that our minds shield us from memories that are meant to stay buried. The brain is its own galaxy, with more cells than stars in the Milky Way. The most powerful organ in the body, it rivals any supercomputer, processing 90,000 to 150,000 thoughts a day through billions of neurons and trillions of synaptic connections. Now that we have found a pathway to retrieving memories that before were inaccessible, we are perfecting its function too quickly.

When I awoke to Diana's screams, I had to hold her to keep her from hurting herself as she remembered Juliana's death. Every cry was a knife in my heart, and I knew I had to sabotage my own study. I will present Renovo as a failed drug and destroy our research. It is the only course left to take. The world is not ready for this. It would end our sense of time, ourselves, and the linear world as we know it.

TWENTY-SEVEN

The first thing Bryan did when he arrived at St. John's was rent a boat. He had no trouble handling it. Bjarni's expertise and passion for the sea now lived inside of him.

The Hunter Vision 32 sailboat was perfect for his needs and the owner had rigged it for single-handed use. Bryan had easily maneuvered it through the Narrows and caught a swift wind that would take him north. He was planning on sailing up the coast, into the bay, and then sighting the new land just as Bjarni had done a thousand years ago.

The last two nights he had slept on deck just like every Viking had before him. This was not the first time that Bryan had roughed it. As he sailed, he remembered previous lifetimes when there had been no electricity, no running water, no modern medicine. . . . Hardship only existed if one knew differently.

Modern conveniences had always felt less necessary to him after he'd experienced a recall. It was because Bryan felt no need for modern comforts that he was able to survive those first years after he had left home—or run away, as his mother liked to say. The day after his eighteenth birthday, he had packed his backpack and vanished in the middle of the night, leaving his parents only a letter saying that he had to go find himself and his place in the world, alone.

For the first year, he had called once a month to let them know he was all right, if only to ease his guilt. After that, he'd limited his contact to an occasional phone call or postcard. A true nomad, he backpacked all over the world, camping for months on end in the wilderness. He spent a lot of time in Europe—so many places there resonated with him. He would camp in a forest and then wander into a nearby city to do street art or play music to earn money.

He traveled across the continent with the money he made, freely tapping into his language skills and speaking whatever was required. Because he could play unusual instruments like the lute, zither, and pan pipe, he'd often join groups of bohemian musicians. If there was a girl in the group, she would usually offer him a place to stay for however long he wanted it, though those relationships never lasted long. Either he'd have an episode and need to move on, or he would recognize someone from a vision. His recalls inevitably complicated things. He'd found out the hard way that only painting and being on his own could keep him sane.

His life changed the year he went to Avignon, where he joined a band of sidewalk artists there and painted with chalk on a street corner. By the end of the week, he could recognize all the regulars who passed by.

He would leave a hat out and listen to coins clank inside it while he worked. There would often be bills too, and one woman always left a large one, every day. Bryan could tell from her designer suits and purses that she came from money. On the seventh day, she finally stopped and asked if he spoke French, and they had a long conversation about technique. She was a collector and asked if he did canvases. Bryan wasn't surprised when he recognized her as Philip the Good, Jan Van Eyck's most powerful patron. It seemed he had found him again.

Her name was Therese Montague. Her husband was the president of a cosmetics company, and she was wealthy in her own right. She offered him supplies and a space to work in if he agreed to do three paintings for her.

He slept on the floor of the art studio and worked on the canvases for several months, feeling as if he was back in Jan's workshop in Bruges. The completed trio exceeded Therese's expectations. She was highly connected to the French art scene, and before Bryan knew it, he had an offer to show in Paris. That was the moment he decided to make a name for himself as an artist, on the chance that the paintings would be the compass that would guide anyone with similar dreams toward him. But as his fame grew, he began to lose hope that anyone would ever understand his world—until he met Linz.

The possibility of her rejection now terrified him. He knew she was starting to question his sanity, and yet here he was sailing the northern Atlantic, believing he was a seafaring Viking who had almost discovered America. Bryan shook his head at himself and took out the foot-long wind instrument he had carved yesterday from a seasoned tree branch. It was something Bjarni liked to do—whistle on the water.

After Anssonno had been born, Bjarni would play his pipe softly to lull him to sleep at night. And when Anssonno had grown old enough to wield a carving knife, Bjarni had taught him how to make his own.

Bryan played his song, listening to it carry over the waves, and he wondered where Anssonno's soul was. There were over seven billion people on Earth—did the likelihood of crossing paths with someone again boil down to random statistics? Or did a soul's path adhere to a pattern, like the connecting lines on a mandala? Bryan seemed to be connecting with certain people again and again. He could only hope Anssonno would one day come back to him. Perhaps it would heal the loss that lived in his heart.

As the boat skimmed over the sea, Bryan sensed the ocean speaking to him. A whale breached in the distance, puffins dove into the water, and a lone iceberg floated to the west like a silent witness. He closed his eyes and prayed to Odin, Allah, Yahweh, Zeus, Shiva, and every deva and deity he had ever worshiped to bring him peace and understanding. This pilgrimage had to be for a purpose.

He opened his eyes and the shore loomed in the distance just as Bjarni had seen it. A national historic site now called L'Anse aux Meadows, Leif Erikson's settlement symbolized the path Bjarni had not taken. If only he had brought Garnissa to the new land, how different their lives would have been.

Bryan's head was still filled with these thoughts as he came to shore and wandered through the park, touring the reconstructions. It was a living museum, and the staff reenacted what it must have been like for Viking settlers. But it became too much for Bryan, and he broke away from the other tourists so no one could see his grief.

The journey had provided no answers, no glimmer of understanding. Before he got back on his boat, he debated calling Linz on a public phone but changed his mind.

Linz went to sleep every night wondering when Bryan would come back home.

Maybe he would just disappear. But she found that hard to believe. While he was gone, she tried to forget about him and get her life back to normal by immersing herself in her research.

Her latest round of candidate plasticity genes had begun to show promise. Using a multiphoton microscope, she had been imaging the same neurons in a group of mice and had finally identified a gene that showed a special ability to absorb synaptic proteins. Identifying a gene's function was always a huge breakthrough, and it usually took years. In the lab, Linz's photographic memory and obsessive tendencies worked to her advantage.

Normally she would have brought a bottle of champagne over to her father's house so they could toast her success, but she limited the celebration to a formal e-mail to him and addressed it to the other directors as well. She did not reply to his congratulations, or his offer to take her out for dinner. He would only want to talk to her about Bryan's file, which she had yet to open.

Her estrangement from her father did not sit well with her, and now that Bryan was consuming her thoughts, work didn't fulfill her as much as it had before. Several times, she found herself cutting short her usual long evenings at the lab to stop by the gallery to visit Derek and Penelope—but really it was an excuse to see Bryan's paintings. Looking at his work, knowing what it meant to him, made her feel closer to him somehow. Afterward, she would go home and work on puzzles, blasting Vivaldi's *Four Seasons* until she couldn't stay awake anymore. She had even wandered over to Harvard Square to play chess with the irrational hope that she might see him, even though she knew he was thousands of miles away. When she went to the symphony, for the first time, she felt the emptiness of the seat beside her. And every night when she fell asleep, she imagined that she was in Newfoundland with him.

Bryan knew it was time to return to Boston. He needed to get back and call this trip an honorable failure. He needed to repair things with Linz—and he needed to find Finn. Finn would have at least some of the answers he was looking for. Together they could confront Conrad.

His flight wasn't until tomorrow, so after he returned the boat, he rented a car for a day to tour the area. He drove to Conception Bay and headed inland. Caught up in his thoughts, he didn't notice the tire blow out until the whole car started to shake. Swearing, he pulled over and got out.

He was relieved to find a spare in the trunk, but there were no tools to change it. He was stranded in the countryside, and it was at least a half-hour walk back to town. Maybe there would be a house on the way, and someone would have a jack he could borrow.

He was about to set off on foot when a white truck slowed down and pulled over. A young woman jumped out from the passenger side and hurried toward him. She had a pixie haircut and was dressed in a colorfully woven skirt, a tunic-like blouse, and was wearing dramatic stone jewelry. The first thing Bryan noticed was her smile.

She saw the rental sticker on the car and gave him a sharp appraisal. "You have a flat tire? We are happy to help." She spoke in English but with a French accent. "I am Claudette. That is my husband, Martin," she said, waving to the driver. "Martin! *Vite!*"

A man—towering well over six feet, with a powerful build and a shaved head—got out of the car. Bryan gaped at him. He looked like Zidane, the retired pro soccer player.

Martin joined them and gave Bryan a nod. Claudette turned to him, "*Chéri,* this poor man has a *pneu* problem."

Martin headed to the truck bed and got out his tools. Within minutes, he had jacked up the little Mazda and was busy unscrewing bolts. Claudette had a hundred and one questions for Bryan and was thrilled that he spoke perfect French. What was he doing in St. John's? What did he do for a living? Was this his first visit? Bryan tried to keep it simple and as close to the truth as possible, explaining that he was a painter and here for inspiration. Claudette became even more animated and wanted to know everything about his art. For some reason, Bryan didn't mind. He found her charming.

In the time it took Martin to fix the tire, Claudette also informed Bryan that they were from France and had been invited to teach at Memorial University in the graduate Archaeology Department. It seemed they were specialists in ethnographic fieldwork techniques. They had only just settled into their new house, which happened to be just a few kilometers away, "and it was very lucky for him because this road got very little traffic," Claudette bounced on. Bryan found himself nodding quite a bit as he tried to keep up.

After the tire was fixed, Claudette surprised him by inviting him to their house for dinner. Without waiting for an answer, Martin threw the tools into the truck and the two of them tore off. Bryan fumbled to start his car and zoomed down the road to catch up.

Martin's car turned onto a long winding drive, which ended next to an old farmhouse. Up close, the building looked to be in serious neglect with its stripped paint, shuttered windows, and tattered roof. Bryan got out of the car and joined them at the porch.

Claudette seemed to sense what he was thinking. "We spent all our energy fixing up the inside."

"No, it looks nice," Bryan replied, bending the truth

Claudette said, "Martin, the porch lights, vite, s'il te plaît!"

Martin vanished inside, and within seconds the porch sprung to life as decorative lights transformed the exterior into something more like an enchanted cottage at twilight.

The minute Bryan walked into the house, he understood Claudette's comment about the outside being misleading. The floors shone with rich mahogany wood, and two sofas were angled around a mammoth stone fireplace. Beautiful artifacts—framed papyrus, a gold scarab collection, Egyptian bowls, glasswork, and a statue of a sphinx—hung on the walls and were displayed on futuristic chrome-and-glass bookcases. Bryan took it all in. What were the chances that his car would break down, and he would be rescued by a couple who had an ancient Egyptian sphinx in their house? "Amazing," he said, speaking his thought aloud.

"*Merci.*" Claudette beamed at him. "My hobby is restoring homes such as this." She stationed herself in the open kitchen. A whirlwind of energy, she continued to talk while she cooked dinner and checked e-mail. Meanwhile, Martin had lit the fireplace and was opening a bottle of wine.

Bryan studied the framed pictures on the back wall. They were all of pyramids. He glanced at Martin, who gave a new meaning to "the strong, silent type." He had yet to say a word. Bryan cleared his throat and pointed to a photo. "Excuse me, where is this?"

Martin put on huge tortoiseshell eyeglasses, looking even more eccentric. "China, the White Pyramid."

"I didn't know China had pyramids."

"Oh, they have hundreds," Martin replied. "The White Pyramid is one of the oldest and largest in the world. I was there in '94. The government has closed the entire region now."

Bryan moved to the next photo, a step pyramid with Martin and Claudette pictured in the foreground. "Is this Mayan?"

"Good guess, but no." Martin poured the wine. "Cambodia, the great pyramid of Koh Ker."

Bryan studied the photograph. "It looks so similar to the ones the Mayans built."

"Yes," Martin agreed, "fascinating when you consider they're over six thousand miles away from each other." He motioned to the next two photos. "These of course are Mesoamerican—at Cholula and Teotihuacán—the largest pyramids in the world next to Cheops."

Bryan moved along the wall as Martin ticked off more sites: Greece, Italy, Russia, Peru . . . He was beginning to reevaluate his first impression about Martin. The man had plenty to say.

"So pyramids are your specialty," Bryan said, beginning to feel the mechanics of destiny at work.

Claudette answered, "Pyramidologist is a bit of a dirty word in our field, but *oui,* when we're allowed . . ." She trailed off, muttering to herself, "Sometimes people can be pigs."

Bryan looked questioningly to Martin, who grimaced. "Egypt's Supreme Council of Antiquities has denied our latest research request."

Claudette called out. "Let's not discuss it. It will ruin my dinner."

"You brought it up, chéri."

Bryan studied a picture of Claudette and Martin at the Great Pyramid in Egypt. Its scale and grandeur took his breath away. The photo had been taken with the sun low on the horizon and the light hit the stones in a particular way, creating a prism-like affect.

As Bryan sipped his wine, he was overcome by a sudden feeling of déjà-vu. He knew this pyramid. "How do you think it was built?" he asked Martin.

Martin shook his head with a slight smile. "We don't know. Many of the stones weigh over two hundred tons each. Few cranes could pick up that much limestone."

Claudette joined in, "There has been fierce debate over studies that show some of the rocks are not natural and are made of nanoscale spheres of silicon dioxide." She shrugged. "Je ne sais pas. Maybe some were cast with cement—and the Egyptians did create concrete thousands of years before the Romans."

"Even if some were cast," Martin added, "there are still thousands of chiseled stones that would have had to have been lifted, and those are perfectly positioned. You can't even fit a hair between the cracks." He turned back to the photograph. "And, just as important—why was it built? Again, we don't know. Traditionalists maintain the tomb theory, but there are over eighty pyramids there and not a single one houses an original burial. All the bodies that have been found were placed there years after the structures had been built—not to mention that the tools that supposedly built these structures have never been found."

Somehow, Bryan knew all these facts on some level, and he found himself weighing in. "The three pyramids at Giza were also built to perfectly mirror the three stars from Orion's belt. And the Sphinx was positioned to face Leo on the eastern horizon. Those stars would have been visible in the statue's eyeline in 10,500 BC. . . ." He trailed off. *Where in the world had that come from?*

Claudette and Martin looked surprised and impressed. "You have an interest in archaeoastronomical theory?" She brought grilled steaks and salad out to the table. "It's a small field, but it's gaining momentum."

Bryan had no idea what she was talking about. He shrugged. "I wouldn't say interest. I think I remember reading about it somewhere."

"It's a fascinating idea . . . a little outside the box." Claudette winked. "But that's the best place to be, I've found."

Bryan and Martin joined her at the table, and they all ate in companionable silence. Martin put away not one but two steaks. "How much longer are you here?"

"I fly back tomorrow," Bryan answered. "I'd planned on touring around a bit and then finding a hotel in town."

Claudette attacked her salad. "You must stay the night. We have a spare room."

Bryan opened his mouth to decline the offer—he didn't want to impose. But Claudette held up her hand. "No, you stay."

Martin chuckled and refilled Bryan's wineglass. Dinner lasted well into the night. Bryan couldn't remember the last time he had enjoyed himself so freely.

Sometime after midnight they declared the meal over. Bryan barely managed to climb the stairs and close the door to the guest-room. Stripping off his clothes, he crawled beneath the goose-down comforter and fell into a bottomless sleep.

The fine mist stayed constant, muting the world around him. Bryan took a deep breath of air, smelling its lushness as he stood on a plateau. A green valley stretched before him.

He knew he was dreaming. The immense pressure in his head made him feel as if he had pushed against the tide of time to have this vision. He looked out at the Great Pyramid of Giza, and he could see no cars, no buildings, no pollution or trace of modern man, just endless green meadows. Whatever memories lived here felt as elusive as the air—all around him and yet untouchable.

The sun glinted off the pyramid, blinding him. When Bryan regained his sight, he saw the Egyptian goddess sitting beside him.

Her whole body radiated power. She pointed a graceful finger encased by a golden spiral ring to the ground and, calling on an invisible force, drew a symbol in the sand.

Bryan felt suspended as he watched. *I know this symbol.* He looked at her and demanded, "Who are you?"

She did not look up from the mandala she was creating. "Who is not the question," she said. "The question is where." She stood up and spread her arms wide and the wind swirled, sending the sand drawing back into the void from which it came.

In a moment of clarity Bryan realized he already knew the answer to her question.

He was at the beginning.

TWENTY-EIGHT

Michael woke up, disoriented. He hadn't meant to fall sleep. Unlike the recalls, this dream had been filled with disjointed images. The Egyptian queen had been with him again, only Michael hadn't been himself, but a younger man—and she had drawn a magnificent symbol in the sand. Why?

Right on the cusp of remembering more, Michael looked over at the clock. He was surprised to see that it was already seven o'clock at night. He sat up with a start and the fragments of the dream vanished.

His back protested as he stretched his legs out on the couch. He had been sleeping on it for the past four days after Diana had locked herself in their bedroom.

The team had stopped talking to each other. All communication had broken down, and even Conrad had vanished. The state of Michael and Diana's apartment now rivaled Finn's. The dishes hadn't been washed for days and no one had done laundry or taken out the garbage. Michael had not showered or shaved. He felt like a survivalist—he couldn't even remember the last time he'd had anything to drink.

He began to review what had happened before he'd fallen asleep. Finn had called and begun questioning him about Lord Asano's death in formal Japanese. The stilted questions had been asked with probing politeness, but they had shattered Michael's psyche. It didn't matter who Finn had been in that lifetime—too many people had been affected by Lord Asano's mistakes. Michael had replied in Japanese with the etiquette of a lord from the seventeenth century. "I remembered Asano Naganori's life. The fall of his house rests on his shoulders alone."

Finn did not speak. Michael felt karma hanging between them like a deadweight and didn't know what to say.

"Finn?"

"I don't know what to do."

"What do you mean?"

"It's unbelievable." Finn stammered, "I-I don't know what to do."

"Do what? You're not making any sense."

Finn started to babble, saying that it was worse than he thought. It took ten minutes for Michael to pry an explanation from him.

"Conrad is Lord Kira. He wants us all dead."

Michael sat down on the sofa and tried to stay calm. He could not give in to Asano's rage. The minute he allowed himself to be ruled by the emotions of these memories, he would go truly insane. He told Finn, "I've already decided to take Conrad off the team."

"It's not enough," Finn argued. "We have to leave. You don't understand how dangerous he is."

But Michael did understand. He had gone to the lab and found three bottles of Renovo in Conrad's desk, and one bottle only had two pills remaining. Michael did the math. Conrad had been double dosing and lying to them all. He knew he had no choice but to shut down the study and extricate Conrad from their lives.

Now that Michael was awake, he wanted to get the confrontation over with, and only hoped that he was well enough to drive. He'd been feeling very out of body for the past several days.

He knocked on the bedroom door but Diana didn't answer. She was still trying to come to terms with Juliana's memories from ancient Rome. She had also remembered Natalia Pushkina's life and was struggling to assimilate it as well. Michael felt helpless, but he still wanted to do something to ease her pain. Maybe they could go to Nantucket for the weekend and rent the old beach house. It had been years since they'd gone, and the place held only happy memories—a rarity these days. Michael wanted joy back in his life.

When he got back from Conrad's, he would sleep in their bedroom again. He would hold Diana in his arms, pull her out of her depression and together they would talk about the future.

A car blared its horn, jolting Michael out of his thoughts—he was driving on the wrong side of the road. He swerved back into the right lane and tried to focus, reciting the mantra he had begun to say more and more lately, "I am here now. I'm here now. I'm here now . . ." Sometimes it helped.

Thankfully, the drive to South Boston didn't take long at night. Michael entered a low-income neighborhood and double-checked the address. Conrad had never invited anyone to his apartment. South Boston was home to some of the oldest housing projects in the country, and most were in need of major repair. It was once a primarily Irish community, but Polish, Lithuanian, Puerto Rican, and Cuban families had begun to settle there and carve out their own territories, creating a blanket of racial tension. It made him wonder what people would do if they suddenly found themselves with the memories of someone they had vowed to hate.

Maybe the world did need a dose of Renovo. It might trigger some empathy and compassion. Michael didn't know what the right course was anymore. All he knew was that Renovo had the power to change human existence, and the responsibility that came with being its creator was paralyzing. Was he a monster or some sort of hero? He didn't know.

Forcing his thoughts back to the present, he located the apartment building and parked, getting Conrad's belongings from the car. Michael had gone to the lab that morning and packed Conrad's things in a box and changed the locks on the doors. He knew Conrad would demand access to all the files now that he was off the team, but those would soon be destroyed. Anything connected to Renovo must not survive.

Michael went inside and found Conrad's apartment. He knocked and sensed someone gazing at him through the peephole.

The door opened. Conrad looked ravaged, as if he hadn't slept, eaten, or bathed in days. He stared at the box with a contemptuous look that reminded Michael of George d'Anthès, the man who had killed Pushkin. Michael took a deep breath, forcing himself to try not to imagine Conrad as anyone else. It was the only way he could get through this meeting.

Conrad's face turned red with anger. "You can't kick me off."

"I'm terminating the project. Do you want to do this in the hallway or are you going to let me in?" Michael asked. But then maybe the hallway was better—if things got ugly, it would be easier for him to leave. Perhaps even coming here had been a bad idea.

Conrad took the box and let him inside. Michael hesitated but followed, remaining close to the door. He glanced around. A large desk dwarfed the small room, and hundreds of books lined every inch of wall space. He assumed the closed door led to the bedroom.

Conrad took a minute to clear the papers from his desk, stuffing everything into folders. Michael could see his hands were shaking. "You can't just shut us down," he said.

"Finn and Diana are in agreement." A boldfaced lie. Michael hadn't even talked to them about it yet. He looked at Conrad's desk again and froze—all of the books referred to Egypt. A feeling of alarm gripped him. What did Conrad know?

"And what about me?" Conrad was asking. "I have no say?"

Michael tried to stay focused. "Officially it's my project. I spearheaded it. I already notified NIA that we're unable to continue second-round testing." He added, "And we've all stopped taking it."

Conrad looked away, making Michael certain that his suspicions about the double dosing had been correct. Maybe there were more bottles hidden somewhere in the apartment.

"So we lose our grant." Conrad sat down, took his eyeglasses off, and rubbed the bridge of his nose.

"This isn't about a grant," Michael argued. "We've discovered a truth that could redefine our very existence."

Conrad said nothing for a long time. Michael waited, wondering if Conrad had forgotten that he was there. Something was wrong.

"What about our real test subjects?" Conrad finally asked. "We're on the brink of a real cure. Do we bury that as well?"

"Do you think the world is ready for this? I can barely speak English anymore and Diana believes you're the third-century asshole who burned her alive."

Conrad opened his eyes and glared at him. "That's ludicrous."

"Finn thinks so too."

"Because you're all trapped in some warped drama of your own making." Conrad pounded his fist on the table with such force that the wood cracked. "It's a distraction. You don't realize what's at stake."

Conrad was not at all himself, and Michael's instincts told him to get out. He started backing toward the door. "My decision is final."

"I have the formula." Conrad trembled with fury. "I can do whatever the hell I want!"

"You can't do anything without us."

With incredible speed, Conrad grabbed Michael by the neck and rammed him into the wall. Trapped in a vise, Michael gripped Conrad's wrists and fought to breathe. Conrad spoke in a low guttural language that Michael couldn't comprehend—his voice sounded like a deep growl. Their faces were inches apart, and Michael could sense a power radiating from Conrad that Michael had never encountered before.

But Conrad also saw something in Michael's eyes that made him gasp. He loosened his grip and stepped back in shock. Michael took advantage of the opening and rammed his knee into Conrad's crotch. He doubled over to the ground in agony.

Michael escaped and raced to the door. "I knew you were having recalls. Stay away from us. This is over." He slammed the door so hard the hinges shook.

Running to his car, Michael fumbled for the keys and got behind the wheel. Conrad came charging out of the apartment building. Michael started the engine and tore off. He looked back in his rearview mirror to see Conrad standing in the middle of the street, looking eerily still, and shuddered.

Whoever Conrad had remembered, Michael was terrified of him now. He drove away, his hands shaking on the wheel. Adrenaline coursed through his body. Suddenly everything had changed. He needed to go home and get Diana. They would meet Finn at the lab and pack up everything tonight. By morning they'd be gone.

Bryan woke up gasping for air. Within seconds it all came back to him in perfect clarity. He had dreamed of being at the Great Pyramid with the Egyptian goddess, and it had been Michael's dream too. Not only had he remembered Michael's confrontation with Conrad, he had experienced a full recall of Michael's entire life— right up to the moment before his death. Finally the tidal wave of memories had come.

Tears coursed down Bryan's face and he buried his head in his pillow. He had to see Linz. He no longer knew if the fact that she was Conrad's daughter would be enough to keep her safe.

He jumped up from the bed. The smell of strong coffee and the sound of Claudette and Martin's voices downstairs brought him back to reality. He sat back down in disbelief. *Shit, I'm still in Canada.*

After rushing to get dressed, he found paper and a pencil and re-created the symbol the Egyptian goddess had drawn. He went downstairs, but before he could say a word, Claudette started to greet him. "Bonjour! We—" She saw the look on Bryan's face and stopped. "Something has happened?"

Without hesitating Bryan showed them his drawing. "Do you recognize this symbol?"

Martin and Claudette both studied it closely.

"I believe it's Egyptian, and very old," Bryan said, watching their faces.

Claudette shook her head and handed it back. "Sorry. This is not something I have seen before."

Bryan's shoulders drooped with defeat. He had been certain they would know.

"But there is someone who may have," Martin said, smiling, "at Harvard."

Claudette nodded, growing animated again. "Of course! Dr. Hayes. He is a wizard of Egyptology."

"If he can't recognize it, no one can," Martin said. "His office is at the Peabody Museum. Tell him you're a friend."

Bryan nodded, his heart a little lighter.

Even in his hurry to leave, Bryan was surprised by how hard it was to say good-bye to his new friends. They exchanged e-mails and phone numbers as Claudette and Martin saw him to his car, and they all promised to keep in touch. A strong connection existed between them, which Bryan couldn't explain. But if everything happened for a reason, he knew they were the reason he had come here.

TWENTY-NINE

As soon as Bryan's plane touched down, he called Linz. She didn't pick up. He hoped she was only avoiding his calls and that everything was all right.

"It's me. I'm back. My plane just landed," he hesitated. "Listen, I'm sorry I took off. I can't explain it right now . . . there was something I needed to do. I hope you'll forgive me. It's critical that we talk. Please call me."

Linz looked at her cell phone and shoved it back in her pocket, as she headed to her desk. The file from her father felt like a brick in her hand. She wanted to read it before she faced Bryan, but her plan stalled when she found Neil and Steve hovering over her computer.

"What are you guys doing?"

Steve turned around. He was conspicuously dressed in seventies attire. "Neil's helping me get that Renovo file you asked for. My security code wasn't high enough."

Linz frowned. "But Neil has the same security access as you."

"Bingo." Neil didn't look up but continued to type. "Which is why I'm using your computer."

Linz pinched the bridge of her nose, not realizing that she was mimicking her father. "So you can download unauthorized files using my access code?"

Neil finished and hit the return key. "Shazam. Piece of cake. It cleared."

Linz put Bryan's file on the desk. "Guys, I didn't ask you to override security codes."

Steve looked crushed. "Sorry. I thought since, well, since it was you."

Neil handed her a USB flash drive with a wink. "Made you a hard copy too."

Linz groaned inwardly as the printer started to spit out paper. Now it would be on record that she had fished for the Renovo file.

"Okay. Thanks for the illegal work," she said, unable to hide her irritation.

Steve looked ready to melt into the floor.

Linz relented and patted his arm. "It's okay, Steve. Thank you for being . . . proactive."

She waited for them to return to their desks and then opened Bryan's file. The first page started with a detailed psychiatric analysis from twenty years ago. It stated that Bryan suffered from a rare form of schizophrenia, and from there the file only got worse. She read page after page, shaking her head in disbelief. Medicor's investigators had done a thorough job. Most of the information here shouldn't even have been accessible. The more she read, the angrier she became . . . at Bryan, at herself, at her father . . . Why hadn't Bryan told her any of this?

She finished reading Bryan's history and stared into space. She had planned to go to his place and talk to him after work. But not anymore.

The printer finished its job. The Renovo file was waiting in the tray.

❧

The Peabody Museum housed the faculty offices for the Archaeology Department. Now that Bryan had Michael's memories of Harvard, he had no trouble finding it. He had called and spoken to Dr. Hayes that morning, and because of his connection to Claudette and Martin, Dr. Hayes had granted Bryan an interview during his lunch hour.

Bryan found him at his desk, reading a stack of thesis papers. Dr. Hayes must have been at least in his seventies. He had owlish eyes that were framed by square eyeglasses, and an angular face that complemented his frail stature.

"So you have an interest in ancient Egypt?" Dr. Hayes asked, barely looking up from his work. "Please, sit."

Bryan sat down and took out the drawing. "I was wondering if you've ever seen this symbol before?" he asked, getting right to the point.

Dr. Hayes blinked twice at it. "Where did you see this?"

Bryan settled on a simplified version of the truth. "In a dream."

"I see." Dr. Hayes looked skeptical. "And why do you think this is Egyptian?" he asked, unable to take his eyes off the drawing.

"Because I was in Egypt in the dream, at the Great Pyramid." He left out the part about the Egyptian goddess or queen or whoever she was drawing it out of thin air with her finger. He could tell he was already walking a fine line with the professor. "Is it Egyptian?"

"Yes. Yes, it is." Dr. Hayes looked confounded. "It's an ancient symbol for Horus."

"Horus?" Bryan asked with surprise.

Dr. Hayes seemed to mistake his surprise for confusion and went on to explain, "According to Egyptian mythology, Horus was the last god, or super being if you will, to rule Egypt." He leaned forward, now fully engaged in the conversation. "You see, academia organizes ancient Egypt into several periods, starting with the Early Dynastic Period, which begins right around 3100 BC. From there, we move forward through the First and Second Dynasties, then through the Old Kingdom, Middle Kingdom, and New Kingdom, etcetera. However, the time before 3100 BC has become a subject of great debate."

"How so?" Bryan asked, curious to see where the professor was headed.

"Our understanding of Egypt's past is based on the works of a Heliopolitan priest named Manetho, who lived in the third century BC. He compiled a history of Egypt by making lists of the mortal kings. His complete text did not survive. But in the pieces of it we do have, he also describes an even more distant past where gods, not men, ruled the Nile. The Egyptians called it 'The First Time of the Gods,' and supposedly, according to Manetho, this time on Earth lasted for over twenty thousand years—well before 3100 BC."

Bryan nodded. He already knew much of what Dr. Hayes had been describing. Origenes Adamantius had studied Manetho's complete and original texts as a young man, as well as Diodorus Siculus and Herodotus' accounts of the history of Egypt, both of which supported Manetho's claims. Even two thousand years ago, Egypt's past had felt just as fantastical and mythical to scholars as it did today.

"Academia has largely chosen to ignore this part of Manetho's tale. Even though his timeline was also complemented by the Greek historians Diodorus Siculus and Herodotus. It would suggest that certain biblical dates are wrong."

Bryan smiled. Martin had been right, Dr. Hayes was a wizard.

"Regardless of whether Manetho's account was myth or fact, Horus was recorded as the last ruler of the 'First Time of the Gods,' the son of Osiris and Isis. And this," Dr. Hayes handed the paper back to Bryan, "is his personal emblem."

Bryan stared at the drawing.

"I hope that was helpful."

Yes and no. Bryan grimaced. He was glad to have identified the symbol, but he still had no idea why his Egyptian guide had shown it to him. He nodded anyway and stood to leave, "Yes. Thank you for your time."

Dr. Hayes studied him with a thoughtful eye. "If you happen to dream up any more forgotten symbols of antiquity, I'd like to see them."

Linz went to turn into her parking lot and saw Bryan waiting on her doorstep. She wasn't ready to face him yet. What could she possibly say to him when she didn't know what she believed?

He waved at her, but she backed away and drove off. Unable to think clearly, she drove aimlessly for an hour until she found herself pulling up in front of the gallery. There was something she needed to see.

Last night she had dreamed she was the girl in Bryan's painting of the Treasury at Petra. The boy standing on the mountain had been her lover and was soon to be her husband. The music he played on his pan flute was an ancient melody passed down by their ancestors, a call to the heart. It had been the same song that Bryan had played to her that day in the Square.

In the dream, Bryan had been the boy and it had all felt so real. It had been so . . . lovely waking up from the dream cocooned in a feeling of warmth and joy. For the first time, she began to really consider what Bryan had been insisting all along—that perhaps Juliana hadn't been her only previous life.

Linz sat in her car, unable to open the door and go inside. A part of her didn't want to see the painting. She leaned back with a sigh, but then jolted upright when she recognized the car parked twenty feet away.

Without questioning her actions, she drove away before she was discovered. It was her father's.

Conrad walked arm-in-arm with Penelope around the gallery. A stranger would have assumed they were father and daughter.

"Linz didn't tell me you were stopping by." She teased, "I would have raised the prices."

"And I would have paid."

"Don't let Derek hear you say that." She patted his arm affectionately.

Conrad stopped to study a lush and detailed depiction of the Shogun's court in feudal Japan. Lords in ceremonial kimonos were gathered around two men, who were fighting. One man had a sword in his hand. Conrad looked at the signature, which was written in Japanese, and the twist of a smile appeared on his face. "What do you know about the artist?"

"Umm, not much," Penelope replied. "Just that he's from Boston. But his paintings speak for themselves. They're gripping."

Conrad's gaze swept the gallery. His face remained unreadable. "Yes, they are." He nodded to the painting of feudal Japan. "Is that one available?"

Penelope couldn't contain her pleasure—he had chosen the most expensive piece in the show. "It is. The painting is based on the story of the forty-seven Ronin. Do you know it?"

"Yes," he said. "Quite well."

THIRTY

The drive home from Linz's passed by in a blur. Bryan was so dev-
astated that he could barely function. Linz had seen him waiting
for her and had just driven away.

By the time he arrived, his initial hurt had turned to anger. When
he walked into his place and saw Michael and Diana's things, he
picked up the nearest box and flung it. He kicked two more, sending their contents scattering, and began to hurl Michael's books
against the wall. He only stopped when the *Dictionary of Neuro-
anatomy* broke the lamp.

He went into his studio and sat on the floor. He took a deep
breath and tried to calm down. Closing his eyes, he sensed the fig-
ures in all of his paintings looking down at him, whispering encouragement. He couldn't let Linz's inability to accept the truth
derail him. His trip to Newfoundland had brought him closer to
something, and he needed to figure out what it was.

His thoughts returned to his meeting with Dr. Hayes and then
settled on Claudette and Martin. What were the odds that their life's
work would be pyramids—and the Great Pyramid in particular—
and that they would move to St. John's only months before his arrival? He decided to research them and was surprised by the number
of links that popped up.

Bryan clicked on a link with the caption: "Leading pyramidolo-
gists launch multidisciplinary study." A student had recorded a lec-
ture they'd given at the University of Paris and posted it online.

In the video, Claudette was speaking at the podium. Martin

was visible, just at the edge of the frame, running a projector. "The Great Pyramid at Giza . . . if you look, inside the King's Chamber, its interior shows signs of being subjected to extreme temperatures. Here, the chamber walls have been pushed out by a powerful explosion," she said, pointing on the projection with a laser, "with a force strong enough to crack the ceiling beams. One theory is that this damage resulted from an earthquake, but if that is true, then why do no other chambers show signs of suffering similar damage?"

She continued as the next image displayed another chamber. "Here you can see a huge buildup of salt crystals found in the Queen's Chamber. Why salt? Why here? Salt crystals are usually the result of a reaction between limestone and gaseous vapors, which suggests that this particular chamber took in fluids. Salt also happens to be a natural by-product when chemicals react to produce hydrogen."

Bryan's eyebrows shot up. *Hydrogen?*

"The evidence points to the real possibility that this pyramid was a power plant, if you will, one that suffered a catastrophic meltdown. We have joined with expert engineers and physicists who are willing to come forward with theories based on hard science. What we're touching on today is just the beginning."

Excitement stirred inside Bryan. It was the study Claudette had been referring to at dinner. This was important. Somehow, this involved him.

A knock at the door interrupted his thoughts. He paused the video and hurried to the door, hoping it was Linz. He opened it— and was met by his mother, holding two grocery bags filled with food.

"I know I should have called first, but you would have just told me not to come."

She took in the mess with a "my God, this place is a pigsty," and disappeared into the kitchen.

Bryan didn't follow her. He stood motionless at the door, overwhelmed by the force of an unexpected recognition—his mother was Anssonno.

Dazed, he sat down on the sofa in disbelief. His son was right here. Immense joy and sorrow overtook him.

"Don't you ever eat?" His mother's question startled him.

Bryan wiped his eyes and called out. "I'm actually starving. I'll be there in a minute."

Ducking into the bathroom, he splashed water on his face and tried to get his emotions in check. He sat on the edge of the tub and closed his eyes, just breathing, and let the grief flow through and out of him. He thought of all the years he hadn't known—had directed only anger toward her—and wanted nothing more than to ask her forgiveness. Anssonno had been beside him all this time, nurturing and caring for him, and he had been blind to it. His prayer from a thousand years ago had already been answered.

After several minutes he was finally able to compose himself, and he joined her in the kitchen. "This looks wonderful. You came at the perfect time."

"I did?" She couldn't have looked more astonished.

"Yes. Thank you." He took her hand and squeezed it, overcome by an incredible love. For the first time, he saw the same love that he had felt for Anssonno mirrored in her eyes. He could finally understand her desperate need to protect him, to give him the best life, to see him happy, because he had once felt the same for her. She simply hadn't known how.

She stared at him, a puzzled look on her face. "You okay, kiddo?"

He looked at all the food spread on the counter and fought the lump in his throat. "Never better."

Barbara rummaged through the cabinets to find a plate, opened up containers and started serving. It felt like Thanksgiving. Bryan didn't even bother to sit down.

"Sweetie, at least sit. It'll digest better." She poured him some milk and headed to the dining table. Bryan chased after her— Michael and Diana's storage boxes were out there.

"No! Mom, I want to eat in here. It's messy . . ."

"What on earth are you doing with this?" she said, frozen in shock, staring at Michael and Diana's portrait sitting on the shelf.

Bryan thought fast. "I found it in a storage box at the restaurant and wanted to do a painting with a similar composition. You know, a technical study."

He winced inwardly at the lame excuse, but his mother seemed to buy it. "Well, you're the artist. These were old friends of your father's. He has their things. Just put it back when you're done."

So she knew. Bryan couldn't hide his surprise.

Barbara gave him a look. "He doesn't know I know. Your father's so worried about upsetting me when it comes to these two."

He couldn't resist. "Why would you be upset?"

"Honestly? I wouldn't. I dated this guy a few times before I met your father and he has this misconceived idea that I was a jilted ex when nothing could have been farther from the truth."

"But you *were* jilted."

Barbara didn't ask why he thought that, but explained, "I was about to break it off. Michael just beat me to it. Your father was his best friend, so it was a little awkward for a while."

"This was the guy whose wedding Dad was the best man in?"

"He was going to tell Michael he couldn't do it, but I talked him into it. They were like brothers—he had to. Diana even called and asked if I would like to come, said she wouldn't mind." She studied the portrait, looking a bit wistful. "A sweet gesture, but I had already planned a trip out to California to see my parents."

It was fascinating to hear her side. Bryan had thought she was just angry and bitter.

She put the picture back. "So tragic, the way they died . . . your father was heartbroken."

"Did you know their other friends? The ones they worked with?" He couldn't help fishing now that she had opened up, but Barbara didn't seem to notice. She was lost in her own memories.

She shook her head. "No. I heard one man was badly injured in the explosion. And another man came by the house one day, asking if we had any papers—journals, that kind of thing. He was a bit of a prick actually. Your father said no, probably because he didn't like him."

Bryan gave a grim smile. Doc had never liked Conrad.

Barbara changed the subject and gave him a knowing look. "So, do I have to pass some sort of secret initiation before I can see your studio?"

Bryan laughed. Maybe she knew him better than he thought. "You passed. Just don't touch anything."

She looked thrilled and disappeared behind the Japanese silk screens. Bryan shook his head, amazed at how she continued to surprise him. He hurried to put the rest of Michael and Diana's things back in the boxes before she returned. Explaining away the portrait had worked, but he didn't want to push his luck.

After he had boxed all the films, clothes, and books, he took Michael's journal and placed it in a drawer for safekeeping. He thought about what his mother had said. Why had Conrad wanted Michael's journals? He already had the formula.

Bryan realized that he also knew the formula and fought to clamp down his excitement. He would think about that later. Right now it was time to join his mother and see her reaction to his paintings. He couldn't put it off forever.

When he walked in, he found her standing before the one painting Bryan had created before he flew to Newfoundland. It was Garnissa holding Anssonno after he had been born. He wondered what affinity she felt for the image, if any. Did her spirit respond to the likeness of a woman who had once been her mother?

"So much talent. Where did it all come from?" Her face displayed a mixture of emotions as she took in the paintings. "You never stopped dreaming, did you?"

It wasn't really a question, but Bryan answered anyway. "No."

"I think I always knew. I just wanted to convince myself you were better, that you had found peace. Because I couldn't help you find it. And that's my job." Her voice wavered. "I just didn't want to put you in another hospital, another study. You told the doctors they had stopped. . . . I wanted to believe you when you said they had stopped. But I knew they hadn't." She broke down. "And you had no one to talk to. No one to believe in you. I'm so sorry."

"Mom, please don't. I didn't want to talk about it anymore—I couldn't."

"But I still feel it in you. The turmoil." As she said it her eyes traveled to the painting of the Egyptian goddess.

Bryan examined it with her. The power of the portrait dominated the room. He looked closely at the goddess's shrouded face. Her gaze seemed to be mocking him, her mouth parted as if to whisper secrets in his ear. He turned away from it and took his mother's hand. "I can't explain what happens to me. And no psychological analysis is going to make me better. You have to have faith in me and accept me as I am."

His words made her cry even harder. "I do love you. So much."

"I know. I'm sorry I haven't made it easy for you."

He embraced his mother for the first time in years. She squeezed him back tightly, and they stood together for a long moment.

She pulled away and clasped his arms. "I'm not going to pry. But I want you to know I am here. Anytime you need me, I will move mountains for you."

Bryan could feel the immense power in her—the power of a mother who would do anything for her child. He found his voice. "Thank you."

They both knew there was nothing more to say for now. Bryan walked her to her car and gave her another hug; he didn't want to let go. Tonight had been a turning point in their relationship. Perhaps on some level she had known her son needed her—and that he needed to know Anssonno had never been lost.

Bryan stood on the curb, long after her car's taillights had disappeared, and let the tears run freely, purging all that ancient pain. He didn't want to go inside. Emotionally spent, he sat down on a park bench across the street and stared up at the night sky. The stars tugged at him, and he remembered all of the moments he had ever looked up at their light. His thoughts veered toward Linz. She had turned his world upside down—a world already skewed to begin with. Where did that leave him now? Incapacitated on a park bench, apparently.

He pulled his pan flute from his pocket and started to play. In their life in Petra, she could recognize his flute anywhere. He closed his eyes and let the notes take over, remembering.

He was so focused, that he almost failed to hear the car pull up. It was Linz. He put the flute down and called out to her. "Nice night."

Startled, she turned toward him, searching for him in the dark. "Bryan?"

He gave her a salute.

She hesitated and crossed the street. "What are you doing out here?"

"Stargazing."

Unable to look him in the eye, she hovered at the curb. "I'm sorry for driving off tonight."

"Apology accepted."

For a long moment, neither of them spoke. She stared at the flute in his hand and cleared her throat. "All your 'dreams' landed you in a string of mental homes as a child. You forgot to tell me that part."

"Who told you that? Your father?"

Linz crossed her arms. "It's true, isn't it?"

"Yes, it's true," Bryan admitted. "I said I went through the therapist mill."

"In a state hospital for the mentally ill. You were diagnosed with schizophrenia."

"I'm not schizophrenic," he assured her, trying to stay calm. "I was in a state hospital. I was in a lot of hospitals. My parents were desperate. It's where you put kids when you don't know how to make their nightmares go away. You had dreams. Is this really what you want to hear?"

"But I never believed I was those people."

Bryan prayed for patience. Yelling at her would not help the situation. "I'm not crazy. Our meeting sparked something . . . awareness, memories. There's a puzzle here, and we need each other to solve it."

Linz shook her head. "Michael—" She couldn't believe she just called him that.

Bryan waited for her to acknowledge what just happened.

Instead she said, "I think it's best if we stop seeing each other."

"You're just afraid," he replied, his voice flat.

"No, I'm not."

"Yes, you are," he insisted, standing his ground. "You know. Logically none of this makes sense and I sound crazy. But I'm not. On some primal level, you know I'm right."

"Look, I didn't come here to do this." Linz tightened her grip on her purse strap. "I just wanted to say good-bye in person. I thought you deserved that much."

"Do you have a pen and paper?"

"What?"

"Do you have a pen and paper?" He nodded to her satchel.

She glared at him and crossed her arms.

"I have to show you something."

Linz fished out a piece of paper and a pen and handed them over. "Show me what?"

"Shhhh." Bryan closed his eyes and took a deep breath. He wanted to write what he saw in his mind but couldn't. His hand wouldn't move—something was wrong.

Linz stepped back into the street. "Okay, look. I have to go."

"No, wait. I have to show you." He stared at the page, willing himself to write so much his hand shook. In that moment he probably did look as crazy to her as she thought he was.

"I'm sorry. This has to end." She walked away and didn't look back. Bryan knew he was about to lose her. He stared at the pen in his hand, and it came to him—Michael had been right-handed and he was left. Switching the pen to his other hand, he tried again. This time the pen flew across the paper.

He heard Linz get into her car and tried to write faster.

Across the street, Linz slammed the door to her car and burst into tears. She knew it made no sense, but she was upset that Bryan had not tried harder to stop her from leaving. But didn't she want to end it? So why was she crying?

Swiping at her tears, she started the car and pulled out—and then yelped and slammed on the brakes as a hand slapped a piece of paper on her windshield.

Bryan stood next to the car, out of breath. Linz squinted at the paper through the glass. What she saw was not possible: an incredibly complex chemical formula that would have taken her hours to comprehend. At a glance, she could make out various compound molecular formulas, notations for weights, melting points, isomers, and a full breakdown of pharmacokinetic parameters.

She turned off the ignition and got out of the car. "You just wrote this?" She snatched the paper from him. "What is it?"

"Renovo. At least it's the original formula." He waited while she studied the page.

Linz hesitated and then reached into the car and pulled the Renovo file from her briefcase. She started rifling through the pages.

Bryan frowned. "What's that?"

"The project file on Renovo. I haven't looked at it yet."

He gave her a quick summary. "It's an experimental drug designed to generate neurons for a potential cure for Alzheimer's. They found a way to stimulate the creation of massive amounts of neurons, which in turn formed new pathways for memory retrieval. They succeeded beyond their wildest imagination."

"And you know this because you created the drug?"

"Just find the formula," he told her. He had recognized Michael's writing on several of the pages she had been sifting through. Somehow she had gotten a copy of the original file. He didn't think it even existed.

He identified the formula before she did. "That page."

Linz pulled it out. Turning on the car's interior light, she studied both formulas: the one Bryan had written and the one Michael had written. They looked identical down to the last pen mark. "You're saying you just wrote this? Right now."

He saw the skepticism on her face, along with something else—burgeoning belief—and shook his head with a smile. "God, you drive me crazy."

He reached across her and pulled another piece of paper from her bag and wrote the formula out again. "I remembered Michael's entire life while I was in Canada, including his work." He handed the page to her.

Like a schoolteacher, she checked the new page against the other two. Every notation was once again identical, including the penmanship. "My God," she said, her voice barely audible.

Bryan waited, unwilling to let himself believe he had gotten through to her. "You believe me."

She sat there for the longest time, staring at the formula. Her eyes filled with wonder. When she spoke, her voice quivered. "I believe you."

Bryan was overwhelmed. He had done it. She was with him now. He was no longer alone.

He kissed her with everything in his heart. Finally Linz broke away and hugged him, resting her cheek against his. But her mind was filled with questions—she needed to know what this meant. "Where do we go from here?" she whispered. "I already tried to speak to my father, but he refuses to talk about anything related to Renovo. We could try together."

"There's someone else I think we should talk to first." He didn't want to get into Conrad, not yet.

"Who?"

"Just trust me."

She pulled away. "Why go to a total stranger over my father? Michael was like a brother to him. He'd want to know that . . . whatever they did had ramifications for you."

For us, Bryan thought. She still wasn't ready to embrace the whole truth. He would have preferred to tell her everything, but he knew it would only put up a wall—possibly one that he couldn't tear down again. "Please trust me." He promised, "I will talk to Conrad, just not yet."

"Who else could be so important?"

"Their other partner."

THIRTY-ONE

Bryan had researched Finn along with Conrad. He had found out that, after the accident, Finn had spent a year recovering at a burn center in Houston. His name had resurfaced ten years ago when The Kauffman Foundation, a private research foundation with offices in both Boston and New York, announced him as its new director.

The Kauffman Foundation was a well-funded private biomedical research company; and judging by the residential address that Bryan had located for Finn in Beacon Hill, it seemed like his old colleague had done well for himself. Bryan and Linz tried not to feel conspicuous in front of the well-lit brownstone. With its antique lampposts and brick masonry, the entire neighborhood had the feel of Old London to it. Finn's home was the biggest one on the block—it almost was the block. Bryan wondered what Finn would think of them showing up at his door.

His butler could well have been a bouncer blocking the entry to a club. The six-foot, three-hundred-pound Japanese man looked more sumo wrestler than domestic worker. "Dr. Rigby doesn't see strangers."

Linz nodded and inched backward. Bryan put his arm around her, anchoring her to his side and apologized. "I'm sorry we didn't call first, but it's very important we see him. Tell him Mandu is here."

"Mandu?" the man and Linz both said at the same time.

"Yes." Bryan gave an innocent smile. The man nodded and shut the door.

"Mandu?" Linz's tone demanded an explanation.

"You'll see."

They waited several minutes. The door opened again, wider this time. The big man smiled, now looking quite friendly. "Please come in. Dr. Rigby is anxious to meet you." He surprised them both by providing house shoes in the traditional Japanese manner and led the way.

Inside, Bryan and Linz were both taken aback by the grandeur. The first room they walked through was constructed entirely of silk screens and gleaming Macassar Ebony floors. An ancient sundial sat mounted in the center on raised marble, adding to the dramatic effect. The next room they walked through was a gallery filled with antiques. Finn, like Conrad, had developed a taste for collecting.

Bryan kept his gaze on the floor and hurried through, not wanting to risk another episode like the one he had experienced at Conrad's.

Off the gallery, two doors slid open to reveal a library. The room had leather walls and towering bookshelves filled with well-worn texts—a scholar's room.

Finn Rigby sat in a big overstuffed chair next to an antique table lamp that cast a soft glow on the room. Bryan stared at him and recognized the Finn from his dreams—only this man was older, and the right side of his face, neck, and arm bore scars from severe burns. His hair was cut short now and it was more white than blond. But he was still Finn. Bryan noticed that he had on eyeglasses with dark-brown lenses and wondered if he still suffered from migraines.

Finn studied them with the same intensity. "Mandu," he said.

Bryan stepped forward. "A lifetime you and Michael both remembered . . . two brothers from the Wardaman tribe in Australia's Northern Territory. Neither of you knew the exact time frame, only that it happened well before the Europeans arrived in the sixteen hundreds."

Finn seemed to have trouble forming his words. "How do you know that?"

Bryan stunned him even further by answering in Wardaman,

an aboriginal dialect that was now almost extinct. *"Because you were my younger brother, Bardo. It was the first recall you ever had."*

Bryan could sense that Linz was about to ask what language he was speaking, and he squeezed her hand in a silent signal to let him finish. *"Bardo loved to play tricks on Mandu . . . always taking his spear and finding ways to torture his brother. Their time together was short. You drowned when you were a boy."*

To the Wardaman, death signals the twilight time, when the soul returns to its birthplace so it can be reborn. Remembering that life had given Bryan a deep connection to nature, to the Earth, and to the power of dreams. The Wardaman believe in a great tapestry of life and see their dreams as memories of Creation Time, when Ancestral Beings had walked the Earth. Mandu's memories and the peace they brought Bryan had come at a time when he had needed them most. It was the reason he had finally felt able to come home to Boston and make peace with his childhood.

Finn remained perfectly still, except for two fingers that performed a staccato tap against the table.

Bryan knew this meant his old friend was deep in thought, and he switched back to English. "I remembered Mandu's life three years ago. Overnight, I knew how to live off the land. I traveled to remote regions of the world, slept under the stars, hunted my own food, and made a fire by rubbing two sticks together—an ancient art long forgotten. It was a year before I felt the urge to see a modern city again." He had only returned to civilization at Therese's urging. When he had called her from some remote outpost near La Rinconada, Peru, to see how she was doing, it seemed that his art had become famous the year that he had been off the grid, and offers were coming in from gallery owners to present his work in Berlin, São Paulo, and New York in solo exhibits. He would never have been able to make that leap of faith without Mandu's wisdom.

Bryan waited, giving Finn time to process everything.

Finn looked to Linz and then back to Bryan and whispered, "My God, it is you. Both of you. How?"

Bryan heard Linz's breath catch at the recognition in Finn's voice.

Finn sat forward. "I thought I'd never see you again. How long have you been remembering?" He motioned for them to sit.

Bryan led Linz to the couch. She was looking a little dazed. He answered for them. "Since we were children. She's remembered Juliana but no one else. I can't seem to stop mine."

Finn absently touched the scar on his cheek. "Extraordinary. Renovo really has worked beyond our wildest dreams."

Linz sat down. "Would someone please tell me exactly what you all did?"

Finn looked to Bryan, a bit of a challenge in his eyes. "Would you like to do the honors?"

Bryan could tell Finn still wasn't sure if this was a hoax. He nodded in acceptance and turned to Linz. "The journey started in 1974, the first year Harvard Medical School partnered with the Medical Scientist Training Program. It was a national program for both MD and PhD students and was created to support the next generation of physician-scientists in biomedical research. We were all accepted. Diana and Finn already knew each other from when they were undergrads. The fellowship supported our individual research for six years." Bryan addressed Finn, "Your research focused on understanding how to limit the release of glutamate, a vital chemical in the brain that, if produced in excessive amounts, kills cells." His gaze returned to Linz. "Diana's work concentrated on developing a way for the brain to produce more acetylcholine—"

"A chemical believed to be essential to thinking and memory formation." Linz finished his sentence, growing impatient. "And Michael's research?" she asked with a frown, as if trying to piece it all together.

"His dealt with brain cell regeneration, which at the time was a little-known field."

A quiet knock on the door interrupted them. Finn's assistant came in and placed a tray of green tea between them. Then the door whispered shut.

Finn nodded to Bryan. "Please, go on."

"Back then, the general consensus was that the brain didn't have the capability to generate new cells, but studies in animals had begun to show otherwise. Michael believed that if animals possessed an innate ability for neurogenesis, humans must as well. His work centered on developing compounds to trigger the growth of new neurons—later it was considered light-years ahead of its time. He wanted to keep things quiet until he was certain of what he had and only shared his results with Diana and you," he said, gesturing to Finn.

"So he never published," Linz said.

"No. But the compounds he created and tested in preliminary animal studies showed four times the number of proliferating neurons as the control animals. And the mice exhibited a ninety percent improvement in memory skills."

Linz looked astonished. Her words tumbled out of her mouth with excitement. "Those findings are phenomenal. Neurodegenerative disease results in the slow death of the brain's nerve cells. If it could be combated, it would revolutionize treatment across the board."

Bryan saw Finn studying Linz with a curious frown, probably wondering how she knew so much. Bryan continued, "Only one other scientist at Harvard conducted research that dealt with neurogenesis." He cleared his throat. "Conrad's goal was to create a protein that would not only keep nerve cells in the brain from dying but also increase their ability to function. In a move that was even more unorthodox, he introduced the protein as a virus."

Linz remained silent at the mention of her father. Finn still had no idea who she was.

"Conrad's approach intrigued Michael," Bryan said. "He reached out in the hope that they could become colleagues."

For the first time Finn interrupted Bryan; he sounded bitter. "Conrad was an arrogant loner who thought he was God's gift to science. I accepted the new addition to the group with less pleasure than Michael, even though I recognized his genius. No one could afford to be an isolationist. When our program at Harvard came to an end, the big question loomed—what to do next. Michael had the idea. Instead of pursuing the usual avenues—moving to a research institute, pharmaceutical company, or a hospital—he proposed that we combine our research and apply for a joint grant."

Bryan remembered the night Michael had pitched the idea over beers at Doc's. He explained, "Michael's protein had proven to be incredibly effective and would be the cornerstone for the whole study. His proposal was to use Conrad's delivery system with his protein to create a virus and couple it with the compounds developed by Diana and Finn."

"Forcing the body's immune system to respond by creating new neurons," Linz summarized. "Basically, you attempted to create a super virus to combat all neurodegenerative diseases." She shook her head in wonder.

Finn smiled. "The proposal Michael drafted was too tantalizing for the National Institute of Aging to resist, and we received a sizable grant. After development, we entered a phase-one clinical trial, targeting severe Alzheimer's patients in a double-blind, randomized control study. Within weeks, it became apparent which subjects took the placebo. The effects of the drug were that dramatic. And once we were well into the trial, we started preparing to present the first-round findings to the NIA review board to determine if we could broaden it. There were twelve test subjects taking the drug. By the final test stages, their symptoms had virtually disappeared."

"They all had Alzheimer's? And it just went away?" Linz's voice rose. "This never went public? Why?"

"Because of what happened after Michael took the drug. By the end, we all had taken it." Finn got up to pour them tea. As he held the teapot, the tremor in his hand was detectable. He set it back down. "When it became apparent Renovo had the ability to repair damaged minds, Michael began to ask what it would do to a healthy mind."

Linz leaned forward and burst out, "That's insane."

Finn gave a grim smile of agreement. "But you can't condemn our curiosity. We had yet to see a side effect on an animal or human. The risk seemed minimal. Within days, we began accessing remote memories of other lifetimes as real as our own, from people who lived hundreds, even thousands of years ago." He stared hard at Linz. "You know your mother as your mother. But what if you suddenly remembered her as your wife? Your sister? Your husband? Your killer? Lifetimes became crossed. The human psyche, the ego, is not equipped to process such information."

Bryan challenged, "And yet *we* are processing it. Look at us now."

Finn nodded, conceding Bryan's point. "Your ability to remember is beyond what we thought possible. Michael died under the drug. His mind must have remained opened and all those memories, that ability his higher mind was perfecting, must have carried over into this life. In essence, you inherited this capability from your previous self. You share the same higher mind. I have no other theory to offer."

"What about Diana?" Linz asked. "Did she die under the drug?"

Finn shook his head no, as if the question were too painful to answer.

"I don't remember things, like him," Linz clarified. "It's just a recurring dream of one life."

"And you can speak Greek," Bryan reminded her, shaking his head. He couldn't believe she was still holding out.

"You have fluency as well?" Finn asked Linz, looking surprised.

"I think she has the ability to remember more, but her mind is holding back," Bryan answered. Linz frowned at that.

"Out of all of us, Diana took the least amount of Renovo, so perhaps her ability in this life is limited. After remembering ancient Rome, Diana was too terrified to move forward." Finn stared at Linz like an exotic insect under a magnifying glass. "You've had that same dream your whole life? Fascinating."

Linz shifted in her chair, uncomfortable with Finn's scrutiny. She changed the subject. "After Michael and Diana died, what happened to the test subjects?" she asked. "In the project file it says they were all from Forest Green Psychiatric Center."

Finn started in surprise. "How did you gain access to the file?"

"My father . . ." she admitted, "is Conrad Jacobs."

Bryan held his breath, unsure of how this little bombshell would impact Finn.

Finn swallowed several times before he said, "Your father is Conrad? You're . . ."

"Linz Jacobs." She nodded, her eyes growing intent. "Did he take the drug too? As much as Michael?"

Finn didn't answer. Bryan explained, trying to fill the deafening silence and keep the conversation going, "Michael took Renovo over the longest period of time, but, yes, Conrad increased his own doses."

"Why has all of this been kept secret?" she demanded. "My father will barely admit he even knew you." The questions tumbled out of her. "What happened the day they died?" Her eyes zeroed in on Finn. "I find it hard to believe you and my father are no longer speaking. You're both happy to leave Renovo buried in Medicor's archives?"

Finn looked like he was at a loss for words. He stammered, "Your father and I lost touch over the years. I'm sorry for subjecting you to the ramblings of a crazy old Buddhist. Now, I'm very tired." He looked agitated and ready for them to leave.

Bryan leaned forward and spoke in Wardaman. "*I know you're afraid. Help me.*"

Finn replied in the same tongue. "*He's a very powerful man now. I didn't realize . . . you need to leave Boston. Right away.*"

Bryan chose to continue avoiding English. "*I can't leave her.*"

"*She's his daughter. You're the one in the greatest danger. He wanted us all dead, but you the most.*"

Bryan frowned in bewilderment. "*Why? Why me?*"

"*Come back tomorrow, alone. We'll talk then.*" Finn stood up and rifled through a book cabinet, looking for something.

Linz sat fascinated and bemused as they carried on in Wardaman.

"*These will confirm everything you remember about Michael's life.*" Finn handed Bryan five leather-bound journals. "*Come again tomorrow. We have much to discuss.*"

Bryan stood to leave. They could talk at length when he returned. He signaled Linz that it was time to go.

Linz held back. She wasn't ready to go yet. "Dr. Rigby, I'm sorry if we've brought back pain from the past, but we really need answers."

"I've already said too much." Finn declined to shake her hand as she held it out to him. "Don't tell your father you came to see me. Please." He left the room by a different door, leaving Bryan and Linz to find their way out.

Linz and Bryan were headed back toward his car when her frustration finally got the best of her. "Can I get a translation please? How many languages do you speak?"

Bryan thought seriously about it before giving up. "I don't know."

She stopped walking. "What do you mean you don't know?"

"I stopped counting a long time ago."

"Well, can you take a wild guess?" she asked, growing even more exasperated.

"Over thirty?"

"Thirty? You speak over thirty languages?" she yelped, on the verge of having a meltdown on the street corner. "Which ones?"

"German, Russian, French, Dutch, Spanish, Chinese—Mandarin and Cantonese—Korean, Farsi, Italian, Latin—"

"Okay, stop." She held up her hand. "Just translate what he said."

"He said to be careful and gave me Michael's journals."

"I know he said more than that. He had a coronary when he found out who I was. Why is he so afraid of my father?"

Instead of answering, Bryan handed her the journals. "These were Michael's diaries. I already know everything in them. They're for you."

THIRTY-TWO

DAY 31—MARCH 8, 1982

Tonight Conrad finally admitted to recalling lifetimes. More than any of us, he has lost his way in the mire of memories. His attack on me was shocking and terrifyingly real. Who had he remembered, another one of the monsters who destroyed my life?

I now believe a soul can hate another soul, wrap itself around the other and suffocate its light, releasing tragedy and pain as its venom.

I can no longer reconcile the lives I'm remembering with my own. I fear I am losing my identity altogether, and I am not sure how much longer I can stay sane.

Last night, when I dreamed of the Egyptian queen, I thought about my death again. I have begun to think it will happen soon. I'm not ready to die, but if I do, then at least this whole experience will be mercifully forgotten.

Diana and I are meeting Finn at the lab tonight to pack our equipment and leave Boston. Simply changing the locks won't do. We need to disappear in order to survive. Conrad is dangerous to us all.

❦

"He wrote this entry the night he died?" Linz put down Michael's journal and thought for the hundredth time, *This can't be true.* Each word had shattered her heart.

Bryan sat next to her on her sofa, remaining quiet. He gave the slightest nod.

Her fingers fidgeted with the journal cover. Something inside of her snapped—she had reached her threshold. She stood up and threw it on the table. "Now I'm not only supposed to believe I'm this Diana woman, but that my father may have killed me?" She knew she was screaming but couldn't stop herself. "Do you realize how insane this is? I can't believe it! I can't!"

"Calm down." Bryan reached out to her. "I know—"

"What I'm feeling?" She jerked away from him. "No you don't. I just read old diaries suggesting my father is Dr. Evil. Hell, you wrote them. Right?" She searched his face. "What happened after this?"

Bryan kept silent. Linz stared at the journals, hating them, hating Bryan, hating herself for feeling what she felt. A bitter seed of doubt about her father had now been planted inside her and she could not stop its growth.

She paced up and down the room, becoming more distraught as she tried to expel the implications of Michael's journals. "If reincarnation is real, maybe I haven't always been a saint either. Maybe I've killed. Maybe I'd become confused, crazy if I remembered everything at once. Who are we to judge?" She angrily wiped away her tears. "How do you even know my father did anything? How can you be sure I'm even Diana?"

"Don't get angry at me. You read it yourself. Diana's memories of Juliana are the same as your dreams."

"So you expect me to believe the worst of my father without any proof? Well I won't."

"Finn thinks if Conrad knew who I was, he'd kill me," Bryan countered.

Linz barked out a laugh. "Please, now that's delusional."

"He told me to leave town."

"Fine. Go back to Canada. Do us all a favor." She winced as she said it. She had never argued like this with anyone in her life.

Bryan had lost all of his patience. "Linz, I am trying to explain to you what the hell is going on. Stop being so damn defensive!" He grabbed her shoulders.

"Get your hands off me." She wrenched herself away from him.

They stood three feet apart. Bryan was yelling loud enough for the neighbors to hear. "The problem is you don't remember! And until you do, we're going to have this wall between us that I can't climb! All I can do is wait for you. And I will! I won't go anywhere.

I don't care what the hell happens to me. I'll wait!" He threw on his jacket and began to leave.

Linz had never seen him so livid. But a part of her took grim satisfaction in it. She wanted him to hurt as much as she did. "Hey," she called out. Bryan turned around, a slight look of hope on his face. Instead she held out the journals. "Get these out of my house."

Bryan took them and left without another word. Linz slammed the door behind him—and her eyes settled on the Renovo file. It was sitting on her coffee table. She needed more answers than Michael's journals had provided and the scientist within her knew this would be the best place to look.

Galvanized, she opened the file and read every page. An hour later, she read it again, this time taking notes at lightning speed, her mind in overdrive as she worked to break down the formula. She could see now that this was the only way.

When she was finished, she gathered her computer, her keys, and the file with quick efficiency. She was ready to get her proof.

On the corner a street bum sang "Some Enchanted Evening" at the top of his lungs.

Bryan put some money into the man's cup and used it as an excuse to look back at the two men following him. After he'd left Linz's, he had driven back to his place, dropped off the journals, and then promptly left to go for a long walk, hoping it would help him cool down. He had become aware of the men's presence five blocks ago.

Bryan kept walking. So did they.

Inside the Medicor building across town, Conrad's office appeared deserted. His computer monitor flashed in the dark, casting a ruby light around the room that made the statue of Atlas look like it was covered in blood. The message on the screen read: "Security Override: Project File Renovo. Accessed by L. Jacobs."

Downstairs in the lobby, Linz walked past the night guard toward the elevators. Her cell phone rang. She looked at the caller ID and froze—he never called her.

She decided to pick up, forcing her voice to sound normal. "Hi . . . sorry I've been out of touch."

"I just wanted to make sure you're okay," Conrad said, shutting the door to his office and heading to the elevator.

"I'm fine," she assured him.

Neither spoke as each waited for the other to say something.

Conrad finally asked, "Did you read the file?"

"I did. You were right. It's better not to get involved. Clean break."

Conrad got into the elevator and pressed the button for the lobby. "Are you out? Do you want to meet for a late dinner?"

"No, I'm already at home. Why, where are you?"

"Leaving the office."

Linz looked around in dismay. She was right smack in the middle of the lobby and sure to run into him. The lights above the elevator bank showed that there was one on its way down, and there was a good chance that Conrad was in it. He asked again, "Sure you're okay?"

"Dad, I'm fine." Trying not to draw attention to herself, she rounded the corner just as the elevator opened. He stepped out.

"Well, I was just worried. Try and get some sleep. I'll call you tomorrow. Love you."

He waved to the guard and walked out the front door. Linz peeked out from around the corner and watched him leave. "Me too."

Bryan took note of his surroundings and saw he had entered the club district on Lansdowne Street. The men had not stopped tailing him. In fact, they were gaining. Bryan looked over his shoulder. This was bad. There was no choice—he broke out into a run.

They chased after him.

Bryan sprinted hard and was wheezing by the second block. He wasn't used to running, and he could feel his body slowing down. He tried to focus his memories on Mandu, who was the fastest runner in the Wardaman tribe—Bryan might not have his body, but he did have his memories. Immediately his breathing began to slow, his legs relaxed, and the earth rushed beneath him as his speed increased.

Stealing a look behind him, he saw the men break into a dead run. They were both in excellent shape. Bryan pushed even harder and managed to put a few blocks between them.

Rounding a corner, he ducked into an alley and dove right into a dumpster and covered himself with garbage. Then he waited.

Five minutes later, he heard the men outside. They were both breathing heavily from the exertion.

One of them said, "Damn, that bastard's fast. Did you see him turn?"

They passed the dumpster and continued down the street. The second man ordered, "Check across. I'll meet you at the next block."

Bryan continued to wait. After ten excruciating minutes, he lifted the lid of the dumpster as quietly as possible and jumped out.

Just then a cluster of teenagers walked by, heading to the T station at the corner. Bryan slipped into step with them, using the group as cover.

He had almost reached the stairs when the two men spotted him from across the street. Bryan flew down the stairs, leapt over the station gate, and rushed to catch a boarding train. He saw one of his pursuers run into the next car. Seconds before the doors shut, Bryan jumped off—an arm came from behind him, wrapping itself around his neck like a vise.

"Nice try." The other man pressed a stun gun to Bryan's side and delivered a swift, paralyzing jolt.

Right before Bryan lost consciousness, he looked down at his hand and realized that he had forgotten to put on his turquoise ring. Just like Pushkin.

THIRTY-THREE

Liquid from a timed burette dripped in slow rhythm into a Petri dish. Linz checked its progress and went back to review the three-dimensional molecular structure displayed on her laptop.

She had been working in Medicor's biochemistry labs and had one or two more hours left before people would start to arrive. She knew her keycard would show she had been there, but by the time anyone got around to questioning why she had been working all night in another lab, it would be too late.

A sound came from outside. Linz froze like a burglar caught in the act and turned off the light. She waited in the dark until she heard the footsteps pass.

Not wanting to take any chances, she finished working by the light of her computer. Forty-five minutes later, she filled a large vial with the liquid from the Petri dish and capped it. Her replica of Renovo was complete.

Bryan sat upright on the bed, constrained by the straitjacket. Everything about his prison—the sterile smell, the white walls, the barrenness—reminded him of the years he had spent in psych wards as a child.

He looked at the camera mounted on the wall above him, sensing that he was being observed. A minute later, someone keyed in the code for the electronic lock and the door opened.

Conrad entered. "Good, I see you're awake."

Bryan knew Conrad had orchestrated his abduction, but seeing him ignited a new rage. "I don't know what the hell you think you're doing—you can't just kidnap someone like this!"

"But I just did." Conrad gave him a patronizing smile. "No one knows you're here, and I own this hospital."

Bryan spoke in Japanese. *"Was it my paintings that gave me away? Did the one you bought hit a nerve?"*

"This conversation is pointless right now."

"Why? I don't seem to be going anywhere." Bryan pulled at his jacket. "Linz is going to wonder where I am and come looking for me. She knows about Renovo. She has the file."

Conrad smiled without humor. "Which I'm quite aware of. Lindsey loves puzzles, always has. But she won't find anything in the file."

"Except the formula."

Bryan could see the hesitation in Conrad's eyes. "I know how to handle my daughter. I've given her the best life, and I will not have her dragged into this. She will not be put at risk. You are never going to see her again."

Inside, Bryan felt a surge of relief at Conrad's words—he was protective of her. "So you know who she is?"

"I know more than you realize."

"That's right. You always were the omniscient one." Bryan couldn't help his sarcasm. Conrad hadn't changed a bit. "It was so easy, wasn't it? All these years—making money medicating the symptoms, never revealing the cure." Bryan was yelling now, but he couldn't stop himself. "We found the cure for Alzheimer's. And you just buried it."

"You said yourself the world wasn't ready for Renovo!"

"Thirty years! I would have at least found a way to reverse the disease. You never even tried."

"You have no idea what I tried or what's at stake. I'm sorry it has to be like this, but you have to disappear. For your own safety and my daughter's."

Bryan tried to change tactics. "Let me go. I promise I'll vanish.

I'll leave Boston. You'll never hear from me again. I swear. Just don't do this. Please."

Conrad shook his head. "I can't." He unlocked the door and stepped out.

Fear blossomed inside Bryan. "Don't leave me in here like this."

Conrad checked his watch. "Don't worry. I'll have them give you something to help you sleep. Tomorrow we'll be starting you on your first round of Renovo. It should go rather quickly, since I've perfected the formula. We need to know everything that's in that head of yours."

Bryan's heart froze in terror. He didn't want to be given Renovo.

Conrad turned back to him. "I'll tell Lindsey you went back to Europe to paint. She'll get over it eventually. I'm sorry, but it really is for the best." The door closed with a definitive lock.

Bryan stood up and rushed the door. "Conrad! I won't let you do this!" He rammed the door with his upper body again and again. His shoulder took the brunt of it.

Outside, Conrad walked away, deaf to Bryan's screams. He stopped at the nurses' station and smiled at the nurse on duty. "Our special patient needs something to help him sleep before his big day tomorrow."

A few minutes later, two orderlies entered Bryan's room. They held him down and administered an injection.

Bryan's body went slack and he stared up at the ceiling as his psychomotor functions began to fail. He was trapped in limbo, and his mind climbed aboard a powerful ship as the drug took him out to sea.

THIRTY-FOUR

It had taken Linz two doses of Renovo and four hours to recall the life of Katarina Rota. Katarina was born in Vienna in seventeen hundred and moved to Cremona with her parents as a young child. It was there that she met and fell in love with Bartolomeo Giuseppe Antonio Guarneri and her life charted a new course. She became a violin maker's wife.

It was not a glamorous or well-paying trade; Katarina and Giuseppe struggled with finances their whole life. She would have been shocked to know that one of the violins he'd created had survived history and become the most expensive musical instrument in the world.

For two hours, Linz stayed in her bedroom, giving the memories time to settle in her mind. Now she was not only fluent in German and Italian but was also the only person in the world who knew that Katarina had helped her husband make his violins in the years toward the end of his life.

Desperately needing to hear one of his instruments, Linz got out her iPod and shuffled through her collection, studying it in a new light. Over the years, she had unknowingly purchased recordings that had a violinist who had played a del Gesù. It seemed that her subconscious mind could still recognize her husband's violins three hundred years later.

She put on Vivaldi's Concerto in G Minor and closed her eyes. It had been one of Giuseppe's favorite scores. He would often test his instruments by having a violinist come to his workshop, and he would always request that the violinist play something by Vivaldi.

Vivaldi had been a contemporary and was a violin virtuoso, and he had understood just what the instrument could do. Giuseppe would hand the newly made instrument over to the violinist like a parent who was letting his child leave home for the first time. He would then watch the performance with a sharp eye and a stern face and only when he began to close his eyes would Katarina know he was satisfied.

A true perfectionist, Giuseppe always told Katarina that some trees had more music in them than others, and he would devote huge amounts of their resources to purchasing the finest wood. He had a well-connected brother in Venice who helped him get access to select maple and spruce from Eastern Europe. Giuseppe believed that, by giving his love and passion equally to the wood itself, he could coax the soul of the instrument to sing.

Over the years, he also made creative adjustments to his families' violin-making traditions. His grandfather had apprenticed with the great Nicolò Amati, and the Guarneri family of violin makers adhered to the "Grand Amati" design. But as he grew in his artistry, Giuseppe chose to deviate from his lifelong training by letting the wood decide the violin's shape. In that way, each of his violins was an original. They were full of power, able to withstand the greatest strain from the hand-driving passion of any player. His varnish was another one of his great secrets, and he took its recipe with him to the grave.

When he became too ill to work, Katarina would have someone come to his bedside each day to play Vivaldi's *Four Seasons*. While she tidied up his workshop, she would listen to the passages from "Spring," "Summer," "Autumn," and "Winter" coming from the bedroom and pray once more for God to give them more time. No one in the world could ever replace Giuseppe, with his incredible genius, his reckless passion, and his artistry. The Lord had put him on this earth to make instruments that could play heaven's music. And here God was taking him away, with no one to inherit his workshop or his secrets.

Katarina didn't know what to do. The unfinished violin sitting on Giuseppe's workbench echoed her silent grief. She went over to it and sat down, wiped away her tears, and got to work.

On the day he died, she roused him and put the last violin in his hands. "Bartolomeo," she whispered. It was what she called him in their most tender and private moments.

He opened his eyes and looked at her, then turned to the violin, studying its craftsmanship, and laid it on his chest with a sigh. "Grazie, amore mio," he whispered.

The violin rose and fell with his breath until he drew his last, and Katarina knew his spirit was gone. Every instrument has a story to tell, and this violin would tell Giuseppe's.

◆

Linz killed the music, ruthlessly pushing Katarina's memories aside. She didn't want to remember her life or mourn the loss of Giuseppe. Neither held answers to the one question burning in her heart: Did her father kill Michael and Diana?

In frustration, she reached for the vial again, refusing to think about what a triple dose might do. She knew she should call Bryan to let him know what she was doing; otherwise, no one would think to check on her for days. She imagined her father walking in to find her dead on the floor with the vial beside her. She didn't know why the thought gave her satisfaction, but it did.

Linz lay back on the bed and closed her eyes, waiting for the Renovo to take effect. Twenty minutes passed and still nothing happened. Maybe she would take a nap instead. Her breathing slowed, and her body began to feel heavy as sleep drew its blanket around her. She was wondering if the third dose would even do anything when she was hit by a stomach cramp.

Linz moaned and rolled off the bed. She felt dizzy and nauseated as the pain inside her grew.

She remained on the floor and slowly crawled to the bathroom. Her only concern was that she didn't throw up the drug.

JAPAN
DECEMBER 20, 1702

Oishi hunched over, unsure of whether he was finished being sick. The sake at the inn had been poor—and today marked the thirtieth night in a row that he had been incredibly drunk. It was a desperate and necessary ruse to ensure that the loud public rumors of his downfall were kept alive.

"The spies are gone!" Hara, his most trusted man, was running toward him, carrying a lantern.

Oishi stood up. When he spoke, his voice sounded gruffer than he intended. "You're sure the surveillance has been lifted?"

"Shiota and Tomimori followed them all the way out of the city. They are returning to Edo."

Oishi smiled. So they had taken the bait and no longer considered him a threat. "Now we are finally free to act. Order all the men to gather in Edo."

Even though almost two years had passed since his lord, Asano, had been forced to commit seppuku, Oishi had been secretly plotting his revenge with a patience few men possessed. All odds stood against him and his men, for their clan's castle, wealth, and lands had been given over to the Shogun after their lord's death. The men had become rōnin—homeless and jobless—and their enemy, Lord Kira, was under the protection of the powerful Uesugi clan. He was now the most guarded man in the country. However, Oishi knew the Uesugis would retract their guards if they believed he no longer posed a threat. Now that they had, Lord Kira's defenses would be penetrable.

Oishi and his small band of followers disguised themselves as silk traders and began the march to Edo. Although it was risky, Oishi needed to gather the rest of the men as a group at their safe house, if only to reaffirm their unity before the attack. But when Hara went to inform everyone of the upcoming meeting, he returned with devastating news.

"Oishi-sama, a third of our forces have deserted us. Now only forty-five others remain."

Oishi nodded. Most leaders would have been disheartened by this latest setback, but Oishi was a master strategist and had planned for such contingencies. The House of Asano had once numbered over three hundred samurai. After the disbandment, the men who were still committed to serving the clan had shrunk to seventy. To hear that now they were even less . . . Oishi was not surprised. If he and his remaining men were caught, they would be executed. He would have continued on with even less.

He looked at Hara and gave him a grim smile. "Forty-seven will do."

On the night before of the attack, Oishi ate a modest supper of *onigiri* rice balls with his son in their small room above the soba shop where they had been staying in secret. He swallowed bitter grief with every bite of rice—how he missed his wife and his other children. He had publicly divorced her so that his family would not be punished for the crime he was about to commit, but his eldest son, Chikara, had begged to accompany him. Oishi had agreed, knowing it was a death sentence for the boy. Only in moments such as these did he feel the depth of his men's sacrifice.

They sat close to the fire to stay warm and waited while heavy snow fell outside. This winter had been Edo's worst, and the capital had received record-breaking snow. The harsh elements would make their attack even more difficult.

All his life, Oishi had been taught that hardship either atoned for the misdeeds committed during a past life or was necessary to obtain enlightenment during the next. He did not know which would prove true in this case. He only knew that he could not bear to live under the same sky as Kira.

At midnight, a knock sounded quietly on the door. Two men escorted Oishi and Chikara to the safe house where the rest of the forty-seven ronin dressed in silence. They draped cloth capes and hoods over their armor, which they would later discard. But for the moment, their disguises made them look like a fire brigade on patrol, in case anyone stopped them on the way to Kira's and questioned their actions.

It was almost 4 a.m. when they began to walk in formation down the deserted streets. Their lantern boxes cast shadows on the snow, reminding Oishi of a Bunraku puppet show—stories that most often ended in tragedy. He tried to brush off these thoughts but worried that they would not reach Kira in time before his men called for help. If they were forced to fight the Uesugi clan, there would be no chance of victory. As it was, the odds against them were mighty. Kira had forty master samurai and one hundred eighty mercenaries protecting his fortress.

When they arrived at Kira's estate, they split into two groups to attack the front and back gates. Oishi led one group and had his son lead the other.

They took out the outer guards without raising the alarm. But they gave themselves away in the courtyard when they broke down the inner door. The house erupted into screaming chaos as guests and servants attempted to escape. The forty-seven pushed past them and battled Kira's guards, fanning out through the dark maze of rooms to find their man. Kira's house had been renovated due to his paranoia, and it now had countless hidden doors and secret rooms—he could be anywhere.

As desperation set in, Oishi saw his son facing off against one of Kira's master samurais; he left the boy to fend for himself. It defied every fatherly instinct he had, but he needed to find Kira before he escaped. Spurred on by the thought, Oishi overcame every samurai and mercenary in his way. Of his men, so far only Hara had sustained any injuries. He had taken an arrow in the chest but broke it off himself, determined to fight on.

After they had searched the entire house, Oishi and his band reconvened in the main hall. It was a miracle they were all still alive. Eighty-nine men lay dead around them, and the rest of the mercenaries had abandoned the fight.

Oishi ignored the moans of the wounded enemy on the ground.

It was dawn now, and Kira had not yet been found. The Uesagi clan most likely had heard of the attack and was en route.

For the first time in his life, Oishi felt the weight of his armor. "We stand so close only to fail?"

Then a lone whistle sounded in the distance: Kira had been found.

The men rushed to the back courtyard. There was Kira, kneeling in the snow with his captor beside him.

A strange calm washed over Oishi. At last, here was his enemy.

Oishi and his men dropped to their knees out of respect for Kira's station. They waited in silence for him to address them.

But Kira did not speak. He looked feeble and old. His body shook with fear.

Oishi finally broke the silence. His words were soft but measured. "Vengeance does not bow to time. We have come to avenge the House of Asano." He pulled out his sword and offered it to Kira. "I will allow you to kill yourself with honor, as my lord did, and I will stand as your Second."

Shivering, Kira stared blankly ahead—any hint of arrogance or belligerence had gone. Oishi frowned, wondering if Kira's mind had become afflicted by disease in the two years since Asano's passing. Or perhaps the man was simply too frightened to die.

Hara stepped forward. "He won't do it. We must take matters into our hands."

Oishi nodded and stood, sword in hand. His enemy still refused to engage him. "I, Oishi Kuranosuke Yoshio, Chief Retainer to the House of Asano, will now take your life."

With one swift move, he severed Kira's head.

For a moment, no one seemed to move or breathe. They couldn't believe they had done it—Kira had been forced from this Earth. The men wrapped his head with extreme care so they could take it with them. Their mission was not yet over.

Maneuvering through side streets to avoid detection, the forty-seven ronin reached Sengaku-ji temple. They washed the head in the temple's well and brought it to Lord Asano's grave. No one spoke. Oishi placed Kira's head next to the stone, and everyone bowed in unison, making new ground for the snow to fall on their backs.

Oishi gazed at the head of his enemy as it lay on his lord's final resting place and, with fierce satisfaction, breathed in the cold air, letting it soothe the fire that had been burning inside him for so long.

He bowed to Asano for the last time and left. Kira's head could remain on the grave. He did not need it anymore.

THIRTY-FIVE

Linz woke up kneeling in the bathroom, doubled over in pain. Her hands gripped her middle as she gasped for breath. The memories bombarded her: she had been a samurai, plotted for two years to kill a man, beheaded him and then, satisfied, had committed seppuku. Her men had died with her—their actions restoring the House of Asano.

She remembered that in Michael's journal, Finn had recognized her father as Lord Kira. The rage and bloodlust she had felt as Oishi warred against her horror and guilt. Oishi won.

With a war cry, she sprung up and began to destroy everything in sight with the strength of a man twice her size.

She demolished her living room, then moved to the hallway, smashing every framed photograph on the wall. The pictures of her father drove her into the darkest field. The urge to hunt him, to kill him in cold blood, pervaded her psyche.

Her body felt alien to her, her senses sharpened. Every moment, every word, every taste, every scent in Oishi's life passed through her like the fiercest wind. It took her rage with it and left her numb.

She stared at the broken frames lying jigsawed across the floor. Only one picture remained intact: a photo of Linz's mother taken just weeks before she had died.

Linz clutched the picture against her heart as if she could somehow embrace her mother's spirit from the other side. She desperately needed her.

Grace and Rhys Jacobs had been buried at Mount Auburn, one of the country's oldest cemeteries. A National Historic Landmark, it was only a fifteen-minute drive from Boston.

They had died in a car accident before Linz had turned one, tragically severing their family in half. Linz had no memory of either of them and had only visited Mount Auburn once when she was sixteen, after she had accidentally found the paperwork for the plot in her father's desk. She knew it was something she was never supposed to see, and she had been too afraid to ask her father why he had never taken her to see their graves.

In their household, there was an unspoken agreement that her mother and brother were never to be discussed, ever. As a child, Linz had naturally been curious about them, but her father would always divert her questions. Over time, she had come to understand that the past was simply too painful for him to discuss, but still, she wished he would share stories about the years before they had died. She would often daydream about how her father and mother had met, what her older brother had been like, and imagine that fateful day when the two of them had gotten in the car and driven away forever.

Linz had gone to the cemetery with Penelope and Derek during her junior year in high school. She had worn a dress and brought flowers. Now as she knelt at her mother's grave, she felt the same energy she had felt then coursing through her body.

Here, beneath the ground, lay someone integral to her life, someone who had given birth to her and then vanished. Had her mother known about Renovo and that her father had suffered from recalls? *Had she loved him?*

Had he killed them too?

Linz closed her eyes and a soft breeze brushed across her face, as if whispering to her to let go of the thought, and she wondered about how different her life would have been if they had lived.

The headstones were cold reminders that she was not yet through the journey, that she had not remembered what she needed to know. But she was getting closer to the truth.

Linz stood up, strengthened. She would return home and take one last dose, come what may. She would remember it all.

THIRTY-SIX

When Bryan opened his eyes, he knew he was dreaming. He was no longer bound in a straitjacket, locked up in the psychiatric ward Conrad had secreted him away to. He was far, far away, trapped inside a hallucination brought on by the drug the orderlies had given him.

He was sitting onboard the T, moving toward an unknown destination. An old couple behind him was talking in Russian, arguing over Nikola Tesla's theory of electromagnetism. Two seats away, another couple was speaking German, debating Freud's construct of the ego, Jung's definition of the collective unconscious, and the demise of the two men's friendship.

Bryan's head started to throb and he grew nauseous. Everyone in the car was speaking a language other than English—and Bryan could understand them all.

The train stopped, and he looked up to see Christiaan Huygens stepping into the car, holding the clock that Barbara had found. He took a seat across from Bryan and stared at him all the way to the next station. The ticking pendulum inside the clock grew louder and louder.

The doors opened, and in stepped Alexander Pushkin followed by Lord Asano.

Bryan pressed hard on his temples and focused on his mantra as the train began to move. *I am here now. I'm here now. I'm here now. I'm here now.*

The train stopped. The doors opened. And in stepped a hundred people from every time in history imaginable. Bryan knew them all.

He could barely breathe. All the people in his paintings had come to life and decided to ride the subway with him. Everyone stared at him—except Michael, who was sitting beside him, looking out the window. Still, the train did not move. Bryan realized they were waiting for someone.

The Egyptian goddess was the last to board. She escorted Origenes Adamantius onto the train and helped him find a place to sit. His frailty stood in stark contrast to her vitality. After she seated the old priest, she started to walk down the aisle toward Bryan.

When she reached him, she leaned in and spoke softly. "You see time as a stream, a continuous river flowing forward, and you are swimming in it, alone. But it is not. Imagine all your lives at once, all the pieces of your soul boarding the same train. Where are you going? Karma is a distraction to keep you sitting here. See your soul outside of time, and you will arrive at your destination."

She picked up a lotus flower that was lying at Bryan's feet. "The door to this train and the flower both open," she said, laying the flower in Bryan's hand. Then she disappeared.

With that, the train departed and sped like a bullet through a tunnel as everyone from Bryan's memories shared the ride. Bryan could hear all of their thoughts and closed his eyes, trying to divorce his mind from the discord. But the voices grew louder and louder until they became a chorus, and the waves of sound washed over him. It reached a powerful crescendo and then faded, leaving a resonance that was soon engulfed by silence.

Bryan opened his eyes to discover that he was no longer on the train. Lotus flowers stretched as far as the eye could see.

HENAN PROVINCE, CHINA
527 AD

Bodhidharma had heard Shaolin rivaled most temples with its beauty. Built during his lifetime in 495 AD on Mount Song's western peak, it had been named for the young forest planted around it. Emperor Xiaowen had spared no expense.

The temple's first abbot had been an Indian dhyana master,

who, like himself, had come to China to spread Buddhist wisdom. Neither had been the first to make the journey. Buddhism had been taking root in China for several hundred years.

It was brought to the country by the power of one man's dream. In 70 AD, a golden man with a halo had visited Emperor Ming in his sleep. His advisors had heard of a teacher in the West called Buddha, so the Emperor sent men to India to inquire about his teachings. They returned with scriptures, sutras, and two of Buddha's disciples to help make sense of them.

Bodhidharma placed great value in dreams—the lotus flowers of the mindstream. He had practiced mediation for many years and had learned the secrets to mastering his body and mind long ago. Each time he meditated, his mind spent more time away from his body, until perhaps one day, he thought, it would not return.

He knew it was time for a long meditation, and Shaolin would be the perfect place. The temple's main entrance was nestled just beyond the trees, in perfect harmony with the mountain. Bodhidharma could tell that the surrounding bamboo forests would be perfect for outdoor exercises. As he walked closer, the incense wafting from the cast-iron bowls called to his senses. Peace and power lived here. Yes, he thought to himself, I will stay a while.

The head abbot, Fang Chang, rushed out to greet him, accompanied by several others. Bodhidharma was shocked to see how round their bodies were. The monks looked like stuffed dolls, and at six feet, Bodhidharma towered over them. His body was in prime condition, and his black robes made him even more intimidating. He knew he must look a sight with his wild dark hair and long beard. He had been given the name "blue-eyed barbarian" more than once in this country—even though he had been born a prince in India and considered a handsome one. Bodhidharma thought it amusing that the Chinese regarded him as quite the opposite.

He didn't need a translator to tell him Fang Chang was denying him entry to the temple. He was well-versed in the language and had spent time at court prior to traveling to Shaolin. The Emperor had taken great pride in paying legions of scribes to translate ancient Sanskrit scrolls into Chinese so that they would be accessible to the public, and he had felt this alone would guarantee his path to Nirvana. Bodhidharma had laughed at the naivety of this assumption, which in turn had cut his welcome short. Word of the Emperor's displeasure must have traveled quickly.

Abbot Fang Chang apologized like a bird chirping too many times. Bodhidharma held up his hand to silence him and asked, "Could you direct me to the nearest cave?"

The abbot looked taken aback. "You want a cave?" He glanced at his men in confusion.

Bodhidharma nodded. "Preferably without bears. I am in need of a meditation."

The abbot snapped his fingers at the youngest monk. "Huike! Show him to a cave, in the next valley. See that he has food and water."

Fang began to leave, but Bodhidharma called out, "Abbot?" The old man started and turned around. "Get your men out into the forest for some exercise. These trees can be wonderful teachers."

To make his point, he jabbed a bamboo trunk. His finger pierced it straight through. The tree did not even sway. The men stood dumbfounded—what they had just seen was not possible.

Bodhidharma bent down and peered at the monks through the hole. "To the cave." Then he took off, assuming Huike would follow.

As they marched through the forest, Huike tripped and stumbled over his robes to keep up with Bodhidharma's long-legged stride. "But the caves are this way," he stammered, struggling to catch his breath.

Bodhidharma didn't speak and soon he arrived at the cave he had already chosen as his resting place. He went deep inside and laid his mat on the ground near the back wall.

Huike hovered at the cave's entrance, straining to see Bodhidharma through the shadows. "Shall I bring food and water?" he asked tentatively.

Bodhidharma did not answer: he had already folded his body into a lotus position. His mind had begun its journey.

Huike stayed at the cave entrance for hours, watching the strange Indian monk meditate. Bodhidharma's body never moved. His breathing was almost imperceptible. Huike came back the next day and then the next, but every day Bodhidharma remained as still as stone.

The monks at Shaolin had never heard of anything like it. Weeks went by. Every day another monk would sneak away from his duties to watch Bodhidharma sit in the cave.

The weeks turned into months, and the monk's initial astonishment turned into reverence. Abbot Fang assigned a monk to visit the cave once a week to make sure the master still lived. Otherwise, he ordered everyone to stay away so that they would not disturb this holy man.

Through nine falls, nine winters, nine springs, and nine summers, Bodhidharma sat in stillness as the elements performed their dance around him.

Bodhidharma took several breaths to ground himself and willed his Chi to expand. As sensation returned to his body, he was surprised to find his neck was stiff. He moved it from side to side and noticed Huike, asleep on a mat at the cave entrance.

His meditation had given him great insight, and Bodhidharma studied the young man with a thoughtful gaze. Throughout his life, he had felt that he must come to China. Now he understood why.

He took a stick from the ground and gently poked Huike until he was awake.

Huike opened his eyes and screamed as Bodhidharma leaned over him, looking like a phantom covered in dirt. Huike scurried backward in a blind panic until he hit the wall and fell.

The master sat back on his heels and scratched his head, dislocating the bugs that were nesting in his hair. "Why do you run away?"

Huike tried to find his voice. "Are you a ghost?"

Bodhidharma considered the question. "A ghost has no hunger. I am ready for food and water now."

The monk gaped at him, dumbfounded.

Bodhidharma reminded him, "You did offer, did you not?"

Huike stuttered, "Yes, but that was nine years ago!"

"Nine years?" Bodhidharma's eyebrows rose. "Then please bring extra rice."

Huike leapt to his feet and ran off.

Bodhidharma called him back. "Huike, why were you sleeping here?"

Huike bowed low. "Sometimes I come here to watch you. I wish to become your student," he confessed.

Bodhidharma picked the remaining bugs from his hair and gave them a new home on the rocks that were scattered about the cave's floor. "Don't be delusional. I have nothing to teach you."

Huike took a passionate step forward. "You have everything to teach me."

"You will not think so in our next life. In fact, you will kill me many times over. I have seen our future."

During his meditation a goddess had appeared before him with the eyes of an Ancient One. She had shared with him visions of his future selves. He had watched them with great compassion, and then he had felt his spirit returning to his body.

Bodhidharma smiled. At hearing this news, Huike had thrown himself on the ground in a dramatic show of servitude.

"Please, I would rather cut off a limb than do you harm," Huike said.

"And yet you still have two arms." Bodhidharma chuckled and stepped over Huike's body. He walked out of the cave.

Huike jumped up to follow him. "Wait! Where are you going?"

Bodhidharma was already halfway down the mountainside. "To pick berries. You are taking too long with my rice."

His back was to Huike, and Huike could not see his smile. The truth was that Bodhidharma would never refuse someone seeking the Way. Their spirits had connected in this life, and although Bodhidharma had seen Huike lost in the future, wandering at the opposite end of the light, he did not judge Huike for his future actions. Bodhidharma vowed to teach him everything he knew.

When Bodhidharma returned to his cave, he found Abbot Chang waiting with a rather large entourage. Huike was missing.

Bodhidharma waved to the monks, calling out, "I was most surprised to find it is summer. The berries taste delicious."

The men stared at him with awe as he approached them. Abbot Fang knelt on the ground. "Please, Enlightened One, forgive our ignorance in not granting you entry to Shaolin. We have come to beg you to stay with us for as long as you are able and bless us with your wisdom."

The Abbot had not aged well. Bodhidharma noted how much more feeble the old man looked. He held out his hand to help him stand.

Abbot Fang gazed at him with wide eyes. "How were you able to meditate for so many years?"

"Quite simply. I can teach you."

All the men nodded, looking most eager. They led him back to the temple, where the monks had readied their best room and prepared a great feast.

Later, after a much-needed bath and supper, Bodhidharma noted that Huike was still absent. He asked the young monk who was assisting him back to his quarters if Huike had left the temple.

The young monk looked startled. "Huike is unwell. We do not know if he will recover."

Bodhidharma was shocked to hear this news. Huike had been vibrant and healthy when he saw him last. "Please take me to him."

The young monk led him through several halls and two courtyards until they were in a small infirmary at the back of the monastery.

The smell of burning incense greeted him first. Bodhidharma walked in and saw Huike asleep on a pallet with an old healer by his side performing acupuncture while reciting a healing sutra. Scores of needles stood upright across Huike's chest and shoulders, and beneath his right shoulder, a huge bandage covered a stump where his arm had been. Huike lay unconscious, unable to hear the prayers of the priest attending him.

Bodhidharma turned to his guide and whispered, "What has happened?"

"Huike cut off his arm. Why, we do not know."

Pain filled Bodhidharma. The monk had cut off his arm to prove his dedication and worth not only to Bodhidharma but to himself. Huike's actions revealed a deep suffering of spirit, even stronger than what Bodhidharma had suspected. Perhaps Huike did sense the darkness Bodhidharma had seen within him and desperately had tried to dispel its mantle.

The old healer looked questioningly at Bodhidharma. Bodhidharma moved toward the pallet and instructed the healer to rest while he continued the sutra. The healer bowed and left, taking the young monk with him.

Bodhidharma watched Huike's restless sleep. As if sensing him, Huike opened his eyes. It was clear he was in great pain. "Will you teach me now?"

Bodhidharma took his hand. "You never had to ask. I said I could not teach you because I knew you would teach yourself."

Huike fell back asleep. Bodhidharma sat beside him until morning, feeling a love for this man as a father would for a son.

In the weeks that followed, Huike regained his strength and left the infirmary to join the other monks in Bodhidharma's tutelage. Bodhidharma had been horrified to find that no one could hold a simple seated meditation.

"Meditation is rigorous exercise and requires great stamina. How can you sit if you cannot even stand? Look at yourselves. You look like hunched monkeys."

Bodhidharma decided that the next weeks would be devoted to strengthening their bodies. The monks spent every day in the forest, learning exercises derived from Hatha and Raja yoga that Bodhidharma had modified further to enhance their bodies' energy flow.

At first, his unorthodox teachings met with resistance. The

Shaolin monks were accustomed to sitting at their desks all day, transcribing copies of Buddhist scriptures. Bodhidharma watched their exercises and shook his head, unsatisfied.

He tried to explain. "Qi is the life force that flows through all living things. Qigong teaches you how to harness this energy and bridge the gap between your body and your mind. But how can you do anything when your thoughts are so noisy? Quiet your mind." He took off his sandal. "You can start by staring at my shoe." He left it on the ground and walked away.

The students looked at each other questioningly. Huike called out, "Master, how long should we stare?"

Bodhidharma answered without turning back. "Until you find enlightenment."

They stared at the sandal for three days. Many gave up, unable to continue without food or water. When Bodhidharma finally retrieved his shoe, only Huike and two others remained.

The next day, he had the monks stare at a rock wall. The following day, they watched bugs mate. On the third day, they stood like trees from sunrise to sunset.

Bodhidharma circled his pupils. He was still unsatisfied. "Concentration. Confidence. Will. This is the path to internal strength. Huike, stop. You are no longer a tree. Take this iron rod and hit me on the head with it."

Huike's eyes widened. "But master, I can't!"

Bodhidharma ignored him and handed him the rod. "You will not hurt me." He stood in a perfect stance, his gaze fixed and focused now on his inward state. "Go on. Strike me with all your might."

Huike remained frozen. Bodhidharma glared at his best student and commanded him again, "Strike me!"

Huike raised the rod with his arm and brought it down hard on his master's head. The rod broke.

"Qigong," Bodhidharma said as he picked up the pieces. "By mastering it your mind can become insusceptible to pain. You possess more power than you can imagine." To drive his point home, he turned and sent his hand straight through a brick wall. "In time, you will be able to accomplish this and more."

Day after day, the relentless training continued. Many monks went to the infirmary to set broken bones and bandage wounds. But over time, they became stronger in mind and body than they had ever thought possible. Eventually they could break bricks, pierce tree trunks, and meditate for days on end as their Qi became more powerful.

At Abbot Fang's request, Bodhidharma dictated his exercises so there would be a guide for future Shaolin monks, and Huike transcribed his instructions. Bodhidharma knew his stay at the temple was coming to its end. He was an old man now, and India was calling.

On a beautiful spring day, much like the one when he had first arrived at the temple, Bodhidharma watched the monks performing their exercises in the forest. Huike stood beside him. Bodhidharma did not look at him as he spoke. "I have waited many years to tell you this and many times thought I would remain silent. . . . I have seen your soul's karma. It is heavy and keeps you from the Way, but that in itself is an illusion. Anyone can transcend their karma by seeing their true nature."

Huike frowned. "I do not understand, Master."

"One day you will remember this life, your earnestness, your goodness, and you will meet the malevolence that binds your spirit. On that day, let go of your shame at having fallen, and allow it to let in the light."

Huike nodded, his eyes bright with emotion.

"You hear these words now, but remember them when the time comes." Bodhidharma clasped Huike's hand. "We both have a long path ahead of us, my friend. Shine bright again one day."

◆

Bryan's consciousness returned to the hospital room with crystal clarity. He was not sure how long he had been under the drug, but he felt every cell in his body react as it tried to force it out of his system.

Bodhidharma's knowledge flooded his mind. Bryan stood up, and in one fluid movement pushed his right arm toward his left shoulder, brought it up over his head, unbuckled the sleeve with his teeth, and undid the five remaining buckles on the straitjacket with his hands. He stepped on one sleeve and tugged it away from his body—all in about fifteen seconds.

Once he was free, he folded the straitjacket and studied the door with a newfound serenity. The rage and fear that Bryan had felt toward Conrad had dissipated.

For the next hour, Bryan performed Qigong stretches to recharge his energy. His thoughts returned to the woman who had appeared before Bodhidharma during his long meditation. Bodhidharma had called her the Ancient One, but she was the Egyptian goddess.

Bryan pictured the symbol she had drawn for him on the ground at the Great Pyramid. He knew memories were waiting for him there. . . . She was trying to show him a life in Egypt. And he had only a few hours to remember it before Conrad came back to inject him with Renovo.

Bryan felt his initial panic start to return. He lay on the cot and forced his mind to quiet. As his breathing slowed and his body began to relax, he was filled with a new resolve: if he did not find the answers before Conrad returned to begin his experiment, he would use Bodhidharma's power to leave his body and never come back.

THIRTY-SEVEN

They threw Juliana into a damp cell blanketed in the stench of rot. A small barred window faced the square below, where the executions were being staged. The screams from outside rang out with chilling clarity over the jeers of the crowd. Juliana found herself drawn to the spectacle in disbelief. Tomorrow her voice would join the cacophony.

"Why do they hate us so?"

Juliana turned toward the shadows, squinting as she tried to see. A young woman was huddled in the corner, clutching a three-year-old girl. They looked filthy and starved.

Instinctively Juliana took a step forward to offer some kind of comfort, but realized she had nothing to give.

The young woman gaped at her. "I know you. You're Origenes Adamantius' lady."

"Pupil," Juliana corrected, quite accustomed to strangers assuming they were lovers. He would not have been the first priest to fall from grace, but Juliana knew that Origenes would never transgress—he couldn't. As a young man, he had castrated himself in an act of deep piety and sacrifice, to ensure that he would never be swayed by bodily desire. His life would be for God and God alone.

Juliana was a Christian lady from a wealthy family and well educated. She had met Origenes years ago when he had come to visit the Bishop of Caesarea. She had been a young woman then and was quite dazzled by his brilliance. They had formed a fast bond while studying the biblical texts she had inherited, written by Symmachus—the original author of one of the Greek versions of the Old Testament. How many nights they talked, until the candles burned low, about how to change Rome. How to spread love. How to bring about a better world. And in her heart of hearts—in words spoken only to God—Juliana had confessed her love for him as a woman. A part of her had always wondered if, had he not castrated himself, Origenes would have been tempted to deepen their bond.

She knew Origenes sensed how she felt. He would often tell her that there were many kinds of love and that, for her, he had reserved the purist. One night, they had become engaged in a passionate debate after drinking several cups of wine. Origenes had reached out and taken her hand and said that God must have known she would come into his life. Why else would he have guided him to perform such a sacrifice with his body? Otherwise, he might have fallen from grace.

Juliana could hear her heart beating like a bird in a cage as he spoke. Then his hand was gone and he went on as if nothing had happened. They never spoke of it again.

"My brother says Origenes' school is the finest in the empire and marvels even those in Alexandria," the young woman said, bringing Juliana out of her thoughts.

"Yes, it does," Juliana replied. But their efforts to teach God's love had brought them here to die horrific deaths. She fought back her panic and tried to focus on the young woman before her.

"Are you to burn too?" the little girl whispered.

Juliana gave the woman a questioning look, not wanting to upset the little girl.

The woman nodded. "Septimus has ordered us both to burn in two days' time," she answered.

Septimus was the government official in charge of the executions, and a soulless man who had allowed the world's barbarity to eat away at his heart. Juliana couldn't understand what she had done to earn his hatred. She closed her eyes, and her thumb traced a circle around her index finger. It was something she often did to quiet her mind. She tried to envision where she would go when she left her body . . . if God would take her and show her heaven, and if she would be born again, as Origenes believed.

She had once asked him why he thought the soul returned to earth, and he answered that God gives us too much to learn in one life. But then Origenes saw the world on a grander scale than most. Juliana believed it was because his mind soared closer to heaven. It was tragic that men like Septimus cared nothing for his knowledge.

She did not know where the guards had taken him, and a shiver coursed through her body. Knowing that he would soon die for his beliefs gave her the strength to cling to her own.

◆

After Linz had returned from the cemetery she had taken another dose of Renovo. Juliana's memories had come minutes later. Bryan's painting was still hanging on the wall across from her bed, and it became her lifeline as she fought to return to the present.

Her hands were shaking as she tried to call him, but he didn't pick up. Her voice sounded foreign to her as she left a message. "Bryan? I'm coming over. Please be there."

She gathered her purse and keys and opened the front door at the same time as her neighbors. The young couple gasped when they saw her.

The man took a step toward her out of concern. "Are you okay?"

Linz jumped back. "Fine. I'm recovering from . . ." *Being burned at the stake? Destroying my apartment?* "A car accident." She closed the door on them before they could say anything else.

"Jesus." *What horrid timing.* She must look certifiable. Her mind was out of control, spinning with multiple realities. Hysterical laughter bubbled up inside her. She was beginning to get an inkling of how Bryan had felt all his life.

She heard someone else in the hall and decided she'd better make an attempt to clean herself up. But when she opened the door to her bathroom, she walked right into Diana's office—the same night she had died.

Diana put the puzzles she had collected over the years in the pile of things that would be left behind, reminding herself she could only take absolute necessities. They had just a few more hours before people would start to show up for work—hardly enough time to pack up years of research. Her office looked like it had been demolished. A mountain of boxes sat stacked near the door.

She could hear Finn and Michael in the lab disassembling equipment. They would put everything in Finn's van and drive it out of the city before dawn. Michael and Diana would follow in their car. All loose ends could be handled by phone or mail. The most essential thing was for them to disappear.

Diana joined the men. "Okay, I think that's everything."

The lab door closed behind her with a bang, startling them. The new deadbolt that Michael had just installed the previous morning clicked decisively. Someone had locked them in.

"What the hell?" Diana ran to the door. Michael and Finn were right behind her. Their keys were in the control room.

Conrad's voice came in over the mic. "You seriously didn't think adding a lock would keep me away, did you?"

They turned toward the glass window to the control room, where Conrad stood in the dark. "This was going to be our great experiment. And now you decide to scrap it all and run away."

Michael approached the glass. "Conrad, open the door."

Conrad leaned forward until his face became fully visible. "I'm here to offer you a second chance. You want full recall, Mike. I can give you that."

Michael hesitated. "What are you talking about?"

"While you were all away having your nervous breakdowns, I resynthesized the formula to make it even more powerful. With one dose you can retrieve everything. Including the lifetime that's eluding you—the one in Egypt."

Michael took another step closer. "What do you know about Egypt?"

"I know you feel the memory eating away at you, like an itch you can't scratch. Every night you go to sleep wondering, what's this life for? What's my purpose? Knowing that something more awaits you. I can help you find it." Conrad smiled, dangling the carrot in front of him.

Diana put her hand on her husband's arm. "He's lying."

Michael didn't take his eyes off Conrad. "You really reformulated it?"

Conrad nodded to the vial sitting innocently on an empty desk in the lab.

"What about last night?" Michael reminded him. "Eight hours ago you had your hands around my throat."

"When you came I wasn't myself. I had just remembered . . . something." He gave them a placating smile. "Simple bad timing. I'm here to offer you an olive branch and proof of what a real scientist can do. Take it or leave it."

Finn stepped in front of Michael and whispered, "He's completely lost it. You can't tell me you're considering this."

"If he has changed the formula, then I want to know what it does."

Diana shook his arm. "But you don't have to take it. That's crazy."

Michael remained silent.

Finn nodded in agreement and started to fidget. He was barely functioning himself. "This is a bad call, chief."

Conrad leaned into the microphone. "Is your little powwow over? Mike, you need to remember Egypt. It's imperative."

"Okay, is it just me or has Yankee Doodle officially gone off his rocker?" Finn erupted. "Mike, you can't be buying this load of crap. He's locked us in!"

"Honey, for Christ's sake, please listen to Finn."

Michael had not taken his eyes off Conrad. "I need to do this."

Diana kept pleading with him. "But don't you see? He was here before us and left that vial there. He was sure that he could get you to do it." She could tell she still wasn't convincing him and tried another tactic. "Is this worth risking your life over?"

"There's something I have to remember—a life. Please try to understand."

Diana spoke to him in Russian as Natalia, Pushkin's wife. *"Just like you had to challenge D'Anthès to a duel? Are you so ready to die again?"*

Michael brushed her hair away from her face and said, *"Forgive me."*

She turned away from him, unwilling to help. She heard him climb onto the table and administer the injection himself.

Michael instructed Finn to hook him up to the EEG. He lay back on the table, and his body immediately went slack.

Finn did as Michael requested and then glared at Conrad through the glass window. "You got what you wanted. Now unlock the door. Let Diana monitor him from the control room."

Conrad looked undecided, but he left the control room. Moments later, Diana and Finn heard the lab door unlock.

Finn turned to Diana. "Go. I'll join you in a minute."

Diana nodded. She did want to monitor Michael from the control room. When she stepped out into the hallway and saw Conrad, she felt sick. Without a word, she hurried away from him, but at the sound of the lab door being locked again she whirled around.

Conrad pocketed the keys.

"What are you doing?" she demanded.

"Making sure there are no interruptions." He saluted her and headed to the elevator.

Fear rose up inside her. "Conrad, open the door or I'm calling the police."

Conrad got into the elevator and gave her a sad smile. "I'm sorry, Diana. This needs to happen."

❧

Diana sprinted to the control room. Through the glass, she saw Finn bent over, checking equipment at the back wall. Michael was lying on the table, but he wasn't moving. She checked the monitors. His pulse rate had skyrocketed and the EEG was going ballistic.

Diana turned on the microphone. "Something's seriously wrong. We need to get him to the hospital."

Michael remained deathly still, his eyes closed.

Finn was still busy with the equipment. He looked tense.

"Finn? What's going on?"

Finn didn't look up. His fingers were fumbling with something. It was the first time Diana had ever seen him in a complete state of panic.

"Finn, talk to me."

"I need a minute here. Find the keys and unlock the door. I'm pretty sure we have a gas leak."

The lab had several natural gas sources: gas spigots, a gas line to the chemical fume hood, and a row of canisters used to fuel the burners. Diana tried to stay calm as she rifled through drawers looking for the keys. Conrad must have taken them all.

She reached for the phone to call the police. "The phone's dead," she said as cold dread began to take hold of her. "You need to get out of there. I'm going to try and break the glass."

Finn ordered, "No, don't. Just come unlock the door. I think I found the leak."

Ignoring him, she grabbed a high-back desk chair with metal legs and managed to lift it chest level—just as the explosion shattered the glass wall into a thousand pieces.

The blast threw her into the air and launched her backward. Her body smashed against the wall of the control room and crumbled to the floor.

It took her a moment to refocus. Her arms were bleeding and covered in shards of glass. The chair had shielded her from the brunt of the blast, and she didn't seem to have any other injuries.

She stood up in a daze and saw that Finn was on fire. Without thinking, she jumped through the broken window and ran to the fire extinguisher. She fumbled with it and finally managed to spray him down. He lay on the ground unconscious.

There was another deafening boom. The fire had found the sodium azide, a dangerous chemical used to synthesize drugs that became explosive under heat.

Diana saw Michael, still immobile on the table. She screamed at him over the roar of the flames, "Michael!" But the fire was about to ensnare Finn again. With strength she didn't know she possessed, Diana hauled Finn's body to the control room window and managed to hoist him up and drop him on the other side.

With Finn safe from the fire's path, she ran to Michael before the flames could separate them. She shook him as hard as she could. "Michael? Wake up."

Nothing.

She struggled to detach the sensors and slide him off the table, but she couldn't pick him up. His body was too heavy. They both collapsed in a heap on the ground. She wrestled with his dead weight and squirmed out from under him.

Grabbing his feet, she pulled him across the room as the fire stalked them. A wall of flames blocked the path to the control room. Her only option was to get to the lab door.

"Come on! Come on!" she shouted at him, even though he couldn't hear her. With superhuman strength, she half carried, half dragged his body to the door and then crumpled against it. Unable to breathe, she took off her shirt and wrapped it around her hand and tried the doorknob. It was still locked.

First she banged on the window, then she tried to break the glass with her foot. "Help! Somebody get us out."

With a sob she realized no one would come. The smoke had encased them like a tomb. They were both about to die.

She cradled Michael in her arms and watched him sleep, wondering where his mind had gone. Was he remembering the life in Egypt that he had yearned for? She was just thankful he would never remember this.

Numb with shock, Diana looked at her feet—her shoes were on fire. She put her lips to Michael's and whispered, with her last breath, "Find me."

When Linz opened her eyes, she was gasping for air, suffocating on Diana's memories—she and her husband just died. Cries came from deep within her soul. She had remembered too much too quickly.

She was sprawled on her bathroom floor. Forcing her muscles to move, she picked herself up. Her hands and body shook uncontrollably as she splashed water on her face. She put her head on the edge of the sink and left the water running. Her chest heaved as she struggled to breathe. Her father . . . she couldn't even think about her father right now, or she would lose every last shred of sanity she possessed. She needed Michael—no, Bryan . . . her mind was so confused.

Unable to drive, Linz took a taxi to Bryan's place. She ignored the elevator and ran blindly up the stairs. But as she approached Bryan's door, she slowed. It was already open.

"Hello?" She walked in and found the place was trashed. Michael and Diana's boxes were gone, the Super 8 projector had been smashed to pieces, and all of the films were missing.

But the worst was the studio. Every canvas had been splattered with black paint—the paintings had been destroyed.

Linz sank to her knees in despair. Only one painting had been spared, a magnificent lifesize portrait of an Egyptian goddess. Linz had never seen it before. It was a masterpiece, clearly the best Bryan had ever done.

Linz gazed at the goddess's face, at the beautiful being created by Bryan's hand. Sobs racked her body. She covered her face with her hands, unable to look anymore. She knew who had done this—and it meant he had Bryan.

There was only one person who could help her find him. And now that she had her memories back, she understood why he had been so afraid.

THIRTY-EIGHT

Ten o'clock on a Friday night was too late to be knocking on Finn's door, but Linz didn't care. She rang the doorbell repeatedly and kept rapping with the brass knocker until the door finally opened. It was Finn who answered, dressed in a robe and dark-tinted eyeglasses.

Her words barreled out at once. "Finn, Conrad has him. I didn't know where else to go. Michael—Bryan's missing. He has him. He—Conrad—he locked the door. It's happening all over again. I barely got you out." She gripped her head in agony and sank to her knees. "Oh God. I'm going crazy. What have we done?" Her body began to shiver.

Finn knelt beside her and took her pulse. "How long have you been taking it?" Linz couldn't stop trembling. He held her arms and asked again, "Linz. How long has it been?"

"Today. Four doses." She realized how she must look to him and started to stand. "I'm sorry. I shouldn't have come here."

Like a hurt animal she turned to leave. But instead, Finn guided her inside to his study. When he spoke, his voice was soothing. "You're adjusting. Trying to assimilate another lifetime with your own—perhaps several. It's incredibly difficult to do. We asked ourselves the same questions."

He sat her on the couch and wrapped a blanket around her. The fireplace was lit, and the room felt warm and safe.

Linz gazed at the flames and shuddered. When she spoke, her words were quiet. "How do I live with what's in my mind?"

Finn studied her a long time, as if weighing a decision. He went to his desk and returned with photographs. "This would have been Diana's last memory."

Linz gasped when she saw them. They were photographs of the lab after the accident, identical to her vision.

Finn hesitated. "I never thought I would be given a chance to thank you for pulling me from the fire," he said, his voice barely a whisper.

Linz looked at him, remembering how he had been before the accident . . . such a beautiful man. She couldn't begin to imagine his devastation.

They sat together in silence. Tears ran down Linz's cheeks. "I've been fighting my heart. I've been fighting my heart my entire life—keeping it dead so I wouldn't recognize the truth. How can I face him?" She couldn't even bring herself to call Conrad her father anymore. "I'm his daughter, but Diana's memories are mine now. And I'm imagining the worst for Bryan. I know he has him."

Finn squeezed her hand. "We'll find him. Think—where would Conrad take him? Someplace safe, where no one would ask questions."

Linz shook her head. She had no idea.

Finn kept pressing her, "What hospitals and research centers does Medicor work closely with?"

Linz answered easily. "Medicor owns St. Mary's, Forest Green, and Park Plaza."

"Medicor owns Forest Green Psychiatric Center?" Finn asked, sounding alarmed.

"It was one of the first facilities he acquired. Why?" Then it hit her. "Our test patients. They were all from there."

Finn brooded. "It's also one of the only facilities that perform psychosurgery and other experimental studies."

"If he's there . . ." Linz tried not to panic. "How do we even find out?"

Finn tapped his fingers on the desk. Linz remembered the gesture well.

"Assuming he is," she said, "I can't just waltz in and sign him out. I'm not a physician."

"Then we need to find one."

Something clicked in Linz's mind—*Bryan's file*. "His mother." Finn gave her a questioning look and she explained, "Conrad had Bryan investigated. I remember reading that his mother is a psychiatrist, a very prominent one. She even does psychiatric screenings for the Boston Police on high-profile cases."

"Then she could help," Finn said. "But what will you tell her?"

❧

Linz drove Finn's Navigator to Bryan's parents' house. The GPS system instructed her to turn right and indicated that the car was almost at its destination. Luckily, Linz had remembered the address from the file. She remembered everything from it.

She turned into a charming residential neighborhood called Newton Highlands, and her thoughts returned to her most immediate problem—what in the world she was going to say to Bryan's mother. No one went knocking on doors in the middle of the night asking people if they could help rescue their son from a mental institution. Especially on a street where every family probably had two perfect children who made lemonade stands in the summer. It was hard to even visualize Bryan growing up here.

The brass plated number on the antique mailbox signaled that she'd found the right address. As she pulled up in front of an immaculate 1920s Colonial with clapboard siding, she noticed the glow of a light upstairs. *At least they were still awake.* Still not quite sure what to say, Linz got out of the car and went to the front door. She rang the doorbell twice.

A minute later a light in the downstairs hall came on, followed by the porch light. A woman's voice asked, "Who is it?"

"My name is Linz Jacobs. I'm a close friend of Bryan's." She could feel herself being scrutinized through the peephole. "I realize it's late. I wouldn't be here if it wasn't urgent. Bryan's in trouble."

The door unlocked and swung open. *Holy shit.* Linz's mind went blank with shock. "Barbara?" she gasped.

"Yes, I'm Barbara Pierce, Bryan's mother. What is this about?"

Linz covered her mouth—she couldn't believe Bryan's mother was Michael's ex-girlfriend. She remembered that Diana and Barbara had met a few times, always with civility. Sometime after Michael and Barbara had broken up, Barbara started dating Michael's best friend, Doc. For obvious reasons the four never did any couple's outings. Now here she was thirty years later.

Linz tried to stop gawking, knowing she must look crazy. "I'm sorry to call so late. May I come in?"

Barbara hesitated a moment and let her in.

Linz entered, still unsure of how to explain herself. She decided to keep things simple. "Bryan is missing. His apartment's been vandalized."

Barbara gasped and headed to the phone.

"Wait," Linz stopped her. "Don't call the police. I know where he is."

"Where?" Barbara demanded, her hand hovering over the phone.

"Forest Green Psychiatric Center."

Barbara didn't put the phone down. "What in God's name is he doing there?"

"I don't have all the answers, but let's just say a very powerful man has taken an interest in Bryan's dreams and is holding him against his will."

"That's unbelievable. How are you involved in all this?" Barbara looked at Linz as if she was the one who had taken him. "I *am* calling the police."

"Barbara, I need you to trust me. I would never hurt your son. I love him." Linz took a deep breath, somehow managing to hold her emotions in check. "The best way you can help him is to come with me right now to Forest Green and get him out before they can do anything to him. You have privileges there." Barbara seemed to be sizing Linz up. Linz pleaded, "You have to believe me."

Barbara hesitated only a moment and grabbed her purse.

Linz tried to concentrate on driving while she listened to Barbara on her cell phone. "No, stay at the bar. I'll call you when I know more." She could hear Doc's voice on the other end. He sounded distraught, but Barbara interrupted him, "Honey, I will call you when I know more. We're almost there."

She hung up. The two women drove on in silence. They had already discussed their plan. Now they just needed to see if it would work.

A simple wooden plaque marked the entrance to one of the country's largest psychiatric hospitals. Linz had never been inside Forest Green, but she had driven past it every day when she had interned at the Health Alliance the summer after her freshman year in college. The serenity of the winding drive and the quaint guardhouse was all an illusion, though. The place was more of a prison than a hospital. Only the most difficult patients ended up there, people in advanced stages of psychosis or mental disease who had no hope of a cure, and were admitted either by their families or law enforcement agencies. The idea that Bryan could be somewhere inside filled her with horror.

Barbara pointed. "Take a left here."

"I know," Linz murmured. A minute later she coasted up to the guardhouse and rolled down her window. The young guard on duty motioned for her to stop.

Barbara leaned over. "I'm here to see a patient." She handed him her ID.

The guard logged her into the computer. "Thank you, Dr. Pierce." He looked questioningly at Linz.

Barbara said, "This is my daughter. I can't drive at night. It's all right if she waits in the lounge, isn't it?"

Linz tried to give him her most flirtatious look. He smiled back and said, "Of course," and hurried to open the gate.

Inside, the nurse at reception logged them in and gave each of them a badge. She looked annoyed at having been interrupted from the show streaming on her iPad. "Which patient are you here to see?"

Barbara quickly glanced at Linz. "He's a John Doe. Brought in yesterday, I believe. We're still working with the police on identifying him. I just got the request for the psych eval, so I'm not sure what room he's in."

The nurse looked even more annoyed now that she had to get on her computer. She scrolled through the log. "Nope, sorry, no John Doe."

Barbara didn't miss a beat. "Then perhaps his identification was found, and I wasn't notified of the status change. Could you look at the list of check-ins for yesterday? White male, age 30."

The nurse gave them a pained look, but she checked the database again. "Sorry, I—" she stopped. "Wait, there's someone unregistered in Room 450, came in yesterday. It has to be him."

Barbara and Linz glanced at each other. Barbara gave the nurse a smile. "Thank you. You just saved me a trip back tomorrow."

She put on her badge and led Linz to the elevators. They stepped in and waited until the doors shut before they said anything to one another. Barbara physically sagged when she spoke. "I could lose my license for this, or worse. This better be my son."

Linz wasn't about to admit that their whole rescue attempt was based on a gut feeling.

The elevator doors opened. Barbara nodded for Linz to wait by an assortment of chairs and sofas that served as a lounge. The hallway was a long row of windowless doors, each equipped with a serious-looking keypad and a small surveillance monitor that allowed visitors to see inside the room.

No one sat at the nurses' station. A chilling silence pervaded the entire floor. Barbara hurried to room 450 and pressed the view button on the monitor. Whatever she saw made her cry out, but she quickly recovered.

Barbara took a second to fully compose herself and walked back to the nurses' station. On her way, she locked eyes with Linz and nodded yes—Bryan was here. She reached the station and hurried behind the desk. She began rifling through the patient files and managed to find the one marked "John Doe: 450" just as the nurse on shift rounded the corner with a medicine tray.

"What are you doing?" the nurse demanded.

Barbara turned around, flashing her badge. "I'm here to check out my patient in 450." Flipping open the file, she scribbled something in the comments section and signed.

The nurse took the file from her and looked at it in confusion. "But he's scheduled for a procedure in the morning. I need authorization."

"A procedure?" Barbara said. "On whose goddamn authority?"

"Conrad Jacobs'." The nurse put her hands on her hips.

Linz could see the situation spiraling out of control. Barbara was about to blow it. She hurried over, pulling out another badge, and said, "Dr. Pierce is coming late to the table. We've decided to postpone the procedure. My father asked me to handle this for him personally." She handed the nurse her Medicor ID.

Barbara looked at Linz's card with as much surprise as the nurse. Linz added, "Please call an orderly to assist us with transport."

But the nurse continued to hold Linz's card in her hand. She didn't pick up the phone.

Linz snatched her card back and tried to infuse her voice with icy displeasure. "If you have a problem, you're welcome to contact my father, but I can guarantee he will not be happy to hear from you."

The nurse looked angry, but she was too intimidated to argue.

Barbara held out her hand. "I need the keycard to the room. Have the orderly bring a gurney."

The nurse handed over the keycard and watched them walk down the hallway. Once they were out of earshot, Barbara hissed, "Why didn't you tell me who you were?"

Linz settled for the truth. "Because I knew it was my father who was holding him and I needed you to trust me."

"He's going to have hell to pay."

"Believe me, I want nothing more. Let's just get Bryan out of here first."

They reached the door and unlocked it. Bryan was asleep on the cot, using the straitjacket as a blanket. Linz rushed to his side.

"Bryan? Can you hear me?"

"Dreaming," Bryan mumbled.

Linz gave him a gentle shake. "Wake up! This isn't a dream."
He smiled. "Yes it is."

Barbara crouched down too, her voice loud and firm. "Bryan, honey, this isn't a dream." She picked up the straitjacket with a repulsed look on her face and threw it in the corner. "We're here to get you the hell out of here."

Bryan's eyes flew open. He was beyond stunned to see them both. Then he looked at Linz and saw a new light in her eyes, and he realized what she had done. She kissed his hand and nodded. His questions would have to wait.

"I need you to act unconscious," Barbara instructed him. "An orderly's on his way."

A minute later a big hulk of a man arrived. His skull and bones tattoos were hardly reassuring. Barbara squeezed Bryan's leg in warning and he closed his eyes, letting his body go limp.

The orderly's face was a stamp of indifference. "Transport?" he asked.

"We're parked at the service entrance," Barbara snapped. "What's he been given?"

"Midazolam. You don't need the jacket? He gave us problems earlier."

Midazolam was a potent sedative normally used on patients who were going into surgery. Barbara looked ready to wrap the straitjacket around his throat. "No. Let's go." She marched to the elevators and gave the nurse a curt nod. Linz followed the orderly and tried not to look over her shoulder.

The nurse watched them leave. As the elevator doors closed, Linz saw the woman looking for something in Bryan's file—most likely the phone number that she should call if anything unexpected arose.

❧

Downstairs in the parking lot, the orderly eyed the SUV with a perplexed look on his face. "You sure you don't want secure transport?"

Linz knew she sounded rude, but their time was running out. "He's unconscious. Can we hurry this up?"

The orderly lifted Bryan like a baby and put him in the backseat. Linz jumped behind the driver's seat and started the car.

Barbara hurried to move the gurney and got into the passenger seat. "Thanks for your help," she said to the orderly, before shutting the door quickly. She turned to Linz and whispered under her breath, "Go, now."

Linz drove just over the speed limit, trying to get past the guard station. His phone started to ring, but he had already gone to lift the rail. By the time he picked it up, Linz had already gunned it out of the drive.

She looked in her rearview mirror and saw him frantically trying to wave her down. She found little comfort in the fact that he didn't pull his weapon or pursue them.

It was far more dangerous that her father knew.

THIRTY-NINE

"Would someone please tell me what the hell is going on?" Barbara erupted.

Linz continued driving, checking the rearview mirror every few seconds. Bryan leaned forward and reached out his hand to his mother. She squeezed it tight. "I have never been so scared in my life. Are you all right? Did they hurt you?"

"I'm fine. I promise."

But Barbara didn't seem to hear the words. She was on the verge of hysteria. "The nurse was talking about some procedure. What in God's name were they going to do to you?"

"I don't know," Bryan lied. The less she knew, he thought, the better.

"Well, they just messed with the wrong family. I'm shutting that place down." She turned to Linz. "And your father is going to jail for a very long time." She got out her cell phone.

"I agree with you," Linz muttered. Seeing Bryan inside that room had broken something inside of her and removed any doubts she had about her father.

Bryan reached out for Barbara's phone. "Mom, wait. No calls."

Barbara gaped at him. "You were kidnapped, Bryan. I'm calling the police and then our lawyer."

"Please don't."

"Why the hell not?"

Linz and Bryan's eyes met in the rearview mirror. Linz answered,

"Because it will be our word against his. There's no record Bryan was ever there. My father will erase every trace of him."

"We can't just pretend nothing happened!" Barbara shouted.

Bryan put his hand on her shoulder, trying to calm her down. "We won't. Just give us some time. I need you and Dad to go away for the weekend, check into a hotel."

"You're joking. I'm not leaving you."

Bryan insisted, "I need to know that you both will be safe. Linz and I are going to deal with her father."

"The man who had you kidnapped? Honey, you can't fix this by yourself. Right now we need the police."

"And the police can't do anything. You don't understand what I'm dealing with. I need to do this my way!" Bryan paused. When he spoke again, he sounded calmer. "Someday I'll tell you everything, but right now I need you to trust me."

They drove in silence the rest of the way, until Linz pulled up in front of Barbara's house.

Barbara turned to Bryan and tried again. "This is not going to fly with your father. He just won't leave like this."

"Then you have to convince him," Bryan said.

"Don't put this on me. Come talk to him. He'll be home any minute."

"He'll only ask questions I can't answer." Bryan insisted, "You need to go pack an overnight bag and be ready to leave when he gets home. You can explain things to him in the car."

Barbara put her hand over her mouth. She looked like she was about to break down.

Bryan got out and opened her door. "Just give me a few days. I'm sorry to put you through this. Thank you for getting me out." Bryan tried to reassure her. "We'll be fine. I promise."

"I want a number where I can reach you, and I want you to check in with me every day." Barbara added, "You have until Monday. Then we're going to do this my way."

Bryan nodded, willing to agree to anything that might buy him and Linz more time. He gave her a hug. "Please do what I asked," he reminded her.

She squeezed him tight. "Be careful."

He got into the passenger seat and rolled down the window. "Tell Dad I love him. I'll call you soon." He tapped Linz's leg—a silent cue for her to drive—and waved good-bye to his mother. As they drove off, he leaned his seat back and let out a deep breath.

Linz looked over at him. "I'm sorry. I couldn't see any other way."

"No, you did the right thing."

They drove on in silence, each of them dealing with the shock of the last twenty-four hours. No more walls stood between them.

Bryan closed his eyes and asked, "Whose car is this?"

"Finn's. He helped. How the hell are you even awake with midazolam in your system?"

"I remembered a life as a yogi. Mind over matter."

Linz gave him a sideways glance. "You're serious?"

He cracked open one eye and peeked at her. "Yeah. You stayed in India. I went to China to train Shaolin monks."

They both burst into laughter, as if that was the most hysterical thing either of them had ever heard.

"I can't believe your mom is Barbara," Linz added, and they doubled up even harder.

"I wish I could have seen your face when she opened the door."

They laughed until they had tears in their eyes. "Stop, I can't breathe," Linz begged. She took several calming breaths and grew serious again. "So what do we do now?"

"I don't know. I'm thinking."

"We need to hide, leave Boston until we can figure this out."

"Agreed." Bryan straightened up. "Where's your passport?"

Linz shot him a look. "My house. Why?"

"Let's get it, then swing by my place."

"Why do we need passports?"

"To go to Egypt."

Linz pulled over and turned on the hazards lights. She was beginning to feel light-headed. "You want us to go to Egypt?"

"Conrad is obsessed with getting me to remember a life there. That's what the procedure was for. The answer to everything is in

Egypt. I've had . . . dreams about it." Bryan refrained from sharing anything else. He wasn't ready to talk about it.

Linz chewed on this information, remembering what Conrad had said before Michael and Diana had died. The key did lie in Egypt.

She thought about the Egyptian goddess painting and realized it had been left untouched to taunt them. Her heart began to ache again at the thought of how his studio had looked, every painting a black void.

Bryan looked at her, concerned. "What?"

"I went to your place to look for you. Someone had broken in, and everything was trashed. All your paintings were . . ." She couldn't bring herself to say it.

Bryan processed the news with little emotion. "They're just paintings. I could do them all over again if I wanted to."

"How can you say that? It's your work, your creations." She could feel herself getting weepy.

"Because I really could paint them all again. They're just memories," Bryan said softly, "road maps to help me get here . . . to get to you. I don't need them anymore. I just need my passport."

"What if it's been taken?"

"I keep it hidden. We have to go to Cairo," Bryan repeated. "You know we do."

"We can't just fly off to Egypt."

"Why not? We both have the money."

"What about Finn?"

"We'll give him an update when we get there," he reasoned. "Say we needed to lay low for a while."

"For how long?" she asked.

"I don't know. Until we have enough leverage against Conrad. Do you have a better idea?"

She didn't. Her mind and heart felt so battered she just wanted to curl up and cry. Part of her was still unable to believe that her father was really capable of hurting them. But he had already shown his willingness to inflict harm on Bryan, and that was enough.

She shook her head. "It's too dangerous to go back to either of our places. He could have people watching them."

"So we send someone else."

"Who?"

"I don't know." Bryan threw up his hands, sounding frustrated. "Penelope? Isn't she your oldest friend?"

Linz was about to voice another objection, but Bryan stopped her. "I know this has to be unbearable for you. You've been bombarded with realities you didn't know existed and are having to face truths about your father . . . about what he did . . ."

They both sat quietly together, dealing with the weight of the past.

Bryan took her hand. "We found each other again for a reason. We remembered for a reason. This journey didn't start with us or even with Michael and Diana. We're locked in a cycle. We need to see beyond it."

◆

Even though it was well past midnight, the lights inside Conrad's home still glowed. He was on the phone in his office. "What time did she check him out? No. It was a last-minute transfer. I'm sorry no one called."

He hung up and went to the liquor cabinet. He was about to pour himself a Scotch but instead threw the glass against the wall, shattering it to pieces.

With a growl, he strode into the next room, took a samurai sword down from the gallery wall, and sliced the air with the blade again and again.

◆

The Holiday Inn was just three minutes away from the airport. Linz and Bryan had already booked their flight to Cairo. Their plane would leave at 5 p.m. the next day. Penelope had agreed to pick up Finn's car in the morning and bring their passports and an overnight bag with some of their clothes. She had a million questions, but Linz had promised her that she would explain everything when she got back. Now all they had to do was wait for morning.

Bryan and Linz got into the shower together. They took in each other's bodies and washed like lovers, as if they had known intimacy for years.

"I was so scared," Linz whispered. "It was like everything was happening all over again, and I wouldn't be able to save you this time either."

"You did save me," Bryan said, moving her hair away from her eyes. "I'm sorry I couldn't tell you everything before."

In answer, she took a step closer and kissed him. All fear fell away forgotten. It was time for their bodies to remember.

FORTY

Sirius, the star of Isis, had been invisible for seventy days. Today would be its last day in hiding. Every year the star vanished for seventy days, and awaiting its return was considered to be a time of preparation for rebirth. On the seventy-first day, the city of Heliopolis held a celebration, where everyone came together and united.

Thoth looked down at the city from his favorite vantage point. He did not mind the rain. Today nothing could affect his mood. He always looked forward to Sirius's return and all of the promise it held, and this year, the celebration marked the happiest day of his life—the day he would finally meet Hermese.

It had taken him seven years to win the chance to meet her. Hermese had been born the High Priestess of the House of Atum—the only child of the Guardian of the Great Pyramid, and the next in line to become Guardian herself.

It was forbidden for anyone in the House of Atum to speak with a commoner. Since the pyramids had been built, they had lived away from the city in a temple fortress—no one even knew how many the House of Atum numbered. The Guardians continued their lineage by taking a lover from the city to conceive a child. They were not allowed to marry. After the birth, the chosen man or woman had to return to their homes in Heliopolis and could never see either the Guardian or their child again.

This practice had been in place as long as anyone could remember, and it was an honor to be chosen. If the next Guardian in line happened to be a female, when the time came for her to choose her partner, the city would hold a great tournament before Sirius's return, and all of the eligible young men would come forward to demonstrate their virility.

These were games of goodwill, and the tournament only allowed the use of wooden sticks; contestants never suffered anything more than bruises or mild injuries. Stick fighting was an ancient sport, and it had ceremonial aspects as well. The warriors wielded their weapons with a speed and agility that was akin to dancing.

Thoth had never witnessed a tournament, although he had trained for one all his life. The current Guardian was a man, and years ago, when he had been ready to sire a child, there had been a grand pageant, where every eligible maiden was presented before him at a dance. Now that his daughter, Hermese, was of age, the city was ecstatic.

The tournament had lasted two weeks—and for those two weeks Thoth had fought for her. In the end, it had come down to him and his older brother, Seth.

They had sparred for hours in the rain, to the wild cheers of the crowd. By day's end, they had each exhausted six sticks. When they simultaneously broke their seventh, the two mud-caked brothers bowed to Hermese and took a break for water and bread.

During the next round, Seth won the match. He was older, stronger, and the more seasoned fighter, and he had been considered the favorite from the beginning. But to everyone's shock, Hermese chose Thoth as her champion. That Seth won the tournament but not the prize caused a great stir—and it strengthened the divide between the brothers.

The rift had occurred after the tragic death of Seth's wife, Kiya, who had died during childbirth, along with their newborn son. Seth had been away on a hunting party and had not been present. Instead, Thoth had been the one at Kiya's bedside, holding her hand through her pain and witnessing the moment her spirit left her body.

Even the Guardian's daughter, Hermese, had come to take part in Kiya's death ceremony. Kiya had been Hermese's playmate as a child, chosen from hundreds to be her companion. She had spent most of her childhood with the House of Atum, where she had been treated like royalty, and when her time at the temple fortress had come to an end, Hermese's family had showered her with gifts and wealth. Thoth had heard Kiya tell countless stories about what it was like growing up with Hermese, whom she had loved more than a sister.

When Hermese came to pay her respects, it was the first time Thoth had ever caught a glimpse of her. She had stood on the tallest dais in the Sun Temple, but even from afar he could not mistake her tears. That had been seven years ago, and he had loved her ever since.

Seth had returned a week after Kiya's passing. He was inconsolable, and his grief gave way to resentment when he discovered that Thoth had been the one to comfort her. He had never forgiven himself, or Thoth, for not being the one by her side. With Kiya and his son gone, his heart had hardened into a bitter seed.

When Seth had announced that he would participate in the tournament for the Guardian that spring, Thoth had hoped this was a sign that the old Seth had returned. But as they sparred, he had seen the look in his brother's eyes, and he realized that the bitterness had grown into something much worse—a dark animus against life. Thoth believed that, if Kiya had only lived, Seth would have been a different man. Perhaps Hermese had sensed this as well.

Thoth planned to ask her why she chose him after their first meeting. He would be allowed to enter the temple fortress tonight, on the eve of Sirius's return.

By that afternoon, the rains had subsided in time for the grand procession to lead Thoth to the Temple of Atum. He would be the only person allowed inside. The pyramid complex was a quarter day's journey from Heliopolis, and the crowd had now begun to gather at the temple gates, which had been adorned with thousands of white lotus flowers for the occasion.

Thoth's father, Ramses, opened the gate. Seth was noticeably absent.

His father embraced him. "Horus smiles on us this day."

Thoth looked at his father, surprised by his choice of words. Horus had been the last ruler of the first settlers of Old Egypt. Horus' parents, Osiris and Isis, had been the original Guardians of the pyramid, and had supposedly lived for centuries. They had died hundreds of years ago, but Thoth still knew the legends: After the Great War, the last of the super beings had journeyed to Egypt, bringing all of their knowledge and wisdom with them. They built the Great Pyramid and its two sisters, along with the Sphinx, the temples, and all of Heliopolis. It was an attempt to salvage the way life had been before the Great War—a time in history that the people called the First Time, a time before the war had brought disease, death, greed, and rage to mankind. The last Guardian who had truly possessed divine powers was Horus, and when he died, the First Time died with him. After that a new age began— the Age of Man.

Thoth had never heard his father speak of Horus before, but his thoughts were interrupted by the arrival of a warrior dressed in full ceremonial armor. He clasped Thoth's arm in a firm welcome and said, "I am Thutmose, Commander of the Guard for the House of Atum."

Thoth looked up at him. The giant man towered over him by at least two heads and had muscles that made him look as if he could take on any army.

Thutmose and his guards led Thoth through the courtyard to the temple's Constellation Chamber—the most magnificent room that Thoth had ever seen. He raised his eyes and marveled at the open ceiling, splayed with a golden, lattice-like web that connected all the constellations in the sky. The design revolved slowly to follow the movement of the stars as they rose and set each night.

Thutmose smiled, surprising Thoth with his genuine warmth. "Welcome, son of Ramses. Impressive, isn't it? . . . Built to watch the night sky and honor the heavens." Thutmose bowed and left him.

Thoth circled the room, wishing he had paid more attention to his astronomy lessons. The study of the stars had always been vital to Heliopolis, and Thoth knew that the astronomer who had designed this room was a master.

"The sky seems lonely without Sirius, our brightest star."

A voice startled him from his reverie. Thoth turned and found himself face-to-face with Hermese. She was even more beautiful than she had seemed from afar. Her long black hair had been braided into a decorative rope interwoven with flowers that hung down her bare back. She was draped in exquisite shimmering robes that accentuated her feline grace, and her eyes were mysterious, colored like the most treasured emerald stone. Thoth stared into their depths and saw a deep wisdom. It overshadowed everything else about her.

He could think of nothing worthy to say to her.

They studied each other for a long time. The air was heavy with expectation, and Thoth could feel himself being judged. It would be the worst humiliation imaginable if she changed her mind now and sent him away.

But instead, she held out her hand to him and smiled. "Now let us dine."

In every way it was like their wedding night, even though once Hermese was with child, Thoth would not be allowed back into the temple. It felt strange that they did not know each other, yet they had the world's permission to be lovers.

Thoth had always known that one day he would do something worthy for his people, something that went beyond being a councilor's secondborn son. He and his brother had grown up in the shadow of their father, who was the leader of the Council of Twelve—the men and women who ruled Upper and Lower Egypt. But there was no greater honor than siring a future Guardian.

Now he sat with Hermese in her private courtyard off her quarters. They were reclining on an enormous royal chaise, dining under the stars. Thoth felt his body grow warm. He knew an aphrodisiac had been put in the wine.

He reached out and touched Hermese's hair, bringing it to his lips. She smelled like sweet spice and lotus flowers. "Is the same potion in your drink?" he asked.

"It's part of the ceremony," she nodded, a dreamy look in her eyes. "In case we don't like each other."

They both laughed and leaned forward. As they kissed, Hermese pushed him down and sat astride Thoth, her long hair covering them both. They made love, unable to satisfy their desire.

Before dawn, they lay on the chaise and looked up at the fading stars to see Sirius—the Star of Isis—return to the sky. A faint drizzle fell and rested on the trees, shrouding their view in mist. The continuous rains were something Thoth and Hermese had lived with all their lives.

Thoth listened to the humming vibrations emanating from the pyramids, something else he had lived with his whole life. But the hum resonated much stronger here than it did in the city, and he knew it would take a while to get used it. Someday he would love to learn how they worked and what the Guardian did to maintain them. He knew Hermese could never tell him, but it did not hurt to dream.

He closed his eyes, feeling more content than he ever thought possible. "Why did you pick me when my brother won?" he asked. "Was it because of Kiya?"

A shadow passed over her face, and Thoth regretted his words immediately. But then it was gone, and Hermese gave him a little smile, shaking her head. "You won during the match," she explained, "when you finished your water and bread and offered the rest to the young boy who was sitting alone in the crowd." Her fingers traced the lines of his face—his almond-brown eyes, his high cheekbones. Thoth was still a young man, his body not yet fully hardened, but she gazed at him as if he were perfect. "The tournament has nothing to do with silly games of strength."

He took her hand and kissed it. "So what will happen now?"

Hermese nestled against him and closed her eyes. "You will stay in the temple with me until I am with child." When he didn't say anything, she looked at him. "You can leave the temple by day if you need to visit the city. But nights, you'll sleep here." For a moment she looked unsure and asked, "Is that acceptable?"

He hugged her to him. "Immensely."

When Hermese was not busy with her other responsibilities, they spent all their time together *fulfilling their duty*, as they came to call it.

Thoth understood that, since she had no siblings, it was vital that she bear a child. On occasion, he had begun to overhear the hushed whispers of a servant or physician coming to give Hermese news of her father. Hermese had tried to pretend that it was nothing serious. But as the days passed, Thoth began to suspect that the Guardian was ill and in fact getting worse, and he realized just how vital it was that Hermese give birth to the next heir.

Since his arrival, Thoth had been treated by everyone else as an outsider and had been under strict orders to remain inside Hermese's quarters. He was not allowed to talk to anyone or explore the temple fortress. Although he accepted the rules and tried not to feel like a prisoner, by the month's end, he was overcome by an overwhelming urge to see his family. Thutmose granted him leave and reminded him that he must be back by evening.

It was the first time he had returned home, but before he could even sit down to dinner, his brother challenged him. "There are rumors that the Guardian is dying."

Ramses gave his eldest son a sharp look. Thoth kept his face impassive, unwilling to divulge any knowledge he had gained inside the temple. He served himself and took his time answering. "I know he is unwell."

In truth, the Guardian would, most likely, die soon, but the House of Atum wanted to keep his illness a secret.

Seth laughed. "Your lover will take her father's place. She's too young and not even with child. The people will oppose her."

Thoth put down his bread. He had begun to lose his appetite. "What do you suggest, brother? That we will no longer have a Guardian? That is heresy."

Seth's voice rose with a passion Thoth had never heard before. "It is an ancient system put in place by elders who are no longer here. If we are truly a free society, we do not need a House of Atum hoarding our forefathers' wisdom—keeping it locked away in a complex we cannot even enter. What gives them the right to control the pyramid and its force, to share none of their knowledge? They want to keep us ignorant and enslaved."

Ramses banged his fist on the table. Both brothers jumped. "The House of Atum wields its power benevolently, selflessly preserving the past and protecting the future."

Seth rolled his eyes—his father was merely reciting one of his favorite speeches.

But Ramses wasn't finished. "The Elders knew firsthand what happens when such a force is exploited. The Guardians were put in place so that it would not happen again. As long as I am councilor, they will never be unseated."

Seth kept his eyes down as he spoke. "Dissension is growing. You are one of the few who oppose abolishing the system."

Thoth could tell that Ramses was about to erupt again and tried to make his brother see reason. "Seth, the members of the House of Atum are the people's last link to a lost history. Someone must be entrusted to be the keepers of this sacred knowledge."

"Why? Why do you blindly accept the law?" Seth shouted. "Only they know the full spectrum of the sciences and arts, which are all but forgotten by the people. They alone control the power of the Great Pyramid, distancing themselves from the outside world."

Ramses banged both fists on the table this time. "To keep what they safeguard from being corrupted by greed!"

Seth glared back at his father. "The Guardians have always been archaic, and they have become pompous in their isolation. Society is voracious, Father. It will always search for a way to destroy anything that exists outside of it."

Ramses bellowed, "How dare you speak such words at my table? Do you think I do not know what poison you are brewing outside these walls? The High Priestess chose your brother to sire the next Guardian. Do not forget you fought for the honor too. And lost."

At this, Seth fell silent. His father was the one man who was still able to put him in his place. A scholar and a warrior, Ramses was also a father to the people. He was as noble as a king, and he possessed a fair and true heart. But Thoth had never seen him angrier.

Ramses took Seth's wine goblet and turned it over, signaling that Seth was no longer welcome to drink at his table. "I am ashamed to call you my son."

"Then I will be no longer." Without another word, Seth stood up and stormed out of the house.

Thoth and his father both sat in silence. Thoth knew Seth was not a lone voice clamoring for change—the threat of which he spoke was real. The opposition would use the transition as an excuse to challenge the balance of power. Still, he tried to have hope. "Don't worry, Father. He will return."

Ramses shook his head. "Your brother is not the man you think he is. Some days, I'd swear Kiya took his spirit with her when she died. I do not know him anymore." He stood up and went to his writing table.

Thoth noticed how painfully he moved. For the first time in his life, his father looked truly frail. "Are you unwell?" Thoth asked.

Ramses brushed off the question with a wave of his hand and returned from his desk with a sealed scroll. "Give this to the High Priestess and no one else."

Thoth held his surprise in check. Only the House of Atum knew how to read the inscriptions left by Heliopolis' ancestors. The people remembered a few of the symbols, but not enough to make use of them—to do what Hermese called reading or writing. Their history had been carried down orally, through the stories told by the priests. Ramses had taught Seth and Thoth more symbols than most parents, but Thoth had not placed much importance in the lessons. He could not imagine why his father had written to Hermese, but had enough self-discipline not to ask. He did not recognize the seal on the scroll. It was neither the council's nor their family emblem.

Ramses handed Thoth the scroll and clasped his arm. "By the powers of Re, may she be with child before the next moon."

That night Thoth made love to Hermese with a ferocity he could not restrain. Afterward, as they lay beside each other, he recounted his visit home and handed her the scroll. She did not open it, but, instead, studied the seal.

"What is it?" Thoth asked.

"An answer." She smiled and put the scroll away in a small wooden chest.

"You will not read it in front of me? What secrets could you possibly have with my father?" he teased.

She laughed but said nothing.

"Fine, keep your secrets then." Thoth grabbed her and pulled her back on the pillows. "I'll share mine. I never want to leave here, ever, or to leave you."

Hermese hugged him close. "My heart feels the same," she admitted, and her voice dropped to a whisper. "I have found a way to give us more time." She reached over to her dressing table and took out a miniature clay pot. Her voice grew softer still. "As long as I drink this, I will not be with child."

Thoth sat up and whispered, "You break every ancient law."

"Then tell me not to drink it."

Thoth could not say the words. He wanted to steal as much time with her as possible.

She poured the dark, viscous liquid into a cup and drank it in one swallow. "We will fulfill our duty, but not just yet," she said and crawled back under the sheets and kissed him. They never spoke of it again.

FORTY-ONE

Hermese drank the potion for six months, and for six months, they pretended that their prolonged union did not affect the world outside the temple fortress. But Thoth could sense the storm coming. Hermese's father had grown more ill, and she spent more and more time away from her quarters making decisions in his stead.

Only the Guardian knew how to harmonize the pyramids' oscillation so that they vibrated in sympathy with the Earth, channeling its energy and resonating with its magnetism. Not only did the pyramids run their civilization, but they also stabilized the Earth's shifting crust by drawing upon its seismic energy. The Elders had understood that the pyramids played a crucial role in helping to avoid cataclysmic events. They had suffered such occurrences before with tragic consequences in the time of the Great War. It was for this reason that Heliopolis had been built—to start again and protect the ancient knowledge before it was lost. The Elders had lived in the First Time and had become Heliopolis's first Council of Twelve—the wisest men and women chosen by Osiris and Isis to lead their civilization. It was the Elders who had created the new laws when Horus died, and the First Time had died with him. And it was they, Heliopolis' benevolent forefathers, who had given the Guardians unconditional autonomy in their duties.

It often amazed Thoth to think that Hermese knew how to control such an incredible force, and yet he had never met anyone more humble or more giving.

It pained him that he now only saw her at night. In the mornings, she had started leaving papyrus scrolls on her writing table for him to look at so that he might have something to occupy his time. He had no idea where they came from, but he had the feeling that others in the House of Atum would not approve of her actions.

Hermese also began showing him the Sacred Symbols. Each one contained within it a mathematical equation that formed the fabric of the universe. She explained to him how all things were made of vibrations and particles of light, and that in the First Time, the Guardians had been able to direct both with the mind.

Thoth could not grasp everything she said, but then she had been trained extensively all her life. She could decipher the Sacred Symbols, and she could fine-tune the Great Pyramid's harmonic oscillation and acoustic resonance much like a master musician would. The more Thoth learned, the more he was in awe of her mind. An entirely new world was unfolding before his eyes, and with it he began to understand just how much power the House of Atum wielded.

Hermese asked him not to discuss these lessons with anyone, including the scrolls he was studying that mapped out the entire pyramid complex, its expansive tunnel system, and the hidden vault underneath the Sphinx. Thoth committed everything to memory in the event that one day he might be called upon to use it.

Every day he began to look forward to discovering what Hermese had left for him, although he could not understand her motives. People on the outside would have killed to know these secrets. On his last visit home, Thoth had learned that Seth had publicly joined the Apophis, those who opposed the council's allegiance to the Guardian. The public saw this as a personal blow to Ramses, whose presence was the only thing that kept the council from falling apart.

Thoth had heard Ramses praying to Re again for the child, and his guilt at his and Hermese's deception grew. He knew his father needed him more than ever, and he swore that Ramses' prayer would not be in vain.

When Thoth returned to the temple that night, he did not

know how to broach the subject with Hermese, but to his relief, he didn't have to. After they made love, Hermese took the secret vial and, without a word, scattered its contents into her garden. She came back to bed, and he held out his hand.

It took two weeks for Hermese to become pregnant, but they wanted to hide the news as long as possible. As soon as the child was announced, Thoth would have to leave the temple.

They spent many nights lying in bed, listening to the soft rain while they debated the name of the next Guardian.

Hermese stroked her stomach. "I think he is a boy."

"Do you?" Thoth kissed her belly.

Hermese's fingertip traced the circle of infinity on her stomach. "I want to name him Amyntas."

Thoth considered it and tried not to feel desolate, knowing well that she could name the child whatever she wished. He would not be with her for the naming ceremony.

"It means defender of all that is sacred," she explained. "If the baby is a girl, she will be Amynta."

Hermese grew quiet, and Thoth knew she was thinking about their impending separation. The law stated that once the child was conceived, the father could never be allowed inside the temple again—if he entered, he would forfeit his life.

As the time of their separation drew nearer, Thoth began to agree with his brother and question why the Elders had created such strict laws. He posed no threat to Hermese, or to her role as Guardian. He merely wanted to be with her and raise their child. Why was such an innocent desire so unthinkable?

He decided it was time to ask the question. "Once you are Guardian, can you not change the law?"

She rested her head on his chest. He could feel her tears. "I took an oath to uphold all the laws of the temple. I can never break them."

Thoth held her, and after a while he said, "Then we will wait as long as we can."

The wait was not as long as they had hoped. By the next month,

Hermese's body had transformed, and her belly had begun to show such that even the heaviest robes could not hide it.

One day, she came back to her quarters, weeping. Thoth did not need to be told what had happened.

"I'm sorry. My father's sister forced me to announce."

Thoth did not know Hermese's family, only that her father had a younger sister and brother who lived elsewhere in the temple with their own children. He heard himself ask, "So our time together is over?"

She nodded and whispered, "The guards are coming."

Her words seized his heart. His time here had ended, without warning, without mercy. He clenched his hands into fists. "They cannot just make me leave. They should give us one night, at least! Sirius returns tomorrow."

"It is the law. We must obey."

"You find it so easy to see me go?"

She cried out at his words. He felt ashamed and rushed to kneel beside her. "Forgive me."

She took his hands and put them on her stomach. "Horus is God of the Horizon. I will meet you there."

Thoth did not have time to question what she meant. Thutmose and his guards had already entered the room.

Thutmose's face was solemn as he said, "Son of Ramses, your stay in the temple is over. May the Gods bless your child and reward this sacrifice."

Thoth turned away from his compassionate gaze, not wanting the old warrior to see his sorrow.

He embraced Hermese for the last time and whispered, "If ever you need me, I will break every law to come to you. I know the tunnels by heart."

She whispered back, "I did not show you the scrolls for my own benefit. That is for your father to explain."

This was the first time she had mentioned his father. Thoth wanted to know more, but the guards were already sending him out. He heard the doors to Hermese's quarters close behind him. It was done.

The forced march through the temple seemed endless. During the day, it always struck him how unkempt and old the fortress looked. Thoth wondered how many people even lived here. He had already discovered that the Atum guards, though they appeared formidable with Thutmose as their leader, barely numbered a few dozen. Thoth shuddered to think what would happen if the opposition ever found out how easy it would be to take the temple—they would crush it in an instant.

It was as if his fear had been whispered in his brother's ear. Seth was outside the gate, waiting for him in an elaborate litter carried by six men.

Thoth hid his shock and hurried through the sheets of rain. He climbed inside and clasped hands with his brother. For the moment, they pretended that there was no strain between them.

Seth signaled to the litter-bearers to move on, then handed Thoth a small towel. "An even bigger storm is coming. The waters of the Nile are already rising."

"So you came to keep me from getting wet?" Thoth jested.

His brother laughed. "No, I heard news the deed is done."

Thoth knew the Guardian had not made a public announcement—his brother must have a spy inside the temple. His fears grew as he watched the temple grow smaller in the distance. "So you've left Father's house for good?" Thoth asked.

Seth answered with a grim smile. "A great change is coming, and he can do nothing to prevent it. I am here to extend the hand of brotherhood and ask you to join me."

Thoth sized up his brother, noting how the last year had altered him. Seth was dressed in an adorned tunic fine enough for any ruler, and he wore an emblem around his neck that Thoth could not identify. It must be the symbol of the Apophis. Thoth had heard rumors of their growing brutality, how they had tried to stage public riots, threatened Heliopolis' peacekeepers, and supported any usurper of the law. It chilled him to think that his brother may now be one of their leaders. "You expect me to help you destroy the House of Atum? After I just sired their heir?"

"Which is precisely why you should. We can rewrite the laws so you and Hermese can be together and raise your child. I know you well, brother. Is that not your heart's desire?"

Thoth didn't speak. Seth would be surprised to know how much he wanted to share that vision of the future, but it was impossible. Hermese would never agree and he could never go against her.

"Just think, we would gain access to the complex." Seth's eyes grew bright with tempered zeal. "No more secrets, no more knowledge that the people can't touch. All of Egypt would join together."

Thoth held his gaze steady. "I thought the people were together. I do not see many complaining."

"Because you've had your head buried in the sand," Seth snapped. "Or somewhere else."

Thoth refused to be baited. "There is a balance of power for a reason. After the Great War—"

Seth interjected, "Spare me Father's history lesson! The Great War has nothing to do with here and now. You gave the House of Atum your seed, did you give them your manhood as well?"

Thoth sat back and crossed his arms—the urge to strike his brother overwhelmed him.

Seth leaned forward and lowered his voice. "Their fall will happen soon, with or without you. Would you not like to have a hand in your lover's fate?"

Thoth began to feel real fear now. He had to tread carefully—his brother had become a threat to Hermese. "I need time to think on your offer. For now I will walk the rest of the way to the city."

Something flickered in Seth's eyes. He gave a sharp knock on the litter door and the men beneath it stopped and lowered it to the ground.

Thoth got out and could not resist saying, "If she had chosen you, this would all be different."

Seth stared at him, and his smile hardened. "No, just easier." He knocked on the litter again, and the bearers moved on.

Thoth knew he needed to talk to his father and find a way to warn Hermese. He feared his brother did not plan to let her, or the child, live. She would forever pose a threat to the Apophis even as a figurehead.

Thoth broke into a run. He realized his brother would strike on the day that was meant to symbolize a new beginning: the return of Sirius—the Star of Isis. He would strike tomorrow.

When Thoth arrived home, he discovered that his father had died three days earlier. He listened numbly as their house servant explained everything and begged his forgiveness. Ramses had refused to let anyone send for him. The servant's continuous sobs carved Thoth's heart up into even smaller pieces. He patted the servant's shoulder and did his best to comfort him. Then he left.

He wandered through the market, unsure of what to do next. His father had been the keystone in his life, and he needed his counsel now more than ever. Even worse, his brother had said nothing of his passing. This was something Thoth could not forgive.

He could feel the people's eyes upon him as he made his way to the Great Sun Temple of Re, where he knew his father's funeral would have taken place. Its size and grandeur made it seem more like a mountain that had been hollowed out by the gods. When he entered, he was not surprised to find it empty. Everyone was busy preparing for tomorrow's celebration.

Thoth walked up to the altar and stood before the eternal flame. It was an homage to the phoenix—the sacred bird of Egypt. As a child, Thoth had been fascinated by stories about them. The last known phoenix had died with Horus and traveled with him to the *Duat*, the Afterlife, but its spirit lived on as a potent reminder of the soul's immortality and the people's past.

He watched the flames, trying to imagine his father's spirit within them. He had never felt so alone.

"Your father was a great man."

Thoth turned around and was surprised to find himself face-to-face with Ptah, the High Priest of the temple. Thoth took a step back and bowed in respect.

The old man continued, "And a dear friend. I have been waiting for you to come."

Thoth did not know what to say. Ptah was the most revered priest in all of Heliopolis. He had been alive for so long that no one even knew his age. Thoth could not imagine what he wanted with him.

The high priest had been staring at him with great intensity, and he appeared satisfied by what he saw. He motioned for Thoth to follow him with a gentle hand. "Come, the others are waiting," he said and turned away. Thoth hesitated—*what others*, he wondered—but hurried after him.

Ptah led him to a hidden door behind the great altar and ushered him inside. They descended a stairwell that spiraled deep into the earth. Thoth thought of the maps Hermese had shown him and knew this must lead to the labyrinth under the city.

They walked through a maze of tunnels. Ptah opened another hidden door to an enormous room, with a ceiling so high Thoth's eyes strained to see it. He saw a huge emblem on the wall and recognized it as the same one that his father had used to seal the scroll he'd sent to Hermese. Below the emblem stood an exquisite round table made from a giant acacia tree. Four people sat around it: two men and two women. Thoth recognized three of the faces.

Bast, a formidable councilwoman who had worked closely with his father and known Thoth all his life, gave him a warm smile. "Welcome, Thoth."

Thoth looked at the man next to her: Ammon, the greatest alchemist of their time, and a man who could allegedly control any element. Thoth did not know him, but recognized him because of his fame.

The third person at the table was Thutmose. Out of all the people who were gathered there, Thoth was most relieved to see him, and he stepped forward, anxious to speak to him alone—he needed to reveal his brother's plans. But Ptah was busy introducing him to the fourth person in the group. "This is Ma'at, our greatest seer, and the Keeper of Time."

Thoth was taken aback. He had heard of Ma'at but had always thought of her as an ancient sage, not the young beauty who stood before him. A deep sadness eclipsed her loveliness, but she gave him a faint smile. As if reading his thoughts, she said, "I am in fact older than you, and you are wondering why you are here." She offered him the seat beside her. "Although he is no longer with us, your father always longed for this day. We are the Brotherhood of Horus. Or what is left of it."

Her words stunned him. Thoth shook his head in denial. "The Brotherhood is only a legend."

"We exist," Ammon said with a mischievous grin. The gesture made him less intimidating. "Your father was one of us. Each of our ancestors sat on Horus' inner council. He entrusted them with safeguarding the Hall of Records, which is all that survived the Great War . . . and the pyramid, the last working energy center of its kind. For hundreds of years, each family has passed its sacred oath to protect them on to the next generation and we have not failed, yet."

Bast touched his arm in a maternal gesture. "So you see, Thoth, the Brotherhood of Horus are Guardians, in secret. Only one son or daughter can inherit the seat. Your father chose you."

Now Thoth understood why Hermese had taught him so much. She had known he had been chosen. The weight of that ancient vow pressed upon him and Thoth envisioned his father's hand reaching through the Duat to help him accept it.

He sensed Ma'at studying him. She frowned and said, "Hermese should have been here by now."

Thoth's heart quickened. "Hermese is part of the fellowship?"

Ma'at nodded. "The Guardian is leader of the Brotherhood."

It took Thoth a moment to comprehend what she hadn't said. "Hermese is the Guardian?" He could see looks being exchanged around the table.

Thutmose answered, "Hermese has been Guardian since her father died four months ago. We were waiting for the child's conception to announce the transition."

Thoth sat speechless. Her father's death coincided with when they had abandoned the potion and she could not even tell him. So she had carried their secret after she had conceived so that they could have a few more stolen scraps of time together. He was ashamed of the anger he had felt when he last saw her.

But she was coming. The underground tunnels connected the city to the pyramid complex and the temple. The knowledge that they would be able to meet each other in secret gave him life again, and now her parting words made sense: Horus was God of the Horizon and she would meet him here . . . with the Brotherhood.

Thoth wanted to laugh for joy, but then he saw Thutmose's worried face and his previous sense of alarm came rushing back. The time for speaking in private had passed.

"I am honored by your trust and inclusion, and I must speak freely now. I was on my way to seek my father's council when I learned of his death . . . my brother is going to make a move against the House of Atum. He has a spy inside the temple. Somehow he knew about the child."

Thutmose swore and jumped to his feet. "I should have never left her alone. When is he planning to strike?" He put on his cloak.

"Tomorrow, upon Sirius's return. I hope I am wrong."

Ma'at shook her head. The seer's eyes grew more unfocused as her mind turned inward. She drew a sharp breath, her face filled with horror. Whatever she saw there was unspeakable. She only could whisper, "He already has her."

FORTY-TWO

Bryan listened to Linz moan in her sleep and felt her forehead again. She was burning up.

On the flight over, she had complained of not feeling well, and by the time they had landed, she was barely conscious. Bryan had managed to get her through customs and into a taxi. Luckily it was just a short drive to the hotel in Heliopolis. He had left her sleeping in the cab while he checked in and then carried her to the room and laid her on the bed. She had not woken up since—and that was twenty-four hours ago.

The fact that he could not rouse her, even to drink water, alarmed him. She had also been speaking in her sleep in a language Bryan had never heard before. If she didn't wake up soon, he'd have to take her to a hospital. *She'll wake up*, he assured himself. She had to.

Thinking that he should have aspirin, food, bottled water, and whatever else Linz might need on hand when she woke, Bryan got dressed and wrote her a quick note, just in case, and left it on the pillow. He hung the "do not disturb" sign on the door and headed to the elevators.

"Is your friend any better?"

Bryan turned around and saw the young housekeeper who was assigned to their floor. She had helped him usher Linz into the room yesterday. He had felt an immediate affinity for her, but could not place her from anywhere in his past. It was like meeting an old friend again and forgetting their name.

She gave him an inquisitive smile, waiting for his response. She was a lovely Egyptian girl with wide almond-shaped eyes and a classical face. There was a natural light about her, as if she was always eager to laugh.

Bryan swallowed his frustration and answered, "She's still sleeping."

"Well, let me know if I can get you anything. My name is Layla." She continued down the hallway. Bryan watched her walk away.

He got on the elevator and headed to the lobby. The Intercontinental at City Stars was more opulent than what Bryan would have chosen. Linz had booked their room in Boston while they waited for their flight. The enormous development center included two other hotels and the largest mall in Europe and the Middle East. With over six hundred stores, two theme parks, and a twenty-one-screen cinema, the shopping mecca was a manifestation of the twenty-first century's voracious appetite for consumerism. Bryan had never experienced anything like it.

As he pushed through the crowd, the life he had come to find had never seemed more unobtainable. Maybe it was a mistake to bring Linz halfway around the world. Running away hadn't solved anything. Bryan had used his credit card to pay for the flights and their hotel room, making it possible for Conrad to find them. Hell, he controlled a billion-dollar pharmaceutical empire. He could find anyone.

Bryan's concerns about Conrad evaporated as he stood in front of the massive mall directory. He counted six levels at City Stars and vowed he would only go up to three—he wanted to get what he came for and get out. Working haphazardly and with hardly a clue as to what Linz liked or needed, he bought her toiletries and food.

On his way out, he found a hobby store and purchased a drawing pad, charcoal pencils, and oil pastels. He knew he wouldn't be going anywhere until Linz recovered. Maybe drawing would trigger something. He was starting to feel desperate.

When Bryan got back to their room Linz was still in deep sleep. She didn't wake from the noise he made as he rifled through plastic bags or react when he called her name.

He felt her forehead, and was relieved to find that at least her fever had broken—a good sign. He would let her sleep until morning and then decide what to do.

In the meantime, he piled the supplies on the table and got out a bottle of vodka he had bought. He poured himself a double shot.

The room had come with a terrace and Bryan stepped out onto it, feeling a night breeze brush across his face. He closed his eyes and, for a brief moment, heard the whisper of the ancient land he had come to find.

A comfortable-looking lounge chair beckoned to him. He leaned back and looked up at the sky; he had hoped for stars but saw only clouds and pollution. As he sipped his vodka, his mind turned to Pushkin. He felt an urge to write a poem but suppressed it. He wanted to recover new memories, not old ones.

Finishing his drink, he poured another, unable to quell his frustration. Why couldn't he remember? He knew there were countless lives in his head, and yet the one he wanted to retrieve eluded him like a phantom. Again, his thoughts returned to the poem. It wouldn't go away.

He went inside, found pen and paper in the hotel desk drawer, and returned to the lounge chair and began to write. He stared at the finished poem before tossing it aside, and in one deft move jumped up onto the balcony's ledge.

Calling upon Bodhidharma's grace, he walked the narrow strip with confidence, feeling his mind balancing on the same ledge. Bryan opened his arms wide and let the wind whip his body. He stood like that for several minutes and felt a calm wash over him.

Suddenly Bodhidharma's voice rang loudly inside his head, commanding him to paint. Bryan jolted and opened his eyes— why was he standing on a half-foot ledge fifteen stories off the ground? He pitched forward and caught himself just in time, jumping backward onto the cement.

"Jesus," he said, feeling breathless yet exhilarated. He went into the room to grab the drawing pad and oil pastels.

Returning to his chair, he stared at the blank paper, not knowing where to start—he had never tried to paint a memory before he had remembered a life. Closing his eyes, he tried to imagine his Egyptian goddess. But ever since he had arrived in Cairo, she felt like a distant dream.

He was alone. And, somehow, he feared that, when it came, this memory would be the worst.

FORTY-THREE

The plan was well under way when they heard the explosion. It made the earth shake with such magnitude that Thoth felt as if the ground would open up and swallow the city whole.

At first he thought Ammon had caused the tremor—the alchemist had left the tunnels to create a diversion outside the temple. But the blast was followed by a deafening vibrational hum. The sound could have come only from one source—the Great Pyramid. Something had gone terribly wrong.

The vibrations shook the air itself. Thoth and Thutmose held on to the walls. They had been waiting for Ammon's signal in the tunnel at the temple's hidden door. The plan had been to create a distraction so that Seth's men would head to the gates. Thoth and Thutmose just needed enough time to slip inside, locate Hermese, and get her below. Meanwhile, Bast had returned to Heliopolis to rally the council, while Ptah addressed the citizens at the Sun temple.

Rocks fell from the underground tunnel's ceiling and the staircase began to collapse. Thutmose launched his body forward and grabbed Thoth to keep him from falling. His voice was barely audible over the deafening hum. "We must go now!"

Thoth nodded, watching Thutmose open the door to the Constellation Chamber. The grand room lay in ruins; the beautiful lattice that framed the stars had crashed to the floor. Then, without warning, the vibrations stopped, leaving an eerie silence—a silence Thoth had never heard before.

The pyramids were quiet; the entire temple was dark. And as

Thoth's eyes adjusted to the lack of light, he understood what had happened. The pyramids had suffered a catastrophe. They stopped running because the Guardian had not been there to save them.

Thoth ran toward Hermese's quarters with Thutmose right behind him. They encountered none of Seth's men, only servants looking dazed and bloodied. When Thoth and Thutmose entered the Grand Gallery, they realized why: the entire House of Atum and their guards had been slain like dogs. Both men cried out at the carnage.

Thoth searched among the bodies, terrified that Hermese would be there.

Thutmose fell to his knees at the sight of his wife and son. Six of his finest men had fallen around them. They had tried to protect their commander's family, even as they faced their deaths.

"Hermese! Hermese!" Thoth called her name as he searched. He turned back to Thutmose. "She's not here. I'm going to her quarters."

"I'll look upstairs." Thutmose forced himself to his feet.

Thoth saw the dead guards' weapons piled against the wall and picked up a *khopesh*, a sickle-shaped sword best wielded with one hand. He found a mace and shield as well, tied them to his belt, and took off running. He prayed she was still alive.

When he saw the body, he was not sure. Hermese lay splayed out on the bed, her robes torn, her skin cut and bruised. Thoth knelt beside her and saw the faint rise and fall of her chest. Blood pooled between her legs, and he knew the child was dead.

Lifting her limp body, he cradled her in his arms. "Hermese, I'm here. Please wake up." He rocked her as he cried.

Pulling himself together, he found a cloak and covered her, but not before he had seen the full extent of the torture she had endured. He knew this was Seth's work, and he was filled with such hatred that any remaining love he had for his brother died.

Thoth carried Hermese back to the Grand Gallery but saw no sign of Thutmose. He could not risk waiting for him; the old guard would have to fend for himself. He could meet the rest of the Brotherhood underground.

Thoth made it to the Constellation Chamber and was almost at the hidden door when Seth and his men entered the front gate. Luckily, Thoth was at an angle where he could watch them without being seen. But in a few moments, Seth's army would cross the main courtyard and they would be exposed.

Thoth could not risk opening the passage and revealing its location. Seth would do anything to know how to penetrate the tunnels. His only course was to delay them until the others could take Hermese to safety. He laid her on the ground next to the door and marched into the pouring rain, closing the distance between them.

"Traitor!" Thoth took out his sword. "I challenge you!"

Seth stopped and held out his hand, gesturing for his men to stand down. "Brother! You have come too late."

Thoth could feel his body trembling with rage.

Seth called out, "She left me no choice. She refused to talk."

Thoth could barely say the words. "You killed my son."

"The decision weighed heavy in my heart." Seth shook his head sadly. "But the boy could not live."

"You are no longer my brother," Thoth screamed, tears blinding his vision. "Kiya and Father are watching you from the Duat."

"There is no Duat—no life after death. This is all we are," Seth answered.

A curtain of rain fell between them. Thoth felt bile rise in his chest. "The pyramid is silent. What have you done?"

For a moment, Thoth saw Seth's mask of confidence slip. Seth shouted, "It can be repaired. After we possess the hidden knowledge, we'll be able to build more pyramids, heralding a new world. No more Guardians, no more secrets."

"And who will be the leader of this new world? You?"

Seth spread his arms wide. "The people trust me because I am one of them. I don't hide behind legends and lost magic. It's time for a new beginning."

"A new beginning in the dark!" Thoth turned to address Seth's men. They needed to hear the truth. "Because that is where you will live—in a world with no light. There is more than one Guardian—a Brotherhood—and on Horus' sacred oath, they will never let you have the hidden knowledge."

Seth laughed. "More than one Guardian? Where are they?"

"Here." Thoth pressed the khopesh to his chest. "Chosen by our father, who was chosen by his father, who was chosen by his— because his father's father had been chosen by Horus himself. I am but one of many. You can kill me, but you cannot kill us all."

With great satisfaction, Thoth watched the disbelief on his brother's face turn to fury. Seth's men looked at each other, wondering if they had chosen the wrong side. Seth drew his sword.

Thoth did not know what would happen next. The khopesh felt heavy in his hand, and he tried to remember his training. In theory, wide slashes would do the most damage. The blade of the khopesh was weighted perfectly so that its user could thrust, jab, or slash at his opponent. Thoth intended to do all three.

He forced his mind to focus. In a moment he would try to kill his brother. Surely Ramses would approve his actions. No man deserved to die more than Seth did.

The brothers circled each other, both blinded by the rain. Lightning flashed in the sky, as if the heavens were angered by the silence of the pyramids. Seth's men grew uneasy. Thoth knew Seth sensed this as well and hoped it would splinter his concentration— otherwise Thoth's chances of winning were slim. The only way to achieve victory would be to use his superior balance and agility to avoid his brother's strength.

Seth attacked, and Thoth willed his body to bend with the air. He feinted right, lunged left, and brought his sword up in a wide arc—and his blade broke skin. Seth jumped back, barely saving himself from the lethal cut. He looked down at the blood flowing freely from his chest. The wound appeared deep.

With a roar, Seth charged, slicing the air. Thoth avoided each strike with the slightest turn. Seth lunged low and slashed at his feet. Thoth jumped high and arched his body, avoiding the blow by launching himself into a back flip.

The rains stopped and Thoth felt the Earth's energy course

through him, causing his fear to subside. Thunder rumbled as if telling him he would not die in this fight—that a greater ending awaited him.

He saw that Ammon and Ma'at had arrived, ready to come to his aid. Seth advanced again, and Thoth avoided each strike until he saw his opening. Swift and sure, he dropped his sword and rammed his elbow into his brother's temple, as his other hand found a pressure point in Seth's neck, causing him to lose consciousness. Seth collapsed.

Before Seth's men could retaliate, Ammon threw a powder into the air that turned into smoke when its dust touched the ground. Everything erupted into chaos. Thoth looked down at his brother. His sword was raised and he was ready to strike, but he could not do it. He prayed to his father in the Duat to understand—and he let Seth live.

Thoth rushed back into the chamber with Ammon and Ma'at following just behind. Hermese was still curled up on the floor. Thoth gathered her in his arms as Ma'at opened the passage.

"Hurry!" she shouted. "We must get below."

As Thoth turned to enter, something struck his body with tremendous force. He looked down at the arrow protruding from his chest, then back to his brother, who lay on the ground with a bow in his hands.

Thoth staggered and Ma'at clutched him to keep him on his feet. As the smoke cleared, Seth's men began closing the distance.

Thutmose came running toward them from the other direction. "Get below! I'll hold them off."

Ammon grabbed Hermese and nodded. "I will see you in the Duat."

The old warrior's smile was grim. "In the Duat," he said and charged at Seth's men with a war cry, wielding a khopesh in each hand.

With Hermese in his arms, Ammon disappeared into the tunnel. Ma'at followed with Thoth and sealed the door. Thoth tried to ignore the blood oozing from his chest. When he spoke, his voice sounded faint. "Now they will know how to enter the tunnels."

Ma'at shook her head. "It's unfortunate, but we are not defeated. This passage will never be used again."

Thoth didn't know what she meant until they'd descended the stairs. While Ammon continued on with Hermese, Ma'at stopped and ordered him to wait. She left him leaning against the wall and slipped behind an alcove. Soon Thoth could hear rocks moving, then the ground above him began to shake. At first, he thought it was another explosion—until he saw the walls of the entire passage above them come together to form a ceiling. Ma'at had sealed the entrance.

Thoth grabbed the arrow's shaft and broke it off so that only a small bit of wood protruded from his chest. He felt like he was about to collapse.

When Ma'at rejoined him, she saw the bloody arrow on the ground. Thoth could read the question in her eyes. He stopped leaning against the wall and tried to stand up straight. "I'll be fine," he said.

She lit a torch to guide the way. The tunnels were in darkness now—as was everything else. The magnetic force that fueled the city—their lights, their machines, everything—was no longer accessible. Thoth couldn't begin to fathom the consequences. The technology his ancestors had fought to preserve was all but lost.

He grew weak, no longer certain that he could make it back to the meeting hall, when Ma'at spoke. "We turn here."

Thoth shook his head. "But the Temple of Re is this way."

"We're not going back to Heliopolis. We're going to the Hall of Records."

Thoth had dreamed his whole life of seeing the Hall of Records, but right now, he could only think of Hermese. Again Ma'at seemed to intuit his thoughts and said, "Hermese is already there."

They continued to make their way through the tunnels. Ma'at forced him to use her body as a crutch. "Your father would be proud," she said.

Thoth gave her an appraising look. "You had feelings for him."

Ma'at hesitated. "We were going to be married. He was waiting until you returned home to tell you."

Her confession couldn't have shocked him more. There was so much he didn't know about his father. . . . What other secrets had he taken with him to the Duat? The torchlight cast eerie shadows on the walls. He did not know if the day's events had overtaken him, but the world seemed to take on a dream-like effect. "Where are we now?" he asked.

"Under Hor-em-Akhet."

So the rumors were true, he thought. Hor-em-Akhet, the great Sphinx, sat above the Hall of Records, guarding its treasure.

They descended more stairs, burrowing further into the Earth. It made him wonder all the more at the divide between the keepers of the knowledge and the people.

Suddenly the stairs stopped. Thoth knew they had arrived, and as he stood on this hallowed ground, he began to understand the full extent of what the Guardians protected. Torches illuminated a chamber filled with thousands of scrolls stored in open wooden boxes. Ancient stone tablets had been mounted on one wall, alongside the most beautiful crystals he had ever seen. Even from where he stood, he could recognize the Sacred Symbols illuminated within them.

He looked up, marveling at it all. The shelves were so high that, even with the torchlight, the tops were shrouded in darkness. Another wall as tall as the Temple of Re illustrated the constellations in a carving that covered every inch of its stone. The intricate rendering showed countless galaxies, measured and notated with mathematical formulas.

"A true map of our heavens," Hermese said.

Thoth turned and saw her sitting at a table made of limestone, her eyes numb. "I could not save the child," she whispered. Thoth came and sat beside her, his own suffering forgotten. Ammon and Ma'at gave them a moment of privacy.

She could not bear to speak of it further and diverted his attention to the pyramid by explaining that its fall had been prophesized. "I never believed it would happen in my lifetime . . . that I would be the Guardian who failed."

Thoth shook his head. "I am the one who failed you. I should have known what was in my brother's heart."

"He is but the hand of a greater enemy. The Elders knew the greed in men's hearts. The bridge to all that we were is broken now."

Thoth wanted to ease her agony, but he had no words to comfort her. He shifted his position—his wound had become unbearable.

Hermese saw the blood and gasped, "Ammon!"

Ammon materialized from the shadows and knelt beside them. He brought his hands together with a loud clap and rubbed his palms back and forth. When he placed his palms on Thoth's chest, they felt hot to the touch and pulsated with unseen energy. Thoth winced. Ammon urged him to relax.

Hermese put her hand on Thoth's shoulder. He watched the alchemist work and felt nothing when Ammon slid the rest of the arrow from his chest. Ammon pressed a cloth to the wound and placed his hand on top of it. Once again, the heat was overwhelming. When Ammon removed his hand from the cloth, Thoth saw that the wound had closed. It still looked fresh and tender, but the bleeding had stopped.

Thoth looked to Hermese and saw that she had been restored as well. He wanted to know what the alchemist had done, but Hermese stood up and turned to Ammon and Ma'at.

"They will be searching for a way in now that they know the tunnels exist," she said.

Thoth began to sense there was a plan in place that he did not know about. "What do we do?" he asked.

Hermese looked at him—she was still the Guardian and in command. "The tunnels were built to connect to the river. We open those doors and flood everything."

Thoth gaped at her, unable to accept what she was suggesting. "So the Hall of Records is to be swept into the Nile? No one will ever remember the Great Past. We will be condemned to live in darkness."

Hermese ignored his reproaches and disappeared down an aisle.

Thoth shook his head in disbelief and sat at the table. Ma'at joined him there and quietly reassured him. "The Hall of Records will be sealed. Everything will be kept safe."

He glared at her. "Safe for no one to ever find."

"If people found the Hall of Records now, do you really think it would survive?" she countered.

Thoth couldn't answer. He had seen Seth's mob and could not imagine they understood what sacred meant.

Ma'at pressed her point. "The knowledge that exists here can move mountains and keep a man alive forever, destroy worlds and alter universes. Do you want this kind of power in your brother's hands?" She hesitated, "What has come to pass today was written long ago. Someday, when the world is ready, we will find our legacy again. It has been foretold."

Thoth didn't care what had been foretold, or when the Hall would be found again. These were abstractions from a past and a future he did not exist in. The present was all that mattered. He looked to where Hermese had retreated into the shadows, and he chastised himself for directing his anger at her. She was not to blame.

He heard movement in the tunnel. Ammon hurried to investigate and came back moments later with Ptah and Bast. They looked just as battle weary as the rest.

Moments later, Hermese returned, carrying a stone box. She set it on the table. Once again, to Thoth's annoyance, everyone seemed to know what was going on but him.

Ptah stared at the box with a sad smile. "So it has come to this."

Hermese looked to Ma'at and asked, "How long?"

"Hours, at most."

Everyone sat in somber silence. Hermese frowned. "Where is Thutmose?"

Ammon answered, "He gave up his life to help us escape."

Hermese drew a sharp breath, fighting to control her emotions. She turned to Ptah. "There is not much time. You must hold services every day. The people will need a spiritual leader now more than ever. Bast, rally the Council to stand against the Apophis.

Ammon and Ma'at will flood the tunnels from above. I will remain here to seal the Hall."

Everyone nodded. They all seemed to know their missions. Thoth could not keep his frustration in check any longer. "And what of me?"

Hermese looked at him and his anger died. "Thoth, as our newest Guardian," she said, "you have the most vital task." She set the box in front of him and explained, "This is a summary of the knowledge in this room, the wisdom we protect. It contains many Sacred Symbols and their keys, how to harness the energy of the Earth, control the elements, and much more. It is a great risk to take it aboveground, but we must—which is why I am entrusting it to you. Look far and wide, follow your heart to find the safest place on this Earth to hide it . . . for one day it will need to be found."

Thoth stared at the box, afraid to touch it. "What is it?"

"*The Book of Thoth*," she answered. Thoth looked at her in confusion. She gave him a faint smile. "Every book has a name. This one has yours."

Thoth studied the box again. "I hide it, but then who will find it?"

"You will," Ma'at said.

Thoth was impatient with their riddles. "I don't understand."

The seer tried to explain. "Time is a circle. There will be a way to come back to this moment and set the path right. We will live again and again, gaining new wisdom with time, helping mankind become ready to receive its legacy once more as we find our way back to this moment. We have only to remember our past in our future—when we do and the two become one, then Horus will return to help heal the world."

Thoth listened to her words, his thumb absently tracing an infinity sign along his index finger. *Horus would walk among us? The time of the Gods would come again?* How could man ever return to such a divine state when all seemed lost? It would take thousands of years if not more to reach such enlightenment, and now that task rested on the brotherhood's shoulders? He was speechless. He could see why his father had loved Ma'at. She was just as mad as he was.

"We have studied the ancient texts," she insisted. "It can be done."

Thoth scowled. "I haven't studied them."

Ammon tapped the box with one finger and winked. "Then read your book before you bury it."

Thoth looked at the box, terrified at the thought of being entrusted with such responsibility.

Ptah seemed to know what he was thinking and put his hand on his shoulder. "You will not fail us, son of Ramses. Your father watches you from the Duat."

Thoth wanted to believe it and wished his father could be with him now. He had been thrust into a world he did not understand, a world counting on him for its survival.

Hermese spoke. "We must go. Time is running out."

They all joined hands. Ma'at and Ammon looked at Thoth as they waited to close the circle. He took their hands and his eyes met Hermese's.

Ptah offered a quiet prayer. "Horus, this is our last meeting in this lifetime. We ask you to watch over us and protect us. Help us find our way through the unknown future and back to this circle once more. Let our light never be diminished."

Everyone embraced one another in farewell. Ptah came to Thoth. "I will hide you in the Temple of Re until it is safe to leave the city. You must travel far and never return."

Thoth looked to Hermese and remembered her mission—to seal the Hall of Records. His resolve to hide the box collapsed. "No!" he shouted. "Hermese, let me seal the Hall. You take the box."

She shook her head. "My place is here."

Thoth crossed his arms. "Then I stay too."

"You cannot," she said. "I was not jesting when I told you the name of the book. It has been called *The Book of Thoth* since its creation. It is for you to take." The finality in her voice crushed all of his hope.

Thoth was unwilling to accept her words, when all he could

hear was what she refused say. He began to plead with her. "You will die down here alone."

Hermese did not try to stifle her tears. She took his hands in hers. "Our fates are intertwined. I will find you again and again until we build a bridge back to this life. Nothing is ever lost."

FORTY-FOUR

Linz opened her eyes. She was in a dark room, and for a moment, she had no idea where she was. Her body was heavy; her mouth was dry. She heard someone breathing softly and turned to see Bryan asleep beside her.

Then everything came flooding back: the plane ride, and the horrible feeling that overcame her on the flight. By the time they had touched down, she thought she was dying. The headache and nausea were like nothing she had ever experienced. She barely recalled the airport, the cab ride was hazy at best, and she definitely did not remember ending up in this hotel room.

She lay in the dark for a long time, assimilating the memories. This time, she did not experience the same anguish or turmoil she had felt after previous recalls because, ten thousand years ago, she had prepared for this awakening.

Sliding off the bed so as not to wake Bryan, she crept to the bathroom and turned on the light. The person in the mirror startled her. Her hair was matted in an oily tangle, her face swollen from sleep, her complexion pale and sickly.

She took a long shower, and the water on her skin revived her. It made her wonder how long she had been asleep. When she got out, she wrapped herself in a towel and tiptoed into the bedroom, letting the light spill from the bathroom so she could see. Her overnight bag was on the table. She took it back into the bathroom.

She didn't think twice about leaving. As soon as she had woken up, she knew she had to fly back to Boston.

After she had dressed, she left the bathroom and located her purse. Next to it was an almost empty vodka bottle and halfhearted sketches of the Sphinx. As she was looking for a pen and paper, she saw the poem Bryan had written. Diana's memories of Natalia's lifetime had made her fluent in Russian, so she picked it up and read it. It was a poem full of longing about a woman whose child had died tragically before it could be born.

The words hit her hard, and Linz let out a deep breath. Bryan was close to remembering. With a steady hand, she wrote her note beneath the poem, struggling to keep her words in English—her mind was not yet fully grounded. There was so much she wanted to tell him, but in the end she kept it brief. She placed the note on the pillow.

She took all the cash in her wallet from her purse and set it on her laptop, which she left behind as well in case he needed it.

She watched him sleep and her heart filled with emotions she could not even begin to describe. Renovo had opened a window, and Linz had climbed through it first. Now it was her turn to wait for Bryan so they could embrace their destiny together.

Linz stood at the elevator bank with perfect stillness. The doors opened and she locked eyes with the person exiting. Linz instantly recognized her.

The housekeeper stepped out and smiled at her with surprise. "I'm so happy to see you are feeling better. Your boyfriend was very worried about you. You were so sick."

Linz took in the woman's hotel uniform, connecting the dots. "I'm much better, thank you. What is your name?"

"Layla. Layla Mubarak."

Linz nodded. She opened her purse and pulled out a business card. "I have to take an unexpected trip back to Boston," she said, offering it to Layla. "Could you please call me if there's any kind of emergency? My . . . boyfriend is under a lot of stress right now. I'm worried about leaving him alone."

Layla's smile faded and she took the card. "Yes, of course." She misunderstood Linz's scrutiny and tried to reassure her. "Do not worry. I will watch over him for you."

Linz nodded and stepped onto the elevator. She had no doubt that Layla would.

The afternoon light woke Bryan. He sat up with a start and then wished he hadn't—his head was throbbing from a hangover. It took a few seconds for him to realize Linz was gone and had taken her bag.

He noticed her laptop and the cash and began to panic, thinking that she'd abandoned him. Then he saw the note on her pillow. He read it several times, trying to make of sense what it meant.

> *Stay in Cairo. You will find answers here. You once told me that, in the future, we would build a bridge to our past. I've remembered Egypt. Now I will help you as you helped me, by letting you face it alone.*
>
> *I'm flying to Boston to deal with my father.*
>
> *Go visit the pyramid. It has been waiting for you for a long time.*

Bryan could feel the tears on his face. She had found the life he had been searching for—but she had found it without him.

He looked again at the signature and didn't know what startled him more, the fact that the name was a man's or that it was a name that had been passed down through legends.

She'd signed it *Thoth.*

FORTY-FIVE

Tonight I dreamed I was a young man painting on a hotel balcony in Cairo. It took two days for the canvas to dry before I could fly home. In the dream I knew I was giving it to Diana, and that when she saw it, she'd know I had remembered.

This dream is telling me to go to Egypt.

Linz was surprised when the plane touched down. The past eleven hours had sped by. She had bought a journal at the airport and had spent the entire flight writing in it. Now she understood why Michael had kept so many diaries—she needed to make sense of her thoughts.

When she turned on her cell phone, she saw that Bryan had tried to call her twelve times and had left three voice mails. She ignored them and got off the plane to clear customs. They peppered her with a few questions about the reason for her quick turnaround.

"I got a call that my father is very ill. . . . I had to cancel a romantic getaway."

The female customs agent studied her passport, noting how many pages had been filled. "And where's the boyfriend?"

"He stayed. At least one of us should enjoy the vacation, right?"

The customs agent stamped the book. "Now that doesn't sound like till-death-do-us-part behavior."

Linz took the passport with a conspiratorial grin. "You have no idea."

Linz rented a car and left the airport, already knowing her destination. It was pointless to put off the inevitable.

She got out her cell phone and made a call, feeling guilty that she hadn't spoken with Finn since she borrowed his car. He answered on the first ring. "Finn, it's Linz. Sorry I haven't been in touch."

He sounded flustered, which made her feel even worse. "Where's Bryan? Is he with you?"

"He's fine. I'll explain in person. I'm on my way to see Conrad."

Finn insisted that he wanted to be there. She was relieved to have his support and gave him directions to the house. He said he could get there in twenty minutes.

He hung up, and Linz tried to focus on the road. It was eight o'clock at night, and she was tired, jetlagged, and exhausted from the past week. When she finally pulled up into the drive, she stayed in the car and allowed herself a moment to think.

Her childhood still resided in this house, along with the man who had nurtured and loved her. The scientist who had killed his partners also lived inside it, as did the Japanese lord she had beheaded, the man who had dueled and shot her husband, and the official who had sentenced her to burn at the stake. She had read other stories in Michael's journals—stories of lives she had fortunately not remembered. Had her father also been Tarr, the barbarian who had murdered her son and kidnapped her? And was he the same brother who had killed Hermese's unborn child?

What could she possibly say to a man like this? A part of her didn't even know if she would survive the confrontation. She had written her will on the plane, as well as a letter explaining her actions.

She got out of the car and went to the front door, using her key to enter. Conrad's car was in the driveway, and she saw that the light was on in his study. Her father was home and likely to be alone. The housekeeper left every day at six.

Linz walked through the foyer, past the living room, and entered the antique gallery. She stood there for a moment and took in the room—so many of Conrad's mementos were now her own.

She toured the showroom like a stranger in a museum, noting the samurai swords, the Persian armor, the ancient manuscripts, a coronation ring, and countless other priceless artifacts.

"History isn't so grand when you've lived it." Conrad's voice came from the next room. Linz reached up and took down a samurai sword she recognized and moved toward his office.

She stood in the doorway. Conrad sat in his favorite leather chair. A sword lay on his desk, along with Michael's journals.

"You re-created the formula," he said. It wasn't a question.

"I had to know the truth."

He stared at her for a long time. "Where's Bryan?"

"Safe. Far away from you."

"I was trying to protect him."

"By kidnapping him and putting him in an asylum?"

Conrad leaned back in his chair and crossed his arms. "It was the safest place."

"From who?"

"From the people who would do anything to know what's in his mind. They were about to make a move. I was trying to protect you both," he said.

"How convenient. Who are these people?" she demanded.

"Put down the sword and I'll tell you everything. I should have done so sooner and that was my mistake. Please," he added.

Linz hesitated. Her father was the master of manipulation and she refused to be swayed. She studied the weapon in her hands.

"This was the most treasured sword in Lord Asano's collection. There's an engraving inside the handle." She took the sword from its sheath and examined the blade. It had rusted and grown brittle with age, but it was so expertly crafted that she thought it could still withstand a fight.

She gestured toward the door with it. "Origenes wrote the *Commentary on St. John* while he taught with Theoctistus. You signed the order for his death, and yet his book sits outside your door like a prize."

Conrad banged his hand on the table. "I was not Septimus!"

"Just like you weren't Lord Kira? You caused Lord Asano's death and the fall of his entire clan."

Conrad's lips formed a thin line of anger.

"You don't deny it, then?" Linz challenged. "You even bought the painting at the gallery. Penelope told me."

He spoke in Japanese. *"Yes, I was in that painting. But I wasn't Kira. I was the Shogun! Tsunayoshi!"*

Linz shook her head in disbelief. "That's not possible. You were Kira."

"Why? Because Finn told you?"

Linz couldn't answer.

"Look at me! See for yourself!" Conrad stood up, pinning her with his gaze. "I will show you."

Linz locked eyes with him and gasped when she saw what he was trying to show her so clearly—he was the Shogun. She struggled to come to terms with what that meant.

"You sentenced Lord Asano to death," she retaliated.

"He broke the law. I had no choice. But I let him die with honor. Who were you?" Conrad demanded with the tone of a ruler.

Linz bowed in spite of herself. *"Oishi Kuranosuke Yoshio, his kerai."* She stood up straight again and looked him in the eye without flinching. Here was the Shogun, whom she had defied, and who had sentenced them all to death. But it was true his mercy had allowed them an immortal place in history. She spoke once more in Japanese. *"Thank you for allowing my men to die with honor."*

Conrad gave a gruff nod of acceptance. *"That lifetime was a chain of unfortunate events best forgotten."*

Linz looked away, beginning to feel confused. Her rage toward Lord Kira could no longer be directed at him. Her eyes focused on the journals and they strengthened her resolve. "You found those at Bryan's after you destroyed all of his paintings."

Conrad shook his head. "I don't know what you're talking about. These were delivered to me today."

Linz's voice seethed with Diana's rage. "You'll say anything to convince me otherwise. But nothing changes the fact that you locked the door and let us burn."

Conrad slammed his fist on the table again. "I didn't know anything about the explosion! I was trying to get Michael to remember a life! If he had just remembered then everything would have fallen into place. I didn't know what else to do. You were all going mad."

"You were taking more Renovo than any of us," she accused him.

"Because in the beginning I couldn't have a recall!" he shouted. "You all thought I was a monster!" He waved one of Michael's journals around and threw it back down in disgust, as if he couldn't bear to touch the pages. "I had to know what was causing everyone to turn against me, to look at me in fear. I began to up the dosage. I didn't care about the consequences."

Linz thought back to her actions after she had re-created Renovo. She hadn't cared either. She would have kept dosing until she either remembered Diana's life or died trying.

"Then, one night, the memories started to come," he continued. "And then they wouldn't stop." Conrad's eyes had grown distant. But when he looked back at Linz, his gaze was searing and honest. "I swear. I was never any of the bastards they believed me to be. But I couldn't talk to anyone. Anyone! Egypt was a turning point. I knew what I was meant to do—who Michael was, our true course— and I thought getting him to remember was the only way. I never intended for you to get hurt." His voice broke. "Never. When I came back it was too late."

Linz's eyes welled up with tears. What she wouldn't give to believe him. "There's no way that was an accident."

"Because it wasn't."

All of a sudden Conrad grabbed his sword and lunged at her with lightning speed. Linz flinched, but she wasn't the target— his blade blocked the sword that was slicing through the air behind her.

Linz whirled around to find Finn at her back. If her father hadn't stopped him, she'd be dead. In one deft move, Conrad knocked the sword from Finn's hand and it flew across the room.

He held his sword to Finn's neck and said, "I always wondered if it was you who turned them against me. Now I know. Thank you for the journals. They were very enlightening."

Conrad stepped back and drove the tip of his blade into the floorboards, so that it stood upright. He would no longer fight. He spoke to Finn in ancient Egyptian. "*Seth. I see you finally crawled out from your rat hole to face me.*"

With a twisted smile, Finn gave a mocking bow. "*Father.*"

Linz stood frozen in shock. *Seth? Conrad was Ramses?* She peered into the depths of his eyes and saw it was true. "*Father?*" she asked in their ancient tongue.

Conrad's eyes grew wide. He whispered, "Thoth? You've remembered?"

She nodded and turned to face Finn and all the remaining pieces of the puzzle fell into place. Linz needed to see his eyes, but he was still wearing his tinted eyeglasses—she needed to know for sure.

"Take off your glasses," she ordered. "Look at me."

Finn gave her a self-depreciating grin, and Linz caught a glimpse of the Finn that Diana had loved like a brother. "It's not pretty," he warned.

She gasped when he removed them.

Finn had begun wearing sunglasses after he had started to remember, but it was now clear the migraines were a lie. The dark lenses had veiled the truth. The eyes were windows to the soul, and Finn had not wanted anyone to see his. They were hideous— livid, bulging, marred with broken veins. His once beautiful green irises were now a muddy violet. Linz could see the hatred of Septimus, d'Anthès, Kira, Seth—so many enemies from her past—but she could also see Finn, in pain, suffocating under the weight of his own soul. "Finn?"

"Finn's gone," he said. "I almost kidnapped you both that first night you came to visit me. It's so easy to hide a sedative in tea. But then I found out who you were—Daddy's little girl. I knew

Conrad would come after me if you disappeared. It's a shame I hesitated. It would have saved me so much trouble."

Linz pointed the tip of her sword at Finn's neck, forcing him up against the wall. "You convinced us that Conrad was Kira and Septimus so we would fear him. But he wasn't. You turned us against him . . . you knew Conrad was Ramses and that he wanted to help Michael remember." She thought back to the moments before the lab explosion. "You caused the gas leak . . . you were willing to kill yourself in the process. You wanted to stop us that much."

Finn scoffed and let out a maniacal laugh. "I only wanted to kill him—the gas exploded before it was meant to. I remembered Seth at the same time as Conrad, and I couldn't have them reunited. I would have loved to have extracted the Guardian's knowledge from Michael's mind, but I didn't know how to, yet. That has taken me many years to perfect. So you see, I couldn't let him remember. He had to die. Conrad unknowingly made it quite easy."

It drove Linz mad to realize that, even now, Finn had tried to turn them against her father—and had almost succeeded. If her father hadn't tried to protect Bryan and she hadn't remembered the past, their present lives would have ended no differently.

Conrad tried to calm her. "Lindsey, put the sword down. You cannot have his death on your hands."

But her psyche was battling with too many alien emotions. She spoke in ancient Egyptian. *"He destroyed our world, Father. You died before you could see . . . we've lived in darkness ever since."* She pressed the blade into Finn's skin, accusing him. *"You put an arrow into my back. But Ammon healed me. I did not die. I lived a long life wandering the world, finding a place to hide the book that bore my name."*

Finn gasped in astonishment. *"The Book of Thoth* exists?"

Linz nodded, feeling she had won a small victory.

A fire flared in Finn's eyes. He took a step forward. "Where is it? Think what we could do with that knowledge."

The thought of him obtaining the book and using it made her want to strike him down with every atom of her being.

"Lindsey Jacobs!" Conrad's voice was harsh, as if he were yelling at a child who had run blindly into the street.

Linz was startled. She didn't take her eyes off Finn, but her father had her attention.

Conrad spoke as Ramses, in a tone as forceful as the leader he had been. "*You once contemplated killing your brother and wondered if I was watching you from the Duat. I saw you spare his life.*" Tears blinded Linz and she blinked them away. "*We are here for a reason.*" He reminded her. "*Do not be seduced by rage.*"

Linz took several deep breaths, struggling to calm herself.

He put his hand over hers and whispered in English, "Stormy Weather, come back. Come back to me."

She dropped the sword and, with a sob, turned to her father. He held her in his arms. His eyes met Finn's.

Finn put his hands in his pockets and gave a mocking bow. "Thank you, Yankee Doodle. This has been a fascinating reunion."

Conrad didn't see the taser in Finn's hand until it was too late. Finn delivered a high-level jolt that paralyzed him. He buckled to the ground, writhing in agony and clutching his heart as his pacemaker failed him.

Linz screamed and dropped to her knees. "Dad? Dad!" She sobbed, then looked up to see Finn picking up his sword. "Please don't do this," she begged, watching her father die. "Don't do this, please."

Finn mocked her. "You always were his favorite."

"Please. We can forget the past. Just help me."

"Forget the past? We are the past."

"You can change who you are. Start over. Just help me save him. Please."

"The Brotherhood of Horus," Finn sneered, "hoarding the ancient knowledge. Do you think you are the only ones who have a destiny?"

"So your answer is killing? Your father? Your friend?"

"And I will do it again. The Apophis only wants to give power back to the people. You're the one who stands in our way." Finn spoke in ancient Egyptian. *"Father never understood that. . . . It was why he had to die. I made sure the poison was slow."*

With a fierce growl, Linz sprang to her feet. She lunged at Finn and attacked him barehanded, delivering a brutal jab to his chest. Finn lurched backward in surprise and retreated to the gallery as Linz came at him like a Fury. There was no time to waste—her father was fighting for his life.

She grabbed a medieval spear hanging on the wall and tested the weight of the weapon. Finn charged at her, sword in hand. Linz avoided every strike, her mind in sharp focus, channeling an Egyptian stick fighter at his best. With a powerful roar, she launched her body and swung the spear, forcing Finn to jump to one side. She spun in the air, leg extended, and crashed into his chest with all her weight. The force knocked Finn backward into the case holding Bjarni's vegvísir. It fell with him to the ground, shattering glass everywhere.

Finn lay on the floor stunned amid the shards of glass. Linz bent over, picked up the vegvísir, and looked down at Finn. She spoke in ancient Egyptian. *"Poor Seth, never able to find your way."*

Using the stone as a weapon, she brought it down hard on his temple, knocking him unconscious.

Linz stared at him and wondered when it would end. Thoth had not killed him in Egypt, and she would not kill him now. She could gain nothing from his death.

She rushed back to the study. Conrad was on the floor, alive but gasping, clearly fighting for every breath.

Linz grabbed the house phone and called 911. "Help me, my father's having a heart attack—he was tasered. He has a pacemaker."

The dispatcher assured her an ambulance would be there in five minutes. She hung up and returned to her father, cradling his head in her lap.

Conrad was cognizant but in great pain. "Finn?" he asked her.

"He's unconscious. Just hold tight, Dad, please." She took his hand. "Why didn't you tell me who you were? I'm so sorry."

He squeezed her hand. "Wanted to protect you from it all . . .

my fault. . . . Renovo is too powerful, so easy to get lost. . . ." He struggled to get the words out. "No time. Listen to me. I built Medicor . . . for the Guardian to return . . . people will try to stop you. So many."

Conrad was fading now, his body shutting down. Linz heard the sirens and knew the ambulance would be there soon, but not soon enough. Her father's spirit was already leaving this world. She had to lean in close to hear his last words. "Find the others. They are waiting."

She saw his soul depart and cried out in anguish. She was not ready to lose him. It was just like it had been ten thousand years ago: they still had too much left to say.

FORTY-SIX

Bryan stood on the ledge of the balcony, performing a series of dance-like stretches. Countless drawings filled the tiny hotel patio; none of them were depictions of Egypt.

He closed his eyes and breathed in the air, letting his mind expand into the openness, hoping to touch upon whatever life Linz had already found. But instead he began to fixate on why she hadn't called him back. He felt like he was in exile.

His scattered thoughts almost pitched him over the edge. Channeling Bodhidharma, Bryan quickly regained his balance. And again the Zen monk commanded him to paint.

Bryan rolled his eyes and, instead, stood up on one toe to prove a point.

"Sir?" Layla stood behind him at the balcony's door holding a set of fresh towels, her face frozen in disbelief.

Bryan pivoted around in a perfect 180-degree turn. "Oh, hello, Layla. I didn't hear you come in."

Layla's mouth opened and closed several times. "Should you be up there?" she finally squeaked.

"Probably not." In truth, he could only tolerate Bodhidharma's exercises for short periods of time, and the look of terror on her face wasn't helping his concentration.

He glanced over the edge, feeling the street rise up to meet him as gravity did its best to pull him down. Somehow, he launched into an impossible back flip and landed right in front of Layla.

She yelped and dropped the towels. It took her a moment to

process what he'd just done. "Are you in the circus?" she finally asked.

Bryan burst into laughter. It made Layla laugh too. "Something along those lines," he said, when he finally stopped chuckling.

"You scared me to death!" She playfully swatted at his arm.

"Sorry." They both smiled at each other.

"I don't think you should be standing on that ledge anymore, okay?"

"No more ledges," he promised.

Layla picked up the towels and took in all the drawings. "You're an artist," she gasped, delighted. "These are so beautiful. You are in Cairo to work?"

"It's turning out to be that way," Bryan said with a rueful smile. This hotel had somehow become his studio, and he had yet to leave it. He stared at her, still trying to determine who she was. "Could I paint your portrait?" he heard himself ask.

Layla laughed in surprise. "You want to paint me?"

"I would pay you, of course, as a model." Bryan could sense her reluctance and hastened to reassure her. "I pay all my models," he lied, having never worked with a live model in his life. Ducking into the room, he found Linz's pile of money. "Five hundred dollars is the usual fee," he offered, counting out five one-hundred-dollar bills.

Layla laughed even harder, making a sound like a duck. "You want to pay me five hundred dollars? Just to paint me?"

Bryan nodded, and found himself laughing again too. All he knew was that he had to keep her with him.

"My clothes stay on, yes?"

"Of course," he assured her, moving supplies off the lounge chair. "You just sit right here. Your uniform is fine."

"Right now? But I'm working." She giggled at his unabashed earnestness. His pastels were already in one hand, and he had money in the other. Bryan's face started to fall with disappointment, and she added, "I have tomorrow and the next day off. I'm happy to come back."

"Tomorrow," Bryan answered immediately. "Here, I like to pay in advance." He wanted to make sure she didn't change her mind. He held out the money.

Again, she hesitated. "This probably is breaking the rules with my job."

"I won't tell anyone. I promise," he said. "It's just a painting."

Bryan had never done a miniature before, but somehow it felt imperative for her portrait to be able to fit in his pocket, and his instincts had never misguided him before. His hand worked with the smallest strokes, relying on Jan Van Eyck's mastery.

Jan had of course painted countless miniatures in his day, along with paintings of every other size imaginable, but Bryan had always preferred to paint on an expanse of canvas. He had no trouble working with a smaller scale, though. Yesterday, he had returned to the art store and purchased half a yard of linen canvas to work with, along with a small set of oil paints and several fine brushes suited for miniature brushwork. He'd created a three-by-three-inch frame to stretch the fabric for the portrait.

He grinned as Layla erupted into her signature laugh when she saw the tiny square.

"Five hundred dollars for such a little thing?" she asked in disbelief. "You're crazy."

Bryan shrugged with a smile, inwardly agreeing, but he grew somber as he studied the lines of her face. He worked in silence a long time, bringing her image to life.

Layla sat still, looking serene as she gazed at the city line from the balcony.

"Are you from Cairo?" he asked.

It was as if his simple question had given her permission to talk and she opened up, telling Bryan all about herself as he worked. It seemed that she felt as comfortable with him as he did with her.

An only child, she was born to elderly parents who thought they couldn't have children. They considered her a blessing from heaven and doted on her, despite the fact that they had little money. Her mother had made jewelry that she sold in the markets, and her father had done construction. But they were both too old to work now, so Layla had given up any dream of going to college and instead found a job to pay the bills. Five hundred dollars would go a long way.

When Bryan had finished, she came over to look at the miniature. "You're really very good," she said.

He shrugged and mumbled thanks, giving his work an objective eye. Jan Van Eyck's gift had served him well, and his signature had never seemed more fitting: *ALC IXH XAN*, "As I can." He willed himself to believe the words. *As I can. I can. I will remember.*

Layla interrupted his thoughts. "Do you have a guide to show you the city? I can show you some sights tomorrow if you like?" She grinned at him. "Help to really earn that money."

"You don't have to do that," he said, though he wouldn't mind the company. He wanted to get out of this hotel room.

"I don't mind. And I promised your girlfriend I'd take good care of you," she admitted, teasing him. "I can't let her know you stayed cooped up here the whole time."

"You met Linz?" he asked in surprise.

Layla looked embarrassed. "She was leaving and gave me her card . . . wanted to know my name. She seems like a very serious person."

Bryan frowned. Linz gave Layla her card? He knew that meant Layla was somehow important—otherwise Linz wouldn't have singled her out.

"I'll pick you up at nine," she said, moving to the door.

"Are you taking me to the Great Pyramid?" he asked.

"Of course. It's the first place we'll go."

The swarm of vendors selling their wares wouldn't take "no" for an answer. Bryan's attention was jockeyed from person to person as he tried to push his way through the throng. But the chaos was oddly comforting. It kept him from focusing on the Great Pyramid towering a hundred feet away.

Bryan followed Layla through the crowd with a faith he didn't understand. All he knew was that he never would have had the courage to come here if it hadn't been for her.

As they moved forward, they almost got separated. She looked behind her and reached out to grab his hand. He gazed into her eyes and suddenly saw himself as a young girl, running hand-in-hand with her—and in that moment Bryan remembered who she was.

She was Kiya.

His heartbeat began to race, as every memory from that life in Egypt began to return to him like blood circling back to the heart. Bryan's pulse quickened as his feet kept moving him toward the Great Pyramid, until he stood just a few yards away from it. He closed his eyes and, as his palms made contact with the weathered stones, he remembered it all: the power of this Sleeping Giant, the untold atrocities that had happened here, and the mission that had been given to him.

Bryan felt Hermese expand within him. She had been there all along—a shadow he couldn't see, a feeling he couldn't describe, a sense of longing he couldn't explain.

He opened his eyes and looked up at the pyramid and his heart filled with joy. Every life he had ever lived sounded within him in perfect harmony. His soul was singing.

The Guardian had awoken.

Bryan turned to Layla and saw Kiya's spirit shining in her. How many times had they played here as children . . . of course, she should be the one to bring him home.

"Are you all right?" she asked.

He nodded, his heart filled with infinite gratitude at the gift life had just given him—all of his memories were now one.

FORTY-SEVEN

Gravestones stretched across the green like a thousand unlit candles. An enormous crowd had gathered to pay their respects to Conrad Jacobs. At a freshly dug grave, a priest performed the burial rites.

Linz stood at the front, with Penelope and Derek at her side. She watched as the coffin was lowered into the ground next to her mother and brother's grave.

She still couldn't believe that he was gone. Her mind had already started projecting into the future, imagining when their paths would cross again, knowing with certainty that, one day, they would. If Bryan had remembered his lifetimes without any help from the drug, then Conrad might be able to as well in his next life. He would find them. Linz had to believe it. She had to hope.

Her thoughts turned to Finn, knowing that they too would meet again—at the trial. She had given her statement and then turned the matter over to the police. The court date had not yet been decided. But even after he was convicted for Conrad's murder, she knew that sitting in a cell for the remainder of his life would not cause him to repent. There was too much malice within him.

Linz stared at the coffin. She didn't want to watch the undertaker cover it in earth or receive condolences afterward. Ignoring Penelope and Derek's distressed looks, she walked away and got into the waiting limo. The driver hung up his cell phone and started the car.

She had met her father's driver on a few occasions over the past few years, whenever she had ridden with Conrad to a function.

But all she really knew about him was that he went by the name Vadim and was originally from somewhere in Russia. He had worked for her father the last ten years, and he had always seemed like a bodyguard more than anything else. She caught him looking at her in the rearview mirror—the poor man was probably worried he would lose his job. It only reminded her of how little she knew about her father's private affairs.

"Where to, Dr. Jacobs?"

"My house for a minute so I can change and then to the office," she said. She had a long night ahead of her.

Linz planned to return to Egypt as soon as Bryan contacted her, and she had to make sure that the company would run smoothly when she disappeared. Yesterday she had held a board meeting and they had mapped out a forecast for the next six months. As for her research, she had placed Maggie in charge of the lab. She knew her team would keep everything moving forward in her absence.

Tomorrow, she would begin to tackle her father's belongings— she was already planning to donate his antique collection to several museums.

Her cell phone rang, flashing a number she didn't recognize. "Hello?"

"Lindsey Jacobs?" an authoritative voice asked.

"Yes." The man sounded like the police. She had finally grown used to them.

"This is Mitch Tanner from TDC Security. I've been instructed to contact you in the event of your father's passing. First, I'd like to offer my condolences."

Linz frowned. She had no clue what this call was about. "Thank you."

"We need to know how you would like to proceed with the warehouses?"

"What warehouses?"

"Your father has three warehouses by the wharf. He didn't tell you?"

Linz rubbed her forehead. "Why does he have three warehouses?"

"As you're probably aware, he was an avid collector of relics and artifacts."

It took Linz a minute to realize that Conrad had amassed a collection so large it required three warehouses. "Mr. Tanner, I appreciate the call, but I'm just leaving the service. I will call you soon to schedule an appointment to tour the buildings. Until then, just keep everything as is."

Linz listened to his profuse apologies and then signed off. She leaned back and stared out the window, wondering what in the world Conrad had kept there. It was just one more item on the incredible list of things she had to deal with. She didn't even want to be in Boston, and she was frustrated that she hadn't heard from Bryan. It had been well over a week since she'd left Egypt—in reality it wasn't that long, but, to her, it felt like an eternity.

Part of her worried that he would never remember his life there. But she had to believe he would. Her mind went back to the portrait of Ma'at she had seen in Bryan's studio. He had already painted the ancient seer without even knowing it, and Linz told herself for the thousandth time to be patient. He had waited for her. Now she had to do the same.

The limo pulled up to her condo, and she saw a package sitting against the door. She jumped from the car and ran to it. As she closed the distance, she recognized Bryan's handwriting.

She ripped open the box and took out the exquisite twelve-by-twelve-inch painting of Hermese standing in her garden in the moonlight, with the Star of Isis—Sirius—shining in the sky.

He had included a note:

I'll be home soon. I hope you remember where you hid the book.

Linz yelled with joy.

Vadim jumped out of the car. "Dr. Jacobs? Are you all right?"

"Change of plans, Vadim," she said. "I'll be staying here." She wasn't going anywhere until she had seen Bryan.

❧

Finn's cell at Suffolk County Jail in Boston was far away from the other inmates. High-profile cases were generally given special treatment. He had been charged with voluntary manslaughter and tucked away there since Conrad's death, where he would remain until the trial and sentencing.

These circumstances had made Bryan's visit possible. He had relied upon Bodhidharma's stealth to maneuver past the security cameras and had used one of Hermese's techniques to disable the night guard. As Guardian, Hermese had been taught that the Earth was one big spinning magnet, and that magnetite tissues existed throughout the human body but were concentrated in the brain. Modern science had only begun to understand biomagnetism during the past thirty years, with the advent of high-resolution electron microscopy. But with Hermese's knowledge, passed down from Horus himself, Bryan inherently understood these connections and how to control them. With the touch of his hand, he had taken the guard's mind from a waking beta state to a delta state in an instant, skyrocketing him past dreamland into a slumbering abyss.

Bryan found Finn's cell and stood in the shadows, watching him sleep. His thoughts traveled back to Hermese and how she had not been able to protect herself from Seth's attack. Seth had entered her quarters while she had been bathing, killed her maids, and then bound her before she could use her powers. He had been wearing armor covered with lodestone, a natural magnet that interfered with her abilities. Somehow he had known how to defeat the House of Atum. Bryan wondered who else had led the Apophis and if their spirits were now at rest. To plunge the world into perpetual darkness was soul-crushing karma indeed.

Finn murmured in his sleep. He was dreaming, and his words made Bryan pause—he recognized the life Finn was remembering. Bryan's enemy had also been his most devoted student once, cutting off his own arm to prove his sincerity. He waited for Huike to wake. Would he remember what Bodhidharma had told him?

Finn seemed to sense his presence and woke up with a start, his eyes wet with tears. He turned to look at Bryan.

Bryan let the silence rest between them for a moment and then swept it away. "You were speaking Chinese," he said with surprising gentleness. "Have you remembered our time together at Shaolin?"

"*You knew.*" Finn spoke in Chinese. "*You had seen our future and you still forgave me.*"

"*Do you remember what I told you that day?*"

Finn nodded, crying like a lost child.

Bryan recited Bodhidharma's words to Huike in Chinese. "*One day you will remember this life, your earnestness, your goodness, and you will meet the malevolence that binds your spirit. On that day, let go of the shame of having fallen and allow it to let in the light.*"

"You can't offer me such peace. I've done too much harm," Finn answered as Seth in their ancient tongue.

Bryan pulled a small, wrapped bundle from his bag and slid it across the floor through the bars. "Life always returns what it takes from us."

Finn looked down at the package with confusion.

"I found Kiya."

Finn choked down a sob and he dropped to his knees in front of Bryan's gift, afraid to touch it.

"She's in Egypt, as vibrant as she was before. This is for you."

FORTY-EIGHT

Linz stood at the center of her sand garden, staring at her latest attempt to re-create the Brotherhood of Horus' emblem. It amazed her that she had been unknowingly drawing variations of it for months. Her brain just hadn't caught up to her mind, and she now understood that they were two very different things.

The doorbell rang. Linz dropped the stick and ran across the garden, demolishing her work and trailing sand everywhere. He was here.

She threw opened the door and they stared at each other, much like they had the first time they had met. The difference was that now they could see past themselves and recognize they were bound by love. It had moved them through time, had been their compass through the brine of life, and guided them against all odds to make their remembering possible. Love had collapsed ten thousand years.

Bryan moved forward to cross the remaining distance that separated them. He took Linz's hand and kissed it, placing it on his heart. They held each other for a long time.

He finally whispered, "I missed your father's funeral. I'm sorry."

"Conrad was Ramses," she told him. "He was waiting for you to remember."

"I know."

Linz pulled away and looked up at him. "How?"

"After I remembered everything, I realized he had spoken as Ramses to Michael that night at his apartment. Michael just couldn't understand him. Finn remembered Seth at around the same time.

When Finn realized who Conrad was, he knew he had to separate us. Conrad's decision to show up at the lab made Finn desperate."

Linz still felt confused. "But how did you know Finn was Seth?"

"The sundial in his home was the symbol of the Apophis."

Linz had forgotten about the sundial, but Bryan was right. Its shape and design were identical to the emblem Seth had worn around his neck.

Bryan saw the worry on her face and gave her another hug. "It'll be all right."

She nodded, her heart welling within her. They had done it. They had built the bridge that could lead to a future few dared to hope for—a future where the Hall of Records would be restored.

The prophecy claimed that the First Time would come again, when the Hall of Records was discovered and Horus returned to help heal the world. The Brotherhood had sworn an oath to pave his way.

"Getting the book is going to be hard," Linz said.

Bryan nodded, growing thoughtful. "We need to join the others first."

"You know where they are?" Her face lit up with hope.

Bryan nodded, unable to explain how he knew. As the Brotherhood's leader, he had sensed their presence like a divining rod. "I found Thutmose and Bast in Newfoundland. They're archaeologists studying pyramids. I only realized who they were after Cairo."

"And the others?" Linz asked, growing excited.

"Ma'at and Ammon are alive, but I'm not sure where they are." Bryan said. He thought about the great debt he owed to Ma'at. She had been the Ancient One visiting his dreams and trying to guide him. Her abilities had been so immense that she had been able to walk in the dreamworlds of the future even then.

"And Ptah?" Linz asked, frowning at the strange look on Bryan's face.

"Ptah is going to be a little tricky," he said, and hesitated.

Somehow Linz knew what he was going to say. "Oh no." She shook her head, hoping she was wrong.

"Oh yes," he affirmed.

Barbara was Ptah. "Somehow I don't think your mother's going to handle the news well. I'll let you figure out how to deal with that one."

"Wonderful." Bryan sighed and shook his head with a rueful smile.

Linz hurried to the hall closet. "We can deal with Ptah later. First we need to see Thutmose and Bast." She got out her suitcase—it was already packed. "Let's go to Canada."

Bryan laughed. "Their names are Claudette and Martin and I called them yesterday."

"Then let's go." She rolled her eyes as she got out her cell phone. "Yes, this is Linz Jacobs. I need the plane ready and a flight plan to St. John's, Newfoundland. Excellent. We'll see you this evening."

She hung up, enjoying the incredulous look on Bryan's face. Owning Medicor came with vast privileges—like having a private jet at your disposal. It would take getting used to, but Linz knew she and Bryan would need all of Medicor's resources in the journey ahead. She could now see how Conrad had prepared the way for them.

"You have your own plane?"

"A Gulfstream 550. We can thank my dad the next time we see him." She grew somber. Bryan kissed her hand.

"We will."

Linz took his hand and led him to the sand garden. On the way, he stopped to admire the chess set she had laid out on the table. It was a Jaques of London original and probably worth a small fortune. He whistled.

"You ready to play me again?" he teased.

"Now that I've remembered how to beat you." She had recalled her life with the great chess master Pedro Damiano. "Guess which other life I remembered?" she asked with a gleam in her eye. She pushed him down into the sand and called him by another name.

Bryan's smile held the shadow of her ancient lover. "Hmm," he murmured softly. "What else have you remembered?"

"Everything," she said, her eyes shining.

The Brotherhood had returned.

AUTHOR'S THANKS

I have many people to thank for this journey to publication. First, I'd like to acknowledge two amazing women: Brianne Johnson, my agent at Writers House, whose brilliance and passion blew me away as she became the captain of the ship and found *The Memory Painter* its home; and my editor, Elizabeth Bruce, who entered my life one unforgettable Monday like an incandescent firework and then continued to exceed my every expectation as we worked together. To both of these ladies, I will always be grateful.

My deepest thanks goes to everyone at Picador: Kolt Beringer, managing editor; production team Lisa Viviani Goris and David Lott; copyeditor Alda Trabucchi; marketing team Darin Keesler, Daniel Del Valle, Shannon Donnelly, Andrew Catania, and Angela Melamud; Executive Director of Publicity James Meader and my publicist, Andrea Rogoff; Devon Mazzone, for handling subsidiary rights, assisted by Hanna Oswald and Amber Hoover; Jonathan Bennett, interior designer; and Keith Hayes, for designing the book's beautiful cover. Also a huge thanks to Lorissa Sengara, my Canadian editor with HarperCollins Canada, who worked so closely with Elizabeth on the editorial front, and to all the international publishing houses who have come aboard.

Thank you to Alan Greenspan, Julie-Ann Lee Kinney, and Todd Eikelberger at International Arts Entertainment, for their feedback and creative support so many years ago when I first started writing this story; Lucy Stille and Judith Karfiol; my first readers: Richard Devlin, who helped enormously as I waddled through the first draft,

Janis Lull, Kate Maney, and Bridget Norquist; my second-round readers: Adam Gonzales, Mark Grimmett, and my father, Leo Womack. Thank you to John Hoffman and Indy Neidell, for research assistance; Bakara Wintner at Writers House, for help during several revisions; photographer JennKL; and web designer Mike Ross.

I would also like to give special acknowledgment to Christopher Dunn and his book *The Giza Power Plant,* as well as Graham Hancock and Robert Bauval and their book *Message of the Sphinx,* for being such an inspiration behind the ancient Egypt chapters.

Infinite gratitude goes to my sister, Alex, who was the first person to hear the idea for this story; all my family and friends; the ever-supportive Julia Burke; Sue Ebrahim; Charlotte Schillaci; Monika Telszewska; Robin Wilson; my mentor at CalArts, Lou Florimonte, for his deep love of story; Rick and Emma Ferguson, for the copper pyramid they made for me so many years ago; fellow writers Kate Maney, Beth Szmkowski, Kelly McCabe, and Cindy Yantis, aka the "Nic Chicks," for the years of encouragement, laughter, and the traveling pants; and my husband and our son, who are my sunlight and inspire me every day.

My final thanks I'd like to give to the reader. I like to think that stories are akin to dreams. Thank you for sharing mine.

ABOUT THE AUTHOR

GWENDOLYN WOMACK grew up in Houston, Texas. She studied theatre at the University of Alaska, Fairbanks, and then moved to California to pursue an MFA in Directing Theatre, Video, and Cinema at California Institute of the Arts. She now lives in Los Angeles with her husband and son. *The Memory Painter* is her first novel.